# THE GOAT GOD
# OF LUST

The young Ariston had seen naked girls before. In Sparta, during the holy rituals, he had danced with them. But Spartan girls always shaved all the hair from their bodies. This girl was different, and the feeling that rose from the bowels of his being was different too.

As Ariston moved toward the waiting girl —naked, and terrible in her nakedness— he felt the claws of the primordial god of lust claw at his body and brain—and he knew, even at this first moment, he would forever be the goat god's slave. . . .

# GOAT SONG

## A
## NOVEL OF
## ANCIENT GREECE

# FRANK YERBY

A DELL BOOK

Published by
DELL PUBLISHING CO., INC.
750 Third Avenue
New York, N.Y. 10017

Dell ® TM 681510, Dell Publishing Co., Inc.
Reprinted by arrangement with
The Dial Press
New York, N.Y.
Printed in the U.S.A.
First Dell printing—July 1969
Second Dell printing—September 1969
Third Dell printing—November 1969

Τί γὰρ σύ, ἔφη, ὦ Κριτόβουλε,

ἐπί τινι μέγιστον φρονεῖς;

Ἐπὶ καλλει, ἔφη.

XENOPHON: THE SYMPOSIUM iii, 7

# CHAPTER ONE

HE HAD BEEN RUNNING a long time, so now there was a sickness in him. The sickness came up from his belly in waves, and it tasted vile. He thought about thrusting his fingers into his mouth in order to relieve himself by vomiting; but to do that he would have to take one hand off the goat kid he had stolen; and besides, there was nothing in his belly to throw up anyhow.

Where he was now, in the foothills of the Parnons, the air was thin and sharp so that to drag it into his lungs made a tearing. Behind him, the mountains were a soaring bleakness, forbidding hope. Off to his left was another blue misting of mountains, the Taygetus, taller, bleaker still, with their peaks glittering whiter than a cry in the morning sun, though spring had long since come to Lakonia. He could see far below him the river which his countrymen, the Lakedaemonians, called the Eurotas, flashing silver like a shield. If he could reach it, cross it, he would be safe. But he knew what his chances were of doing that. Slight. Or none.

He looked back to see if the villagers had given up the chase. But they were still lumbering along behind him, clad in their goatskins, bearded, filthy, looking for all the world like a horde of lesser demons escaped somehow from Tartarus, such minor fiends as Lord Hades employed to torment the shades of the wicked among the dead. And it came to him with a sudden contraction of his breath, his heart, that they weren't going to give up. Not now; not ever.

Poor as they were, a kid was an important thing to them. But that wasn't the main point. The main point was that he, Ariston, shouldn't have climbed so high into the

1

mountains in the first place, alone and weaponless, in his famished search for food. Up here they could kill him without any of the homoioi, the citizen class of Sparta, ever finding it out. And they would. What man, be he slave or free, who lived beneath the pitiless rule of that city-state where even the money was coined in iron, would not happily offer burnt sacrifices to all the Chthonic gods for a chance like this to kill a Spartan? And with impunity, at that?

Ariston ran on. His stride was long and supple, a picture of grace. If it hadn't been for the weight of the little goat, he would have been beyond the villagers' reach long ago. He was a melliran, son of a citizen; his body had been subjected to the exercises that killed you or left you a machine of iron, ever since he was seven years old. But even so, what was in his lungs now was very bad. He had been running for nearly two hours with that fat little kid in his arms. He thought about putting it down to see if the villagers would be satisfied with recapturing their possession. But he knew they wouldn't. He knew that because, in their place, he wouldn't have either. They were Perioeci, the Dwellers Round; and though they were freemen, there was very little to distinguish the way his lordly race treated them from the treatment meted out to the Helots, who were slaves. And the measure of that treatment was that both Perioeci and Helots frequently risked death by torture, rising up almost annually in hopeless attempts to throw off the Spartan yoke. Again, he couldn't blame them. Again, he realized that in their place he would do the same. And that, in its turn, was the measure of something else— of, you might say, the corrupting influence his uncle Hippolytus had had upon his mind.

But now, along with the suffocating agony inside his chest, there was a new thing in him. He could smell it rising through the stench of rancid oil mingled with sweat which was his normal scent, since, like all Spartans, he almost never bathed, holding the practice weakening, but achieved cleanness of a sort by rubbing himself all over with oil, and then having a companion scrape it off with the crescent-shaped strigil. And the name of this new thing,

2

stronger than his own body's overdriven stink, stronger than the aroma of the goat, was fear.

It was a crippling sensation, draining the strength out of him, causing him to reel, to stumble. He was a Spartan youth; he was not supposed to know the meaning of the word. But now he was afraid. And the shame of knowing, realizing it, was worse even than the fear itself. For he, Ariston, was of that race, that country, that had produced the men of Thermopylae, where a mother's parting words to a son marching off to war were: "Return with your shield, or on it!"; where a boy allowed a hidden, stolen fox to devour his entrails, and died without a cry of pain.

But he was seventeen years old, and he didn't want to die. Not now with fame unearned, with glory still before him. And especially not by this stupid, ignominious way of dying: to be put to death by wild mountaineers for the crime of stealing a goat! But behind these youthful sophistries there towered the ugly truth: He didn't want to die because he was afraid of death itself; because he could not face the thought of annihilation, of ceasing to be, that his live, beautiful body should become food for worms, that his high, bright dreams be reduced to naught. "Why think you men invent gods, Ariston?" his uncle Hippolytus had said.

He put the kid down now, and began to run faster than ever. At best, he might be able to reach one of the outlying farms. At this time of the year, the owner might be there, supervising the work. Then he would be safe. The Perioeci wouldn't dare kill him before another Spartan. But if the owner were not there? If there were only the Helots, more brutish than the beasts they tended, smoldering with their sullen hatred for their betters?

He dared not think of that. He dared not think at all now. He shrank his whole being down into his heart, concentrated all his soul into his running. Then a stone whistled by his head. Another. He stumbled, a prey to sickness. For the Perioeci had taken their slings out of their belts, and were whirling them about their heads to send the stones whipping after him. The Perioeci were among the best slingers in the world, because, among the

3

many burdens their Spartan masters had imposed upon them was that of serving the polis, the city-state, as light-armed troops in times of war. Having denied them the heavy armor that made the Spartan hoplite supreme, their masters had trained them well in the use of lesser weapons: the bow, the flung javelin, and, above all, the sling.

Ariston fairly flew now, in that downhill race. His terror lent his feet the sandals of Hermes. He all but forgot the laboring torture in his chest. He ran as he had never run before in all his life. But it served him for nothing. Above him, a shaggy oaf of a Perioeci stopped, whipped his leather sling around his head once, twice, thrice, released one of the two thongs. The white stone blurred sight, arcing out. Then its hard, straight trajectory coincided with that of the flying Spartan boy. Ariston felt red fire explode inside his head. On far off Olympus, immortal Zeus thundered. Then Tartarus opened beneath his feet. With something like a sigh, he fell fathoms deep into darkness, into nothingness, into utter night.

He came back to the feel of jolting. His head ached damnably. But the pain in his wrists, his knees, his ankles was almost as bad. He opened his eyes. The rays of the midmorning sun stabbed into them like white-hot spears. He closed them again; but the sun drove through his eyelids, making a redness, a burning. The jolting, the swaying, went on. He seemed to be swinging from something with all his weight. And now a shadow of a rock outcropping fell across his face, bringing a blessed coolness. He opened his eyes. Saw at once what the pain in his wrists, knees, ankles was. The Perioeci had bound him to a sapling pole like a slaughtered boar. The ends of the pole rested on the shoulders of two of their stoutest oafs. They carried him like that, slung between them up that mountain goat track. And suddenly everything—the fiendish ache in his head, the leather thongs biting into his flesh, the jolting, the swaying, the emptiness of his belly, the deathly congestion of his overdriven lungs, and, most of all, the smell of the villagers—got to be too much. Ariston turned his head sidewise and vomited upon the stony ground.

"Ha!" one of the Perioeci said. "Even the gods spew

bile! You'd do well to keep your muck, Spartan. You'll need it."

Ariston didn't answer him. Truth to tell, he could scarcely understand the mountaineer's speech, for the Perioeci spoke a sort of Achaean dialect older than the language of Homer. Compared to them, his own Dorian race were upstarts, newcomers and invaders in the hollow land of Lakonia, which was but another reason for the hatred that the subject Lakedaemonian tribes felt for everything Spartan. Besides, his mind was busy trying to devise some way of escape. He was still afraid, but now his fear no longer ruled him. That was one of the advantages of Spartan training. It had many advantages: Physically, as a result of it, the homoioi, or equals, as Spartan citizens called themselves—meaning only that they were equal to one another, for their superiority to every other race on earth, be it of Hellas or barbarian, was to them so evident that they felt no need to mention it—were demonstrably stronger man for man than any enemy they would ever meet; mentally, they were far more clever, cunning—

"Or rather cruel, stupid as donkeys, and dull as earthen clods!" his uncle Hippolytus' mocking voice cut through Ariston's mind. "We're trained to hypocrisy, treachery, and deceit. And mark me well, my boy: I should rather be a slave in Athens than one of the two kings of Sparta!"

With an effort, Ariston put his uncle Hippolytus from his mind. This was no time to entertain the corrosive mockery of that fat, clownish fool, whom nevertheless he loved. He suspected that his uncle was right about a good many things, among them being that the price you had to pay for the privilege of being a Spartan was a voluntary surrender of civilization. He had copied out with his own hands the poems Uncle Hippolytus had brought back from Attica and Lesbos; but when the buagor, the group captain, had found them hidden among Ariston's scant belongings, he had reported the youth to the paidonomos, the manager of the boys, who, after having spelled out enough of them—reading was not a ready Spartan accomplishment—to determine that they were not martial odes but rather erotika, love songs, had ordered Ariston whipped, and, what was to him worse, the poems burned.

5

Yet now, trussed up like a hog, slung upside down like a savage boar, what he needed was not the infinite subtleties of his uncle Hippolytus, for all that they touched a responsive chord deep in his nature, but the iron manhood that the training his uncle despised—perhaps because Hippolytus himself had been such a miserable failure at it—had ground into his soul. Some ruse then, some cunning deceit, some matchless Spartan treachery to make them cut him down, turn him loose, let him go back to the banks of the Eurotas—where summer and winter he slept naked among his fellows in order to harden his body—was what was needful now. But nothing came to him. His head ached too much from the place where the hard-flung stone had opened his scalp; and though the blood had clotted in crusts amid his dark blond hair, the flies that buzzed maddeningly about the wound were no help to thinking. He closed his eyes again, murmured a prayer to Zeus, Averter of Flies. The jolting went on. He felt sick almost unto death.

For one thing, he hadn't eaten anything in nearly three days. He had no idea how strange that fact would have seemed to any other Hellene who was not of Sparta. That a youth, son of a rich man, of aristocratic race and blood, would be taken from his home at the age of seven, forced to take part in man-killing exercises daily, to be reduced to a single garment worn summer and winter, to have to sleep naked on the rushes by the river's bank in all seasons no matter how inclement, to engage in duels almost to the death with his companions in order to prove his courage, to be whipped upon the slightest infraction of the rules—and at times, for no infraction at all but simply to teach him to endure pain without a murmur; and, worst of all, to be kept forever in a state of semi-starvation, periodically, as now, having his rations totally cut off so that he had to steal to stay alive—all this would have seemed to the citizens of any other polis in Hellas, to an Athenian, a Theban, a Corinthian, or a Syracusan, say, incredible.

But that was the way young Ariston of Sparta, son of a member of the Gerousia, the Council of Elders, had been brought up, in common with all his fellows. And it was because of this exercise in foraging, in living off the country—"Hummph! Plain thievery!" he could hear Uncle

6

Hippolytus snort—that he was presently going to die. Though, his subtle brain told him, the robbery of the goat was but an excuse. What he was going to die for, actually, was being a Spartan. For being a member of that master race who, numbering barely thirty thousand all told, women and children included, nonetheless ruled with absolutely merciless severity over one hundred thirty thousand Perioeci, and twice that number and more of sullen, snarling Helots.

More immediately, what he was going to die for was his failure, for his mistakes. For instance, had he been willing to risk the humiliation of another whipping, he could have stolen a goat from the more nearly civilized Perioeci of the Plain, close to the city itself. There too, of course, they would have chased him, but his life wouldn't have hung in the balance upon the outcome of a footrace. Because the Dwellers Round About of the Plain would have been in no position to kill him, would not, in fact, have dared. The worst that could have happened down there, if he had failed to shake off their pursuit, would have been for the Perioeci to enter the gymnasium, which, as free men, they had the right to do, and accuse him to the manager of the boys. Whereupon the paidonomos would have ordered the kid restored to them and Ariston whipped until the blood ran down his back. That was a part of the code. If, on the other hand, Ariston had succeeded in escaping his pursuers below in the hollow valley of Lakonia, the selfsame paidonomos would have stood him up on the dais and lauded his bravery, his astuteness, to the stars. For, as Uncle Hippolytus justly put it, the crime was not stealing, but rather getting caught.

"Fool!" he cursed himself silently, "tender fool! To risk your hide for love of him who despises you! Lysander will not even weep upon learning you've been torn to pieces by these wolves. Nor, doubt it not, lift a languid finger to avenge you!"

He didn't want to think about Lysander now, because those memories, too, were crippling things. But he couldn't help it. He had been in love with Lysander ever since he was twelve years old and big enough to feel the torments of the blood, the anguish of desire. In this he was not alone. Lysander was almost unbelievably beautiful, and over three-quarters of the boys in the gymnasium were in love with him. Nor was his fame confined to the gymnasium: Every time he exercised, throwing the discus and the spear, wrestling, boxing, running the long race, with his matchless body totally naked, as the custom was, a crowd of older men came to watch, and even some women, too. It was disgusting to hear some bald-headed, skinny-shanked elder citizen declare aloud his passion for the boy, and to beg Lysander to grant him but a single night. All the more disgusting because that was precisely what he, Ariston, longed to do himself.

He remembered how he had wanted to die when he'd learned that Lysander had finally taken a lover among the older men. But the very next day, with youth's inability to surrender hope, he was trailing behind the beautiful boy again, like a spineless lackey, or a fawning dog. And that boundless, hopeless passion for golden-haired Lysander was, at bottom, responsible for the fatal situation in which he found himself now. For, if he could have brought his fat goat kid home to his regimental mess, he would have been a hero to his fellows. Then perhaps Lysander would have deigned to look at him, granted him even the favor of a smile. But more, it had been the desire to avoid all risk of being whipped again with Lysander looking on—his languid, poutingly beautiful face indifferent, or even mocking, a thing that had happened all too often now—that had driven Ariston to range so far afield in search of a gift to win his beloved's favor. So now, because of his romantic folly, here he was at the very gates of the Underworld, about to be transformed into a shade and sent to whimper forever in the gloomy dark.

The uphill climb to the village of the Perioeci, high in the Parnon Mountains, took all day. The distance he had run in some two hours in his wild downhill race had to be won back inch by stubborn inch against the trail's steepness. Besides, they were burdened with his not inconsiderable weight. Slender as he was, he was nonetheless rock solid. So it was dusk before Ariston knew by the smell of hearth fires that they were nearing the village. Then he heard a great gabble of women's voices. A moment later he and his captors were surrounded by them.

He kept his face still, trying to show no fear, while the Perioeci women gathered about and stared at him. For once he wished he were an Athenian, because there, his uncle had told him, women were not allowed to wander about as they would but were kept carefully locked up, as was fitting. But a Lakedaemonian female, whatever her social status, was the freest woman in all the world. Citizen-class Spartan ladies shocked visitors from other parts of Hellas with their boldness, until the visitors learned that in actual practice their manners meant nothing, that they were among the most chaste maidens and faithful wives upon the face of earth.

He stared back at the shaggy, unkempt, filthy Perioeci females. In truth, his feelings about women were ambivalent. He adored his mother, Alkmena, with all his heart; but apart from her and the slave girls he had no other contact with the other sex. And not even with them any longer since he had reached his seventh birthday and been removed from the softening influence of the home. He knew some of the older boys had used them, lain with them, and even boasted about that feat, claiming that it was a great delight. But it was inconceivable to him that one might *love* a woman. It was very nearly inconceivable even to those boys who had bedded with them. A woman was a brood animal, whom, when you reached age thirty, the Gerousia forced you to marry in order to breed more soldiers for the polis. That having sexual intercourse with one could be pleasant—he suspected that physical love was always pleasant no matter with whom or with what you indulged in it—he didn't doubt; but how could you love a creature without a mind? Besides, women were ugly, with their narrow shoulders and wide hips and great globes of breasts. So far, he hadn't slept with anyone; but when he did, he hoped his partner in delight would be Lysander.

In fact, it had been the exclusivity, the concentration of his love, that had so far kept him chaste. For, in sober truth, he himself was almost as beautiful as Lysander and had had more than his share of attention from boys, men,

9

and even girls. There was in this a detail upon which, although he didn't know it then, all his fate would presently hinge: Alone, among all the boys of the school, he and Lysander were truly blond.

His people, the Dorians, were Northerners, possibly even of Balto-Teutonic stock; but after centuries in Hellas they, despite their boasts of racial purity, had been drowned in a sea of darker peoples, though less in Sparta than elsewhere. Among the boys, blue and gray eyes were not uncommon; many of them had hair that was noticeably brown, especially when contrasted with the inky tresses of the aboriginal Hellenes; but by some freak of breeding, every so often a Doric youth or maiden would revert to the original Nordic type. And that was Lysander's good fortune, and his. For so extravagantly were blonds admired in Hellas that the makers of bleaches and dyes had become wealthy in every polis in the land.

His head ached from the gabble of the women. He closed his eyes and lay there in the dirt, where, still trussed up, he had been thrown by his captors, sapling pole and all. The smell of the Perioeci was making him sicker than ever, especially now that to it had been added the peculiarly insupportable stench of unwashed femininity. But he was conscious suddenly of a warm, garlic-laden breath stirring against his cheek. He opened his eyes, and stared into the face of a girl.

She was as dirty as the rest. She smelled not one whit better; but somehow, suddenly, her aroma was exciting. The tangled mass of her hair would have made the river Styx snowy by comparison; her eyes were blacker than the deepest pit of Tartarus. She licked her lips, leaving them outlined in white where her tongue tip had washed away the soot and grime encrusting her face. And Ariston saw that those lips were wine dark, full, sensuous. From the considerable amount he could see of her body through the flutter of filthy rags she wore, it occurred to him suddenly that she, if scrubbed for at least a week, might serve to test some of his fellows' theories about the excellencies of girls.

From where she knelt beside him, she arched her little head upward. Despite the lines of dirt ground into her throat, Ariston found the motion enchanting. She moved

10

with as much grace as Lysander did. No, more. The thought was singularly disturbing.

"Father," she said—and her voice was very low and sweet—"what is he? Man—or god?"

He heard the heavy boom of bass laughter. But none of the women laughed. They were all staring at him the way the girl was. One of them in particular caught his eye. She was very tall for a woman, and slender, and somehow different from the others. After a moment, he saw what that difference was, or he thought that difference was: This woman was far, far cleaner than the rest. But then he perceived it was more than that. More, even, than the fact that she was an attractive, even a handsome female. There was a tension in her, a straining tautness, so that he could almost hear her nerves screaming beneath her skin. As she stared at him now, a visible pulse showed at the base of her throat. He tried to take his eyes off it, but he could not. He lay there gazing at the great vein in the hollow of her neck that stood up and beat and beat until it seemed to him he could hear it. And the sound of it was the sound of his own doom.

"Father," the young girl whispered, her voice awed, dark: "Why have you tied up a god thus? To bind him to your will? For men don't have eyes the color of the sky and hair like—"

"He's but a man, you silly chit!" a shaggy old goat of a Perioeci said. "Man and thief. So get you up from there!"

"Father," the girl whispered, "are you sure?"

"Immortal gods! Deliver me from women!" the old Perioeci roared. "I tell you, Phryne, he is but man. Don't make me prove it ahead of time!"

"No, Deimus," another Perioeci said, "not man—but something less, it appears to me. A boy. A very pretty boy, of the kind our august masters love to use instead of women. Ha! Maybe we should finish him off that way! We could take turns at him until we've drowned him in our seed! A fine sport, eh, friends?"

"Ho, Epidaurus!" a burly brigand cried. "Don't tell me you've such delicate appetites! Oho! Come to think of it, you've been married to Lycotheia these seven years, and her belly's as flat as ever! Never a boarling or a little sow to show for your labors. Come now, Lycotheia, tell the truth: Does the Shaggy One neglect you? I'll bet my prize ram and two ewes against a stinking billygoat that he goes around poking his weapon into dainty, effeminate boys like this towhead, here! Tell us, girl—is our Epidaurus given to the lordly Spartan vices?"

The thin woman shrugged, but kept her mouth shut.

Lycotheia, Ariston thought; a she-wolf. How apt that name is!

"Go home, woman!" Epidaurus howled; and Ariston heard the furious shake that had got into his voice. "And you, Pancratis! Just because your mother horned your old fool of a father with a bull or a bear or some such monstrous beast, don't go too far! There are ways of pulling down even overgrown, muscle-bound oafs like you! By Zeus, I'll—"

"Afraid she'll talk, O Shaggy One?" the big man laughed. "A dead giveaway! Come, Lyco, my girl, tell the truth, and I'll protect you! Is our Epidaurus a man?"

Lycotheia looked away from the colossus, Pancratis. Her gaze came away slowly, slowly from the huge man's face. She stared at her husband coolly, speculatively, for a curiously halted, dead still time. Ariston could see the Shaggy One—for that was what the name Epidaurus meant —paling under his matted hair, behind his beard. When the woman spoke at last, her voice was absolutely venomous.

"A man?" she said calmly, judiciously. "No, I think not. Not much of one, anyhow."

Epidaurus leaped forward then and hammered her to the ground. As he started to kick her where she lay, all the square was loud with the bull bellow of male laughter; and now the women's harsh, high-pitched shrieks joined in.

So must the Erinyes' laughter sound, Ariston thought. Then all his breath caught in his throat, halted by the recognition of the appalling enormity of his offense. "I beg your pardon, Dread Sisters!" he prayed; "I meant to say Eumenides!"

But it was too late now. He had called the Furies by their right name, which, as any Hellene born knew, was to earn their undying anger. And now, in his helpless state, needing as he did the favor of all the gods, of every supernatural being, he had used the forbidden word "Erinyes," Furies, instead of the propitiative title "Eumenides," Kindly Ones.

"Fool!" he all but wept. "Now you've done it! Now you've doomed yourself!"

But then again, his uncle Hippolytus' mocking voice cut through his mind: "Think you, nephew, that the Erinyes are such dullards that they can't see through human deceit? Call them Eumenides all you like, but pretty names won't change their nature. They'll hound you to earth at last, they do all men born. Nothing living escapes them in the end, my boy. So dance to the Goat Song while you can; hark to the panpipes on the hills. Put vine leaves in your hair, drink deep; clasp in hot embrace fair youths and maids! For no man escapes them, no man at all."

Epidaurus was still kicking Lycotheia. Ariston could hear the dull sound of his buskined feet thudding into her flesh through her dress. Why don't they stop him? he thought. Can't they see he'll kill her?

As though she read his thought, the girl who knelt beside him whispered: "Lyco's a foreigner—from Attica, Father says. That's why they hate her so. I—I've tried to be friends with her, but she won't let me. She—she despises me. I don't know why—"

"Because you're pretty, Melanippe," Ariston said.

She stared at him.

"That's not my name," she said.

"It is now," Ariston said; "for I have named you that. Melanippe—little black mare, the loveliest creature the gods have made."

Swine! he mocked himself inside his mind; swine and he-goat and worse! To take this dirty, unknightly way out! But then—what's her innocence against my life? Which, immortal gods, has the greater value in your sight?

"I am called Phryne," she said primly. "And I don't like this name you've given me, captive. Men ride mares. And I am vowed to Artemis—so no man will ever—" She clapped her two hands suddenly to her face, so hard that the sound cut sharply through the bestial roars of the Perioeci as they applauded Epidaurus' murderous beating of his wife.

"Forgive me, my lord captive!" she whispered; "I don't know what's come over me! I have never before even thought such a wicked thing! And now—"

Ariston smiled at her, slowly, carefully. Went on smiling until the corners of his mouth hurt. It was the first time in his life he had deliberately made use of his great beauty. Most of the time he was totally unconscious of it. No more than a week before, when his uncle Hippolytus had been bemoaning his own lack of grace—it seemed one Ioxus had scorned him; but then both women and boys were always scorning fat-bellied Hippolytus, who had no luck in love at all—he had laughed aloud at his uncle's envious cry to the gods to grant him such beauty as Ariston's, be it but for a single night. But his uncle had cut off his burst of laughter.

"Don't laugh, whelp conceived in a haunted glen!" he said. "In this delicate sport, you have all the advantages. Your beauty is so far above that of the commonality of men that it could be called godlike, whatever that means. And after all, no one can *prove* that the divine Dionysus wasn't your father, as my idiotic sister claims—"

Ariston had smiled at his uncle then.

"Do gods exist?" he said.

"No. But don't go around babbling that to everyone you meet! The concept's too useful in the gentle art of bilking fools!"

Like this tender one, now, Ariston thought. She seems a kindly maid—and sweet. 'Tis a pity to— But he went on smiling at her, in spite of the shame his own deceit awoke in him.

"Father is wrong!" she whispered. "You *are* a god, aren't you, captive? Far-shooting Apollo, surely—because your hair—"

He shook his head a little angrily. She really was too stupid to be endured.

"Do gods bleed?" he snorted, "or stay tied up with thongs made by ordinary men? Don't be silly, Phryne! I'm as human as you are. Human enough maybe to even fall in love with you if I could make out what you're really like under all that dirt."

"Oh!" she said. "I bathed no more than a fortnight agon, and—"

14

"Where I come from women bathe every day, but no matter. Look, Phryne—your friends don't seem to be exactly gentle. People who'll watch a man kick a woman to death and never lift a hand—"

"He's not kicking her now," Phryne pointed out.

She was right. Epidaurus wasn't kicking his wife at the moment. He was merely grinding his heel into her face, a feat which the women seemed to find particularly delightful. Likely because she's far better looking than they are, Ariston thought.

"Anyhow, I don't think they'll treat me kindly," he said, "when that Olympiad is over and they get around to my case. If a woman can be beaten to death for sneering at her husband, what will they do to a thief who's robbed them of a goat?"

"Kill you, likely," Phryne said; then: "Oh, no! I won't let them! I'll stop them somehow; I'll—"

Ariston smiled at her, only half in mockery now. It was a bad, even a monstrous thought that had come to him then; but was not death more monstrous still?

"They can kill me," he said calmly. "but they can't make me stay in Tartarus. Hades will release me the minute he sees me. Because although my mother is mortal, which is why I bleed and cannot escape these bonds, my father is the god Dionysus, and I have his powers of resurrection. And, when I do come back, I'll wipe these swine from the face of the earth unless—"

"Unless what, my lord?" she breathed.

"Unless you save me, Melanippe-Phryne," he said. "Go get a knife. Cut me free and—"

"They—they'll kill me!" she wailed.

"I'll protect you. I—I'll reward you greatly! Believe me, I'll make you blessed among all women, if—"

She stared at him.

"Blessed—how?" she said.

He smiled at her in wry self-mockery. Because, all of a sudden, he couldn't go through with it. It was just too rotten. He had a sudden flash of insight as to what life would be, lived out upon the memory of this swinishness. So wildly, idiotically, he threw it away from him by mak-

15

ing it outrageously inacceptable; an offense against her obvious maidenhood, an insult. Yet somehow, saying it, his voice deepened, made grave music, slow, yet playful and tender, as he said:

"I shall give you a child, Melanippe, O little black mare of my heart! And he shall be immortal, and a god!"

She clapped her hands to her cheeks again, as if to contain the heat visibly flaming there. But what she would have answered, what effect his cruel stratagem had had upon her, he did not then discover, for Epidaurus' rage, or his strength, or both, had gone from him, and he paused in his efforts to kick the surprisingly durable Lycotheia to death, so that the sound of Phryne's palms smacking against her own face in a gesture, Ariston realized, habitual to her, attracted her father's attention. Deimus turned away from a spectacle rapidly losing all interest now that it was clear that the Shaggy One would leave his wife not only alive, but not even crippled, and stared at his daughter. He locked his horny hand in the great black mane of her hair, and jerked her to her feet. Holding her like that, the old man slapped her stingingly across the face.

"By Cypris!" he roared. "Has a daemon driven all you bitches mad?" Then he looked quickly at the crowd.

Pancratis, the colossus, had stepped forward now, and caught Epidaurus in his arms.

"Enough, O Shaggy One!" he said good-naturedly; "You've punished your woman sufficiently. And the offense doesn't warrant killing her. Besides, where would you get another piece this fine? Take her home, but hurry back. We've got to decide what to do with the towhead whelp."

Deimus gave Phryne a stiff-armed shove. He was, Ariston saw, sick with worry that some of the others might have noticed how long his daughter had been talking to the captive—and how intimately. Strange, the boy thought; even among goats and monkeys like these, questions of prestige and pride enter in. . . .

"Get you gone, wench!" the old man hissed. " 'Fore Zeus himself, you shame me, girl!"

Phryne stalked off then, her young back very stiff and

16

proud. So the ancient queens must have walked, Ariston thought. Helen and Hecuba and—

But she turned in the doorway of that filthy hut of mud and stones and looked at him. And what was in her eyes was a thing so great, so pure, that for all the time she gazed at him, it stopped his breath, his heart.

He knew one thing then, at long last, and very surely: Women might be, as the men of his polis claimed, brood mares upon whom joylessly a man's sons must be got; but this one, at least, was capable of—no, even suffered—love.

# CHAPTER TWO

HE HAD BEEN IN THAT CAVE a long time. Until the sun had set, he had heard the rumble of male voices debating his fate. But he couldn't make out what they had said. And now it was night; it had been dark for above an hour. They had untied him from the carrying pole; but then they had promptly bound him once again to a tree trunk set into a pile of rocks in the middle of the cave, which was some improvement, but not much. Before the opening, they had put Epidaurus and another man, called Argus—perhaps because of his keen sight, since all the names of this clan seemed to be related to some personal attribute or another—to guard him.

The two men had rumbled away a while; but now, he was sure, they slept. Certainly they had put away enough wine to make them sleepy. The strangest part about it was that Lycotheia had fetched them the wine. As a peace offering to quell her husband's wrath, Ariston guessed.

He leaned back against his pole and closed his eyes. He wasn't hungry any more. Just before dark, they had brought him food, loosed his hands, and stood over him with drawn skinning knives while he ate. It had been surprisingly good: a broth of goat's flesh and lentils, hot and savory. It had put the strength back into him.

"I give you thanks, O Perioeci!" he had said politely.

Whereupon Epidaurus had grinned at him, growled: "Tomorrow you won't, pretty youth! Eat well. The famished die too quickly."

But he had gone on eating with good appetite, despite that. For the well-fed also have the strength needful for escape, he reckoned.

18

Leaning there against the tree trunk, he tried to work loose of his bonds. If he could do that he would be able to step over the snoring, drunken oafs at the door, and before daylight he would be beyond all pursuit. His fingers tore at the leather thongs, but they had been tied by experts; he could not loosen them. It was maddening. The way to life lay open before him, and because of a few rawhide strips, he could not take it. Then he remembered how he had called the Furies by their name, and his heart stood still within him. He fought for hope: The Erinyes were not, after all, gods; he had offended no god, so—

He opened his blue eyes wide. Then, very slowly, he bent his head and wept. The shame in him was a great and terrible thing. To tell poor little Phryne lies in order to save his life was, according to the code of Sparta, acceptable. But when those lies involved a god? Would not the divine Dionysus require of him his life tomorrow under the most fiendish tortures these mountain wolves of Perioeci could devise, for such a blasphemy?

If, indeed—and his bright young head jerked upright, his eyes flared—it were a blasphemy! What if his mother, Alkmena, had been telling the truth? She could have been— that is, if you didn't listen to scoffers like his uncle Hippolytus. Had not great Zeus in the guise of a swan got fair Leda with child? And once more, as a bull, the father of the gods had taken the lovely Europa and—

"Ho!" he could hear his uncle Hippolytus roaring. "A bull, you say, Nephew? And he didn't split her in half?"

But it was better not to listen to rationalists like his uncle. For the alternative in this case was not to be accepted even in thought. He'd got the story from a garrulous slave girl, one Iodama, who'd paid dearly for the looseness of her tongue. For when Ariston had asked the august Telamon about it, that soldier, statesman, member of the Senate, had flown into so great a rage that the beating he had laid upon poor Iodama had scarred her back hideously for the remainder of, and came close to ending her life.

Two weeks later, when Iodama had recovered enough to crawl about the house like a wounded dog, Telamon had called in the slavedealers and sold her. Now she worked in

19

the household of a schoolmate of Ariston's, one Simoeis, a brutal lout who was always making indecent advances to him and whom, as a consequence, he hated. But since both he and Simoeis were members not only of the same bua, or herd, but also of the much smaller ila, or pen, these being the semimilitary classifications into which all the boys in the school were divided, Ariston had to fend off his attentions daily. That the same attentions from Lysander would have delighted him changed matters not at all; at the basis of all morality are such imponderables as instinctive repulsion, while most chastity is accidental, depending largely upon one's *not* encountering any of the various lovers who could melt it with a look, a smile.

But Ariston had to accept his mother's version of his birth, first of all because she herself obviously believed it with all her fervently devout soul. His mother was chaste! She was! There was nothing of porna, or auletride, or hetera about her! Neither whore, nor flute girl, nor courtesan. She, his beautiful, beloved mother, Alkmena, was an angel in the very flesh; a woman of almost awesome purity. And yet—

And yet he, Ariston, had been born two weeks after Telamon's return from diplomatic missions on behalf of Sparta to Euboea and to Megara, said missions being, in part, the cause of the dreary war that had been going on between Sparta and Athens ever since Ariston was twelve years old. And, to the immense delight of every evil old crone in the wall-less city—at least until Telamon had found the means to silence them—the mathematics of Ariston's conception, gestation, birth escaped even two-handed reckoning on their withered fingers. For Telamon had been absent from his hearth fires on those great and momentous affairs of state for two long years. Even if they included their grimy toes, they could not count it up. No, it was very clear: Soldier, statesman, member of the Senate, honored by all Sparta though he was, stern, august Telamon had a new decoration to add to his store—a fine pair of horns, awarded him by his loving wife.

Ariston knew now, bitterly, the rest of it: how Telamon had bided his time until he, Ariston, had been born. Then the man whom all his life he had respected and feared, if not loved, had ordered him thrown from a cliff on Mount Taygetus, as the custom was for disposing of weakling and defective boys, or any girl whose father so saw fit. But his uncle Hippolytus had saved Ariston from that. Before Telamon's sentence could be carried out, that fat clown appeared, serious for once, with the State Council of Eugenic Inspectors in tow. They saw what a magnificent baby Ariston was, and overruled Telamon's jealous rage. Such fine human material must be preserved for the greater glory of Sparta, they declared. And they chided Telamon sternly, quoted great Lycurgus to him on the folly of sexual monopoly. "For is it not absurd," Sparta's great lawgiver had written, "that people should be so solicitous for their dogs and horses as to exert interest and pay money to procure fine breeding, and keep their wives shut up, to be made mothers only by themselves, who might be foolish, infirm, or diseased?"

Then they added insult to injury by pointing out to Telamon that he was well stricken with years; and though wedded to Alkmena on her thirteenth birthday, until now, when she was all of twenty-three, he'd given her no child. Better to bow his head and accept this bounty, than to have his soul howl homeless down the winds for lack of a son to give him the proper funeral rites.

So Telamon had given in. But he had strung poor Alkmena up by the wrists and beat her until all the floor was bedewed with blood to make her name her partner in sin that he might kill him. But until she fainted, and even after she had revived and he started in to beat her once more, she persisted in whimpering, sobbing, screaming:

"The god! It was the great god Dionysus!"

It was said that Telamon continued to beat her at measured intervals for half a year without ever being able to shake her story. Then, seeing that he must fail, he sent a priestess of divine Artemis, goddess of chastity, in to her, knowing that to such a one she'd dare not lie. And heard, as he listened secretly at her door, her voice lifting, soaring, filled with pride:

"I swear it by the white-armed one you serve, O holy votress! There came upon me an ekstasis, a going forth of my soul to meet the god amid those green and mystic

21

groves. And I felt the knowledge of the god within me! Wild music played: flutes, panpipes, lyres, and citheras! I was surrounded by light more brilliant than that of Helios, the sun god! And then—and then I knew no more. But I awoke knowing the god had possessed me, that I had lain enraptured in his great embrace! So, though my husband beat me to death, as he will, he cannot make me deny this glory: My son, sweet Ariston, is half-divine!"

After that, Telamon had grudgingly accepted his bounty, had endured Ariston's presence in his house until, at age seven, the boy had been led away to the gymnasium to join what was at one and the same time his school class and his regiment for life.

Though you'll have to put up with me no more, august Telamon! Ariston thought, for surely, though you punish them for it in all due form and severity, the news that these mountain wolves have butchered me, will delight you to your soul!

The thought was a bitter one. He had spent a goodly part of his few years trying to gain the love of the man he had believed to be his father. And even after Iodama had told him why that was impossible, he had gone on trying to win it. But now, no more! his rebellious young heart cried out within him. What I have to gain now is my life!

He lifted his head toward the roof of the cave.

"Father Dionysus," he prayed, "if you are really my father, save me. If you're not, I ask you still, for my mother in all honesty believes you are. If she were deceived by man or satyr casting upon her mind a spell, the fault is neither hers nor mine, so why then should I die for it? And if I have by thoughtlessness offended the Kindly Ones, I pray that you intercede for me before great Athena, who saved my ancestor Orestes from them, establishing thus the rule of law. I dare not pray to her, since my polis is at war with her chosen city. But I am too young to die! I beg you, divine Dionysus, save me, if you will!"

He stopped, listened. The silence was a weight upon his ears. Were there gods? Did they answer prayer? Or was his uncle Hippolytus right in his belief that they were but the invention of cowards afraid to die?

I must not think these terrible things! he thought. They're impieties and—

And then, at that precise moment, he heard the dull sodden thudding sound. Another. A groan rolled hollowly in from the opening of the cave. A choking, strangling gurgle. The beginning of what he was sure was going to be a scream. But it was muffled suddenly. The thudding sound came again. And again. Ten, twelve, twenty times. Then silence rode in upon him, louder than Zeus's thunder.

He saw the flickering little flame coming toward him. It was a clay bowl filled with oil, in which a length of cord was alight. Above it, the woman's bruised and swollen face was absolutely terrible. Her eyes were fixed upon him, glaring, penetrating, wild.

"Lycotheia!" Ariston said.

"Yes, it's me," Lycotheia said. "Who'd you expect, bastard of god—Phryne? Ha! That simpering little filly hasn't enough womanhood, or enough plain bitchery—call it what you like—in her to do what I've done for you. And for myself—why should I lie? The final impiety! Yes, yes—I've killed for your sweet sake, Ariston! I've butchered a swine. No, two. A double pig-sticking before the high altar of your beauty. That hairy pervert I was forced to marry; he who left my warm and willing bed to go hide behind rocks on the trail in the mere hope that some defenseless little boy would pass his way. And with him that fool who boasted of his keen sight. By now he's keenly gazing on the naked shades in hell. I drugged them first. I steeped poppy seeds in their wine. Added the juice of the flower to make sure. Which made the operation painless. Or almost. Kind of me, wasn't it? So now you must reward me, son of Dionysus, or else—"

"Son of Dionysus?" Ariston said. "Did Phryne—?"

"Tell me that? No, O divine youth, divinely beautiful! I overheard her. She screamed it out to her fearful old fool of a father when she learned of the fate these foals of she-goats covered by asses plan for you tomorrow—as if it were possible to kill the resurrecting god!"

Mad, Ariston thought. Better to humor her. . . .

"What fate is that, Lycotheia?" he said.

"One only such cowardly dogs as the Perioeci would have thought of," Lycotheia said contemptuously. It came to Ariston then that she did not consider herself one of them. Why should she? he thought. Phryne said she is a foreigner, and besides, she's more than a cut above them in a good many ways.

"And that is?" he said.

"You're to be stoned. Since none of them trusts the other, they decided upon that. Or else, as they know only too well, some treacherous swine or another would betray the rest to your people for a handful of rusty iron coins. This way no one will dare, because your blood will be equally upon his hands. But enough of that folly! Will you reward me, son of a god?"

"Reward you how?" Ariston said.

"Take me with you," Lycotheia said. "As your wife, or your concubine, I don't care which—as long as it is away from these dung-smelling sons and daughters of all filth. Take me to Sparta, so I can live again—as I used to in Attica. As a woman, rather than a she-beast. Give me the ultimate glory—of being beloved of a god!"

"But I'm not—" Ariston began.

"Ha! With that beauty of yours that has driven every woman in the village mad? I tell you, son of Dionysus, that not one of these Perioeci she-asses has escaped having her unwashed hide mottled with a few more bruises for your sake, this night. Because you put such sweet dreams of immortal rut in their itchy loins—that's where they wear whatever brains they have, anyhow—that one and all they started in to nag their he-goats of husbands, giving them ten thousand reasons why you should be let off, which naturally only succeeded in getting the oafs wild. Poor, silly Phryne—they say she's going to die, old Deimus whipped her so."

"No!" Ariston said. "Don't tell me that! Immortal gods! I'll—"

"You'll ruin your chances by making me jealous," Lycotheia mocked. "I never could abide that little black-maned filly, anyhow. Too close to being human. I suppose her mother got her with a Spartan behind old Tremble-Tail's back. Forget Phryne; you'll never have her. Besides,

24

you'd better remember that you're still tied up like a hog, with only me to cut you loose. Do you promise?"

Ariston did not answer her. The temptation was great, but—

She lifted her hands and touched his face. He both smelled and saw the thick ropy blood with which they were covered, and recoiled from her in horror. For among the Hellenes of any polis whatsoever, murder was not only a crime but a veritable blasphemy, an offense in the nostrils of the gods who had given men life. And it was not alone from outrage that he rejected the wolf-woman now, but also from a sure conviction that her help would be no help at all, would in fact damn his shade forever.

"Get away from me, she-wolf!" he howled. "Don't touch me with your bloody hands!"

She stared at them as though she were seeing them for the first time. Then, very quietly, she turned and went out of the cave, stepping like a sleepwalker over the butchered bodies lying there. When, five minutes later, she came back, her hands were clean. She bent forward and sought his mouth. He thrashed his head from side to side to avoid her lips, but she imprisoned his face between her two hands, icy from the water of the mountain stream in which she had washed them, and clung her mouth to his endlessly. Her breath was fetid. It stank of rotting teeth, garlic, leeks, even of—of blood. Instead of arousing him, her kisses sickened him unto death.

She took her mouth away and ran her cold hands over his body under his single garment, committing finally the impiety for which, he knew, women in olden times were condemned to death, fondling the sacred organs of his maleness, trying thus to incite him to lust. But he would not, could not respond to her. She stepped back, stared at him, her eyes sick with rage.

"Since that's what you want, die, dog!" she said. "I thank Zeus I didn't untie you first!"

Then she went back through the opening, stepping carefully over the bodies of the men she had slain, and left him there.

God's son or not, Ariston of Sparta bent his head and wept.

He wept a long time, until the weariness in his body overcame him. He sagged against his bonds, slept. Only to be wakened almost instantly, it seemed to him, by a feeling of looseness, the cruel biting of the thongs at his wrists and elbows gone. He tried lifting his hands and found that they were free.

"Quiet, my lord!" that soft, sweet voice came over to him. "Do not make a sound until I cut your feet loose, so that you can run."

"Phryne!" he said. "But she—I was told that you were near to death!"

"Hush!" Phryne hissed. "Your guards will hear us!"

"They're past all hearing now," Ariston said. "Tell me, my Melanippe, is it true that your father beat you because—"

"It doesn't matter," she said. "I only pretended to faint so he wouldn't watch me too closely, thinking me too badly hurt to move. My father's very old; the strength's gone from his arm, now. But your guards—"

All Ariston's Spartan training in deceit told him to lie now.

"They're drunker than Athenian lords," he said. "Zeus Thunderer couldn't wake them up now, after all the honeyed wine they've swilled. Let's go, little dark one—"

He took her arm, started toward the cave's mouth.

"Not that way," she said.

"There's another way?" Ariston said.

"Yes. I found it last year when a kid got lost from my father's herd. At first I thought the wolves had got him, but then I heard him bleating. He'd fallen down a hole. I went down to get him out, and got lost myself. This cave is bigger than anyone knows but me. I came out on the other side of the mountain—where those terrible far trails are. They're haunted, you know, my lord—"

"Don't call me my lord. Call me Ariston. Haunted by what?"

"Demons. And the shades of all the people who were buried in the avalanche. Three whole villages perished. Now nobody goes that way anymore. Not even Pancratis, big and strong as he is. But you can, seeing as how you're half divine. So come on—"

26

When they had gone a considerable distance beyond the place where the Perioeci had had him bound, she took out of her robes a little box. In it she had the materials for fire-making: a lump of iron, a piece of flint, some dry, half-charred rags. Expertly she knocked the iron against the flint, caught the sparks, blew them into flame. Then she put her hand into a crevice in the rocks and drew out a lamp, which surely she had left there before coming to free him.

She lit it, and by its soft, flickering glow, he saw a small miracle. They were in a lovely grotto where the stalactites and stalagmites had formed a temple fit for the Olympian gods. And Phryne was startlingly, spotlessly clean. She was clad in an ankle-length homespun dress of white lamb's wool, with an equally snowy peplos draped about her shoulders, and no trace of smoke, soot, or grime remained upon her.

He stared at her. Her face was lovely. She was as beautiful as Lysander, though in a different way. And now, very simply, she lifted her mouth to his. They kissed, long and deeply. When he tore his mouth free at last, there were panpipes in his blood, nymph song, bacchanalian flutes, soaring, wild.

But she pushed him gently away from her.

"Come, Ariston, my lord," she said, "for there is no time."

He reeled along beside her like a drunken man. Certainly neither Lysander nor any other boy, no matter how beautiful, had ever made him feel like this. He understood suddenly why the man the Gerousia had condemned to death for ravishing a woman of the citizen class had committed his mad act. Women had a magic in them, an enchantment that boiled the blood inside your veins, tormented your very soul into madness and—

But he was to suffer worse. For suddenly, ahead of them, he heard the sound of running water. Phryne stopped, clapped both her hands to her face in that characteristic gesture of hers.

"O Ariston!" she wailed.

"Now what?" he said.

"The river! The river! I forgot all about it!"

He stared at her. His uncle Hippolytus said there was no comprehending women, and he was beginning to realize that his uncle was right.

"Didn't you come this way?" he said.

"No! I came in through the hole my kid fell into, but we can't go that way. It's on the far side of the village so we'd have to go straight through the square to reach any trail at all. That's why I thought about this one. Because, as I told you, it comes out on the demon-haunted trail where the shades of those people, who had no relatives left to make the sacrifices and give them the proper funeral rites, moan and gibber at you from behind every rock. Only—"

"Only what, Phryne?"

"You—you got me so upset that I forgot about the river. I spent the whole evening scrubbing myself—I didn't want you to call me dirty any more—and thinking about you. How—how beautiful you are! With your skin and hair both golden, and your eyes like the heavens are in October, just before the rains come. That's why I didn't remember about the river. O Ariston, how stupid I am!"

"I'll carry you across it," he said. "We're trained to swim across the Eurotas while clad in a full suit of armor, Phryne. In comparison to that you weigh nothing at all."

"I can swim," she said. "In fact, if I had to, I could carry you across a river, armor and all. It's not that—"

"Then what in the name of all the Chthonic gods is it?" he said.

"We don't have to merely swim across the river, Ariston my lord. We have to swim down it—a long, long way. More than a hippicon, I'd guess. . . ."

"So?" he said.

She stamped her foot.

"How thick-headed you men are! Don't you see if I tried to swim in this long robe, it would drag me down and I'd drown? And without me to lead you, you'll never find the way. It has many branches, this river. . . ."

"Then take off your robe. Leave it here," Ariston said, reasonably enough.

She stared at him, and her eyes were big with horror.

"Oh, Ariston, I—I couldn't!" she said.

28

"And why in the name of cloud-bearing Zeus can't you?" he demanded.

"Because—because then I'd be naked!" she wailed.

"So?" he said, amazed at a scruple totally incomprehensible to a Spartan. "What difference does that make? I've seen naked girls all my life. In the greater Dionysia all the maids dance naked in the processions, and so do we—the boys, I mean. Nobody thinks anything of it. Lycurgus, the Lawgiver, put that in his laws so that all Spartans, men and women alike, would be encouraged to have fine bodies. That's why our girls are the most beautiful in all Hellas— they diet and exercise daily so that when they take part in the sacred rites they won't have to be ashamed of having ugly bodies. Yours is nice, I think. You don't look deformed or crippled or anything. Do you have scars or blemishes? Here, let me see. My uncle knows an iatros capable of removing any mark from the skin without a trace, so—"

"Ariston!" she cried. "Don't you touch me! Don't you dare!"

He stood there looking at her, and now his blue eyes were dark with sudden hurt. She saw that, and came to him at once. She put her arms around his neck and peered into his face, but her gaze was troubled with a kind of anguish he couldn't begin to understand.

"I—I love you, Ariston," she said. "Only—among us, nakedness is a shameful thing. I—I'd heard that the boys of Sparta exercise entirely naked—and that the girls marched unclothed in the processions. But I didn't believe it. I didn't—and I don't—see how any girl could stand to dance and fling herself about with nothing on before the eyes of men. I—I'd die. Tell me—do you love me?"

"With all my heart!" he said. And it was almost true.

"All right," she sighed. "I'm your wife—or I will be when you come back for me. And I have to show you the way. Where we come out, it will be already light, because that's near the other entrance, and the sun will be up by then. So you'll be able to see me—before we've said any vows or offered up burnt sacrifices on the high altar, which is a terrible thing! Will you promise not to look at me?"

That, he realized, was going to be a promise difficult to keep. So he offered her what seemed to him a perfectly acceptable alternative.

"Could you swim in my chiton?" he said.

"Why—why, yes. It's very short and light. But—you?"

"Here, take it, then," he said, and whipped it off.

She took a backward step, both hands clapped hard to her cheeks.

"Ariston!" she gasped, and turned her back to him.

"Immortal gods!" he said. "Deliver me from women! Now what have I done? I'm trying to preserve this famous Perioeci modesty of yours, and you—"

"But, Ariston—dearest—I'm not supposed to see you either!"

He laughed then, gaily. Put out his hands and caught her by the shoulders. Turned her about to face him.

"Well, now you have," he said. "Am I repulsive? Deformed? Blemished? Ugly?"

"No!" She wept. "You—you're beautiful! I've never seen a man naked before, but I think only a god could have such a form. Only, my lord Ariston, for a woman to look upon a man who is not her husband without his clothes on is a terrible sin! Now something awful is going to happen to me! I know it! I feel it in my bones!"

"Nonsense," he said. "Give me your peplos."

She turned her face from him, took the shawl from about her shoulders, held it out blindly in his direction. He took it, bent and found his cord belt, picked it up. In half a heartbeat, he had fashioned a loincloth for himself.

"Better?" he said.

"Yes," she whispered. "Now turn your back—oh, Ariston, please!"

In his chiton, she made a fetching sight. Carefully she rolled her long robe up and placed it in the cleft of a rock. Then she blew out the lamp and laid it beside her robe.

He saw a dim white flash, heard the water leap up as she dived. He followed her at once. The water was icy. It was blacker than the Styx, than the stream of Lethe. Yet she seemed to know exactly where to go. He was an excellent swimmer, as good or better than his boasts; but she drew ahead of him effortlessly. They swam a long time, so long that he became conscious of the beginning of an ache in his arms. Then he saw the light ahead. He could see her white arms stroking powerfully, the swift flutter of her feet kicking. They reached the rock bank. She climbed up and put out her hand to him. But he hung there in the river, paralyzed. For his chiton, soaking wet, clung to her like a second skin. And never before had he seen a female body as lovely as this, in any Dionysian procession, or at any of the games.

"Great Cypris, aid me!" he prayed, and climbed up beside her. But desire was in him like a brand, so he dragged her into his arms. At once his fingers felt the ridges, the welts upon her shoulders. He whirled her around and dragged the chiton down about her hips. Stood there and stared at the horror her young back had been reduced to now. And try as he would, he could not keep back his tears.

"For me," he whispered, "you suffered—this!"

She pulled the chiton back up over her shoulders before she turned to him. Then she put up her arms and laid her hands along the slant of his jaw, just beginning to show a faint blurring of the golden down of his first beard.

"For you, O son of Dionysus, I would die," she said.

"Phryne—" he groaned.

"No, Ariston," she said. "There is no time! I won't—lend you my body at the cost of your life. Perhaps you *can* rise from the dead, come back from dark Tartarus—but I'd rather not take a chance on it. I want you living and in the world with me. And—and I know I'm not of your station, nor of your race—but I—I want to be more to you than a concubine. I want the vows said, and the sacrifices made. I want to hear the chants lifted to Hymenea and know the gods approve—" She laughed suddenly, impishly. "Besides, with my back in ribbons from my father's beating, I couldn't, anyhow! So kiss me, and go—I hope—"

"What, little Phryne?" he said.

"That you—you won't forget me. Leave me here to pine away until, like poor Echo, there's nothing left of me but a voice. Oh, Ariston, son of the god, will you really—"

"Come back? No. I'll send my father to call formally upon yours to ask your hand for me, which is the way it should be done, according to our customs. Since you're poor, he'll ask no dowry. For you are dowry enough for me, my sweet."

He found, to his utter astonishment, once those words were out, that he meant them—meant them with all his soul.

"Oh, Ariston!" she breathed, and clung to him. What saved them both at that moment was that their bodies were dripping wet and blue from cold. "How will he come to us?" she said. "Won't his glory blind us? Will we even be able to see him? I've heard that to mortals, the gods—"

"I mean my foster-father, who is a senator and a strategos, a leader of armies," Ariston said. "Hence he is mortal. And now, little Melanippe—"

She stamped her foot.

"Don't call me that!" she said.

"Melanippe, Aganippe, Anippe, Arrhippe, Leucippe, and of all my Leucippedes, Leucippoi, Melanippedes, and Melanippoi, the mother to be!"

She laughed then, gaily. For in one breath he had called her black mare, mare who kills mercifully, queenly mare, best of mares, white mare, and mother to be of all his fillies and stallions, black and white together—which was a thing that only the marvelously rich and flexible tongue he spoke was capable of. But then he bent and kissed her. A long time. A very long time. Until they were no longer cold.

She tore free of him and ran to the riverbank, dived very cleanly into the black, icy waters. He stood there watching her arrowing downstream, swift, sure. But at the last moment, she trod water and blew him a kiss. Then she dived beneath the dark river and disappeared. He knew she'd come up beyond the bend, but terror knifed his breath. Because he couldn't live without her now. The very thought was a little, anticipatory death. With a great sigh, he turned and went through the opening into the light.

He had been going downhill for half an hour when it came to him. If he returned to the gymnasium empty-handed with no stolen prize to explain his long absence, the paidonomos would order him whipped again. And suddenly the very thought was an outrage. His body was no longer a machine for killing, but a temple where bright and pure there burned the sacred flame of love. He'd not have Lysander, languid, pouting, gaze upon him as he twisted in silent pain, nor that gross lout Simoeis, whom he'd never been able to beat at wrestling, jeer as the lash sang and bit. Over one single night, he had changed totally. And the nature of the change was this: that it was no longer the agonizing pain of a whipping that troubled him, but the total, intolerable indignity of it.

He hung there, thinking: Those Perioeci owed him a goat in recompense for all they'd put him through. And now that the advantages were all on his side, he'd best make the most of them. For, over these dark and forbidden trails, he could approach his former captors' huts from behind and above. He'd be able to see them long before they caught a glimpse of him. And, doubtless—he exulted at the thought—they were all away from home by now, pounding down the normal trail in search of him!

So thinking, he turned in his tracks and started once more to climb. As he did so, he occupied his mind with arguments to use upon his foster-father. How would he ever convince that stern, forbidding old man that he should be allowed to marry a lowly Perioeci girl? The more he thought about it, the worse his chances seemed. Telamon, senator and general that he was, simply could not permit the boy whom all the world—except the fair Alkmena, her brother Hippolytus, and the members of the Eugenic Inspection Board, who naturally had kept their mouths shut about it—believed to be his son, to so dishonor his house. Then Ariston shrugged off his gloomy thoughts. What mattered it if he could marry Phryne or not, as long as he could have her? And no power on earth could prevent that. He had only to descend fully armed upon the village in the night and carry her off by force. In Sparta, he could set her up in a little house. Telamon, who had no patience at all with the growing modern tendency to tolerate homosexual love, would not only approve, but chuckle at his son's manliness, and fix an allowance for her support. . . . Of course, at age thirty, he, Ariston, would be forced to marry a proper Spartan maiden; but she would have no power to make him give up his love.

Besides, thirty was a long way off. To each day its own sorrows!

He could see the village now, lying below him in the sun. It seemed deserted. Not a soul was in sight. Odder still, no single wisp of smoke climbed up from the lintels of the doors, for these mountaineers, subjected to the torrential rains and snows of winter, dared not cut a hole in the roof as city dwellers did to let the smoke out. It was this, in fact, which accounted for the usual sooty griminess of their clothes and skins. But the absence of smoke indicated that not even the women were at home, and that was very strange indeed.

Have they joined the men in chasing me? he thought. Then he decided it didn't matter. For just beyond the village a herd of goats cropped grass, entirely untended, in the sun.

He had taken the goat kid in his arms—the same one so that they would know that it was he who had robbed them after all—when he heard those cries. He hung there, frozen, listening to them. Then it came to him that there was not a male voice among them. Maenads, surely, he thought. Harpies, perhaps or—or the Kindly Ones!

"Let us be off, little stinker!" he said to the kid, and started up the back trail. But he had gained no more than twenty rods above the village, when he saw it. A lone woman—no, a girl, clad only in a short shift, more like a man's chiton than a woman's longer robe, stumbled drunkenly out between two houses into the clearing. She was literally covered with blood. Her shift was soaked with it. Her long black hair was matted, dripping tendrils of black scarlet down her cheeks. Ariston stood still. His breath stopped within his lungs. His heart no longer beat. She reeled, and, raising her face toward the heavens, gazed straight up at him. Gazed at him dumbly, imploringly with the one eye she had left, for the other hung against her cheek like a bloody onion on a string.

She opened her mouth to call his name, but all that came out was a rush of blood. Then the other women came out from between all the houses. They had stones in their hands. Reaping hooks. Kitchen knives. All of them, except Lycotheia. She had something else in her hands. Then

Ariston saw what it was: Phryne's robe. The same one she'd put on to come to save him. Doubtless her best one, the dress she saved for religious ceremonies, festivals, games, dances. But how in the name of the dark and terrible Chthonic gods had this she-wolf—

Then he knew. Lycotheia had followed them. Had stopped, baffled by that Stygian underground stream— very likely she couldn't swim—until she had seen the robe carefully folded, lying there. Had snatched it up and—

Now slowly, ceremoniously, the wolf-woman spread it out. It too was stained; but on it the splotches were dry, gone black.

"The blood of my poor husband!" Lycotheia intoned like a priestess, "shed by this she-goat that she might wallow in her filthy lust! Avenge him, O my sisters! Avenge poor Argus, too, who has no wife, no sons to do him honor, so their shades suffer not the torments of the unavenged!" Then her voice rising, grating, shrilling, she screamed out:

"Kill her!"

Ariston did not see who threw the first stone. But then all the air was white with them. He couldn't move. He could not breathe. He hung there, his blue eyes stretched wide, staring upon that horror.

Phryne went down under the impact of half an hundred stones. She lay upon the earth, shuddering a little still. Step by step Lycotheia approached her. There was no stone in the wolf-woman's hands. No reaping hook. No knife. There was nothing in her hands, nothing at all. Then with a howl that drove ice slivers through Ariston's heart, she hurled herself upon the unconscious girl. Her clawing fingers locked into Phryne's matted, blood-slimed hair. She jerked the girl's head back, back. Her own head came down in a she-wolf's lunge, and there before their eyes, she sank her ugly, fanglike teeth into Phryne's slim throat.

Ariston could see his beloved's head jerk, as Lycotheia worried at her throat, snarling doglike, wolflike, through locked and savage teeth. Then all the others were upon Phryne, too, in an avalanche of thick, black-skirted bodies, a lifting, a glittering of blades.

He saw, just before night crashed down upon his head, before his own vomit strangled him out of consciousness,

35

something lifted high in triumph. Then he saw what it was: one of the long, sweet legs that had pressed against him for an all too brief moment in the cave, promising what now he'd never know—

The women of Parnon had hacked it off at the hip.

When he came to himself again, all his body covered with the vile stink of the products of his nausea, he didn't remember it at first. Then memory drove brine and ice and fire and gall into his bowels. He screamed aloud, his voice high, woman-shrill, wailing. He got up very slowly, stumbling to his feet without using his hands. He didn't want to look down into that village, but he couldn't help it.

The women were gone. The only living things left in the clearing now were the dogs. And they—

God God God God.

He whirled, his eyes sunblazed, blind, and fled down the farther, forbidden trails. He did not realize then that it would be these that his life would thenceforth forever take.

And, as he trotted wearily down the outlying streets of the wall-less city, his biceps ached dully, unaccountably, as though they bore a weight. Looking down, he saw they did.

He still had the little goat clasped tenderly in his arms.

# CHAPTER THREE

FROM WHERE HE SAT, near the head of the table—the richness of his prize having gained him that honor—Ariston looked out over the faces of his companions. They were roaring with laughter. For, in one of the rare and capricious moods of indulgence to which he was occasionally given, the paidonomos had allowed them to make a feast with the spoils of their raids. But as always he had mixed in a dash of bitter with the sweet: Before the boys now, four Helots staggered, reeled, fell, crawled on their bellies, wallowed hoglike on the floor, mouthing thick-tongued stupidities in their countrymen's dialect, even befouling their already filthy rags the more with vomit and urine.

By this object lesson the paidonomos meant, it was clear, to demonstrate to the boys the folly of drunkenness. A Spartan must be cool-headed, clear of sight. Witless sots do not win wars.

Ariston watched the sickening display. But he could not help wondering which was more sickening: the antics of the drunken Helots, or the type of mind that thought nothing of debasing men out of humanity to serve as horrible examples, to prove a point.

"Because," his uncle Hippolytus had said, "even the Helots once were men, before we demeaned them, reducing them into beasts of burden, forcing them to wear those ridiculous badges of servitude: the sheepskin mantle and the dogskin cap. They and the Perioeci are exactly the same race, except that the Perioeci escaped to the mountains and thus freed themselves, to some extent, of our control. Though some of the Perioeci bear our blood through intermarriage, and many of them are gentle folk, even civilized—"

Gentle. Civilized. Whose women had torn Phryne limb from limb. Tossed her butchered, dismembered carcass—unrecognizable as anything human, so much mangled meat, hacked and broken bones—upon the ground to be devoured by dogs. And he, Ariston—

Sat here at the banquet table, and ate well and slowly, fighting back his nausea. No one there could tell from his young face's total impassivity that he lay under a sentence of death, by himself imposed, to be carried out by his own hand before another sun should rise.

For he was a Spartan, and he had played the coward. In Sparta, the penalty for cowardice was death. What mattered it that no one on earth knew what was within him now, what screamed and gurgled blood and seared his lungs with alternations of ice and fire? He watched the drunken Helots; but his private daimonion spoke softly, sternly, flatly in his inner ear:

"You left her. You stood there and watched it. You saw them disembowel her, scatter her entrails to—"

"I was alone!" He wept inside his mind. "I had no weapons! They would have killed me too—just as the maenads kill any man who stumbles upon their revels! I could not have saved her in any case! They'd have torn me limb from limb—"

"So?" his daimonion said.

That was all. That was the root of it. For, under those circumstances, his simple, inescapable obligation had been to die. Only by facing that pack of she-wolves bare-handed; only by accepting their stones, their reaping hooks, their knives upon and in his naked flesh, standing tall there above and in defense of her who had honored him with her love, her trust, could he have preserved his arete, his manhood, saved in himself those qualities without which it is not possible for a man to live: his honor, and his pride.

So now? He watched the drunken Helots, ignored the banter of his fellows. He was oblivious of the fact that the beautiful Lysander was at long last studying his face with some care. He had to die. He would go to the Temple of Artemis, goddess of chastity, and fall upon his sword before her altar in penance for not having defended the chastity —for the way the women of Parnon had killed Phryne was a kind of violation as well as murder—of a maiden vowed to her service.

No. He couldn't pour out his blood in libation before Artemis now. The goddess would reject his sacrifice with scorn. For he had made poor Phryne renounce her oath, would even have robbed her of her virginity itself, had his base preoccupation with saving his own precious skin allowed him the time. More, he had called down the gods' wrath upon her dark-maned head with his lying, blasphemous, deceitful promises. Was it not likely that Dionysus had struck her down for entertaining the impious hubris, the vanity, of believing she could become the mother of a god?

So she had believed that! What was there so terrible in such a belief? Could not any Hellene name scores of women who had lain with this or that lecherous god, and borne as a consequence a glorious, semi-divine son? Had not many of these bastards of gods been granted immortality? More, had not dozens of them been permitted after their mortal lives were over to rise again from the dead and ascend to cloudy Olympus, becoming gods themselves?

That she had believed him showed only that she was devout. At worst, her sins—if they were sins—were credulity, accepting a Spartan's lies, a country lass's naive pride. No more than that. No more!

His blue eyes went black in his face. "Great Dionysus, father of mine or not," he raged, "if you—if all the gods—punish such petty faults with such awful penalties, I curse you all! Send the Erinyes—no, let me call them by their names, making the impiety complete—send Alecto, Tisiphone, and Megaera, who haven't an iota of kindliness about them, down upon me; and I curse you still! But of one alone among you would I retain until the dawn some favor—to him to whom presently I'll offer up my life! Tell me, Father Dionysus, who shall it be? Ares, god of war, who despises cowards? Hermes, god of liars, thieves, and cheats? Or dark Hades, ruler over Tartarus, the Underworld, he whom men deceitfully call Pluto, the Rich, Lord of Death?"

"To no god," his daimonion, his familiar demon, told him quietly. "Nor must you die by your own hand—"

"Then," he whispered, "how—"

"You must return and honor Phryne. Think you that Deimus, whose very name means 'The Fearful' will dare gather up his daughter's scattered bones to give them pious burial? Can you upon your cur-dog cowardice stand to pile impious neglect? Would you condemn the shade of her who in all honor is your bride to wander pale and fainting through the dust, the heat of summer, whimpering through the winter rains for the lack of a kinsman, lover, friend, to appease the vengeful gods by the proper funeral rites? Would you leave her memory forever dishonored by Lycotheia's lies? Will you lift no pallid, trembling hand to avenge her? Will you not do these things, Ariston, do them though you die, and by such a death redeem your manhood, uphold whatever pretensions you may have to honor? Or think you to accomplish such an end by this quick and easy dying, by a suicide's cowardly blade?"

Ariston pushed back his stool to stand up—for the Spartans did not recline upon couches while eating as the more effeminate Athenians did—when something caught his eye: One of the Helots, a red-bearded giant of a man—so Odysseus must have looked, Ariston thought—gazed straight into his face with calm, untroubled, alert blue eyes. Ariston halted then. Two things came home to him that instant: This man must have Doric, Thracian, or even Macedonian blood, because no Lakedaemonian who was not of the conquering Dorians, or who came, in fact, from any of the southern Hellenic tribes, would have had his fair and ruddy coloring; and he was not—even slightly—drunk. That he wallowed with the rest was but a ruse.

How had such a one, whose face betrayed intelligence, had, even, a certain comeliness, been born among the Helots? Or perhaps he was a former Perioeci, from one of the scattered towns where Dorian colonists, preceding by some generations the general invasion in which their tardy kinsmen had overwhelmed the Peloponnesus, had settled and mingled their blood with the darker aborigines. Such a one might well be reduced by debt, minor crime, or some other misfortune to helotry. That would explain it.

What was beyond explanation, however, was why he was gazing upon Ariston's face so, with an expression of tor-

40

tured longing commingled with what was surely pride. It was this unfeigned emotion at the sight of the boy that had made him forget his role, reveal the fact he had somehow managed to evade drunkenness—likely by holding his wine in his mouth, and then spitting it out unobserved, Ariston thought.

But the abrupt arresting of Ariston's motion, his long, careful stare at the Helot, did not go unobserved. Simoeis, who rather fancied himself as a composer and singer, paused in the drinking song of his own gross and bawdy invention, and gazed, too.

"That swine's not drunk!" he bellowed. "Is he, Ariston?"

Ariston shrugged. Nothing could persuade him to agree with Simoeis about anything whatsoever.

"How would I know?" he said. "Since I'm not inside his belly, how can I measure how much wine he's got there?"

Simoeis grinned at Ariston then. The opportunity, to him, was priceless. Nor did he neglect it. For it was not more than a week ago that, lying upon Iodama's plump and pleasant breasts, with her stout thighs but beginning to relax their hold about his muscular rump, he had wormed out of her the means to destroy Ariston forever, destroy this beautiful golden youth who had scorned all his advances for years, rejected the love that burned in his great and clumsy body, granted him not even an occasional kiss or a furtive bodily caress, the way that the even more beautiful, but somehow less exciting, Lysander now and again did.

"Yes, Ariston, you're right!" he roared. "You're not inside his belly—not now. But very likely you came out of it. Or at least the seed that made you did!"

The babble died. Every singer halted in midnote. Even the most intemperate admitted to themselves that Simoeis had gone too far. For such an insult, Ariston had the perfect right to kill him. If he could. Which was where the rub lay. But Simoeis was not done. He had to pile outrage upon outrage, make his meaning entirely clear.

"Ho! Helot!" he bellowed. "You're the god Dionysus in disguise, aren't you? Come back to visit the son you got upon the fairest of your handmaidens? For, friends and lovers, it is fitting and pious that we all bow down before the golden Ariston! For though, in his modesty, he would deny it, it is known to all men that he is a son of the god!"

"Simoeis—" Ariston whispered.

"How else would you account for it, Ariston? For your beauty is not the beauty of mortals. Were you not born in the thirty-seventh year after Thermopylae? And where was the august Telamon in that year, O lovers, friends? And in the thirty-sixth as well? From where did he return scarcely a fortnight before the beautiful Ariston first saw the light of day?"

"Simoeis—" Ariston's voice was less than sound.

"Two years absent from his hearth fires was the august Telamon! Unwise, was it not, my lovers? Or, perhaps, wise. For else, how could a man well sunk in years even then, with age snowing his inky beard and hair, have sired this glorious, golden beauty? The lovely Alkmena—Dionysus witness she is fair enough even yet that, were I her son, I should be tempted to the sin of Oedipus—grew restive, did she not, O son of the resurrected god? So she, your fair and neglected mother, wandered up into hills to join the maenads, and there—"

Ariston's chiton came off his body in one long ripping sound as it tore away from the fibula, the pin that held it together at his left shoulder. The rope belt at his waist, but loosely tied, burst free at once, fell to his feet. The chiton made a whitish blur as he hurled it to the floor. Now entirely naked, as the Spartan custom for hand-to-hand fighting demanded, he started toward Simoeis.

Simoeis grinned, and threw off his short robe in his turn. Fell into the wrestler's crouch, his huge hands curving into bear paws, ready to rend, to tear.

"Come, my beautiful, golden one, my love!" he crooned, "that I may serve you as the god, or some herdsman, or even this slave-dung here—note well his hair is red, his eyes blue!—served your mother! Come unto me that I may decide which of your tender orifices to ream out for you with my mighty weapon: the toothless, or the toothed! Come let me delight you, golden Ariston, son of the god, or of god knows whom!"

The rage in Ariston was a deadly thing, but most deadly in this: that it was cold. One who has lived through the sights, sounds, even smells—nameless now, unspeakable in the precise physical sense that had anyone asked him to tell what had happened to Phryne, describe her violation out of life by the women of Parnon, the muscles of his throat would have corded, locked, shutting off his breath; the blood and bile rising from entrails literally torn by grief, by horror, would have risen to his mouth and choked him —is proof thereafter against any lesser outrage, has had mind, sense, heart, and even soul numbed, or armored, or both, against excess of grief or rage or pain.

Grapple with this huge ox, and he will maim me, he thought, his brain clear as the icy waters of a mountain stream. But I am far quicker than he, and if—

"Ares aid me!" he prayed aloud. "To you, O mighty god of war, I dedicate this blood sacrifice! To the death, Simoeis! You hear me? To the death!"

Big as he was, Simoeis paled a little at the way Ariston's voice sounded, saying that. Then he recovered and boomed out, his bass shaking noticeably:

"So be it, bastard of god or man! To the death!"

Then he hurled himself forward, a bull charging, an avalanche of dark, sweating flesh, roaring down upon—

Nothing. For Ariston was not there. The motion he made, dancing aside, was incredibly graceful. As Simoeis thundered by him, he went up on tiptoe, his two hands clasped together to make a double fist, and hammered down with all his strength on the back of that bull-neck. Simoeis crashed down across one of the tables, reducing it to firewood, to faggots, splinters. Lay there, dazed. When he got to his feet, his great barrel of a belly was besmeared with the remnants of the feasts, but what gushed from his nose and mouth was blood.

The roar the boys sent up at that sight racked sound out of existence. Nearly all of them had suffered at Simoeis' hands. They had endured him because, until now, his size and strength had made him invicible; but seeing him blood-ied, shaken, his knees trembling, they were like a pack of wolves howling at the very prospect of the kill.

And now Ariston smiled, his mouth curling in an expression cruel as death. He moved away from Simoeis, skipping backward almost as fast as most of his schoolmates could have run forward. When his broad young back struck the wall, he seemed to rebound, to leap forward like a stone whipped from a sling. Even while his hurling, burnt-golden body blurred sight in that forward rush, he saw, out of one corner of his eye, out of the matchless peripheral vision of the trained fighter, to whom not to observe all quarters of the field at once is to pay the forfeit of carelessness with his life, that although three of the Helots lay beastlike on the floor, the red-haired one had come erect now, was watching the fray with interest and with care. Then Ariston left the floor like something winged. He arched through the air, horizontally, feet first. His hard young heels crashed terribly into Simoeis' face. They heard the sickening sound of the facial bones crushing inward, breaking; the wet sodden smash of Simoeis' big body against the further wall. He hung there as though nailed to it, then slowly he slid down it to sit spraddle-legged and dazed upon the floor.

"By Herakles!" Lysander laughed. "You've chosen his sire ill, O Simoeis! A Titan surely, if not the wearer of the lion's skin himself! What ails you, lout? Up from there, and fight!"

Simoeis put down his hands and pushed. Ariston stood halfway across the hall, watching him. When, at long, long last, the gross lout swayed there, barely able to keep his feet, again Ariston launched his matchless young body through the air, but head first this time. Like an enraged ram, his hard young head sank into Simoeis' greasy paunch. And, as he rebounded, leaped away, he saw Simoeis bent in half, offering in libation to all the darker gods every blessed thing he had eaten and drunk that day.

But to butt like a billy goat had been a mistake. Ariston had forgotten the rip the Perioeci's stone had made in his scalp. The impact opened it again; a gush of scarlet stood amid his burnt-honey-colored hair, rained down. He staggered dizzily; the ache in his head was very great. Then he shook his head to clear it, rushed in.

For he had to finish Simoeis before that lout recovered, and before his own strength drained out of him. He went to work on his foe with both hands and both feet; brought him to earth with an avalanche of blows whose wet, sick, smashing sound was drowned out by his fellows' bestial bellowings.

And now he leaped high, came down upon Simoeis' barrel chest with all his weight. Even above the roars, the sound of those great ribs going was clear and sharp. Ariston leaped again—mercy, pity, humanity, sense gone from him. Another dull, cracking, muffled, board-breaking sound silenced even his penmates' voices. He stood back, measured the distance, caught Simoeis on the point of the chin with one hard kick. The big head jerked back, but not far enough; Simoeis' thick neck still held. Ariston drew back his foot again, but great arms pinioned him round about; and struggle though he would, in that Heraklian embrace he was totally helpless. He twisted in silent fury until he stared into the face of the red-bearded Helot. The man was frowning at him. Sternly. As though he had authority over him.

"That's enough, by Ares!" he said, and it seemed to Ariston then that his voice sounded like the crash of one of Zeus's thunderbolts. "There's nothing about the ugly business of murder that becomes a man. And nothing that justifies it, not even this insult to your lady mother. So stop it! Cease using your feet like a wild ass, and employ your head, if there's anything in it, which I doubt. Stop it! You heard me, Ariston. Stop it!"

"Let me go!" Ariston raged. "Take your swinish hands off me, Helot!"

"Whose hands these are, and of what quality, you don't know, melliran," the Helot said grimly. "But be assured they'll hang onto your wild donkey's hide until you promise not to kill this overgrown clown. Do you?"

Ariston stared at him. There was something about this man. A quality of—of authority. Of godliness. A force you sensed, deep hid, controlled, but enough to shake down a city, if he should care to loose it.

"Aye," the boy said sullenly. "I promise."

The Helot released him, stepped back. Said in his surf-boom, tropic-tender voice.

"Go with god, my son; for I fear me there will be trouble from this night's work—"

45

And, as if in answer to his words, the paidonomos came flying into the hall.

"What's going on here?" he cried. "Immortal gods! Who has done this thing? Who has killed——"

"Fly, lad," the red-haired Helot said.

The house of his foster-father lay not above four and one half hippicons from the gymnasium; but Ariston knew better than to go there now. When he came out of the gymnasium into the palaestra, the exercise grounds, a hypothetical watcher would have scarcely noticed that he paused, so fast was his decision made. Almost surely it was influenced by his experiences in the cave with Phryne, by the accidental means he'd been forced to take to escape the Perioeci. Be that as it may, his decision was one of those supremely intelligent weighings of pros and cons that can with some justice be called inspired. For he realized at once, no matter how fast he ran, on the flat and level plain of Lakonia, his flying figure would stay in plain sight, diminishing, of course, but clearly visible for far too long a time. Long before he could reach the mountains, the horse guards would have caught him, cut him down. What he needed to do was vanish into thin air, or have the ground open up and swallow him. Since both were clearly impossible, he took the available alternative: he changed his course a little, slanted his arrowed flight to the left, until he came to the banks of the Eurotas—at that spot not ten rods from the palaestra—and dived very cleanly into the placid waters. They were still icy, but that troubled him not at all. The essential point was that a swimmer leaves no tracks, nor even any scent for dogs to trail, and can, within certain severely limited bounds, quite literally disappear.

He took a calculated risk, of course, because even an indifferent runner can overtake the fastest swimmer alive. But he was gambling upon a shrewd belief that the pursuit would not start at once; that the paidonomos would question the boys at some length; that shock would hold them paralyzed for a while, unaccustomed as they were to witnessing assassination; that—and this most surely!—the red-bearded Helot would set himself between any would-be pursuer and the door, impeding his passage. Ariston didn't know how he knew that, but know it he did, beyond any possible doubt. So now to put a good stretch of river water between him and the school before the boys burst out of the gymnasium into the palaestra, and halted, staring in every direction to catch a glimpse of his running figure in the distance. Which, he thought, with a kind of grim joy, is just what they aren't going to see. But, in any case—

He filled his lungs with air and dived. Opened his eyes in the murky depths of the river. Swam swiftly, powerfully, under water, trailing an iridescent wake of bubbles behind him. He went on swimming like that until he was sure his lungs were going to burst, and even after that, as long as he could endure it. Then he surfaced, close to the near bank, where the tall reeds would hide his bobbing head.

There was, as yet, no pursuit. He had gained almost a quarter of an hippicon under water. He hung there until his breath came back, dived, swam on, surfaced again, repeating this stratagem over and over until he was around the broad sweeping bend of the river, and out of sight of the school.

Still, he could hear them as they boiled out into the palaestra, shouting his name. But knowing they could not see him, he did not dive again. Instead he began to swim in deadly earnest, his strokes smooth, powerful, silent, scarcely making a splash, his feet flutter-kicking, driving him on. It was a tribute to the superb training that Sparta had given his young body that when he climbed out of the river, one full league, or six hippicons, from the school, he wasn't even breathing hard.

But his troubles were far from over, he knew. He supposed he had killed Simoeis, which caused him only the smallest twinge of regret. So now his own life was forfeit. Simoeis' father and his brothers were honor bound to avenge his death, though nowadays most people left such matters up to the polis. Scant difference that made! His own foster-father, in order to demonstrate the impartiality of the Gerousia's justice, and his own, would be compelled to vote the death sentence upon the boy commonly believed to be his son. That was so certain as to admit no slightest doubt.

Ariston smiled at the thought.

"I've given you your second chance, haven't I, Father?" he murmured. "And nothing my uncle Fat Belly can say will stop you this time. The opportunity's too good, isn't it? You'll be forever rid of this hateful face that only serves to make your forehead ache—though deny it as men will, my uncle Hippolytus says, that particular decoration's always earned. And deserved. So be it. I'm a dead man. Remind me to learn to moan and whimper like a shade. Tomorrow. Some other time. I've a few small things to do before crossing the Styx, Senator Telamon, General Telamon, even Farmer Telamon—husbandman of a crop by another sowed! So let me see—let me see—"

A farm. With barns and even haystacks in which to hide. Until night, at least. And then—

He turned away from the river, struck boldly inland. Ten minutes later, he sighted the low stone and sun-baked brick buildings of the farm.

When he left the farm, it was already dark. He strode along boldly, confident that even if his pursuers chanced upon him, they'd never recognize him now. For he'd profited greatly from his long training in thievery. No longer was he naked. His hard young body was covered, not only with a lamb's-wool chiton, beautifully embroidered, but he had a chlamys wrapped about his shoulders to protect him from the night's chill. The lead weights sewn into the four corners of this short horseman's cloak to keep the wind from lifting it tapped pleasantly against his chest and back. But the one attribute of his stolen finery that would cause his schoolmates or the city guard to pass him by without a second glance was the hat he wore—the broad-brimmed petasos, favored by farmers and travelers, made a perfect disguise for him whose dark-honey-colored hair had been invariably exposed to sun, wind, and rain since the hour of his birth.

Nor had he neglected his belly. In a sack slung over his shoulder he had a huge round loaf, a great cheese, two or three handfuls of olives. Upon such provisions he could cross the world. But where he was bound at the moment was, in all good truth, much closer than that: he was headed for his foster-father's house, his object further thievery—or at least, a sort of borrowing without permission, for were not the arms and armor he meant to take from his foster-father's storeroom his by right of inheritance?

So thinking, Ariston came up to his former home. He knew he should steal Telamon's arms at once, for soon the soldier-statesman would come home to sleep. All day, in his capacity of strategos, Telamon had been consulting with the other generals, planning the annual summer attack upon the lands and outlying villages of Attica. They had been doing that every summer for nearly six years now; and, as far as Ariston could see, they could go on doing it for another hundred for all the effect it had upon the outcome of the war. The fools! Couldn't they see that the only way to beat Athens was to destroy her fleet? As long as her mighty walls kept her connected with her port at Piraeus, her seafarers would keep her well, even abundantly, fed. What mattered the burning of farmhouses, the cutting down of olive and fig trees, the trampling of millet, barley, wheat, the running off of livestock? Children's games! But then, as his uncle Hippolytus had always declared, the one impossible feat on earth, a labor at which even Herakles would have failed, was to get a new idea into a Spartan's head.

There was no time; but still he couldn't go without at least gazing for the last time upon his mother's face. Because at that time the possibility, remote as it was, that he could do what he had to do and escape alive had not even occurred to him. He wouldn't let her see him, of course, for if he did he'd never get away. He knew only too well how great the grief the news of his death was going to cause her; but that couldn't be helped. He was a Spartan; his duty was clear: to give decent burial to the bones of her who would have been, had the Furies and the Fates permitted it, his companion for all his life, thus granting peace to her shade, and thereafter to avenge her. His mother would weep long and bitterly for him, but it was the destiny of women to weep, just as it was the fate of men to fight and die. And already Clotho had spun out the thin thread of his life as far as it was meant to go, Lachesis had measured it on her rod, and terrible Atropos stood with shears agape ready to snip it off. So be it! But first—

He circled the house, which, like all Spartan houses, was small and plain and rather dingy, until he came to the window of the gynaekeia, the women's quarters. At once he heard his uncle Hippolytus' voice. As Alkmena's brother, he had the right to visit her in her sitting room, an act which, attempted by a man not of her blood, would have earned his instant death.

"So when he comes home," Hippolytus was saying fretfully, "tell him to give himself up. The worst he can expect is a whipping and some months of imprisonment. That overgrown ox won't die, though I must say, Sister mine, that he won't is hardly Ariston's fault! Zeus witness your darling tried hard enough to kill him! And in *your* defense, Alkmena—Athena forgive you for your lack of wit!"

"In my defense?" Ariston heard his mother's limpid voice murmur. As always, it was curiously serene.

"Yes!" Hippolytus snorted. "Seems that young oaf started giving the whole school lessons in elementary arithmetic, addition and subtraction both, to wit: that two years are twenty-four months; that gestation from the moment of conception to the hour of birth takes but nine; that a man, even an august strategos, who is absent from his wife's bed upon weighty affairs of state for two long years, and who, upon his return, finds his wife about to be delivered of a man-child has had, shall we say, assistance in his husbandly duties—in short, his stately forehead has been adorned."

"Oh," Alkmena said sadly. "Then why didn't Ariston simply tell them who his father was? Surely no blame attaches to me because of that!"

"Goats and satyrs!" Hippolytus roared. "Listen, O she-ass of an assininity most complete and total! You went up into the hills—despite the fact that every polis in all Hellas has forbidden those orgiastic rites, that there's not a city-state in the whole land which has not established these hundred years or more a festival in honor of Dionysus in which the god can be worshipped in stately processions, dance, drama, and song—in a word, sensibly, and with civilized moderation—you, I repeat, my chaste, fair sister, married to this dull clod, who nonetheless is an honorable man—stole from your home, went up into the hills, joined the maenads, indulged in the drunken bacchanalian rites at which acts are performed that the lowest pornai upon the ports at Piraeus, those poor bedraggled wenches whose favors cost but an obol for a full night, would with indignation refuse to do—from which gay occasion you returned with a beatific smile upon your silly face, fully determined to tell poor Telamon that you have adorned his forehead with the keroesses by work and grace of the god! That the bastard brat you carried in your belly—"

"Hippolytus!" Alkmena said.

"Was not the offspring of some goatherd with a phallus bigger than that of Priapus himself, who chanced upon you lying dead drunk upon your dainty fundament, and availed himself of the opportunity to roll your chiton up above your navel, tug your thighs apart, and get to work. Don't blame him. Who wouldn't have? The point is, silly Alkmena, that no one has ever brought forth one iota of proof convincing to any man with wit enough to avoid falling over backward into a latrine as he squats to relieve himself that gods exist, and certainly not that they have no more important things to do than to spend every available instant bumping bellies with female fools! So will you cease to insult my intelligence, Sister? There are more serious matters at hand. Ariston is in trouble! Bad trouble. That fat lout could take a turn for the worse and—"

"He won't," Alkmena said serenely, "because no evil can befall my golden boy. His life is forever safe. I had that promise of his father, the divine Dionysus—"

"Eros and Aphrodite!" Hippolytus raised his full-moon, sparsely bearded face toward heaven. "Now she's going to tell me she saw the god! Felt him, I grant you—thumping away right lustily. But saw him? I ask you!"

"But vaguely," Alkmena whispered. "I was, as you've said, Brother, much the worse for wine. But I remember that he was huge, with hair like a forest afire in a dry season, and eyes like the summer sky. He was very gentle with me, though I don't remember much—"

"He was lucky to get home with his hide intact. I

wouldn't go up there! That's what I could never understand. By Pluto-Hades, Lord of Tartarus, by three-headed Cerberus, howling before the door! For what reason did you want to guzzle wine and run up and down hills with a bunch of wild women, most of them mother-naked, shrieking and dancing with vine leaves in your hair? And if some poor fellow had chanced to fall afoul of your insane band of harpies, likely as not you'd have joined them in tearing him limb from limb, and afterward—oh, how sweet the gentle rite!—eating of his flesh, and drinking of his blood! Ugh! I like not cannibalism, Sister, even when it's disguised as a holy of holies! Yet you— Aha! So that was it! Less drunken than the rest, you thought to save him from your savage sisterhood—and found the lad comely, eh, Alkmena? And—"

"You, Hippolytus," Ariston heard his mother snap, "have an evil mind! Have you never *looked* upon my Ariston?"

"Aye, and Apollo witness he is fair. At times I've had to remind myself he is my nephew."

"Boy lover!" Alkmena said scornfully.

"What's wrong with loving boys?" Hippolytus said, reasonably enough. "They never come home with bellies looking like they've swallowed a half-grown hog, and grant one the delightful privilege of spending one's hard-earned drachmae in bringing up the fruit of another's pleasant labors. But enough of this nonsense! If you haven't even wit enough to worry about Ariston, I—"

"Poor Hippolytus!" Alkmena said gently. "You don't understand. It's not that my wit is small, but that my faith is great. Believe me, accept my word: No harm will befall my Ariston. His father, the god—"

Ariston backed away from the window then.

No harm will befall me, Mother? He wept inside his heart. By two risings of the sun we'll see what has become of your insane faith! For where was my father, the god, when Lycotheia was worrying my Phryne's throat like a wolf? Where was he when they sawed and sawed with their dull blades and tugged at that sweet flesh and tore—O Mother, Mother, you are a child! I, who have seen my own flesh—because she was that—butchered like a goat, flung to the dogs, tell you that! And now—

He turned and went toward the storeroom where his foster-father's heavy armor was.

# CHAPTER FOUR

ARISTON STOOD in his foster-father's storeroom, looking at the strategos' armor. He couldn't decide which suit to take: the ordinary, darkly oiled fighting armor that Telamon wore when going into battle against the Athenians; or the ceremonial dress armor, reserved for parades or military rites. The dress armor tempted him more because it was so highly ornamented. The helmet, shield, breastplate—in fact, the whole cuirass, front and back—as well as the greaves, were richly worked with gold inlays depicting warlike scenes and portraits of the gods. Which was why the strategos never wore it while in the field. In addition to attracting the attention of every archer and slinger in the enemy ranks, ornaments of this sort had the fatal defect of catching spear and arrow points that would have glanced harmlessly off the smooth and rounded surfaces of simpler plate.

Yet Ariston thought that its showy splendor might well be a help in the peculiar circumstances in which he found himself. He could picture how he'd look in it: ablaze with gold and polished silver; the dyed horsehair crest nodding from his helmet; shield on his arm; spear in hand; the short, thick-bladed, two-edged Spartan sword slung from the right side of his belt; the short dagger from the left. He'd appear a hero striding into life straight from the blind bard's mighty scrolls; no—more than even that: Clad in Telamon's dress armor, he might well seem to the credulous a glorious young god. And that, precisely, was the point: Since what he had to do must be done alone, why not raise up a host of invisible phantoms to his aid, said phantoms being the Perioeci's superstitions and their fears?

So thinking, he bent to pick up the dress armor—and

stopped dead, appalled. It was monstrously heavy. He guessed it weighed at least two talents. He could picture in what a state he'd arrive at the village of Parnon if he had to lug all that useless ornamented iron up the mountainside.

The ordinary suit, then? But now his head had descended abruptly from the clouds. He had had plenty of experience with fighting armor: He remembered how his limbs ached after a day's forced marching while clad in it. And slowly time was beginning to mercifully blur the intolerable, unspeakable details of Phryne's death—thus always is sanity preserved, so hope was quietly, softly, stubbornly beginning to awake in him. He wanted to give her bones a proper burial; he wanted to avenge her; but he wanted, if possible, to do both, and to live. Under all that iron, he'd be a tortoise. The Perioeci would surround him and crush him inside it with their stones.

So, in two heartbeats, he surrendered godhood, and prepared to fight, and run, as a man. He took a sword, a dagger, a bundle of javelins, a long cloak—nothing more. Thus armed, he set out to face a host of foes, hoping to outwit them at first, outrun them at last, and die only if he couldn't help it. For Phryne had wakened a wild, sweet torrent of feeling in him; or more truly, turned the one already murmuring through his veins into its natural channel: He realized now that, for all his people's endless slandering of them, women could be enchanting. And certainly this aching business of girls couldn't be looked into by a dead man. He'd honor her as was fitting, mourn her in the deepest niche of his heart lifelong; but he sensed that the scroll of his days was not to be rolled up for many a year; he was young and alive, if sorrowing. He had some future right, he thought, to joy.

Thus, with all youth's imprecise and contradictory thoughts burdening his mind, his heart, he hurried away from his foster-father's house, so belatedly that he had to dash into another street to avoid the procession of elders, strategoi, and common hoplites who lighted the august Telamon's way to his home. He flattened himself against a wall and hung there trembling until they had all gone by. Then he set out again in a long, easy, running stride that pushed the hippiconoi behind him, devoured the leagues between him and his goal.

He crossed hollow Lakonia in the darkness, gained the foothills of the Parnons, began to climb. But fighting and swimming and running had bred weariness in him. He knew it was foolish to arrive at the village worn out. That it was more foolish still to get there in broad daylight—which was what was going to happen if he stopped to sleep—did not then occur to him, so he stopped, wrapped himself well in his stolen himation, the full-length cloak, against the cold mountain air, and lay down in a little hollow in the rocks. Lying there, he poured out some drops of wine in libation to the gods, ate sparingly of the goat's-milk cheese and bread, topped off his frugal meal with a few olives, and closing his eyes, tried to sleep.

But sleep was slow in coming. His thoughts, his memories, tortured him into painful, tingling wakefulness. It was already close to the hour when rosy-fingered Eos, goddess of the dawn, should harness Lampus and Phaethon to her chariot and mount the eastern sky, making way for her glorious brother, Helios, the sun, when finally Ariston slept, only to wake within the hour, the dawn glow in his eyes. He took that as a good omen: All the world knew of Eos's incurable passion for young men. Perhaps now she would favor him.

Some hours later, from the high back trail over which he had come, that shade- and demon-haunted path that no one but he had trod these twenty years and more, he looked down once again upon the village. Wood smoke spiraled upward from all the lintels of the houses, but no one was about except a boy who was herding some goats on the edge of the grassy square.

Ariston could see the white scatter of Phryne's bones, half-hidden in the grass. But her skull was nowhere to be seen. There was no trace of the delicate little globe that, living, had cradled dreams and hope and tenderness. Only the long thigh bones, the hacked and broken ribs, the curved pelvic arch which, had not the village harpies murdered her, would have been the nesting place of an unborn—god. Yes, yes, a god's life would have sprung from those tender loins. It was no blasphemy to dream it, think it, for how could any lesser being be born of a love as great as that which she had offered him?

Before he turned back, he marked well the spot where each bone lay, for, it having finally occurred to him what suicidal madness any attempt to perform his self-imposed mission by daylight would be, he was going to have to find them in the dark. Still, the absence of the skull troubled him. The flesh melted away after death in any event; but what effect could rites have performed over bones with so vital a feature missing?

And, one more thing: For her crime, Lycotheia must die. That he had to let the rest of her band of villainous harpies escape all punishment, he regretted to his outraged soul; but there was no help for that. Considered coldly, they were but blades in the hands of the murderess; they had been lied to, deceived. And, by their customs, the double slaying of which Lycotheia had convinced them Phryne was guilty merited such a death, or worse. But the wolf-woman herself had been coldly, cynically aware of what she was doing. For her there existed neither palliative nor excuse. Immortal gods, but she had planned it well! She had followed Phryne and him through the winding labyrinths of that cave, surely; dogged their footsteps like the she-wolf she was. Only the river had stopped her; doubtless she was afraid of water, couldn't swim. And there—

She had found Phryne's robe. Took it up, retraced her steps until she came to the mouth of the cave. Bent and dipped that white fine-spun dress that had clothed innocence, chastity, tenderness into the thickening horror of her husband's and Argus' blood. Used it as evidence to convince those stepdaughters of the Furies, the Parnon women, that Phryne—

"Ready your boat, Charon!" he swore softly. "For by grim Hades, your lord, you'll have a passenger, or freight, this night!"

But that, too, was going to be difficult, he realized, as he sat before his fire in the far opening of the cave. He had no idea which of the huts was Epidaurus'. In addition to searching for poor Phryne's skull, he'd have to creep from window to window, peer inside, try to make out which of the sleepers was Lycotheia. The thing was impossible on the face of it; quite simply, it couldn't be done.

He sat there before the fire, brooding over his problems. Well did it seem to him that the gods had imposed more labors upon him than they had even upon great Herakles. If there were only some way, some way—

Suddenly, he leaped to his feet, for it had come to him in one of those onslaughts of clarity of which he was capable that the way not only existed but was relatively simple. By now, it must be hard upon high noon. The men would be returning from their rocky fields, their goat pastures, to eat the noonday meal. He had only to watch which houses they entered to reduce the number of windows he'd have to look into that night to two. For, he was aware, every man in the village was married except Argus. Therefore, one of the huts into which no man would go, now that Argus was dead, would be the house of the Keen-Sighted One; and the other, since there was no man of marriageable age to replace the late, unlamented Epidaurus, nor even sufficient time passed for her to be freed of the mourning rites, Lycotheia's.

So thinking, Ariston left the cave and raced back up the trail. From the heights above, he looked down on the village. And Eos or Artemis or Athena favored him: He saw Lycotheia herself, striding queenly and tall across the square. He had the sudden, shame-ridden feeling that the wolf-woman was compellingly attractive. Seen by daylight, with her arrogant face in repose, the swelling gone from it now, the bruises fading, it came to him that—that to lie with her must be a great delight, the more so because, as always, she was clean.

And now the shame in him was like vulture claws tearing his entrails. To think such a thing of her who'd butchered Phryne! Who'd sunk her teeth into—

But someone else evidently agreed with him. For, as Lycotheia passed by, the colossus, Pancratis, sauntered out of his doorway and fell into step beside her. From where he crouched, many rods above the village, Ariston could not, of course, hear what they said to each other; but it was evident from Lycotheia's expression and her gestures that she was rebuking the giant for his presumption. At which Pancratis only laughed and caught her to him, cupping her buttocks in his huge hands. Ariston saw the knife flash. The big man reeled away from her, clapped his hand to his face. Took his paw away and stared at the blood with which it was filled. Lycotheia had slashed open his cheek from his ear to the point of his chin. All his great bushy beard dripped red.

Ariston saw her smile, saw her lupine and voluptuous lips shape words. He could not hear her, but he could read on her face what that phrase was.

"The next time it will be your filthy gullet, he-goat!" Lycotheia said.

Then she turned away from the reeling giant and marched straight across the square to a certain house. Ariston marked it well.

The day dragged on endlessly. The first two or three hours of darkness were longer still. But the boy contained his impatience. He was sure that the Perioeci, like all countrymen, went early to bed; but he had to make sure that sleep lay heavy upon them before he dared enter the square to gather up poor Phryne's bones.

But now it was time. He did not know whether to thank the gods or not for the fact that there was a full moon silvering all the sky. It would make the dreadful task of playing pious scavenger easy, that was sure. Yet, on the other hand, it would make his own position untenable if he had to stand and fight.

No help for it now, he thought. Great Artemis, I ask your help, for she was both chaste and fair. And yours, too, divine Aphrodite, for, by my soul, I loved her. Of you, Dionysus, my father, the resurrecting god, I ask only that I may be spared to live out my days in honor. And of you, immortal Ares, I ask valor with which to fight, by which, if need be, to die.

So praying, he spilled out in libation all that remained of his wine. Then he picked up his weapons and started up the trail.

It began well. Too well, which should have warned him. So conveniently was everything arranged for him that it was oddly like the trick that bad playwrights used at the drama festivals of the greater Dionysia to get their hipokritoi players—and, be it said, themselves—out of the dilemmas they had written themselves into: the mechane which creaked up beside the skene, that little building representing now a temple, now a castle, now a swineherd's hut, or even more obviously beside the orkestra, the dancing place of the chorus, and let a god down on quite visible ropes to work a miracle by which all troubles were resolved.

The moonlight pinpointed Phryne's scattered bones for him, giving them a soft and pearly glow. He gathered them up, fighting the deathly sickness in him; for neither the ravenous hunger of the ill-fed village dogs, nor the crows, nor the swarming insects, had been enough to leave them entirely clean. Here and there a shred of hardened, black-red flesh clung to them, flesh of his own flesh, reduced to this! And they had about them a faint odor of putrefaction, that sweet, sickly smell which is past any man's bearing. But Ariston persisted, endured this torment. Tenderly he wrapped them in his cloak, one by one, until he had all, or nearly all, of them.

Except her skull. Grimly he quartered the field, searching ever wider. But there was no sign of that delicate little globe, no sign at all. And it surely should have been the easiest of all her scattered bones to find. Yet—

Then it was, it seemed to him, that the hypokrite god creaked down upon his hypocritical ropes. For, raising his eyes, he saw light streaming from the window of one of the houses. He caught his breath. But he'd fixed the position of that particular stone and mud and wattles hut too well in his mind to be mistaken now. The house from which the light came was Lycotheia's own.

He moved toward it, step by cautious step. Beside the door, he laid his macabre burden down. Chose one of the javelins, the lightest, best balanced of them all, laid the others alongside Phryne's bones. Loosened his sword, his dagger, in their sheaths. Now ready, he stole toward the window. But, before he reached it, Lycotheia's voice came out to him.

"So this is your vengeance, Pancratis?" she was saying, her tone light, playful, mocking. "For that scratch I gave you on your face, I should lie with you? Tell me, what would your darling Sterope say to that?"

Pancratis' taurine bass came over to Ariston now, saying a thing which bears no repetition, but whose import was that a certain obscenity should be performed upon Sterope, his wife, or that she should perform it upon herself.

Lycotheia laughed clearly, gaily.

"But that, my dear Pancratis," she purred, "is precisely what you promised the gods to do nightly, when you made the nuptial sacrifices. So get you to it! Don't tell me that plowing and harrowing that Stubborn One is such a chore! Zeus witness you've brats enough. So what need have you of me?"

"Need?" Pancratis rumbled. "I tell you, girl, that I'm afire! And not because you notched my jaw a little, but because you're the finest piece of hot and juicy she-meat who ever made a man pant after a little wallowing. So be reasonable, Lyco! Who'll ever know? I don't want to be rough with you, but——"

"And if you pump my belly up with your emblem of Priapus?" Lycotheia said.

"Look, Lyco, you were married to old Shaggy Hide all of seven years and——"

"But you, great Pancratis, are hardly Epidaurus, now, are you? He was secretly a boy-lover. He scarcely ever touched me, while you——"

Ariston could see them now. Lycotheia had her back to the window. She was quite naked, probably because she slept that way. She was holding a blanket up to her breasts, letting it trail down so that it hid her body from Pancratis' eyes. But Ariston's view was unobstructed. He decided that she was very fine.

And now, suddenly, she laughed. The sound of it was harsh, chilling.

"All right," she said. "It's not worth fighting over, is it? And what would I be defending, anyhow? The memory of what I gave away when I was twelve years old to a slave in my father's shop? Ha! The only reason I even remember him is because the oaf ripped me apart so that I bled for a month. And you, ugly monster, might have strength enough to—to content me. Though I doubt it. No one man could do that. It would require an army. Some wine first? A cup of my brew—Bacchus witness that it's potent—to put some iron in your weapon? Don't smile! You'll find you'll need every jot of brute force you've got, to mount and ride this she-wolf, friend!"

"Don't be long, girl," Pancratis rumbled happily, and sat down. Deftly Lycotheia wrapped the blanket about her form. She moved across the room to a cupboard.

Ariston heard the soft gurgle of the wine, but he could not see what she was doing. Then she whirled, letting the blanket slide down off her, standing there naked and terrible, a Stygian nymph, holding out in her two hands that bowl.

"Drink, Pancratis!" she hissed, and her voice was a coiling and writhing of serpents, "drink, O huge and lusty one! Drink deep—if you dare!"

Ariston heard the rasping outrush of Pancratis' breath. Then, in one long tearing howl, like a man pursued by shades and demons, the colossus was up from his stool and out the door, his big feet shaking the very earth as he pounded away from there. And as metallic and harsh and chilling as the clangor of a sword clashed hard against a brazen shield, Lycotheia's laughter followed him.

Ariston hung there, staring at her. It was quite true, as he had told Phryne, that he had seen naked girls before. In Sparta, it was a sight you couldn't escape. At the religious festivals, all the girls danced naked in a group, singing the maiden songs, and after them, the boys, equally naked, danced, whirling to the flutes, the lyres. But, as he stared at her, he knew he had never seen a female body as—shocking—as Lycotheia's was. Because the girls of Sparta, before appearing nude in public for the festivals, carefully shaved all their bodies, or used depilatories of arsenic and lime. So their white forms moving, dancing, swaying in stately rhythms were curiously statuelike, and there was nothing particularly exciting about them.

But Lycotheia—Aphrodite and Eros!—the difference was slight, really: just three wild spiraling and sudden splotches of inky pelt to emphasize startlingly her body's whiteness, to convert her nudity into nakedness. Just enough of the ancestral goat-god retained to shock his senses into the

62

recognition that woman, too, was animal. A she-thing with blood in her, and heat and desire. Not a living statue covered all over with pearl powder so that you couldn't see those twin dark cherry buds puckering, pointing under his gaze as she raised that bowl to drink—

What? Wine or nectar or—blood? What could she, would she drink from that bowl? That bowl.

Inside Ariston's bowels something screamed. The cry was as high and shrill as a maenad's maddened upon divine wine. Obscene claws tore at his entrails, his heart, his breath. A night cloud drifted down upon his eyes.

Then it cleared. He drew the javelin back and hurled it with all his force. But something, a slight motion on her part, the haste with which he had thrown, the hand of some mocking, ribald god, turned aside his aim. Instead of taking her in the throat, as his intention was, the javelin went through her left shoulder, and pinned her to the wall.

She did not so much as cry out, or even moan. She merely hung there and stared at him as he came through the door, his short Spartan sword already drawn.

He put his point against her throat. Then, quite suddenly, he couldn't. A weakness was in him, a sickness unto death. He had never killed anyone before. He had never even so much as dreamed of killing a woman. And now—

The smell of her came up and took him in the nostrils. His entrails churned with the anguish of that torment, that pitiless warfare in him between shame and desire. She said no word, made no motion to beg of him her life. She hung there, spitted upon his spear, and searched his face with eyes filled with mockery, with contempt. For she knew he was going to spare her, realized at what a price, and despised him for it. Her eyes, blacker than immemorial sin, were cool and sure, filled with a wearily acute knowledge of the debility of any man of woman born, probing into his one soft-cored, rotten spot with certainty, with the icy, abysmal contempt she felt for any man possessed of the slightest weakness, and hence for all men upon the face of earth. Then, very slowly, she smiled at him.

It was too much. The bland, contemptuous, weary cynicism of her sensuous mouth got home to him. Blind with sudden rage, he plunged home his blade. He drew it out. A

63

great gush of black scarlet followed it, flooded down, dyeing her breasts. He could feel her eyes boring into his, and he knew he would not forget them until his dying day. Without knowing why, he tore the javelin free as well, allowing her to fall. She writhed, whipped her limbs about, made the convulsive flopping motions that a fowl does when its throat is cut. Then she was still. She turned her face toward him, and her lips moved, forming words; but no sound came out. Her breath whistled through the rent in her throat; it would not reach her mouth to give audibility to what she said. But Ariston could read it upon her hateful, dying, tortured mouth.

"I curse you! From this hour on, you shall never—"

Then, quite abruptly, she died.

Ariston stood there, completing her unfinished phrase in his mind. She need not have mouthed it, for already he had laid that selfsame doom, that death-in-life, upon himself.

"You shall never from this hour know peace. You who slaughtered a helpless woman in her blood. Guilty though she was, you should have shown her mercy. You should have stood tall above your barbarous Lakonian customs, your savage Spartan mores. Cried out to the one true god hidden behind all this polytheistic mummery that—"

But it was no good. Quietly he bent down and retrieved poor Phryne's skull. Stood there holding it, seeing with awful clarity how well Lycotheia had prepared it, scraped it, cleaned it, polished it until it shone to make her monstrous drinking cup. Then, bearing it, he went outside into a night from which even the moon had fled, leaving no light at all.

He buried Phryne's bones upon the high trail, erecting a mound of stones above them to protect them from the wolves. He sprinkled his own blood from a cut he made at the wrist, in libation, in sacrifice, having nothing else. Then he knelt and prayed to all the high Olympian gods to receive and bless her tender shade.

He got to his feet, stood there, his blue eyes filled with tears. Turned a little—not much, but enough, perhaps, to save his life.

For he stopped thinking now. Stopped breathing. Hung there, reeling under the tremendous impact of Pancratis' blow; under the fiery anguish of the big man's blade. The change of position he had made, turning, had caused it to miss his vitals, limited its penetration. Yet it was deep enough in all good truth to bring his life gushing out with it, when Pancratis drew it forth. He whirled then, trying to come to grips with his foe. And the sudden twisting of his hard young body snapped the badly tempered, brittle knife off at the hilt, leaving the blade buried in his back. In one smooth motion Ariston drew and thrust out with his sword. Pancratis bellowed like a bull as the blade plunged through his huge belly to emerge beside his spinal column. Ariston yanked it free, and upon a foaming red tide, Pancratis' life followed it.

Ariston stood above the big man, looking down. But he couldn't really see Pancratis now. It was too dark, and, besides, there was a red mist before his eyes. They refused to focus. He turned and strode away from there, step by willful, stubborn step, erect, proud, curiously godlike, tall.

He reached the bend of the trail, passed beyond it, before he fell. He clawed himself upright again by pure indomitable will, moved on. A scant yard or two further on, he fell again. Got up. Once, twice, thrice, a dozen times. When he could no longer rise, he crawled. On and on through that red mist, through that utter dark, with white-hot fire probing in his back, seeking his pneuma, his breath, his life. He was still crawling when those great arms caught him, lifted him up, and by then Eos was riding the sky, beating the night back with her horse's pale, broad wings.

Through the dawn haze, he stared into that face of brooding sorrow, ringed about by that great brush fire of red hair and beard, into those deep blue eyes that were too brilliant now, glazed, shifting, wet.

"Don't cry, great Dionysus," he mumbled, thrusting the words out on a rush of blood. "Don't cry for me, my father. The gods don't weep, and I—"

Then, abruptly, the light spilled out of the sky. It was very dark, and he was freezing cold.

"Hold on, my son! Clasp your teeth together tight, lest your pneuma flit between them like a little bird. That's it! That's it! Now I shall take you home," the red-haired Helot said.

# CHAPTER FIVE

LIFE, TALOS THE HELOT had long since learned—for he had reached his forty-seventh year—put no greater burdens upon a man than the iron necessity of making decisions. And, because his own existence had been hard, among the things that had been hammered into his skull was that a man's choices were never between alternatives as simple as good and bad, but usually between bad and worse, said choices being helped not one iota by the gods, who sat forever upon their immortal bottoms on high Olympus and mockingly denied the slightest hint by which a man could guide himself in the subtle art of determining which was the bad and which was the worse. That is, when he didn't have to choose between the worse and the worst.

As now.

Should he run down that steep and slippery trail like a blasphemer with the Furies after him? There were at least three answers to that question, all of them negative. No, because if he did, the jolting might well drive the blade deeper into the boy's back and find his life. No, because running greatly increased the chances of his slipping, falling. And even if he were lucky enough not to go over the edge of the trail, plunging straight into the bowels of Tartarus without even having to cross the Styx, dropping the boy would finish him then and there. No, because if he tried to run all the way down to Sparta with Ariston in his arms, he'd collapse from weariness long before he reached the city.

An impressive series of no's. But the alternatives? Should he go slowly and cautiously? No, because if he delayed too long, this glorious, golden youth would surely die. Should he attempt to draw out that blade? No, because he had no means at all to stop the great rush of blood that would follow it. Should he leave the boy here, making him as comfortable as possible, until he could return with an iatros, a doctor-surgeon, and stretcher-bearers to—? No. By the time he convinced the city guards he was telling the truth—if he ever did—and returned to find Ariston, the boy would be dead.

He put his great fiery-maned head back and laughed aloud—a paean of wild and bitter laughter that boomed among the gorges like Zeus's thunder. The sound of it started a slither, a skittering of small loose rocks showering down from the peaks above. Talos closed his mouth. Mountain-bred himself, he knew only too well how easily the vibrations of a cry could start an avalanche.

"As if I didn't have troubles enough without being buried under a rockslide set loose by my own jackass bray," he muttered and started down that trail. Almost at once he fell into a rhythmic dogtrot, neither slow nor fast, consciously trying to cushion the jolting by lifting the boy in counter measure to each jogging step. He kept it up for hours. When he no longer had any breath in his lungs, and the ache in his arms, the muscle jerk of his weariness, made it impossible for him to go on, he stopped and rested; but for as short a space of time as was necessary to regain some measure of his strength.

Fortunately for Talos, the trail was downhill all the way. Even so, it was a tribute to both his body and his will that he reached the city with some reserves of strength left with which to complete his self-imposed task. For now, with Sparta in plain sight on the horizon, he had to make his final decision: Dared he swing half around the city in a long detour in order to enter the polis by one of the secret routes he knew, with the ever decreasing chances of getting Ariston to a physician while yet the boy lived, or should he go straight forward and accept the risk balanced perilously upon the choices open to the city guards: to listen to his explanation of how he, a dog of a Helot, happened to be carrying a wounded Spartan youth in his arms; or to cut him down upon the spot and investigate the circumstances later?

Then Ariston groaned, and the choice was made: Talos started to trot again, straight toward the wall-less city.

Twenty minutes later, he entered it at last, with Ariston unconscious in his arms, both of them covered all over with dust. At once the guards stationed all around Sparta at intervals to guard against the unlikely contingency of an Athenian attack—a contingency in which no one believed, since in this tiresome war in which Athens commanded the sea and Sparta the land, a direct and decisive blow by either polis remained, in that sixth year of largely seasonal hostilities, a dream eluding the strategoi of both sides—leaped upon him with drawn swords.

"Dog!" their captain howled. "Helot swine! You dare come into the city, bearing—"

Then he stopped, for even as slow-witted as Spartans usually were, it was apparent to the ilarch that he had answered himself. No Helot alive, in his right mind or out of it, would dare do such a thing. Any slave brute who had wounded or killed a melliran would be running for the hills now as fast as he could force his big feet to carry him. It followed, then, that this red-bearded animal was performing a meritorious action, or—and the captain's eyes narrowed, since suspicion was a Spartan's second nature—seeking to ingratiate himself with the relatives of the wounded youth, in hope of a reward. Which meant that he was both bolder and more intelligent than a Helot had any right to be. The ilarch marked his features well. He'd keep this fiery-maned canine in mind, have the Krypteia, the secret police, dog his tracks from this hour on.

"Sheath swords!" he commanded. "Now, Helot, speak!"

"Begging the ilarch's pardon," Talos said, "speak I will, but not until I've got this young master to the nearest iatreion. Right now I haven't the breath. And if I don't get him to a clinic soon, I'll have no tongue to speak with. Nor, begging your august pardon right humbly again, good ilarch, will you, if the son of the noble Telamon dies because of the delay *you're* causing. The great strategos will see to that!"

The ilarch's hairy hand flew back to drive the Helot's

insolent boldness down his throat along with his teeth. But then he held it there. Leaned swiftly close, peered into the boy's still face.

"By Apollo!" he said. "The dog's not lying! It *is* the beautiful Ariston! Ho, Iphiclus! Ixion! Oebalus! Phegeus! Prepare the lance shafts and the shield!"

It was quickly done, for the act itself was a part of Spartan training. A shield was lashed between the shafts of two spears. In its hollow, the captain laid his blood red himation—for Spartan military cloaks were always red so that their wounds would not show to give encouragement to their foes—then right tenderly they placed Ariston face down upon it.

"Take care not to jolt him too much, my masters," the Helot said, "lest you drive the blade deeper and it find his life—"

The way his voice sounded, saying that, caused the ilarch to look at him harder than ever. But at that moment, Ariston opened his mouth, vomited up a clot of blood.

"Dionysus, my father," he groaned, "I hurt! I hurt! The pain—"

Talos bent swiftly beside the boy.

"Hold on, my son," he murmured. "We'll have help soon now, soon . . ."

Again the ilarch stared at red-bearded Talos, but now his gaze traveled from the Helot's face to that of the boy, and back again, very slowly.

"By Menelaus, father of all cuckolds!" he muttered. "I'd swear—but no; 'tis too rude a thing to even think—"

Then, raising his voice, he roared out:

"Forward, march!"

But the hoplite at the front end of the shield litter stared at him. There were many iatreia—clinics—in Sparta. And he was but a citizen-soldier, not a mind reader.

"March where, my captain?" he said.

"Donkey!" the ilarch bellowed. "Mule and son of a mule! To the iatreion of the great Polorus, naturally! D'you think I'd take our commander in chief's son to any sawbones who was not of the Asklepiad? Now lift your hooves and move!"

They bore the boy through the winding, narrow, cobblestone-paved streets of Sparta until they came to the quarter of the Phoenodamas, which is by interpretation, the quarter of the restrainers of slaughter, where the physician Pelorus had his clinic. In the center of the square, Talos could see the temple of Asklepios, god of medicine; and on every side there were evidences that this quarter was wholly dedicated to the healing arts. There were statues everywhere: of Apollo Alexikakos, Apollo chaser of ills; of Paeon, the iatros, or physician, of the gods; of Hygeia, goddess of health; of Panacea, healer of all ills; even of Pallas Athena, goddess of wisdom, though men seldom prayed to her now, since it was held that she favored the Athenians in the war. And before the entrance of the temple itself stood a massive statue of the centaur Chiron, who, legend had it, had taught the god Asklepios the secrets of medicine, his brawny man's body blending almost imperceptibly into the forequarters of a mighty stallion.

"It's from old Horse's Ass that most iatroi are descended," one of the hoplites jibed, "and from the south end of him at that, considering the number of patients they put below ground!"

"Silence, fool!" the ilarch said, but without heat. He was too busy observing what Talos' eyes did as they played over the signs above the doors, announcing that herein dwelt this or that healer or traveling practitioner or root-cutter-herbist, or the shops dedicated to the manufacture of stelae, votive tablets to offer the god in hopes of, and of anathemae to be dedicated to him after, the cure. Several of the signs proclaimed the iatreia of the more famous iatroi; and it seemed to the ilarch that Talos' gaze lingered over these with especial care.

No, the ilarch thought. It can't be! A Helot who can read? It's against all nature. Still—

But now they had come to the sign announcing the iatreion of the iatros Polorus; and, without a word from anyone, or even a sign, Talos stopped before it. The captain shook his helmeted head sorrowfully. He was beginning to conceive a certain fondness for the handsome and sturdy Helot. One could see that in his youth Talos had been beautiful, too—as beautiful, perhaps, as their inert burden was now. A pity. For the Helot was already a dead man. He, Orchomenus, ilarch of the Tenth Ila of the city guard, had to denounce him to the Krypteia now. With such a one to lead them, what might the Helots not accomplish? Even this business of saving the august Telamon's son displayed a nerve, a cunning that—

Orchomenus leaned forward, staring into Talos' face. Was it possible that this red-bearded animal had himself stabbed the boy in order to provide himself with the opportunity to win his freedom or—?

But then the ilarch saw what was in Talos' eyes, perceived the brooding, anguished tenderness with which the Helot gazed upon the wounded youth. No. He straightened up again, retreated into confusion, because what his eyes, his instincts, his intelligence told him, he had to reject. It was just too monstrous! A Helot—and the daughter of one of Sparta's first families? A Helot and a Spartan general's wife? No! By all the dark and terrible Chthonic gods, that simply could not be!

They bore Ariston into the clinic then, and laid him down. A slave girl went sullenly, and slowly—until a spear point jabbed into her seat awakened her respect for the military—to fetch her master, who was sleeping.

The physician came, aquiver with rage, and at the sight of him, Talos' heart sank to the tops of his buskins. For the iatros was very old. His hands shook, and his voice broke and quavered in his fury.

"How dare you!" he squeaked. "To awaken me just because one of your armored louts has been carved up in a tavern brawl! Over some porna or other, doubtless! Get you hence—all of you! There's an iatros down the street who's fair enough surgeon for this kind of case. I don't take—"

"Silence, quack!" Orchomenus bellowed. "Hold your feeble tongue if you'd keep it in your ancient head. This lad's highborn, as if that mattered. What matters is the punishment meted out to those who break their vows to Asklepios, or don't live up to their Hippocratic oath! The boy's at the banks of the Styx now. Your duty is to save him. So hop to it! Or else—"

The old man stood there.

"Very well," he snapped. "But my services are dear, Ilarch. That I am forced to warn you! And who's going to undertake the cost of the sacrifices? I consider them essential. Without the gods' favor, what iatros can work a cure? That's an awful lot of sacrifices. There's Apollo Alexikakos, and Paeon and Hygeia and Panacea and the centaur Chiron and Pallas Athena and Asklepios himself! And I may have forgotten somebody. Oh, dear me! I just know I have. This won't do. The gods get awfully angry when they're forgotten. Let me see—let me see—who—"

"Telesphorus," Talos the Helot said.

Again Orchomenus stared at the red-bearded one. Telesphorus, the elfin boy who accompanied the god Asklepios about his rounds, was the most obscure of the healing gods —if he even was a god, a point in much dispute. Only a man of considerable erudition would have known of him at all. Everything about this ruddy Helot was wrong! His voice, his accent, his—

"Aye, Telesphorus!" the doctor squeaked. "Knew I'd forgotten somebody! Tell me, Captain, who's going to pay for all that?"

"Don't worry your ancient addled pate about it, Iatros," Orchomenus said. "You'd better concern yourself with who's going to undertake your own funeral rites and sacrifices if this boy dies while you're arguing with me. Because his father, Telamon, Chief of the Gerousia, Head Strategos of the Armies and the Fleets of Sparta, will see that your death in such a case will be both slow and highly unpleasant. You heard me; to work, Sawbones!"

Polorus' face went white as death. The shaking in his hands was far more noticeable now. Talos looked at Orchomenus with imploring eyes.

"Aye, you're right, Helot," the ilarch muttered. "I'm afraid I've gone too far—scared the old quack into uselessness." He turned to the ancient iatros, and said in a much more kindly tone:

"On the other hand, I'm sure you can count upon your weight—or the boy's—whichever is greater—in gold, as a reward, if you save him. At least two talents, Polorus! What say you to that?"

The effect was magical. For, although in that fifty-fourth

73

year after Thermopylae—for the Spartans, like all Hellenes, reckoned time from some memorial event in their history—officially the money of the polis was still the huge cartwheel-like iron coins cunningly designed by Lycurgus to discourage greed (since they were too heavy to carry around and far too big and too valueless to hoard), the creeping luxury that was to destroy all Hellas, weakening and effeminizing her sons before her barbaric foes, had already begun to invade stern Sparta. Lycurgus' famous laws to the contrary, every homois had managed to get his hands on an ounce or two of forbidden silver, or even gold. And a talent was almost one thousand ounces; nine hundred and twelve, to be exact. Two talents would make the iatros richer than Croesus—at least in his own mind.

The trembling stopped. Color returned to that withered face. The dark eyes shone.

"Here!" the physician said. "Put him up here where I can examine him. That's it, that's it. Hmmmmmnnn—"

"But the sacrifices?" Talos said.

"Don't bother me with that superstitious nonsense, Helot! Don't you see there's no time?" great Polorus said.

Despite his age, the physician proved that his hand had lost none of its skill. First of all, he forced a brew composed of mandragora and jusquiam down Ariston's throat. But, after waiting half an hour, when he touched the wound, the boy groaned aloud. Thereupon the iatros added a draft of belladonna. Still, it was clear that the patient was still sensitive to pain. Polorus resorted to drastic measures: He administered a quarter drachma of opium. That did it. Even when his forceps grasped the broken blade, the boy gave no sign. But when the physician drew the blade out, the rush of blood was terrible to see. And nothing would stop it—none of the usual astringents employed by the iatroi of Hellas at that time of the first flowering of medicine, when the immortal Hippocrates was still present among men to inspire and guide his fellows, neither oak bark, nor sanguis draconis, nor grenadine had any effect at all. Finally, old Polorus did what he had to: He applied a red-hot iron to the wound. When he did that, in spite of all the stupefying brews and concoctions in him, Ariston split the heavens apart with his scream.

Talos dropped to his knees beside the bed. And the ilarch saw the tears in his eyes.

Poor devil, he thought. Patriotism be damned. He's too tender-hearted to be dangerous. I'll not put him to the torture. What information I need, I'll trick out of him—

Thereafter, the iatros washed the wound with boiled wine, pushed clean thorns through its edges to hold it together, placed a bandage over it.

"Will he—live?" Talos whispered.

"Don't know," Polorus snapped. "You want me to cut open a chicken and look at its guts?"

The boy was resting quietly now. A slave had been sent to Telamon's house, and another to the Gerousion, to inform his parents of the news. So now, with time available, the ilarch, Orchomenus, led Talos the Helot out into the street before the iatreion and began to question him.

"Do you know who stabbed him?" he began. "That is, if you didn't do it yourself in hopes of gaining a reward by saving the life you almost took—"

Talos smiled wearily.

"I don't think you're so poor a judge of men as that, my lord Ilarch," he said. "You *know* I wouldn't hurt him."

"Aye, I do know it, Helot," Orchomenus said. "Your mystery lies deeper than that. Are you his lover?"

"A dog of a Helot like me, good Captain?" Talos said.

"Stranger things have happened. You're comely enough, Red Beard, though you wear the dogskin cap. And there's no accounting for tastes—or else there'd be no Mothones, now would there?"

Talos' lips tightened. The insult was deliberate and calculated. Mothones were the bastards Spartans got upon the helpless Helot women who dared not refuse them their favors.

"No," he said evenly. "I don't suppose there would be."

"Well," Orchomenus said, "are you his lover, or not?"

"No," Talos said.

"Then there's no connection between you?"

"None," Talos said.

"And you just happened to find him wounded?"

"No. I followed him. I was in the gymnasium when he—"

"You were in the *gymnasium!*" Orchomenus roared. "What in the name of—"

"The annual lesson against drunkenness, good Ilarch. They chose ill. I have an unusually good head—and belly, too, for that matter—for wine."

"All right. You were in the gymnasium, wallowing on the floor like a hog, drunk as an Athenian, or pretending to be, and—"

"He fought a lad who'd insulted his mother. And, in spite of the fact that he'd almost killed the lout—who richly deserved killing, good Captain!—I could see he was still so upset that he was likely to do something rash. So I followed him. I wanted to prevent that."

"Why?" the Captain said.

"Out of the respect and admiration I bear that great lady, his mother. She was kind to me once. Very kind."

The ilarch's hand flew downward to the hilt of his dagger. Sweat stood and sparkled on his forehead. A great vein at his temple rose and beat with his blood.

"If I thought—" he growled.

Talos looked him straight in the eye.

"But you don't, do you, my master?" he said. "Such thoughts are a blasphemy against divine Artemis, as well as an insult to the Lady Alkmena herself. So let us not indulge in them, shall we? I think you have wiser, nobler questions to ask."

"Aye," Orchomenus muttered. "For instance: *Who* stabbed him?"

"I don't know. I lost his trail for a night. On those rocky ledges in the Parnons, one doesn't leave tracks, you realize, Captain. When I found him, it was too late. He was crawling down the trail with that broken knife in his back—"

The ilarch glared at Talos.

"Fat lot of help you are!" he said. "Still, I'd better put down your information. The ephors are sure to want it. I don't suppose I have to warn you not to lie. You're intelligent enough not to want to risk torture—"

"You're right, there, my master," Talos said.

Orchomenus took a wooden tablet coated with beeswax out of his belt, and a stylus. Painfully he began to write, gripping his tongue between his teeth. The date, the place he'd met the Helot carrying Ariston, other details. Talos kept back a smile. From where he sat beside the ilarch, he could see the tablet. And as they nearly always were, even in those Spartans who had a pretense towards culture, Orchomenus' spelling and grammar were atrocious.

"Your name, Helot!" the ilarch barked.

"I am called Talos," the Helot said.

Orchomenus looked up from the tablet.

"I doubt it," he said dryly. "You've changed your name, haven't you, Helot?"

Talos gazed at the cobblestones. Looked up again.

"Yes," he said simply.

"And before it was—Phlegyas, wasn't it? From the color of your hair?"

"It was Phlogius, my master, which means almost the same thing. So I changed it to Talos. More appropriate to my condition, don't you agree, good Captain?"

"To agree with a Helot is a form of treason to a soldier, dog!" Orchomenus said. "You know the law!"

"Aye," Talos said. "But I also know men."

"Meaning?" Orchomenus said.

"That you, good Ilarch, are less—hard than you'd appear. This law now—what does it mean? We're slaves, and powerless to remedy that condition. Yet every year the ephors formally declare war upon us, as though we were an enemy polis—"

"You're enemies enough!" Orchomenus said.

"You make us so," Talos said quietly, "because you refuse to learn that the one way men can't be ruled for any length of time is by the lash."

"Then how can they?" Orchomenus said.

"I think—by love," Talos said. "But I only think that. I don't know it. Because so far, no polis has been intelligent enough to try it."

"Talos the philosopher!" Orchomenus mocked. But the mockery was false. Talos could see that, despite himself, the ilarch was intrigued.

"In a way, I am," Talos said. "Take your law, Captain. What is it but a subtle acknowledgment of the fact that you *know* you're wrong?"

"Dog!" Orchomenus roared. "I'll—"

But Talos' blue eyes moved compellingly over the ilarch's face.

"Why don't you listen, Captain?" he said. "You know the opportunity's priceless. To deal frankly and freely with the truth always is. It'll hurt, because there's no pain equal to that of being forced to think. I've learned to endure that pain. So even in my filthy mantle, under my dogskin cap, I remain a man—"

"And I, a donkey in armor?" Orchomenus said. The phrase came too quickly, Talos could see he'd thought it, alone, and bitterly, many times before.

"If I thought that," he said evenly, "I wouldn't waste my breath on you, Ilarch. I see intelligence in your face, humanity in your eyes—which is why, forgive me for saying it, my master, I pity you."

"You pity me?" Orchomenus all but whispered. "You, a Helot, pity *me?*"

"Yes," Talos said, "because, even so, having both qualities, you're forced to remain—a Spartan."

Orchomenus dropped the tablet. His dagger flashed in the sun as he drew it. Talos didn't move. He sat there, smiling at the Spartan. He didn't so much as glance at that high-lifted, glittering blade. He seemed to know it would stop at the apogee of its upswing, hang there. The ilarch glared at him, but it was not Talos who lowered his eyes. Instead, it was Orchomenus' hard stare that broke, shifted, gave, shattered against the armor of the Helot's serenity.

"You know I can kill you, dog?" he said almost wonderingly.

"I know you're permitted to," Talos said.

"Meaning?"

"Your famous law. The ephors declare war on us yearly, so that the young men of the Krypteia may butcher us as an act of war without being charged with any crime.

Which, as I said, is a prior acknowledgment of your sense of guilt. Because, if you didn't know you were wrong, you'd just kill us without making this elaborate formal excuse for it beforehand. But there's a difference between 'may' and 'can,' my young master. You may kill me with that dagger you've got in your hand. Only, you can't."

"Why can't I?" Orchomenus snarled.

Talos smiled again.

"Because you're you. So put your silly, cruel toy up, and sit down, my son. Stop trying to be what you're not—a donkey in armor—I thank you for that phrase—and start practicing at being what you are in your heart, what you've got to be: a humane and kindly—man."

Orchomenus stood there, staring at him. The warfare going on inside his mind, his pneuma, his spirit, was the cruelest he'd ever faced. He was tempted to kill this strange and compelling red-beard, and thus free himself from the conflicting currents that tugged him now this way, now that. Or else, he suspected, his whole life was going to be ruined. The only trouble with that oversimplified solution was that Talos was right. He couldn't.

Slowly he sheathed his dagger.

"You fear us," Talos said gravely. "And your own recognition of the injustice of the burdens you heap upon us is the cause of your fear. That's why I changed my name. Since I want to live, I thought it wiser to be called Sufferer than Fiery One."

"But you remain Phlogius in spite of all," Orchomenus said. "And that name refers to more than the color of your hair. Talos, by interpretation, 'He Who Suffers'—Ha! It's others you make suffer, Red Beard! And I think the Helots have found their champion in you, though they had to reach far above themselves to do it. For your speech isn't their bestial mumblings, and everything about you is, for a Helot, wrong! Your skin's too fair, your hair and eyes are those of the northern barbarians, and the way you carry yourself—"

Talos shrugged.

"Men's conditions change, my young master," he said. "Mine has, several times. I was once a 'donkey in armor' attached to the guard of the king of Macedonia. Which

79

there—as here—means that a boy has to be gently born. But I was Phlogius, the Fiery One. I killed a companion in a witless, drunken quarrel over a tavern wench, and had to flee to Thrace. But as the Thracians don't love us Macedonians, they took me, sold me as a slave. To an Athenian, bless them!"

Orchomenus' eyes danced in sudden anger.

"You prefer the Athenians to us, then?" he said.

"Yes, my son," Talos said simply. "Oh, I know they're somewhat effeminate, hopelessly corrupt, a bunch of idle chatterboxes, but—"

"But what?" the ilarch said.

"They're free men. The freest men the world has ever seen."

"While we?" Orchomenus whispered.

"Are slaves. Slaves even to us, who are your slaves. Slaves to the hourly necessity of keeping us down, to subjugating the Perioeci. Slaves to your stern training that doesn't even make you good soldiers. All it does is make you brave. And the Athenians, who are cowards, beat you time and time again, because being free, their minds are flexible. They can improvise. They are free even to throw away their shields and run like human, fearful men, thus sparing themselves to return and beat you on a better day. But you, slaves to your iron discipline, must stand there like iron donkeys, and die—"

"Go on," Orchomenus said.

"You have no walls because the bodies of your sons suffice. But the Athenians, shut up behind the long walls you forced them to make, shake all the world with the immortal force of ideas. Where is your Sophokles, Euripides, Aeschylus?"

"Poets? Ha!" Orchomenus said.

"Poets. Who set the pneuma free to soar. Nobler than plunging a sword through a man's guts, my son. And when you destroy Athens, as you one day will, being stubborner, stronger, harder than they are, and—worst of all—dimwitted enough to do it, men in all future generations will remember you *only* because you did that—in infamy, as the destroyers of what you are incapable of: civilization. Forgive me, but among the things that Talos the Sufferer can do is to see and speak the truth. While that hot-tempered billy goat Phlogius, with his flaming hair, could only kill people. No fit occupation for a man, son Ilarch—this butchery of meat you can't even eat."

"If you're such a lover of the Athenians, why didn't you stay with them, then?" Orchomenus said. And though he didn't know it, there was a note of hurt in his voice.

"I did," Talos said. "Only, my master was a merchant —by trade. At heart he was a poet and a philosopher. He taught me all I know of life, the arts, sciences, men. We sailed the Ho Pontos far too late one year, bound for the polis of Syracuse in the island of the Sicelu near the toe of that great buskin-shaped peninsula where the Italiotes dwell. There was a storm. Our vessel wasn't large. In fact, it was only a penteconter because, being much more a philosopher than a merchant, my master never managed to scrape together enough money to buy a bireme. The first wave that caught us broadside turned it over. I swam ashore, dragging my master along beside me by his beard. But when we reached the shore, his shade had already departed. And that shore was the Peloponnesus, so—"

"You became a Spartan's, rather than an Athenian's, slave," the ilarch said.

"I became the slave of a rising young buagor, soon to become a strategos, named Telamon," Talos said with a smile. "Who put me to herding goats upon the hills of his further estate. But then—some seventeen years ago, it was —he took a strange and unaccountable dislike to the color of my hair and beard. So he sold me to another. Since then, I've been bought and sold several times. My present owner is a widow who depends upon me to keep things going for her, the poor dear lady. So she allows me a certain degree of freedom. But enough of my sad, dull history, young master! Couldn't we go inside once again so I may have a look at the boy?"

"He'll sleep for hours yet, Talos," Orchomenus said. "And there's one more thing I'd get clear: Just what is your relation to our General's son? Were you his paidaigogos?"

Talos got to his feet, glanced quickly up the street. To Orchomenus' surprise, a noticeable shake had gotten into his voice when he answered.

"I have no real connection with the beautiful Ariston at all," he said, "except, perhaps, the respect and gratitude I owe his mother. Please, good Ilarch, couldn't I go inside now?"

But the ilarch, who was no fool, had already followed the light locked pointing of the Helot's gaze. He got up in his turn. Looked toward the regally tall and slender woman who was coming toward them now, her face veiled, her arm resting upon the shoulder of a little slave girl, as convention demanded, but walking a good bit faster than custom permitted or than was commensurate with dignity.

"The lady whose name has been in your lying mouth all afternoon, eh, Talos?" he said. "His mother, great Telamon's wife. I've never seen her before. And you, it would appear, don't want to. Why?"

"You've got it wrong, son Ilarch. I don't want *her* to see *me*."

"Why not?"

"Because I don't like killing things—not even dreams. She's kept one fine bright one these eighteen years. Allow me the gallantry proper to my former state. Don't force upon her a brutality she doesn't deserve. I beg of you, young master!"

"You talk riddles!" Orchomenus said. "Oh, all right! Get you inside. I'll receive the gracious lady."

Talos dived into the doorway of the iatreion, moved into the room where Ariston lay. Swiftly he knelt beside the boy. Ariston mumbled something. Opened his eyes. Looked upon Talos' face with great melting tenderness.

"Dionysus, my father—" he murmured. Then he closed his eyes again. Slept.

"May I wait in the slaves' quarters, great descendant of the healing god?" Talos said quickly. "I'm dead of weariness and—"

"And famished, and athirst," Polorus said, not unkindly. "Of course. You deserve something for having saved the boy. Down the hall. Tell Arisbe to give you food and drink, but nothing more. She has a hard time keeping her chiton down, the slut; and you're most fair favored. Still, you'll be whipped if you avail yourself of her, Red Beard. I warn you!"

"Have no fear of that, great Iatros!" Talos said, and was gone.

He had no sooner left the room than the Lady Alkmena came into it on the ilarch's arm.

"Chaire, gentlemen," she said serenely.

Orchomenus stared at her. In all his life, he had never seen a more beautiful woman. She was, he guessed, about forty years of age; but only the wisps of silver in her dark hair revealed it. Her face was that of a woman of twenty-five. No, even less.

But it was not her beauty that struck the captain with the greatest force. He'd seen lovely women before, even had one or two as bedmates for a night. Besides, like the majority of the young men of his time, his inclinations were confused. He'd been greatly stirred by Talos' masculine splendor as well. What impressed him, even shocked him, was her calm. Her greeting to the company, conventional as it was, seemed to him singularly inappropriate in the present circumstances. "Chaire"—"Rejoice"—with her son lying at death's door, was marvelously ill chosen; and the word kalokagathoi, "gentlemen"—too all inclusive addressed to a group which included common soldiers, a doctor—who, after all, was no more than a demiurgos, a skilled worker, useful to the people, in the official view— servants, and slaves.

While it was true, as Orchomenus well knew, that high-born Spartan girls were almost as sternly trained as the youths, and that that training left them with a self-control unmatched by the women of any other polis in Hellas, this was *not* self-control. The lady Alkmena was not—even slightly—worried about her son's fate, nor was she—again not even slightly—afraid he'd die.

She knelt but the briefest instant by Ariston's bed, kissed his too-cold cheek, and got up again.

"You'll be rewarded for your work, good Iatros," she said in that marvelously serene voice of hers. "You'll find my lord and me both disposed to be generous toward one who has worked so nobly on behalf of our son. Tell me, how long will the cure take?"

"The cure?" Polorus gasped. Then he straightened up. After all, he was an Asklepiad, which was to say that he was a member of that noble house who claimed direct descent from the god Asklepios, and whose eldest sons were always dedicated to the practice of medicine—and a Spartan. Besides, questions of professional ethics aside, it was wiser to tell the truth. High-born people deceived by doctors could do much damage in their disappointment and their rage.

"My lady," he said bluntly, "let us speak of cures when he's up from there—if he ever is. It has been my experience that from wounds of this nature, the patient nearly always dies."

Alkmena took a backward step. For the barest perceptible instant, her face paled. Then her head came up, her color returned.

"No, good Iatros," she said, "he won't die. I know he won't, though I can't tell you how I know. In any case, I have already sent half a talent to the silversmith to have votive stelae made to be placed in the Temple of Asklepios in my son's behalf. And I command you to make me a drawing, or better still, a model in clay, of the wound, that I can have the goldsmith copy it in an anathema of solid gold to be thrown into the fountain at the god's feet in recompense for his granting my Ariston his life. Though, I must say, he hasn't any choice in the matter—a much stronger god than he commands him."

Mad, poor thing, Orchomenus thought; stark, raving mad!

"Now, with your permission, good Iatros,"—this phrase, the ilarch saw at once, was pure courtesy; what this madwoman meant to do, she'd do with permission or without it—"I'll have my slaves remove him from your iatreion to take him to the abaton of the temple, that he may rest this night at the god's feet—"

"No!" Polorus screeched. "You'll do no such idiotic thing, woman! Moving him will kill him surely, and the cold in that stone ice box will bring on a congestion that—"

Alkmena stared at the physician.

"Have you no faith, good Iatros?" she whispered. "Don't you even believe in the gods?"

The iatros Polorus stood there until the insupportable

84

agony of a lifetime of enduring fools got the better of his prudence, his good sense.

"No, my lady," he said, "to both questions, no."

Alkmena's black eyes opened wide.

"How—monstrous!" she breathed.

"Less than murder by superstitious cant, my lady, which is what you propose to do!" Polorus howled. "All right! Say there are gods. What evidence have you ever had that they care one jot about what happens to men? Don't you live in this world? Have you *ever* seen virtue rewarded—in any consistent way I mean—or evil punished? What's punished in life, my lady wife of the senator-general, is stupidity and weakness; and morality is an irrelevancy to your hypothetical gods! So I forbid you to remove this boy to kill him with your insane nonsense! What on earth have carved tablets of ivory, silver, or even gold with pretty words on them to do with curing this death wound? And that's all your stelae are! What does it serve to make a clay representation of this ugly stab wound and the area around it, spending above a talent in gold, which could feed two whole villages of starving Perioeci for more than a year, upon your equally useless anathema to be thrown into the fountain of Asklepios, where it will presently be fished out by your fat-bellied priests to be spent upon a fish fry, wine guzzling, and on whores! I tell you—"

Ariston's cry cut through his angry voice.

"Father!" he screamed. "Dionysus, my father! Don't leave me! I die! I die! Come back to me! Come ba-a-a—"

Alkmena whirled, her face paling now, her black brows flying upward.

"He means the Helot who saved him," Orchomenus, the captain of the guard, said. "For some reason he seems to have got that red-bearded animal confused with the god."

"Father!" Ariston screamed again. "By the love I bear you! Please!"

Polorus turned to one of his slaves.

"Go get the Helot," he commanded. "In cases like this, it's better to indulge their whims. Delirium, of course, but if the Helot's presence helps—"

The slave went out. Came back again, alone.

"He says he's afraid to—" he began.

Orchomenus nodded to two of the hoplites.

"Bring him!" he said. "Bodily, if you have to!"

The soldiers returned, shoving Talos roughly ahead of them. When he saw the Lady Alkmena, he tried to turn away his face. But there was no way to. The Fates had spun their tangled web full round.

Alkmena stared at the Helot. The color drained out of her face then, so slowly that Orchomenus could see it go. Now even her lips were whiter than the snows atop Mount Taygetus.

"You!" she said.

Talos took off his dogskin cap. Bowed to her.

"Yes, my lady," he said, "I—who was once a herdsman in your august lord's employ, upon his further estates, high in the hills. And once—for a single hour—I dreamed I was—a god. But the dream passed. I returned to sweat and pain, and sorrow. So now—"

But Alkmena's great dark eyes tore away from his face. She took a tottering step toward Ariston's bed, another. Stood there looking down at the twisting, sweating, semi-conscious, pain-wracked boy.

"I've killed you, haven't I, my son?" she whispered. "It's for my sin you suffer, is it not? For having a—a porna for a mother. A creature so unspeakably vile that—"

"My lady," Talos groaned, and put out his hand toward her. Great and muscular as it was, that hand trembled visibly.

Alkmena shrank away from it. Stood there staring up into his eyes with an expression of such utter loathing that she performed the sad miracle of making her face ugly.

"Swine!" she hissed. "Helot swine!"

"My lady, please!" Talos all but wept.

She swayed there beside Ariston's bed. Then slowly, slowly, her legs gave way beneath her. It was as though her bones were melting within her flesh. She knelt there a long time beside her wounded son, before she bowed even further in a long, shuddering swoop until her forehead touched the floor.

Then loudly, terribly, she screamed.

# CHAPTER SIX

ARISTON WAS COLD. In all his life, he had never been so cold before. His teeth chattered. He tried to stop them, but he couldn't. He hadn't even strength enough to do that.

And now he looked up and saw Hades, ruler over the Underworld, standing at his side. Hades was dressed in somber colors. His robes were wet. They dripped dark water. But the mist-gray, fog, and night-shade robes the god wore were very plain, and not of very good quality.

"Why do men call you Pluto, then, my Lord Hades?" Ariston asked him. "You don't look rich to me."

Hades smiled at him.

"I count my wealth in the shades of men. In that coin, I am very rich indeed," he said. "In fact, I've come to add yours to my store, son of Dionysus."

Ariston considered that. He was very cold, but he wasn't afraid any more. Just cold. Too cold.

"All right," he said to the Lord of Death, "since there's no help for it, all right."

"You seem sad, son of Dionysus," Pluto-Hades said to him. "I'll wager men have told you lies about my abode. Besides, not having been much of a sinner, you'll be sent to the Asphodel Meadows, not to Tartarus itself. And Asphodel is not all that bad. A mite gloomy, but not too bad. Most shades are quite content there. And now there'll be one who'll be very content indeed. She'll stop crying when I lead you to her side. That's why I came for you. I want her to be happy. She's a good little shade. She deserves the best."

"Who?" Ariston said.

"Phryne, of course. Didn't you know?" Hades said.

"Oh," Ariston said.

"Don't you want to go to her?" Hades asked him.

Ariston thought about that.

"Yes," he said.

Hades smiled at him.

"That's the proper answer. You're a good boy," he said.

Then the god knelt at Ariston's side. He put out one huge finger and touched the boy in the back. The finger didn't stop. It pushed on through his flesh, deeper, deeper, until the pain in him was very bad, the worst, absolutely insupportable. He opened his mouth and screamed. The sound of his scream was the sound of darkness. Night crashed down upon his head.

After that, he wasn't sure of anything. It was very dark, and he was freezing cold. He was in a boat, and a very old and ugly ferryman was rowing him across dark waters. On the far shore, a dog howled. Ariston had never heard a sound more terrible. It seemed to him that the dog howled louder than a whole pack of boarhounds giving tongue together. Then he saw why. The dog had three heads.

And now he noticed without surprise, taking it as a matter of course, that the dog wasn't there any more, and the ferryman wasn't either. He was alone and he was going down a steep, rocky trail. The trail was inside a cave. It was very dark in the cave and he was freezing cold.

Then he saw Phryne. She was all together again. None of her was missing. She came running toward him with her arms outstretched. Her long black hair floated out behind her like a cloud. She was laughing and crying at the same time and calling his name.

He couldn't hear her, but he knew that. He could see her lips move, but he couldn't hear her.

Then, suddenly, the god Dionysus got between them. The god was very tall and strong and beautiful. His hair and beard were red. Ariston loved him very much. The god smiled at him and put out his hand.

"As I was reborn from great Zeus's thigh," he said, "I am proof against death, and so are you, my son. Therefore you must come back into life with me. I bid you come!"

Then Ariston saw that the god had on a filthy sheepskin mantle and a ridiculous dogskin cap. He couldn't understand why a god wanted to dress like a Helot, but he took his hand all the same. The two of them went up the steep rocky trail together.

"Don't look back, my son," the god said.

But Ariston looked back. He saw Phryne kneeling on a rocky ledge. She was weeping and imploring and calling his name.

"She'll just have to wait, that's all," the god said. "Come—"

It was very dark, and he was freezing cold.

But now there was pain. The pain was very bad. It was in the middle of his back between his shoulder blades. Yet there was something different about that pain. He lay there, trying to decide what that difference was. Then he knew. The pain hadn't changed. It was just as bad, or worse. What had changed was his awareness of it. Now he felt it as a living man feels pain. With all his senses. He was alive and now he was beginning to remember it, starting to recreate in his mind, scene by scene, the insane interlocking of causes and results that men call fate. He was alive and he didn't really want to be. But he was. He had a feeling that he was even conscious. And he didn't want that either. Because, being conscious, he was presently going to recall even more of it, even the parts so bad that his mind had thus far locked them out.

He opened his eyes and stared up into the face of the god.

"Dionysus, my father—" he said clearly.

"You see!" Talos the Helot said. "We've come in time. Have your slaves put him on the litter, my lord Hippolytus."

His uncle Physcoa—Uncle Fat Belly—turned to the physician Polorus.

"Is it safe to move him, good Iatros?" he said.

"Safe, no," the physician said. "But safer than leaving him here to die of cold. I told your sister that it was unwise to lay a boy so dangerously wounded in the abaton of the temple. But she wouldn't listen. She changed all of a sudden from being absolutely sure he'd live to being equally convinced he'd die. Your sister's—well—odd, my lord Hippolytus . . ."

"Alkmena's daft," Hippolytus snorted. "I only hope she'll have wit enough to nurse him."

Polorus looked at the fat little man. "I wouldn't take him to her house, if I were you, my lord."

"Why not?" Hippolytus said.

"Because your sister's more than daft. She's—mad," the iatros said.

"But I'm not married," Hippolytus said. "I have no woman in my house to—"

"I'll send you my slave Arisbe to attend him. She's very good at nursing. Of course, when he's stronger—if he ever is—you'll have to send her back to me. He's much too handsome, this boy; and Arisbe's a randy she-goat. Now, have your slaves put him on the litter."

Ariston felt their hands. He was being lifted, and they were tearing him in half. A tongue of flame plunged through his back, reaching for his heart. He opened his mouth to scream, and stared straight into the face of the god.

Not Dionysus, but another god. Asklepios, from the looks of him. Then he saw the god was only a statue. A chryso-elephantine statue, which meant that it was made of gold and ivory. He wondered tiredly if the gods were ever more than that, ever anything else but man's fear and his megalomania frozen into a replica of life by a sculptor's hand.

Then the slaves moved off, bearing him out of the cold, dark abaton of the temple into the soft spring night, under the light of the stars.

"Uncle," Ariston said, "what is life?"

Hippolytus looked at his nephew. Ariston was very pale and thin, lying there propped up against the pillows.

"A mystery, Nephew," the fat little sybarite said, "into which it makes no sense to pry. Or worse, Pandora's box, which, once opened, lets loose all kinds of evil on the world. Why do you ask me that?"

Ariston didn't answer him. Instead he looked out of the window into the glaring August heat. The outlying village where Hippolytus had his house—for Sparta was not really a city in the sense that Athens was, but rather a collection of villages that had run together as they grew so that the lines of demarcation between them had become unclear—was a poor, unpretentious sort of place. Naturally, being the type of man he was, Hippolytus couldn't afford better.

"Uncle," Ariston said now, his voice reedy, thin, "why is there evil in the world? Why do the gods permit it, I mean?"

"By Pallas Athena, sprung full armed from the forehead of Zeus!" Hippolytus said. "What do you think I am, boy? A philosopher?"

Ariston smiled at him. But that smile was a painful thing to see. It resembled, if anything, one of the grimaces that men under torture adopt in order to fight back a scream.

"I think you're wise, Uncle Fat Belly," he whispered, "wiser than any man I know—except my father."

"Hmmmpht!" Hippolytus sniffed. "I don't consider that a compliment, boy. There may be, somewhere on earth, a duller clod than the august Telamon, but—"

"I don't mean him," Ariston said quietly. "I mean the Helot."

Hippolytus stared at his nephew. For once, the voluble little man could find no word to say.

"He doesn't dare visit me, or else I'd ask him," Ariston went on. "Therefore, I have to ask you. What is life, Uncle? Why is there evil in the world? Why do *I* exist, who am evil's self?"

"Ariston!" Hippolytus said.

"I loved a girl. She was torn to pieces by a pack of she-wolves. Have you ever seen anything like that? It's very interesting. They pulled her legs apart. As wide as they could get them. As though they were going to—to make love to her. Then an old, white-haired woman chopped at her middle with one of those thick cleavers that butchers use. It sounded like someone chopping wood wrapped in rags. Wet rags. And she was alive, Uncle. But she didn't scream. She didn't make a sound. She just lay there looking up at me with her one eye—they had knocked the other out with their stones—and let them chop at her, until her legs came off. I think she died very quickly after that. Then they threw her legs to the dogs."

"Nephew—" Hippolytus moaned.

"And even then they weren't done with her. They cut off her head. Hacked her body into pieces. You know what it looked like, Uncle? Like a goat's. You couldn't even tell she'd ever been a girl. A very pretty girl. The prettiest girl I've ever seen. I loved her."

"My boy, listen!" Hippolytus said. "I—"

"So I, in my turn, killed their leader. I cut her throat. Did you ever see a woman die with her throat cut? The air comes whistling out through the rent. You can hear it. It blows little bubbles in the blood. She flops about like—"

"Stop it!" Hippolytus said.

"Or a man when you've put a sword through his belly? He dances, Uncle. He clutches his belly with his two hands, trying to keep his guts inside. But the blood spurts out between his fingers in little jets. So he hops about clutching himself and roars and roars until he dies. A comic sight, Uncle. Makes you laugh."

"Ariston—" Hippolytus whispered.

"How did they kill the men of Parnon, Uncle? How did my foster-father arrange that general slaughter on behalf of a bastard whom he hates? Oh, I know; it was the law. They'd lifted hands against a Spartan. So the women and children were sold into slavery, and the men—butchered. And all because—"

"Who told you that?" Hippolytus said.

"Simoeis. He came to beg my pardon for insulting my mother; and to grant me his, for my almost having killed him. So now we're friends. I let him kiss me. He didn't know he was kissing a Mothone."

"Ariston, by Zeus!"

"What else am I? Or have you another name for it, Uncle? If a Mothone is a bastard got by a Spartan upon a Helot woman, what do you call a bastard got by a Helot upon—"

"Ariston, I forbid you!"

"Aye," Ariston said. "You forbid me. But nobody forbade my chaste, sweet mother, did they? To lie like a swineherd's woman on the ground, to open her thighs, her life to—"

Hippolytus crossed the room in one quick bound. His

fat little palm made a brief explosion as he slapped his nephew stingingly across the mouth.

Ariston lay there without moving. But now tears glazed his eyes, brimmed upon his lashes, began to fall.

"I thank you, my uncle," he whispered. "I deserved that slap."

"Nephew, Nephew!" Hippolytus groaned; "I—"

"Forget it. Why hasn't anyone come today? Neither Lysander, nor Orchomenus, nor my mother? I like Orchomenus better than Lysander now. I don't love him, of course, because he's ugly. But—it's strange—"

"What's strange, Nephew?" Hippolytus said, relief moving through his voice. This turn Ariston's thought had taken seemed to him less dangerous.

"I don't love Lysander either, anymore. He—he's beautiful; but, by Athena, he's stupid! While Orchomenus—"

"Has the rudiments, even the beginnings, of a mind. A fact he never would have discovered if—"

Hippolytus stopped short, his round, sparsely bearded face mirroring confusion.

"If Talos, my father, hadn't taught him to think," Ariston said, calmly, "just as you taught me, Uncle Physcoa. I've seen people in love before, but never anyone so in love as Orchomenus is with—my father. And yet—he swears there's nothing—well—bodily—between them. It seems my father is of those who find physical love between man and man repugnant. Odd, isn't it, Uncle?"

"Very," Hippolytus said. "In a way, I prefer boys to women, though I have to admit that females can be very fine abed."

"I suppose so," Ariston said indifferently. "Orchomenus says that my father is the wisest man on earth. A true philosopher. He goes to visit him twice a week at his little farm. Generous of my foster-father, wasn't it? I mean to buy Talos his freedom, make of him a freedman, give him that little tract of land—"

"No," Hippolytus said, "it wasn't generous."

Ariston stared at his uncle.

"You're right," he said slowly. "It wasn't, was it? Because, if he hadn't, people would have called him mean, wouldn't they? And somebody would have seen soon enough how much I look like Talos. Orchomenus did. So, in a way, it would have been admitting to the whole polis that he suspects or knows—"

Hippolytus shook his head.

"No," he said dryly. "It would have been admitting it to—himself."

"Oh!" Ariston whispered.

"Think no more of it, my boy. And we've talked enough unpleasantness for one day, considering your state. Besides, I've most absolutely got to go—"

"Where?" Ariston said.

"To call upon Sarpedon, the father of Lamia. You know I turned thirty a few months ago? Now I'm forbidden to attend the processions, according to the law. An homois of the age of his majority who refuses to undertake his sacred duty to the polis, that is, to wallow nightly with some unappetizing cow of a woman in order to produce future soldiers for the glory and defense of Sparta, is deprived of all his privileges. So no longer can I feast my famished eyes upon Ixion's or your Lysander's lovely naked forms dancing in the sacred rites! Nor, for that matter, upon Theope's, Thebe's, or Philomela's—you know I've no prejudice about the sex of my lovers. Anyhow, week after next is the festival of Artemis Orthia, so—"

"Rather than miss the festival, you'll marry a girl you hardly know, not to mention love!"

"Love is the worst possible reason for getting married, Ariston, my boy. And I do know Lamia. Quite well. How well, it ill behooves a kalokagathos like me to say. Anyhow, she suits me. She's round, rosy, plump, and greedy—in both senses. Unfortunately, Sarpedon's a stingy old bastard. He's been haggling over her dowry for two months, now. But I'll best him, never you fear! In any case, when your mother comes, treat her more kindly, will you? She's a lovely thing, but she *is* your mother. So contain your brute male jealousy, Nephew! After all, what did Oedipus solve by killing Laius? And he killed him first, without knowing why. So forgive Talos his spot of fun on the rocky mountainside. Dominate life. Be irreverent, unchaste, and a mocker, like me—in other words, civilized. Then you'll never again feel called upon to kill people. Chaire, Nephew. I go!"

A scant two minutes after Hippolytus had gone, proving she had been impatiently awaiting his departure, Arisbe, the slave girl the physician Polorus had loaned Hippolytus to nurse his nephew during his convalescence, came into the room. She bent and kissed Ariston long and lingeringly upon the mouth. He made no resistance. He liked the way Arisbe kissed. She was very expert. Then she committed the gross impiety of tactily exploring the result of her kisses upon him. Stood back, grinning at him impishly.

"Another two weeks and we can give it a try," she said.

The day that Arisbe's two weeks were up, Ariston was walking in the garden with the ilarch Orchomenus, and he didn't have Arisbe in the back part of his head.' Orchomenus was telling the outrageously funny story of how he'd rescued Ariston's uncle Hippolytus from a pack of Spartan women bent upon beating him up, or worse, just the day before.

"They had him down in the mud," the ilarch said, "and were pummeling him right merrily. One fat, dignified matron sat upon his head. So what did old Physcoa do, you ask me? He took a man-sized bite out of the harridan's seat. The screech she let out brought the Eleventh and the Thirteenth ilas on the run. They thought the Athenians had finally got up the nerve to attack. And believe me, Ariston, we needed their help! Not even the Kindly Ones themselves could have been worse than those stately Dames of Sparta!"

Ariston laughed. The oddest part about it was that Orchomenus was telling the truth. The matrons of the homois class regarded continued and stubborn bachelorhood on the part of a citizen as an insult to their collective dignity —probably, Ariston realized, because there were so few eligible males of suitable rank for their marriageable daughters. And by ancient custom, they were freely permitted to make life utterly miserable for a man who'd reached his thirtieth birthday without taking a bride. Which was why there were no thirty-one-year-old bachelors in Sparta, not to mention any of more advanced age. Even widowers were not allowed to grieve too long. The rule had no exceptions; there was no alternative, no escape. For if Hippolytus, for instance, did not accept stingy Sarpedon's miserably small dowry for the plump and lascivious Lamia before next year's Greater Dionysia, the august Spartan Dames would hurl him into a darkened room in which waited all their crossed-eyed, skinny-shanked, flat-chested, or otherwise ill-favored daughters who had reached their twentieth birthday and more without having been asked for. And from that room one bloody, naked, triumphant Amazon would emerge, dragging poor half-dead Physcoa by his beard or his hair, having won him as her prize for life in a no-holds-barred battle in which not only were teeth, nails, elbows, knees, feet, and fists employed to such effect that three-quarters of the contestants reposed in the various iatreia of the city upon the morrow, but upon rare occasions, sadly enough, a weaker sister or two had been known to die.

"He now swears," Orchomenus chuckled, "that he'll accept Lamia without any dowry at all. At least she's good to look at, and promises to be a merry bedmate—which, if you ask me, your uncle Fat Belly already knows."

"Wouldn't doubt it," Ariston said. "But tell me, friend Orchomenus, what did you really come to tell me? I'm not the Helot's son for nothing, you know. I can see through pretense as easily as he does."

"Pretense?" the ilarch said. "Why, Ariston, I never—"

"Rubbish. Pretense is the exact word. You're a solemn creature by nature, my friend. Yet all afternoon, you've been—a trifle too gay. And that gaiety is forced. You think my life's in danger, don't you? You believe that the Perioeci will do anything to revenge themselves upon a man who was the direct cause of more than thirty deaths, and the enslavement of nearly twice that number of their people. Don't blame them. I—I'd welcome their daggers, friend."

Orchomenus looked away from him; looked back again.

"It's not that," he said. "So far the Perioeci are quiet, Zeus be praised."

"Then what is it?" Ariston said.

Orchomenus' dark eyes searched his face.

"Well—" he began, and stopped.

"Out with it!" Ariston said.

"It's—it's your mother. It seems that she's greatly troubled by your attitude toward her. Or she was. I don't think she's troubled by *anything,* now . . ."

Ariston looked at him.

"Continue, my friend."

"And the august Telamon's in Attica, as is usual this time of year, raiding the Athenians. So she had no one to turn to. You understand that, don't you? Certainly a mocker like your uncle Hippolytus wouldn't have been any help . . ."

"Go on," Ariston said.

"So she asked me to tell Talos to come to see her. I—Athena, goddess of wisdom, pardon me my folly!— pointed out to her that for Talos to enter the strategos' house during his absence was a form of suicide. A highly unpleasant form, at that. So she asked me to ask him whether he would receive her at his place . . ."

"Go on." Ariston's voice was less than sound.

"By hades, Ariston, understand it! They're not broken-down old wrecks, but people in the full glory of their maturity! She went to his little farm to ask him to see you, talk to you, so that you'd cease to accuse her with your eyes . . ."

"The whore!" Ariston said.

"That's an impiety, and you know it! She's still your mother, and as sweet and innocent a woman as ever drew breath. If she hadn't been so extremely innocent, she'd have realized what was going to happen. Ariston, Ariston —they've kept the dream of each other these eighteen years, unsullied in their hearts! And Talos—you should see him now—in clean, soft-spun robes, his red beard trimmed and curled, his red hair washed, combed, perfumed, falling like fire about his shoulders . . ."

"You love him," Ariston said.

"Yes. I am not ashamed of it. But I accept his reasoning when he says that men shouldn't lie with men, that the gods made the male body and the female to complement each other. We've the sword, and they the sheath, we've—"

"Stop it. So now—they've become lovers again, haven't they?"

"Yes." Orchomenus whispered.

"I'll kill him," Ariston said quietly. "By Hestia and by Artemis, I swear it!"

Orchomenus stared at him.

"I'm sorry I told you," he said. "I—I thought you'd help them—procure a sum of money so that they might flee Lakonia, go to—"

"Help a porna and her paramour?" Ariston raged. "Help a she-goat and her satyr once more to dishonor my house? Immortal gods! I—"

Then he stopped short, for Lysander had come through the gate into the garden. He stood there with an amazed expression on his beautiful young face, looking from one to the other of them.

"Chaire, Ilarch," he whispered. "Chaire, Ariston. I—I'm not interrupting anything, am I? I'll go away. I—"

"No, stay," Ariston said lightly. "I was merely telling Orchomenus that I have to cut a pair of throats. What do two more slit gullets matter to hands that already reek of human blood? Come in, come in. Don't stand there looking so foolish and so gloomy. Here, let me kiss you. There —is that better?"

"Much!" Lysander smiled ruefully. "But I'm afraid I can't stay. I only came to tell you—"

"What?" Ariston said.

"I—I've drawn the black pea. So tomorrow I—and Simoeis, who drew the other one—have the great honor of being whipped before the Upright Artemis until we bedew all the stones at her feet with our blood. So, kiss me once again, Ariston, for by Eros himself, I love you! And I have the feeling that—"

"That what, fair Lysander?" Orchomenus said.

"That it will be the last kiss I'll ever give—or take," Lysander said.

"Nonsense!" Ariston said, and kissed him. "You're as strong as a horse, Lysander. Look, I tell you what! I'll give you a note to my iatros, Polorus, telling him to make you a stupefying brew that'll keep you from feeling the pain—"

Lysander shook his bright blond head.

"No. That wouldn't be honorable, Ariston. Now I have to go to the Temple of Herakles to pray for strength to endure it. Chaire, friends!"

Then suddenly, shyly, Lysander kissed both of them, like the maiden he was at heart, and ran blindly through the garden gate.

"Poor devil!" Orchomenus said.

"Aye," Ariston whispered. "Poor, poor devil! But then, who isn't? What man is happy in this world? Tell me that, Orchomenus! What man at all?"

"Not I, at any rate, not now," the young ilarch said. "Ariston—listen to reason! They married her off at thirteen to a man who could have been her grandfather! The love that produced you is both pure and holy! It's the other that's a monstrosity! I tell you—"

"Orchomenus," Ariston said.

"Yes, Ariston?"

"You value my friendship?"

"Yes. Why yes, of course—"

"Then go before you lose it," Ariston, the Spartan, said.

# CHAPTER SEVEN

THAT NIGHT THERE WAS NO MOON. That was strange. Usually at the beginning of the festival of Artemis Orthia, held the second week in Hecatombian, that midsummer month with which the Hellenes began their year, the moon was at the full. There weren't any stars either. The night was overcast, hot, thick, almost unbreathing. The room in which Ariston lay was utterly lightless, totally black.

"Like the hearts of men," he murmured, "like your sins, my mother!" Then he bent his head and wept.

He wept a long time, but very quietly. His uncle, as usual, wasn't at home; and it was impossible for Arisbe to have heard him from what was going to be the gynaeceum when Hippolytus finally brought his Lamia home. Yet Ariston was conscious suddenly of the sound of breathing not his own, a ragged, staccato gasp and hiss and whistle, halting in midnote on a choked-off little sob, and looking up, he was aware by a curious kind of purely instinctual perception, since sight just wasn't possible in that room, that the slave girl was bending above him in the dark.

He lay there, staring toward the source of that ugly sound: that torn, unrhythmical, dumb she-beast's mute imploring bleat; and now he could smell her, too—that acrid, nostril-stinging odor that fear gives to human sweat; the reek of his uncle's perfumes which she had stolen, mixing them with a wild, undiscriminating hand; her own hot, thick bitch-in-heat stench that halted his breath in a curious mingling of nausea and excitement.

"Oh, my lord Ariston!" She wept. "I—"

He went on staring at that patch of utter darkness, at the trembling—how did he know that? How?—source of those gut-gripping female sounds and smells. Then he said:

"Why not? What other swinishness haven't I already done?" and dragged her down beside him.

Long after midnight, they heard the noise of someone at the garden gate.

"It's your uncle." Arisbe giggled. "Drunker than an Athenian owl, as usual. Turn me loose, my sweet lord. I'd better slip on my robe and go let him in. Oh, I'll come back, I promise you! Just as soon as he's abed and snoring off his wine. You don't think I'm not going to make the best of this night, after all the weeks I've had to wait!"

Ariston looked at her. He couldn't see her; it was much too dark; but he looked toward where he knew her face was.

"Was it worth it?" he said.

"Worth it?" Arisbe laughed. "You have to ask? I'll bet they heard me in Macedonia that last time! By Goat-Pan and all his satyrs, nobody'd believe they were about to slip the obol beneath your tongue to pay old Charon to ferry you across the Styx a scant five weeks ago! Tireless is the word for you, my lord! Inexhaustible. Now just you lie there like a good little son of Priapus till I come back. Say a prayer to Aphrodite. And to Eros. Ask them to tie Eos to her bed so she can't get up to wake her brother the sun. I want this night to last ten thousand years, for you—"

"Oh stop chattering, wench; and go let my uncle in," Ariston said.

It was darker than ever. The heat was oppressive. Sounds moved through it dully, slowly: Arisbe's skip and scamper, the scurry of her bare feet upon the tiled floor as she went to let Hippolytus in, the creak the door hinges made.

And then, it seemed to Ariston, he slept. And dreamed. He knew he was dreaming because now it was his mother who lay there, sweat-drenched and naked at his side.

"Ariston, my golden boy," she crooned, "my lover, my inexhaustible one—"

Which was an impiety so terrible that he burst the chains of sleep and looked up to see Arisbe's form, a sort of moving darkness upon the deeper dark, standing beside his bed.

"Ariston," she said. Her voice was strange somehow. It didn't sound like her own voice anymore. It was thick-toned, humid—as if, he realized suddenly, she were crying.

But he was sleep drugged, and his monstrous dream had left him irritable. He felt both angry and afraid.

"Come, whore!" he said. "Don't waste time!"

Then he caught her roughly by her arms and jerked her forward so that she fell heavily upon him. She had her robe on, now. What was more, she wore both a peplos and a himation.

"What in black Hades' name is all this?" he said. "You've dressed for a journey? By Persephone, I'll have you out of these swathings soon enough!"

Then he reached out his hands and ripped at her clothing.

"Ariston!" she gasped. "Have you gone mad?"

"Aye!" he said. "Mad! In a world of swine, is it madness to be a boar? In a universe of rutting goats, why shouldn't I—"

Then he stopped, his breath caught in his throat; for the echoes of her cry had at last penetrated his mind, stabbing into his consciousness with accents remembered, familiar, loved, known to him since long before he was born, having entered into his very bloodstream through his umbilicus before the cruel obscenity of birth had torn him from her entrails, forcing him—against his anguished will—to have his being apart from her, separately to breathe, live, feel pain.

"Mother!" he groaned; "I—"

And then, of course, in accordance with the law laid down by the more-than-goddess Ananke, Necessity, to whom even great Zeus must bow, that coincidences always occur precisely when they shouldn't, the slave girl Arisbe came through the door with a lighted oil lamp in her hand.

She stood there staring at them, the expression of shock on her small round face making her look even more stupid than she generally did, which was something of a feat.

"A—a mother—and her son!" she whispered. "Immortal gods, save me! Save me, divine Artemis! Save me, Hestia, great Hera! The impiety's not mine! I didn't mean to witness it!"

Alkmena's hands came up, clawing her torn peplos over her bared breasts, which, in her fortieth year, were still beautiful.

"Listen, my child," she said, her voice breathless, fluting, dark. "It was a mistake—a terrible error. There was no light, and my son, he—You mustn't think—"

But Arisbe was of Boeotian peasant stock, than which there was no more stupid race in all the world.

"Think!" she shrilled. "What's there to think about, my lady she-goat? I have eyes! Rutting with your own! I'm going to leave this house—house, ha!—this den of iniquity— right now! For surely the Eumenides will destroy it, and everybody who lives in it as well! And you, my lusty young lord! Wasn't I enough for you? Don't tell me you prefer this raddled old sow at whose dugs you pulled to my sweet flesh! Why—"

Then she stopped, for Ariston had gotten out of bed and was coming toward her. He paused only an instant at the side wall—just long enough to draw from its sheath the ancient Minoan bronze dagger his uncle had hanging there. He put the point of it against Arisbe's throat. She didn't cry out. She didn't dare. But very slowly her knees gave way beneath her, so that she slid inch by inch down the door frame in the midst of all that thick, oppressive silence, unbreathing still. Ariston kept the point of the dagger pressed against her throat, flexing his arm so that the blade followed her downward slide.

But he didn't thrust it home. He couldn't. There was too much remembered horror in him still. And yet he knew very well that he had to kill Arisbe, that death alone would silence her wagging tongue. He had to break through the private horror which was the only thing that stayed his hand. For he had absolutely nothing else to fear: As a Spartan, he held the power of life or death over any slave.

Arisbe saw his blue eyes darken in the light of the oil lamp she still held terror-frozen in her hands. Very carefully she set the lamp down on the floor, in order to free her hands so that she might raise them to him in the attitude of supplication. Then she saw that even that wasn't going to be any good. She found her voice, screamed:

"Don't! Don't, my sweet lord! I—"

Then Alkmena was upon her son. She was almost too late. Her clawing hands turned his thrust aside so that the ornamental blade, dating from prehistory, from Cretan times, being of bronze and thus lacking the kind of edge that can be achieved and maintained only in steel, ripped downward across Arisbe's throat and left breast almost to the nipple, making a huge and shallow tear that wasn't really dangerous, but that was hideous to look at, and that bled frightfully.

"I'm dead!" Arisbe shrilled. "You—you've killed me!"

"Not yet," Ariston said grimly, "but I'm going to."

"Fly, child!" Alkmena cried. "Immortal gods! Can't you see he's mad?"

Then Arisbe was up from there like a doe that hears the pack give tongue. With a leap that would have gained her a prize at the Olympian or the Isthmanian games, she was out the door and gone before Ariston could free himself from his mother's grip.

"Oh, Ariston, Ariston," Alkmena moaned. "What's come over you, my son?"

Ariston looked at his mother.

"A sudden rise of my Helot-dog's blood to my head," he said lightly, pleasantly. "Or maybe it was the smell of whore that got me wild. Forgive me, will you, Mother? I didn't know it was you. After all, it's hard to tell one porna from another in the dark. You should wear a sign around your neck, maybe. To identify you, I mean. But then, what would it be but more pornography, whore scribblings; and who could read it, anyhow, once the lights were out?"

He bent and picked up Arisbe's lamp from the floor and set it on the table.

"Ariston! Ariston!" His mother wept. "My son! My son!"

"Aye, Mother. Your son—who bears your blood. I was proving it just before you came. That is, I was making the beast with two backs with that unwashed Boeotian heifer. Zeus, averter of flies, how she stinks! Which is why I was confused. And you, Mother? Where do you come from at this charming hour?"

104

"Ariston, I—" Alkmena quavered.

"Don't bother. From a dog kennel. A Helot dog's pad of straw. Great sport, nevertheless, eh, Mother? Rut is rut, in bed, on the floor, or in the high groves visited by red-bearded gods in dogskin caps. Have you made me a brother? I thank you, but it's too late. I should be accustomed to being alone by now, don't you think? Why do you look at me like that? Haven't you ever seen a Mothone before? Well, maybe not a Mothone. It's an interesting linguistic problem, isn't it? If you were my father, and he my mother, I'd be a Mothone. But since it's the other way around, I'm—a bastard. Bastardy is universal, isn't it, Mother? And a bastard is a bastard no matter how piously got—"

"Ariston!" She sobbed.

"Goodnight, Mother. Go back to your Helot stallion kept in stud to cover—Oh, I beg your pardon! Go back to the god Dionysus, my father, and tell him I've become a worshiper of my half-brother Priapus. My brother demands of me a sacrifice—from our mutual father. A blood offering, accompanied by a little meat. The parts that made me, say. What are you waiting for? Don't force me to play Orestes to your Klytaemnestra! But no. I am more nearly Oedipus, am I not, as this night I almost proved? So go, my lady Iocasta! Tell your red-haired, beautiful Laius that his son comes with the patricidal daggers ready. Let's fulfill all the ancient legends, play out every skene-full of impiety, incest, madness, death!"

"Ariston, you don't understand! You've no right to abuse me so—you, who've never loved!"

"I—who have—never—loved. You wrong me, Mother! I loved—and was offered a true feast of love. That is, I could have feasted, had I been prepared to get down on all fours and dispute my beloved's entrails with the dogs! Such dainty little guts she had, Mother. So long and pink and slimed with blood. I thought they'd never finish pulling them out of her, rod by slippery, glistening rod. A feast fit for kings. Dogs kings. And her legs. They'd have been better roasted, of course, with a helping of leeks and lentils on the side. But even raw they were—"

"Ariston!"

"Appetizing enough. All bloody—and torn—with the white bones showing through—Aye, Mother, Mother! Have you no mercy in you? Why not play Medea and butcher me as she did her children? By all the gods, I'd welcome it! Here. Take this dagger, for before great Zeus, I swear I'd no longer live!"

Then he was kneeling before her and holding the Minoan dagger out to her hilt-first; and she, kneeling too now, crushing him to her uncovered breasts; and the two of them weeping not as men weep but as the gods do, with so terrible an outpouring of grief, anguish, pain that Hippolytus, returning from a little prior sampling of a bliss he had no right to before the nuptial rites and sacrifices were celebrated—said rites and pious offerings to the gods having that same afternoon been set for the conclusion of the Greater Eleusinian Mysteries in the month of Boedromion some sixty days hence—had the wine-bemused, pleasantly weary thought—a reversal of his former belief—that boys were all right in a way, but a swivel-hipped tornado like Lamia, praise be to Pan, god of lechery, was finer still, knocked completely from his head.

He hung there staring at his sister and his nephew. A rush of nausea hit the back of his throat. For now, sadly enough, poor Hippolytus had become the victim of his erudition, which was vast. He knew the story of the children of Aeolus; he'd got by rote the ancient legends. What they disguised in their shaping of the tales of Oedipus and Iocasta; Orestes and Klytaemnestra; Elektra's response to the death of Agamemnon; Antigone's to the slaying of Polyneikes; what actually had caused Phaedra's false accusation of his own legendary ancestor and namesake, and her subsequent suicide—was to him blindingly clear.

So he leaped to the same conclusion Arisbe had come to: that here the sternest, most ancient of all tabus had been violated; and by his closest, dearest flesh and blood. For what was their wild and bitter weeping if not the blackest wave of remorse? What that dagger pressed between them if not the instrument of incipient suicide?

And all that came to his mind—his agnostic skepticism completely vanquished by his fear—was the sound of the

Furies' wings beating down upon his house; all that burst from his quivering, slack-jowled, weakling's mouth, was:

"Not here! In Zeus's name, not here!"

Alkmena looked up at her brother. Then she said with awful dignity, her voice emerging from its black ocean of tears, serene and clear.

"No, Brother. May the gods preserve your house for you and your bride. And may they forgive both this my son and me for our several, but always separate, sins. Rejoice, Brother! Chaire, my son! I go!"

Ariston's face was a hypokritos' mask, the one worn at the tragoidia, the Song of the sacrificial goat, a monstrous distortion of his beauty by grief and pain.

"Then go!" he howled. "Hades take you, Mother! Go!"

At dusk of evening of that next day, Ariston set out. Despite the Spartan prejudice against such practices, he had bathed and perfumed himself, largely because the various male and female carnal odors, products of his and Arisbe's labors, lingered upon him and revolted him to, and even past, nausea. He wore a red military himation over his chiton, not because he needed the cloak—the heat had lessened only slightly since last night—but to conceal the pair of daggers he carried in the belt about his waist.

He moved on very quietly, his face no longer wearing the twisted, tortured expression of the mask of tragedy, rather, it resembled another mask, the one the hypokritos wore when called upon to play a god. It was as still, as expressionless, as beautiful, and as terrible.

But in order to reach the little farm that Telamon had given Talos—having, in the culmination of life's insane irony, half-knowingly rewarded his wife's lover for saving the life of the bastard said lover had fathered upon her, thus adding new gloss and luster to his horns—Ariston had to pass through Sparta itself; since his uncle Hippolytus' house was on the extreme south side of the polis. So it was that he had gone less than half a parasang, when he heard the slow beat of muffled drums coming toward him, and halted where he was, unable to move or breathe as the funeral beat of that instantly recognized military dirge came over to him, bringing with it a renewed rising of brine and blood into his throat, as his agonized mind shaped the question:

"Which? Lysander or Simoeis?" Knowing that he couldn't stand it no matter which one it was: Lysander for the memory of the love he'd borne him so many years; or Simoeis, because only his own brutal punishment of the young colossus could have weakened that oxlike body to the extent that a mere whipping had caused his death.

He stood there, and all his mind could form was the image of the ugly idol stolen from the Temple of the Taurians by his own ancestor Orestes, with the help of Orestes' sister, Iphigenia, and of Pylades who afterward became husband to Orestes' other sister, Elektra. It was of wood and black with the centuries-old accumulation of human blood that the Taurians had offered it. And even afterward, when Astrabakos and Alopekos, princes of the royal house of Sparta, found it in the thicket where Orestes had hidden it, held upright by a tangle of willow branches (hence its two names: Orthia, "Upright," and Lygodesma, "Of the Willows") the Spartans continued to propitiate it with human sacrifice, first out of dread of its ugliness, which had driven the two young princes mad, and afterward because of the murderous quarrel that broke out between rival bands of devotees of Artemis over which band should have the right to guard and tend it. The quarrel was terminated not by the hecatomb of dead bodies their rioting strewed about the temple, but rather by the plague which followed hard upon this minor religious civil war, and which came close to ending Sparta as a polis. So, having had these triple proofs of the Upright Artemis' awful power—the madness of their beloved princes, their own sudden seizure of not entirely explicable bloody fury, and the plague—they continued to sacrifice a youth to her every year upon the date she had been found. It was great Lycurgus who put a stop to that. He decreed that the blood the greedy idol demanded should henceforth be drawn from the backs of Spartan youths by the lash. And ever since, the melliranoi of Sparta had competed yearly for the great honor of proving their manhood by receiving an incredible number of blows; the one who endured the most without crying out being honored as a hero.

Had Ariston been then capable of thought, he might have wondered how such obscene savagery had ever come to be attributed to Artemis, who, though she was goddess of the hunt as well as of feminine chastity, was fierce only in her defense of purity, and implacable only against its violators. But he had by then gone past all the limits of rationality; he could only stand there and watch as the Tenth City Ila, with his new friend, the ilarch Orchomenus at the head of it, came toward him with the points of their spears turned earthward, slow marching to that ominous funeral strain, bearing those two figures upon the shield litters, lying still, too still.

The eyes that Ariston turned upon Orchomenus were two blue wounds like rents in dead flesh after the bleeding has stopped. Orchomenus halted his columns with a half-audible command, and watched what Ariston's eyes did as he looked toward those two covered bundles on the shield litters. They seemed to usurp the function of his voice, and scream.

Orchomenus could almost hear it. And even his re-creation of it in the darkness of his mind wasn't to be borne, so the ilarch opened his mouth, forced breath, sound through the laryngeal constriction caused by the horror that was choking him too; horror of which, a scant month ago, before Talos had come into his life, he would have been incapable, that then, in fact, would never have entered his completely disciplined head. It's because I've ceased to be an ass encased in iron, he thought, and become—a man. In Talos' sense of the word, not Sparta's. But, immortal gods, how it hurts!

"Yes," he said softly. "Both of them. Lysander, now—I can understand that. He was strong enough, but he had a woman's heart. But Simoeis? By Hades and Persephone both, that's a thing beyond all reason! Why—"

"*I* killed him," Ariston said, his voice flat, even, calm, controlled. And suddenly Orchomenus, whom Talos had cursed with sensitivity, felt in his own entrails the Furies' claws ripping, slashing, tearing; tasted in his own throat—

by a projection of the imagination, sympathy, even humanity the Helot had fostered upon him—the brine and blood that was gurgling in Ariston's, rising from bowels torn now by horror, grief.

"No," he said harshly. "You had nothing to do with it, Ariston. The goddess was unusually greedy this year. She kept crying out, through the priestess who held her: 'More! Harder! Can't you see you weigh me down?' "

"I killed them," Ariston said in that flat dead calm voice. "Both of them. Lysander because I'd ceased to love him. He must have sensed that. And Simoeis because I broke his body, weakened him too much to bear it, for the slight offense of calling my mother the whore she is. So, now—"

"Ariston, in Zeus's name, you can't! You've no right to make of yourself a pharmakos to be sacrificed for the guilt of all the world! Say rather—that Sparta killed them, by refusing civilization, by clinging to these ancient, savage rites of blood and pain."

Ariston smiled at him bleakly.

"Now you're quoting Talos. Or my uncle Hippolytus— or both," he said. "And your words are treason to the polis."

"Hades take the polis! Any state that whips youths to death for this filthy, irrational, insane—"

"Stop it, Orchomenus. May I—see them, now?" Ariston said.

Orchomenus stared at him.

"Sure you want to?" he said. "They're not pretty."

"I want to," Ariston said.

Orchomenus stared at him again.

"I wouldn't, if I were you," he said.

"Do you forbid me, Ilarch?" Ariston grated. "If so, you're within your rights."

Orchomenus sighed.

"No, as Ilarch of the City Guard, I don't forbid you to see them, Ariston," he said, "though, as you've said, it's within my powers to. But, as your friend, I suggest you shouldn't. You've been badly wounded, ill, and this—"

"Might unseat my reason? What makes you think I've any left?" Ariston said, and lifted the himations from the faces of his friends.

110

Orchomenus was right. The bodies were unlovely. They lay face down upon the shields. Their backs were so much shredded meat through which, here and there, the rib cage showed. Their faces, turned sideways, were blue. Both eyes and mouths were opened wide. And both screamed still, even in death, in a terrible silence, louder than all sound.

Ariston knelt in the dust between the two shield litters. He bent to kiss Lysander's mouth. The stench of blood rising from it made him giddy, sick. Then he saw why: The dead boy had no tongue. He'd bitten it off so as not to cry out under that awful, intolerable hell of pain.

But Ariston kissed him in spite of that. Kissed both him and Simoeis on their mouths long and lingeringly, as lovers kiss. Then all the sky roared. Inside his own bowels, Cerberus howled, high and mad, like a maenad, like a woman in childbirth, like the Erinyes yelling at a matricide's heels. He opened his mouth and yellow bile gushed out of it, followed by a foaming tide of hot, salt blood. He bent forward until his forehead touched the earth, knelt like that, shuddering, muddying the ground beneath his face with bloody vomit, soaking it with his tears.

"Ariston," Orchomenus whispered. "Ariston, my friend, my love—"

But Ariston shook off his hand, lurched to his feet, reeled away from there, running in a zigzag—grief-drunk, tear-blinded, mad.

I'll come after him, Orchomenus thought, as soon as I've borne these two poor butchered lumps of carrion to their homes. But I'd better be quick about it. The way he is now—

Then he turned to the hoplites.

"Up litters! March!" he barked. And the muffled drums took up their beat, muted, earth deep, sad. A trumpet keened suddenly, wildly, against the edge of night. The column moved off, bearing Lysander and Simoeis toward where their mothers waited dry eyed. It was beneath a Spartan woman's dignity to cry.

And one more thing. As he reeled through the town, his himation reeking of vomit, of blood, Ariston attracted the

111

attention of more than one citizen who knew him well. But when they approached him to question him, what blazed in his eyes stopped them, made them sense somehow that to pry into a thing so great, so terrible, was at least an impiety, if not worse. But one among them had finally the sagacity, the wisdom, the wit, or their direct opposites—for which it was only the forever silent gods can tell—to report the matter to the Krypteia.

Now the buagor—more than captain; commander, colonel, say—of Sparta's Secret Police, had long since decided upon his own to keep an eye upon august Telamon's son. Since suspicion was second nature even to any ordinary Spartan, it is not difficult to imagine how overdeveloped that trait had become in the head of such an organization as the Secret Police. Besides, Perimedes, buagor of the Krypteia, could not get out of his mind what he had found when he had gone up to Parnon to investigate the stabbing of this selfsame beautiful, golden, highborn melliran. On the trail behind the village, the one that Orchomenus' report had caused them to take, lay the body of a giant of almost legendary proportions. It was hard to determine what had caused his death because the wolves, the crows, the vultures had been at him far too long by then; but beside him lay a sword, its blade black and crusted with blood. And on the hilt of that mighty weapon, the personal device of the strategos Telamon himself. Then, in the village, one hut that no Perioeci would go near. Entering it, they'd met a stench powerful enough to floor an ox. The naked woman on the floor had not, of course, been torn by beak or fang; but she was swollen drum-tight with the internal gases of putrefaction, while from mouth, nose, eyes, ears, the nether orifices of her body, fat maggots crawled, and choked with one great white squirming mass the wounds in her shoulder and her throat.

So, Perimedes reasoned, it would not be amiss to keep an eye upon this beautiful—assassin. Of course, killing Perioeci wasn't a serious enough crime to trouble one's head about, except that, good detective that he was, the buagor was intrigued by the apparent absence of motive. What if this youth were—mad? What if, from killing Helot

112

dogs and Perioeci swine, he graduated to homoioi, Spartans, men?

Therefore, when Ariston peered into the lighted windows of Talos' house, in the soft whispering of the early night, he was not alone; though he didn't know it. All around the house, lying on their bellies in the grass, the grain, the corn, behind the olive trees, the ghost-silent members of the Krypteia watched.

Which was to say that death itself lay hushed and waiting in the dark.

Through that window, Ariston saw his father and his mother. Talos was holding Alkmena in his arms. She was clinging to him and soaking his chiton with her tears.

And suddenly, with absolute certainty, Ariston knew he couldn't kill them. They were such beautiful people. Both of them. He studied Talos' changed dress and appearance with some care. What a noble, knightly man his father was! And his mother, outweeping Niobe now, how queenly!

Yet, someone had to die. The most sacred of all vows had been broken. Hera, Hestia, Artemis, and Hymenea had to be appeased. If the claims of disreputable Olympian riffraff, gods though they were—Aphrodite, herself a licentious strumpet and habitual adulteress, or her son Eros, who was a bastard, probably the fruit of incest with Zeus, her father, and hopelessly wild; or Goat-Pan, lord of lust, or Aphrodite's other son, hideous Priapus, fathered upon her by Dionysus, Priapus who, despite his parents' beauty, was totally repulsive, being the proud possessor of a set of genitals so huge he needed a cart to carry them lest they become sore from dragging on the ground—were placed ahead of those of the four chaste defenders of the home, marital honor, and the nuptial bed, the very fabric of society would be torn to shreds; and hot, goatish lechery would reduce men and women to rutting beasts.

The sin was terrible. And it had now been twice repeated. But he, the fruit thereof, was hardly the Nemesis called upon to avenge it. His jealousy of his father drained out of him now, replaced by love; his passionate, too hot, almost unnatural feeling toward his mother softened, changed,

**113**

transmuted itself into a nobler emotion, at the sight of a thing so obvious, so lovely, and so right: that the beautiful were made for each other; that against the offense they'd unwittingly offered to the angry gods, one had to set the gratuitous cruelty hurled down by the gods upon them, long before they'd ever met, not to mention sinned! A beautiful, wellborn youth, reduced to helotry; an exquisite, highborn, tender maid given lovelessly to an old goat of a general who could have been her father!

And yet, Ariston knew well, the gods didn't reason like men. They'd call for blood, demand a sacrifice . . .

A sacrifice! What better offering than the first fruits of that self-same impious, though understandable, love itself? What was it that Orchomenus had said? That he couldn't be the pharmakos, the freely offered substitute for the actual sinners, taking upon himself the iniquities of all the world. But for this one sin—yes. For this lovely, lovely sin that had shaped him, made him, given him form, beauty, life, he, who now had far too much weariness, horror, pain in him, could die.

So thinking, he drew one of the two daggers from his belt, put the point to his own throat. Then he stopped. He was, at that moment, demonstrably mad. He'd die—and they would weep for him. But, by Zeus, he wanted to see those tears. He wanted to gloat over the suffering his descent into Tartarus would cause them; hear his father's groans, his mother's cries.

Therefore—not now. He'd do it before their very eyes, after he'd tormented them first with bitter words. Plunge that blade—but no. The risk was too great. Quick and strong as Talos was, the red-beard would prevent it, surely, leave him perhaps with only a bad and painful wound—he who'd already suffered that sort of minor hell these past six weeks now.

Therefore—the craftiness of madness whispered through his mind—enter the house already wounded unto death, but with such a hurt as brought death slowly, such a stab as could be concealed.

Then, without hesitation or remorse, he brought that blade down and slashed both wrists, almost to the bone.

Then he drew the other dagger, let it and its twin drop upon the earth, pressed his bleeding wrists beneath his armpits, and thumped with elbows on the door.

Talos opened it, saw who he was. Smiled at him, said:

"Enter, my son! I'm very glad you came."

Alkmena took a backward step, her face gone white.

"Chaire, Father," Ariston whispered. "Rejoice, my father! Why do you look at me like that? Aren't you going to kiss me?"

"Talos—" Alkmena said. "Look at his face! He's mad, I tell you! He spoke of—of Orestes—of Oedipus—I—I'm afraid he'll—"

With a deft motion, Ariston looped the folds of his blood red himation over his flooding wrists, and flung it wide.

"See, my lady mother," he said lightly, pleasantly. "No daggers! I come in love—in filial devotion to ask your blessing. And yours, Father. It's not your fault that I had neither your love nor your guidance—nor my mother's that she was outraged while drugged, asleep—"

Alkmena stamped her foot.

"I was not!" she flared. "Ariston, you listen to me! I came awake and saw him standing there—as beautiful as a god—the image of the god Dionysus, I thought he was. So I put out my arms to him—drew him into my embrace. That, Son, is the truth! Despise me if you will, but I'm not ashamed of it! For the first time in my life—after ten years of marriage to that senile old goat!—I knew what love was. And when my Talos was gone from me, I had only you, my son, to love—his image, his reflection, the duplicate of his beauty. If this be sin, I'm prepared to die for it, though not by your impious hand. Because—"

"Because what, Mother?" Ariston said. He could feel the life draining out of him now, the soft, deadly cold rising up.

"Because I want you to live. To live and be happy! I want you to leave Sparta, go to a fairer, less cruel land. Lesbos or Thebes or Boeotia—or even—Athens. Marry, get sons, forget—"

Ariston could scarcely see her now. There was a mist before his eyes.

"Mind if I sit down?" he said; "I'm very tired—"

115

"Of course," Talos said, and shoved forward a stool. "Some wine, my son?"

"No, Father," Ariston said. "Father—will you kiss me? You never have, you know. I'd have your blessing. Strange —that wasn't what I came to say. But it's what I mean in my pneuma, in my soul. I love you. I love you, too, my mother. What you did doesn't matter. It was right and good. I thank you for it. I thank you both for getting me under the blue sky in mutual joy. Now kiss me. You hear me, kiss me! For I—"

"Ariston!" Talos thundered. "In Zeus' name, what ails you, boy?"

Ariston smiled at him.

"Nothing, Father. It's merely—that—that—I'm dying. For your sin. And my mother's. I'm your pharmakos— your sacrificial goat. And this, I suppose, is the—tragoidia —the goat song, isn't it, my father? Only I'll die silently, without a single bleat. As my Phryne died. As Lysander did. As Simoeis. The world is so full of—death, isn't it, Father? It reeks of it. I can't get that smell out of my nostrils. Did you know that, Father? Lysander's mouth was full of— blood. But I kissed him, in spite of that. So now—"

"He's mad!" Alkemena whispered. "I told you, Talos! He's—mad . . ."

"Mad, Mother?" Ariston said and flipping the sodden folds of the red himation off his wrists, held them out to her.

"Ariston!" Alkmena screamed. "Oh, Talos, look!"

"Son," Talos said, "this is folly. Come, let me bandage up your hurts. There is no need for you to—"

But Ariston stood up, reeled drunkenly, kicked the stool away from beneath his feet, skipped backward toward the door, plunged out into the night. With a lion's roar, Talos followed him, only to crash full length on his belly as he fell over the leg that Ariston, knowing that in his weakened state, he couldn't outrun his father, cunningly thrust across his knees as he came out of the house.

By the time Talos got back some of the breath his fall had knocked out of him, the boy was a flicker of white, disappearing beneath the olive trees. Talos got to his feet,

116

swayed there a moment. Alkmena came out of the house and took his arm.

"You go that way," Talos commanded before she could open her mouth, "and I'll go this. Perhaps between us we can head him off, before—"

He didn't finish that thought. There was no need to. Then they were both off in the moonlight, running hard. Ten minutes later Alkmena, still flying along like Artemis herself, despite her years, caught sight of Ariston at last. He was zigzagging, reeling, stumbling along like a blind man amid the olive trees. She lifted her head and cried: "Talos! Talos! I've found him! Here he is!"

And almost at once Talos came crashing along from the direction of the wheatfield and started pounding toward the reeling, not really conscious, boy. But as he came abreast of Alkmena, being only a little more than a rod to her left, Talos halted abruptly, and turning her head, Alkmena saw the Krypteia spearman poised to throw. She did not hesitate even that immeasurably brief flicker of an instant that thought would have taken—she did what she had to. Knowing instinctively perhaps that it is far easier to die for, than to live with, love, that what the already hurling javelin would do to her poor, bruised, tender heart was kinder than the slow stifling out of hope and joy that proximity, reality, and the years would inevitably inflict upon it—she leaped to offer all she had: her life. The hard-flung javelin blurred sight, made lightning in the moonlight. What came from Alkmena's mouth was less a scream than a long, ecstatic sigh. She surrendered unto death as to a lover. Talos caught her in his arms, eased her down. He tried to pull the javelin free, but he could not; there was no strength left in him at all. He bent and kissed her mouth, bathing her still face with his tears. He was kneeling there, crushing her to him with that spear shaft protruding from her back when the members of the Krypteia surrounded him with all their weapons drawn and ready. So he laid Alkmena's dead body down upon the earth and stood up, looking from one iron-hard, remorseless young countenance to another, into those faces of automatons out of which the last vestiges of humanity had been trained or bred.

The buagor, Perimedes, came through the trees and stood there looking into the red-beard's face with a slight, ironic smile.

"I am a free man, Buagor!" Talos said. "And a Macedonian. Though now you don't know what that means, one day you will. I ask of you a freeman's right: the loan of your dagger. Since your murdering young mindless dog has already taken from me—my life—I'd be deprived of breath by no other hand. As you are a kalokagathos and a Spartan, I demand of you this thing!"

The buagor went on smiling. There was a certain beautiful fitness about the red-beard's proposal. A tidiness. An economy. His hand went to his belt, came out with his dagger. He reversed it, held it out.

"The gods receive you, Neodamode! I have not met your like before," he said.

It was Orchomenus who, arriving too late to prevent the disaster he'd seen in the boy's eyes, found the orphaned, unconscious Ariston lying face down amid the trampled grain. In his rage, his grief—for he'd come to love Talos beyond all measure—he drew his dagger, swung it high. But, at the apex of its upswing, he halted it.

"No," he muttered, "it's as Talos used to say: Life is the punishment, not death. So come, patricide! I consign you to life—and to the Furies! One day you'll beg me on your knees for the stroke I've denied you now. The Erinyes will see to that. And if they don't, I will. So come . . ."

Then the ilarch sheathed his blade, picked Ariston up, and walked with him toward the other searchers, moving very quietly through the soft and starry night.

# CHAPTER EIGHT

PERIMEDES, COMMANDER OF THE SECRET POLICE, sat gazing out the window of his office. What he was contemplating was not the smiling summer landscape, but the chilling certainty of his own death, approaching him with every hoofbeat of the messenger's horse, surely drawing near to Telamon's camp by now, surely almost there.

He sat by the window without moving. His mind reeled, halted before the enormity of the things that had happened to him within a single hour: that one of his men had accidentally killed the lady Alkmena, the great strategos' wife; that he, Perimedes, himself, buagor of the Krypteia, noted throughout the polis for the infinite subtlety of his intelligence, his foxlike cunning, the iron hardness of his heart had allowed himself for the very first time in all his life to give way to a sentimental impulse—permitted himself to be moved by a neodamode's, an ex-Helot's, bearing, manhood, dignity to such an extent that he had granted that beautiful, fiery bearded animal the privilege of taking his own life, instead of putting him to the torture, wracking out of him—

What? In Zeus's name, what could they have torn from Talos that they didn't already know, that wasn't evident on the very face of things? That he was Alkmena's lover? That he had fathered the beautiful, golden Ariston on her? Through the lighted windows, they had seen the general's lady clinging to the ex-Helot, as ivy clings to an oak. And the resemblance between the dead freedman and the three-quarters dead boy, when they'd laid them side by side on the shields to bear them down to Sparta, had risen up to high Olympus to make a stink in the nostrils of the goddess Hera, protectress of the home.

119

That knowledge served for nothing. True, the punishment for adultery on the part of a wife was death; but, in the case of a citizeness, that punishment was customarily inflicted by the injured husband himself. Or in the rare event that he failed to either kill or pardon her she could only be put to death by the official executioner of the polis, after a formal trial before the ephors. Certainly no mere spearman of the Krypteia had the right to slay her as though she were a Perioeci bitch or a Helot sow, no matter what she had done.

Even the truth was useless: Who would believe that that fool Xanthus had accidently killed her while trying to rescue the boy from what had seemed to him——the utter idiot——a criminal attack by a lust-besotted pederast? No one. In five minutes of questioning, the ephors would establish the obvious fact that Talos had surely been trying to save the boy, who had surely slashed his own wrists in his outrage at his mother's monstrous, inconceivable demeaning of herself, her impious rupture of her nuptial oaths, her——

Very understandable surrender to that gorgeous male animal whom he, Perimedes, would have been delighted to take home to bed himself.

But comprehension was worse than useless now. What the buagor had to decide upon was an unassailable defense of his own conduct or, failing that, a quick and painless way to die. Because Telamon's uxoriousness was celebrated; he had never even so much as been accused of either other women or boys. He would surely demand no lesser penalty than Perimedes' as well as Xanthus' death.

Perimedes loosed his dagger in its sheath, drew it out, stared at that cruel blade which but a few hours before had bit into Talos' splendid flesh, had at once, and soundlessly, found his life. And now——

But he couldn't do it. He couldn't! He loved himself too much, with a soul-deep love, passing that of Narcissus. He had never loved anyone else, not even the various apparatuses of male and female flesh which for whim or momentary lust he'd taken to bed. And now, to have to end his own life because a magnificent, red-bearded animal of a neodamode had suddenly and unexpectedly moved him

120

was too much! He'd wait a while, think, exercise his cunning. Surely something would turn up. Surely—

And, because the gods love pure evil, something did.

The ilarch of that ila of the Krypteia which had gone with Perimedes to Talos' farm entered the room and saluted smartly with his sword.

"Speak, Peleus," Perimedes said.

"My commander," Peleus said, excitement playing havoc with his self-control, breathing all sorts of trills and runs through his voice, "there was more to it than we thought! Much more! It seems to me that—"

"Hades take what it seems to you, dolt! The facts! I'll decide what to make of them," the buagor said.

"Very well, my buagor! We took the boy to the iatros Polorus, as you commanded. He says it will be difficult, but that he doesn't think the strategos' son will die. He dressed his wounds, calling for a certain slave girl to aid him. But she, when she saw who the patient was, let out a screech like an Athenian owl and hauled her nicely rounded little tail out of the iatreion as though the Eumenides were breathing down her neck—"

"And you, naturally, my good ilarch, had her pursued and brought back again?"

"Exactly, my commander. But, when my hoplites dragged her back into the room, she was bleeding like a pig. I reprimanded them severely for using excessive force —because if she bled to death, she couldn't tell us anything useful—"

"Very right. And what did your hot-headed young idiots say?"

"Swore up and down they'd kept their weapons sheathed. Then the iatros spoke up in their defense. He said the girl was already wounded—rather mysteriously—night before last—"

"So?" the buagor said. "You begin to interest me, Peleus! What then?"

"I told the sawbones to stop her bleeding, which he did right handily and at once. Then I put it to her fairly: 'Look, slut,' says I, 'Who carved up your pretty tit like that?'"

121

"A commendably delicate way of putting it," Perimedes said dryly. "And then?"

"She didn't even hesitate, my commander. She pointed straight at the boy and ripped out nastily: 'He did, the unnatural swine!' "

"Ha! All that means is he refused her, Peleus. Have you ever seen a wench who has failed at trying to push a piece off on a lad—usually to saddle him with the responsibility for the bundle some other fleet-foot's left her with—who *didn't* immediately accuse him of sodomy?"

"Not this time, Commander. The golden Ariston, for all his pretty looks, had banged the wench about to her entire satisfaction. She admitted that with some show of pride. What got her wild was being superseded by—a rival. A woman considerably older than herself. She, according to her tale of woe, came into his room without knocking, and found him abed with—"

The ilarch Peleus leaned swiftly close, whispered into his buagor's ear. Perimedes' eyes took fire. He threw back his head and roared.

Peleus laughed too, out of respect for his commander, though truth to tell he didn't see what the buagor found funny in such an enormity.

"Did you bring the girl along?" Perimedes asked, wiping his eyes with the back of his hand.

"Of course, my commander! I know my duty, I hope! Shall I put her to the torture?"

"No. Of course not, you dolt! Treat her right tenderly. Have the company surgeon treat her wounds. Feed her well—and, above all, don't let your louts ravish her, even though the word's probably euphemism in her case."

Peleus stared at the buagor.

"If it's not an indiscretion, might I ask—why?" he said.

"It *is* an indiscretion, but I'll tell you all the same. I want her in condition to put on one damned fine show when the august Telamon arrives," the buagor of the Krypteia said.

"Look, Brother-in-law," Hippolytus said. "With all due respect to your rank and your white hairs, I'd let the matter drop if I were you. Quietly."

The strategos looked at his late wife's brother. That she was sister to such as this, he thought, should have been enough to warn me! But he did not relax his iron control of self, not for a single instant.

"Why?" he said.

"Nor would I ask that question," Hippolytus said.

Telamon went on looking at his fat little brother-in-law.

"But if I persisted in asking it, would you answer it, Hippolytus?" he said.

"No," Hippolytus said.

Telamon stood up. He was very tall for a Hellene. Standing, he was imposing. He had then the satisfaction of seeing fear leap into Hippolytus' eyes.

"Don't worry, Brother," he said quietly, "for, by your very refusal, you have answered me already."

Hippolytus' round, infantile mouth began to tremble. Pure desperation tore him. Dolt! he thought; you'll ruin everything! Yes, yes, you've been horned again! Yes, she let another invade her ever-bleeding female wound that can only be stanched by plugging it with man meat, brute male flesh! That would occur to you! The wearers of the keroesses always know or sense when they've been awarded what they so richly deserve! But you don't know, cannot imagine that—

"Look, General," he said, "if I told you that you're wrong, would you believe me?"

"No, Brother," Telamon said.

"Very well. Then I won't tell you that. You're right. You've been right all these years. Where you were wrong was not to kill him."

Telamon looked at Hippolytus a long, slow time.

"Did you—know?" he said.

"Then, no. Else *I* should have killed him," Hippolytus said passionately. "I only found out when I saw him and the boy together in the temple. The resemblance was—remarkable. But by then the occasion for killing was long past. I was concerned with saving life, not taking it. And my poor sister had not then autumnally renewed her springtime folly. When I found out about *that*, both she and Talos were—dead."

"You pity her, don't you?" Telamon said.

"I pity all of humanity," Hippolytus said. "Born as we are to lust, folly, madness, grief, and pain. But Alkmena less than you'd think. She at least had the courage and the sense to live. And now, her troubles are forever over. Whom I pity are—those she left behind: my nephew, beautiful son of a herdsman-slave; myself, a fat little expederast, turned uxorious husband-soon-to-be; but most of all, I think, my august senator-general, great Telamon, esteemed Brother-in-Law, I pity—you."

Telamon stared at Hippolytus.

"You—pity—*me?*" he said.

"Yes. For what are you but your reputation? You man of honor! You creature of unassailable probity! You—Spartan! You've never lived, Telamon. You've never known how sweet sin is. You've never felt your guts melt inside your belly sack at a lover's lightest touch. Touch, Hades! At his—or her—look, glance, frown, smile. If my bride horns me—as she probably will, given the slightest opportunity—she'll only be horning a horner. I've crowned with the keroesses the noblest brows in Sparta, Eros be praised! And, likewise, thanks be to Aphrodite, I've wept my eyes bloody red nightlong for anguished, unrequited love. I've been a swinish glutton, a practicer of filthy vices, a lover—in short, a human being, while you—"

"While I," Telamon said, "have been—as you've said—a Spartan."

"Yes, Zeus pity you. Hear me, Brother; let this matter drop! Alkmena was unfaithful to you; let her death go unrevenged. Let that be her punishment for her infidelity. Consider yourself for a change, my august brother! Show yourself the mercy we all need, and must show ourselves, because the gods—if they exist—never do! I'm not asking you to have compassion for either me or the boy. But for yourself, yes, Telamon; you, who've never lived, have need of mercy! To name but one simple, minor thing: Tell me, how can you maintain discipline in your ranks with your officers and men snickering behind your back and making the sign of the keroesses with their fingers above your head? Tell me how?"

Telamon's smile was bleak.

"I've already resigned my commission, Hippolytus," he said quietly. "And at this very moment a slave bears my letter to the Gerousia, telling the august members of that august body that I can no longer serve among them. In a way, I'm glad of this opportunity, Brother. I am sixty-seven years of age. I tire of both statesmanship and war. I tire even, I think, of life. What I've seen of it was hardly pleasant. I mean to go into exile. I've thought about that for a long time. In fact, I've acquired a farm in Boeotia—a great expanse of pasture land with many cows. As soon as I've had the satisfaction of seeing Perimedes and his butchers brought to trial—someone should curb the Krypteia's ever growing power, you know—"

"I agree," Hippolytus interrupted, "but somebody else. Not you."

"Why not I? They've given me the opportunity—"

"They've given you no opportunity at all, General! Except to cause Ariston's death, which, I believe, you no longer want—if you ever really did—"

"No. Let the boy live. He's a pretty lad, who certainly didn't conceive himself or arrange his mother's adulteries. Besides, he might even amount to something someday, though I doubt it. You were saying?"

"That the Krypteia has given you nothing at all, except the chance to murder the boy by indirection, to drive yourself—if you've one iota of humanity in you—mad; and, very likely, an unassailable motive for following Talos' example. Hear me, Telamon! You mustn't! You can't!"

Telamon eyed his fat little brother-in-law long and quietly.

"Then there's more to this than—"

"Mere adultery? Yes, Brother. You see this dagger? I am a coward. Next month I shall be wed. I love life—I have a perfect horror of blood, pain, death. Yet before I'd say to you, or to any man, what that more, that something else is, I'd push it to the hilt into this paunch I've loved and cherished all my life, and disembowel myself here before your very eyes. Is that clear?"

"Very," Telamon said.

"Then will you let the case drop?"

"No," the ex-senator, ex-general, but eternal Spartan, said.

So now, there was no hope at all. Ariston lay upon his bed in his foster-father's house, guarded day and night by members of the Tenth Ila of the City Guard, lest he should attempt again and more successfully, the impiety of self-murder. At first, he had to be fed by force; but later he sullenly consented to take a morsel or two of bread and a sip of water daily. The result of which, naturally, was that he was a pitiful sight: a human skeleton, glaring out at all the world with eyes of blue fire like the sacred flames that burn at Delphi.

What no one at all could get him to do was to talk. He replied to neither greetings, salutations, nor idle chatter. And when the ilarch Orchomenus ventured to question him about his parents' deaths, he quietly turned his face to the wall.

Therefore, he had to be brought before the ephors on a litter; though no man could say for what his silent presence would serve in the court. For he could not be forced to speak against his will; he was still a melliran, a son of—at least officially—a homois, a Spartan. He couldn't be tortured without first being reduced to slavery. And that, in its turn, could only be accomplished by the ephors' publicly proclaiming Alkmena's guilt, admitting to all the world the unthinkable: that Spartan ladies, wives, mothers were after all as other women are.

Which would be to destroy the very soul of Sparta.

So Ariston lay there on his litter in the Gerousieon, as safe, as unassailable as Zeus himself. In the first place, everyone agreed, he was not even on trial; Xanthus, the Krypteia light-armed trooper, was. In the second, everyone agreed again, what would happen was a foregone conclusion: Telamon would wear his horns with grace, defend the legitimacy of the boy he knew perfectly well—Goat-Pan and all his satyrs witness it!—was not his own; Perimedes would wiggle out of the consequences of his errors, somehow; and that poor devil of a secret policeman—Xanthus, would die—quickly, quietly, and cleanly.

Everyone knew that. But everyone was wrong. Appallingly, terribly wrong.

For Perimedes arose and addressed the court with easy calm.

"August Ephors!" he began. "Kalokagathoi! Strategoi! Equals! Since it is to the interest of the polis that this case terminate at once before the ugly gossip running through our streets destroy all that is fitting, beautiful, and Spartan in our lives, leaving us weakened in our pneumae and morally defenseless before our enemies, let me say at once that the sphaireis Xanthus, a noble youth of high birth, as —need I remind this court—all members of the Krypteia must be, did indeed kill the woman Alkmena—"

"The woman!" Telamon said.

"Yes, my lord general! The woman! You'd have me call her lady, wife? As you will, august Strategos! I'll call her that, out of respect for your years, honors, fame. For she *was* your wife, was she not? That she was guilty of adultery and worse—"

Telamon was on his feet now. Ariston's eyes made blue coals in his pitiful head.

The chief ephor raised his staff.

"Gentlemen," he snapped, "I beg you to respect the dignity of this court by observing the decorum proper to men, equals, Spartans!"

Perimedes bowed.

"My apologies, great Ephors, august Strategos," he said smoothly. "I allowed my indignation to carry me away. Just as Xanthus' did when he overheard the true cause of why Talos sought to kill his own son—"

"My lords!" Telamon said.

"I withdraw that statement," Perimedes said at once, "for though I and all present in this court *know* it is true, it cannot now be proved. Amend it, then, citizen clerk, to read, 'Why Talos sought to kill the son of the woman—lady! wife!—Alkmena.' For that I can prove. I plead, therefore, extenuating circumstances: that Xanthus' horror and outrage at this—this lady's, this wife's—monstrous behavior was natural enough and worthy of his upbringing as a Spartan. Besides, her death was largely accidental, anyhow; Xanthus sought to save the boy from Talos' clutches—"

One of the ephors raised his staff.

"You've said that the neodamode Talos sought to kill the melliran Ariston," he said, "who, you claim, was Talos' natural son. As an ex-member of the Eugenics Board, I have some knowledge of that aspect of this case; but out of respect to the august Telamon, whose services to the polis merit our consideration, I suggest that we leave the question of paternity aside as being presently irrelevant to this case. Agreed, gentlemen?"

Solemnly all the ephors lifted their staffs.

"Agreed!" they chorused; but all the same, Perimedes had made his point.

"Now, my question is this," the ephor went on. "For what reason did Talos want to kill the boy? Would you say, my lord buagor of the Krypteia, that the neodamode did not share your belief in the milliran's true parentage? Wait, my lord strategos! It is not the question of that parentage itself that I raise here, but Talos' belief or lack of belief in it, which is quite another thing and does have bearing on this case."

"Very well, august Ephor," Telamon said.

"He shared it," Perimedes said with a half-suppressed chuckle. "His reasons for believing the boy his own were —shall we say?—excellent."

"And yet you say he wanted to kill a boy he was convinced was his own offspring. Rare. Very rare. Might the court be informed—why?"

"Out of—jealousy, my lords," Perimedes said.

"Jealousy?" the ephor echoed.

"Yes, jealousy. The common, base jealousy that a man —displaced—feels for his successful rival. Intensified in this case by the delicate relationship existing among the three. By outrage, my lords. The same outrage that so blinded my poor Xanthus that he hurled his spear without giving thought—"

All the ephors were on their feet now.

"Buagor!" the chief ephor thundered. "Do you know what you're saying?"

"Yes, my lords," Perimedes said; "I'm saying that the

128

tale of Oedipus, Laius, and Iocasta has been repeated here. With variations, of course. Oedipus did not kill—his father. At least, not directly. And my lady Iocasta did not prepare her noose of silken cords—my Xanthus spared her that—perhaps—for I've no evidence she felt remorse at all. And Oedipus remains unblinded—though we'll credit his slashed wrists as fitting substitutes for smashed eyeballs, shall we not, Kalokagathoi? After all, the lady wore no golden brooch with which he could batter out his eyes."

Telamon crossed the floor with a speed surprising in a man of his years. His hand flew to his waist, came away empty. No weapons were permitted in the ephors' court, except those worn by the guards outside the door and those brought into it by the torturers when it became necessary to force a confession from a stubborn slave, though in the latter case they were more nearly implements, tools of a very specialized trade, than weapons.

"Strategos!" the chief ephor cried. Telamon halted. The years of discipline were stronger even than his rage. But no one was looking at him now. They were all staring at Ariston. The boy had turned on his side and was vomiting blood.

Which didn't help Telamon's case at all.

"My lords and peers," the general said, "I ask that an iatros be brought to attend this bo—my son. And that he be removed from this court. If he has to listen to much more of this sort of thing, I'm afraid that, in his weakened state, he'll die."

The ephors consulted among themselves in whispers. Then the chief ephor spoke, addressing himself directly to Perimedes.

"My lord buagor of the Krypteia," he said, "do you formally charge the melliran Ariston, said to be the son of strategos Telamon, with the crime and impiety of—incest? Think well before you speak! This is a serious matter, the most with which I've been confronted in all my years of service as an ephor. More than this boy's life is at stake. For when this is noised abroad—as, inevitably, despite our best efforts, it will be!—it will represent a defeat to our beloved polis equivalent to losing a major battle. All men, Hellenes and barbarians alike, fear Sparta. But other nations have been feared. Persia was, until Thermopylae! The difference is, Buagor, that all men admire and respect us too. Our honesty, our probity, our honor—the chastity of our women have never been questioned! But now they will be! In face of all that, do you, noble Buagor, make this charge?"

Perimedes did not hesitate at all.

"I do," he said.

Telamon got to his feet.

"If it please the court, may I ask the buagor if he is aware what the penalty for false accusation is?" he said. "Or that for the impiety of impugning the good fame and the honor of—the dead?"

"I do," Perimedes said.

"And you—persist?" Telamon whispered.

"I persist," the buagor said.

The silence was immense. It had thickness, texture. It could be felt like a weight of darkness.

"In that case," the chief ephor sighed, "the boy cannot be removed from the court."

"But—but," Telamon's voice was barely audible, "the doctor—at least?"

"That, yes. Let the iatros Polorus be brought," the chief ephor said.

Telamon was aware now of the magnitude of his error. It was immense. For, when the ephors had asked him if he wanted the slave girl, Arisbe, put to the torture, his rage at her insolence, at the boldness with which she made and repeated her monstrous accusation, got the better of his good sense. It would have been, he saw now, far better to have cross-questioned her, tricked her into contradictions, statements damaging to her probity. Because as well he knew, there was no more stubborn beast on earth than a Boeotian peasant. The way Arisbe stood up under torture was—magnificent. She screamed, of course. She couldn't help that. What the official torturers had done to her by now would have made a goat vomit. But each time Telamon waved them away and said:

"Do you still say that my son——" She spat out:

"Yes! He did! I saw him!"

130

Telamon nodded to the ugly, sweating brutes. Arisbe's screams tore the night apart, destroyed the very fabric of sound. Telamon looked at Ariston. His heart halted, his breath. What was in the boy's eyes now was enough to stop even time.

Ariston pushed down with his hands. Stood up. He had had no strength in him at all, when they brought him into that court. He could not have lifted a square of papyrus scarcely big enough to write his name on. But now he stood up, tottered, swayed, took one step toward the torturers, another. The sound of Arisbe's screams beat about his ears—Ho Pontos in winter, a gale rising; the Erinyes in full cry. He took one more step, stopped there, swaying like an axed-through oak. Then he fell, crashing full length to the floor.

The physician Polorus ran to his side, knelt beside him. But the first, tentative motion of the iatros' hand was arrested, blocked, cut off by that glare of ice-blue flame.

"Don't touch me," Ariston said.

Then the boy put down his hands. Pushed. Sweat beaded on his forehead. Blood made twin tendrils out of both his nostrils, penciled scarlet lines downward from the corners of his mouth. But he came erect in the midst of all that silence, still unbreathing, swayed there on his feet, treated them to the spectacle of an authentic miracle, for the sight of the human spirit standing tall amid the tattered rags of his martyred flesh, dominating pain, horror, grief, vanquishing even the death that was in him was at least that, if not more.

He lurched forward, collided with one of the sweaty beasts. His hand flew downward, closed about the hilt of the torturer's dagger. They saw it flash. Then he was standing before the charred, bloody, broken, still living thing that had been a human being, a woman, with that blade in his hand.

"Arisbe," he whispered; "they won't—hurt you—any more. I—won't let them. Now, tell—the truth—You know —I didn't—make love with—my mother. I tore her robe. All. That was . . . all. Thought . . . she . . . was . . . you. Dark. So dark. So tell them—"

Arisbe's face twisted. The hatred in her eyes were absolutely bottomless.

"You did!" she screamed. "I saw you! You were naked. She was on top of you, with her skirt up! And you—"

It was then that Ariston thrust out wildly, blindly with that blade. But the artificial, momentary strength lent him by horror, anguish, need was gone from him. The point of the dagger penetrated less than half an inch into Arisbe's blistered, welted, seamed, broken, charred flesh. He drew it out, stared dully at the dripping point. Then he turned it upon himself with no better fortune; he had not even force enough left for that.

A burly torturer was upon him at once; with one hard wrench he tore the knife from the boy's hand. Then both of the torturers looked at Telamon, jerked their shaven bullet-heads toward the dying girl.

Slowly the strategos nodded. The case was lost now, irreparably lost. Either gesture of Ariston's would have been enough to convince the court of his guilt, convict him before all men of this unspeakable impiety; both were indisputable. Better, then, to grant the slave girl the mercy of a quick end to all her pains.

One of the torturers killed Arisbe with a single, marvelously expert thrust. She died so fast that her final scream became a gurgle in midflight, and then a silence. The ephors and the witnesses bowed their heads. To condemn her was Telamon's right: She was a slave; he, a Spartan.

Very quietly, Telamon got to his feet.

"August ephors," he said, almost gently. "My lord buagor of the Krypteia, gentlemen. I have a proposal to make. I have, you will allow, rendered some little service to this polis, I beg your leave to give one more and final proof of my devotion to great Sparta—to undertake alone the preservation of her honor. This, my son, stands condemned, though whether he is truly guilty or not no man can say. For what homois, strategos, or even ephor can tell what went on in that poor, mad bitch's mind? I think she lied. If you had known—the Lady Alkmena—as I knew her, you'd know as I do that this monstrous impiety was foreign to her very nature. But so be it! Let that pass. . . .

"My lord buagor, I'd strike a bargain with you! I withdraw all charges against you and your man and award you two silver talents in concept of damages, if you will in your turn agree not to object if the august ephors consent to surrender my son into my custody, leave his punishment in my hands. As you know me, know my honor, I will not fail in this!"

Perimedes smiled. He had won. His victory was complete. Not only had he saved his own hide and Xanthus', but he had made himself rich!

"I agree, great Strategos! *Your* honor was never in question. I have no objection," he said.

"My lords, august ephors, will you grant me this?" Telamon said.

The chief ephor frowned.

"My lord strategos," he said, "do you *know* what the penalty for this—monstrous impiety is?"

"Yes. It is death, august ephor," Telamon said. "But, if I know the law, as I think I do, there is nowhere stated what manner of execution must be meted out in such a case. Am I right?"

The chief ephor's frown deepened. His gaze dulled, turned inward, as though he were searching his own mind.

"No," he said; "no exact manner of carrying out the sentence was ever specified. Since not even great Lycurgus dreamed this unspeakable obscenity could ever really happen, he did not make his intent clear. What do you propose, my general?"

"That I—and my son—be permitted to render one last service to the polis. Give him into my custody, let me see that he is attended, his hurts cured. Then, when spring has come again, when fair Thargelion goes flowering through the land, both he and I will march off to war. He shall be placed in the forefront of the ranks. And from that first battle, neither he—nor I—shall return. Upon my honor as a soldier, I swear it!"

"But, the sentence of this court?" the chief ephor said uneasily. "We have to hand one down, lest the populace believe our authority has been flouted! And that we cannot permit, for—"

"You formally declare that no decision could be reached for lack of sufficient evidence. So, therefore, the boy has been released under my surveillance. Thus, august ephors, you preserve Sparta's good name from a scandal that can only do her harm, and leave justice—if such this be!—in hands that have never failed you. Do you agree, my lords?"

The ephors looked at one another, relief showing in their eyes. One by one they lifted their staffs.

"Buagor Perimedes, soldier Xanthus!" the chief ephor thundered. "Do you also bind yourselves by your honor as Spartans to this?"

"We do, my lords!" Perimedes said at once.

"So be it!" the chief ephor said. "You may take the boy home, great Telamon!"

"I thank you, my lords," Telamon said; and turned to Perimedes, looking at the buagor with the ice-cold contempt he felt for a man vile enough to use such a defense as this even to save his miserable life. "I will send the talents to your house tomorrow morning," he said. "You have my word. Now, if your man will be so good as to send in my slaves to bear the boy—"

"Father!" Ariston's voice was faint, but very clear.

"My boy?" Telamon said gently.

"I thank you—with all my heart," Ariston said and catching the general's hand raised it to his lips.

"Enough of sentimental folly!" the general snorted. "Come!"

# CHAPTER NINE

ARISTON MOVED THROUGH THE SPARTAN CAMP. He walked with his back bent, his shoulders hunched forward, his head down, almost creeping, in an effort to avoid attracting attention to himself. He did that from pure habit now. Between the trial's end and the beginning of the annual invasion of Attica, he'd tried so hard—out of real necessity —to become invisible that he almost was.

Which was why the two grizzled old soldiers grumbling to each other under the awning of a tent neither heard nor saw him. The gray-blue glint of his armor was one with the misting rain that was the second item on the long list of things the two old campaigners were grousing about. The first was that they, like all the Spartan forces, were very nearly starving. It was very cold and wet and miserable in Attica that fifty-fifth spring after Thermopylae. So they hadn't been able to rob the Attic peasants of their grain as usual. In the fields, the barley, millet, wheat stood green.

"The old fool!" one of the old soldiers said, and stopped, chewing with meditative anger over his words. And now Ariston could see that he and his companion were both enomotarchs, the lowest rank among the officers, having command of a unit limited to thirty men.

Ariston stopped where he was, waiting for the enomotarch to start talking again. Then he could move on past them without their hearing him.

"Who ever heard," the bald-headed old veteran went on grumbling, "of launching an attack in Thargelion? We're supposed to live off the country, aren't we? Well, I ask you: when in Black Hades' name has there ever been a crop ready for harvesting this time of year? And in Attica, at that!"

"Soldier," the other enomotarch said. "I've been in this man's army as long as you have. But if you'd stop waggling your toothless jaws and listen, you might learn something for a change. Like, for instance, that the august Telamon hasn't got any other ranks in his mind, either. Fact is, he's out to get himself killed."

"Wha-a-a-a-a-t?" the enomotarch Sphaerus said.

"You heard me. The polemarch's out to get himself killed. Him and that pretty boy his old woman dropped on him along with the finest pair of keroesses in living memory. We don't count. All we've got to do is to shut our traps and take a javelin through the guts along with him. Then we lays down and dies. Quicker than starving to death, anyhow."

"You mean to tell me that the august Telamon—"

"Aims to get his? Right. His and the boy's. He ain't got no choice in the matter, Sphaerus. He promised the ephors he'd do himself and that pretty little mother-lover in."

"And why in the name of the sweet, ever wiggling tail of Aphrodite did he promise them that?"

Ariston went on by them in one swift, intensely silent rush. There was no point in listening to what he already knew. Besides, he couldn't bear hearing it again. He was past the stage of self-torment, of subjecting himself to gratuitous cruelties. For he had already borne so much that he had settled the matter by accepting the necessity of his own death. He had had nearly a year to get used to that idea, not that he had needed so long. He had been so close to dying twice now that he knew the process itself; the physical pains accompanying it weren't so bad that you couldn't bear them with dignity. Life drained out of you very fast, and a long time before consciousness left you, your capacity for feeling had diminished so much that the whole thing became almost peaceful. No, dying wasn't unbearable. Living was. Living and remembering.

He recalled pitilessly and in detail those months since the trial. He counted them off in his mind. The trial had taken place the last week in Metageitnion; so, therefore: Boedromion, Pyanepsion, Maimakterion, Poseidon, Gamelion, Anthesterion, Etaphebolion, Munychion—Thargelion. Nine. Nine months, not the nine centuries it had seemed.

From the very first, he had dedicated himself eagerly to the task of recovering his strength. Because, he had realized, the faster he got well, the sooner the life he no longer wanted would be over. Yet despite his desire, his will, it had been slow going. Of course, his slashed wrists healed rapidly, and only a twinge or two in his back reminded him now and again of the stab wound Pancratis had dealt him. But the mysterious interior wound characterized by bloody vomiting stubbornly refused to heal until Telamon had called in a priest of Apollo Alexikakos to see what could be done. The priest had made the sacrifices, even, as the custom was, inspected the livers of various sacred chickens and handed down his solemn command:

The patient was to sleep in the abaton of the temple of Apollo, and to obey to the letter the instructions the god would reveal to him in a dream. Then, assuredly, he would be cured. That said, the grave and sanctimonious old idiot took his fee and departed.

Remembering that now, Ariston thought suddenly about his uncle Fat-Belly. Hippolytus was absolutely convinced that rationality ordered the universe, that everything was subjected to changeless natural law. Yet that ancient sacerdotal ass had been perfectly, totally right.

Except that it hadn't been far-shooting Apollo who appeared to him in the dream. Instead, it had been divine Artemis, the god's virgin sister. That, he'd supposed in his dream, was natural enough: the temples were the earthly homes of the gods, and brothers and sisters were quite free to visit each other even among the most backward tribes of men. But when the goddess bent above him, he'd torn all the night with the great horror of his cry.

For chaste, fair Artemis wore his mother's face.

"Peace be unto you, my son," she'd said in her own loved, remembered, marvelously serene voice.

"Mother!" he had wept. "I killed you! I—"

"No," she had said then. "Each man's death is fated from the beginning of time, Ariston. You had nothing to do with mine. I'd come to the end of my days, that's all. And so had Talos. So remember—"

"What, Mother?" he had said, all his heart, his breath shredded with anguish, with love, with grief.

"That you must forgive yourself, my son. Because only you can. There's no one else to do that. Sin is a part of the nature of man. And so is remorse. But you mustn't give too much importance to either. A man without enough blood in his veins to sin once in a while would be a monster, as your ancestor Hippolytus—the one your dear uncle was named after—was, which was why Aphrodite killed him. And a man forever sunk in remorse is less than a man. In fact, he's a fool. The future is yours, my son. Forgive yourself! Then forget, forget—"

"Mother!" he cried out, but she was already fading away into the surrounding dark. And he woke in the morning with his mind cool and clear. Within a week, the belly pains and vomiting were gone.

But after that the rest of it was quite insupportably bad. First of all, when he'd recovered enough strength to return to the school, the paidonomos turned him away. He, it seemed, was no longer fit company for the youth of Sparta.

That recourse denied him, he went to the palaestra, the public exercise grounds, to train away the awkwardness, the torpor, the slowness his wounds had left in him. But once there, he found himself in sole possession of it; for at his approach every single citizen athlete training there picked up his javelin, his discus, or his shield, clothed himself, and left.

In a way, it would have been better if he had been subjected to violence, taunts, or threats. Anger would have flamed in him then, rebellion would have stiffened his nerve, his will. But he wasn't. Nor was he simply ignored. He was—rejected, with studied, subtle cruelty. Wherever he went, a silence fell. It was as though death itself had entered that tavern, that hall, that street. If he asked for a cup of wine, it was handed over without a word. But when he tried to pay for it, clinked his iron obol down, the tavern keeper shook his head, left the dull, heavy coin lying on the purple-stained boards. And when he'd downed the heavy, honey-sweetened draft, that apron-clad swine smashed the cup before his very eyes.

Only once was he offered abuse or violence. During the month of Gamelion, in his ceaseless, lonely wanderings, he stumbled upon a group of girls practicing their dances for the minor feast of Lenaea in honor of Dionysus, then but a few days off. He stopped to watch, for Phryne had left his heart, his mind, acutely sensitive to female beauty; and these parthenae, maidens, were for the most part acceptably fair. One or two of them, with but a small degree of indulgence, could have been called lovely. To Ariston in his solitary state being more alone by then than any human can bear to be, they seemed nymphs and goddesses at the very least.

Then one of them saw him standing there and pointed him out to her companions. In any other polis in Hellas under those circumstances, a group of all but naked girls surprised at their gymnastics by a youth would have run away, squealing. But these girls were Spartan maidens. They ringed him round about, crowding in until their fair, young, sweaty bodies were but a handspan from his own. Then, each one in turn, they spat into his face.

He endured that. He had endured so many things. But now, Zeus willing, some Athenian spearman, archer, slinger would make an end of it. His private Erinyes would cease to pursue him. Death would come as a mercy, a blessing.

He shook his helmeted head to clear it of such thoughts. Then he saw Orchomenus standing a little way off, his hoplite's armor beaded with raindrops, and went to join him. Orchomenus was the only living creature he didn't flee now.

Orchomenus didn't greet him. He simply nodded curtly, and went on staring at the walls of Athens, so close to where they were now that they could see the horsehair crests on the helmets of the Attic hoplites atop them, tossing amid the silver slant of the rain.

"Cowardly dogs!" Ariston said.

"Who ever told you that valor is necessarily a virtue?" Orchomenus said.

Ariston looked at the hoplite—for Orchomenus was no

139

more than that now having voluntarily surrendered both his ilarch's rank and the total security of his position in the City Guards to take part in this campaign at his young friend's side. Friend? Ariston thought. On the night death finds me, will it not be through the rent his dagger makes, striking from behind?

"Isn't it?" he said.

"Not always. That was one of the points your father—your real father, not this gray-bearded donkey in armor who leads us—labored to get through my thick skull. Nothing is immutable. Circumstances change all things. There are times when cowardice can be a virtue—"

"Name one," Ariston said.

Orchomenus thought. Then he smiled. In the brief time the Helot had had him as a disciple, Talos had trained him very well indeed. One proof of that was that he hadn't even protested when they hadn't made him a pentecostye, which was his equivalent rank in the regular army, but he had accepted being broken down to an ordinary foot-slogger with a shrug and a smile.

"If I were the poet Euripides," he said, "and I had in my mind a masterwork for the next Dionysia, I should be fully justified in saving that work for the benefit of humanity, even though it meant saving my poor, pitiful carcass along with it. Or, if it falls better on your Spartan ears, losing my honor. In such a case, an act of pedication be performed upon my honor! If I had such genius, I'd gladly throw away my shield and run."

Ariston went on looking at Orchomenus.

"Yet," he said, "you're here—and so far you've been brave."

Orchomenus shrugged.

"The Athenians aren't very frightening," he said.

Ariston's eyes made a somber flickering, like a sacred blue fire, in his darkly burnt young face. I'll have to provoke you, comrade Orchomenus, he thought, because the waiting is bad. With such foes as the Athenians, I'll live to join the Gerousia. And life—my life—is a burden I'd be quit of, friend.

"Orchomenus," he said.

"Yes, Ariston?"

"Give me an example of—justifiable—incest."

Orchomenus' mouth tightened, made a line. A vein at his temple stood up and beat with his blood. But when he spoke his voice was quiet, controlled.

"I'd say that when the guilty couple didn't know of their kinship, as in the case of Iocasta and Oedipus," he said.

"I didn't say 'excusable,'" Ariston said. "I said 'justifiable.'"

Orchomenus thought again, long and deeply.

"Say that there were—a—a catastrophe. A flood. A plague. And you and your sister—"

"I and my mother," Ariston said.

"All right! You and your mother—were the only members of your polis left alive. The—preservation of the race —would justify your lying with her. There have been many such cases in history—"

So you don't provoke, Ariston thought.

"Orchomenus—" he said.

"Yes, Ariston?"

"Why haven't you killed me before now, hating me as you do?"

Orchomenus stared at the youth. But when he answered his voice remained as quiet as before, as controlled.

"Because that's what you want," he said, "because death would be a kindness. That's why I volunteered. To be at your side. To save you a thousand times if need be. So you'd go on living. Go on—suffering. Can you think of anything worse?"

Ariston lifted his head. Looked toward the long walls of Athens. Upon them, an Attic archer drew his bow, but because, after two centuries and more of fighting the Scythians, who were the world's finest archers, the Hellenes' boundless contempt for all things barbarian hadn't allowed them to even so much as notice what a Scythian bowman did when he shot—which was to draw his bowstring to his ear, instead of to his belly the way all the archers of Hellas did—the Attic bowman's shaft, naturally, fell far short of where they stood splendid and glittering in their rain-washed armor, like two young gods.

"Can you?" Orchomenus grated.

"No," Ariston said.

It was that same night that the messenger from Sparta came. What he said to the polemarch Telamon—for Spartan messages were always verbal, the messengers being trusted to die under torture before revealing them—they didn't find out until nearly three days later. It is likely that Telamon confided it only to his lochagoi, colonels, commanders over five hundred. The lochagoi snarled a simple order to the pentecostye, captains, commanders over one hundred twenty-five hoplites, and they in turn roared it at the enomotarchs, lieutenants, who bellowed it at the men.

"Strike tents! Pack gear! Ready weapons! March!"

They had it done within half an hour. Then they stood in formation, mute and trembling, hearing with astonishment, with pain, that trumpet call no Spartan in memory had heard except on the practice grounds. The retreat. The trumpeter was blowing the retreat! But they were Spartans. Without a word, they turned their backs to the walls of Athens and marched away from there.

On that homeward march, Telamon almost broke their hearts. He kept force-marching them until they dropped in their tracks. He drove them from Athens to Eleusis the first day, from Eleusis to Corinth the second. But, leaving Corinth, the next logical stop was Argos, some twelve parasangs further along the road to Sparta. Only they couldn't stop there because, although Argos was a Peloponnesian polis, she was an ally of Athens. So they had to bypass her. But late that afternoon, Telamon, seeing how utterly spent they were, displayed the intelligence, the heart he was sometimes capable of: He assembled all the troops and told them frankly and freely what the trouble was:

The Athenian fleet, under Eurymedon and Sophokles, had invaded the Peloponnesus itself, had captured the peninsula of Pylos on the western coast, leaving a garrison there commanded by the Athenian strategos Demosthenes.

At his last word every hoplite was on his feet shouting:

"Call the beat, enomotarchs! We march!"

They bypassed Argos in the night, continued clanking along at the double until the dawn. One hour's rest, and they took it up again; and, though the distance from Argos to Sparta was all of sixteen parasangs, one hippicon and three stades, they covered it in fourteen hours; for, though they had been in sight of the lights of Argos at ten o'clock the previous night, they were nonetheless reeling into the wall-less city by high noon.

They were not sent out at once to Pylos, for Sparta had already summoned her fleet from Corcyra. But Telamon reminded the ephors of his oath, and thus obtained berths aboard a trireme for himself and his son. But in spite of the ephors' orders, they almost didn't sail. In the first place, Telamon outranked by far the captain of the ship, one Brasidas, then only a triarch, though afterward he became Sparta's greatest general. For among the Hellenes there was no division among the various services; a man might be a navarch one day and a strategos the next. In Athens, in fact, the word navarch, admiral, wasn't even used, the commander of their fleet being called a general just like the leader of the land forces. Normally, therefore, Brasidas should have given up his command to Telamon; but this he politely, but firmly, refused to do. With all his Spartan's respect for age, Brasidas was confronted with the fact that the Lakedaemonian fleet was a newborn force, created within the last few years to meet the threat of Athenian naval power. A man of Telamon's years, therefore, would know absolutely nothing about sailing; worse still, as a noble, he would surely despise it, as the nobles, conservatives to the marrow of their bones, despised all things their great-grandsires hadn't had or seen or done. This graybeard, the young triarch was achingly certain, hadn't even a sufficient vocabulary of nautical terms to give the necessary commands. So in bitter despair, young Brasidas opposed Telamon, knowing that by law, by custom, by morality he would be forced to give way. What he didn't know was that Telamon was a living dead man, past all such petty considerations as rank and honors. The ex-strategos smiled bleakly at the handsome young triarch. Then with awesome dignity, he stripped from his armor his insignia of rank and threw them in the sea.

"Put me in the galley, if you will, my boy," he said calmly. "I know how to cook."

In the second place, at the sight of Ariston the sailors set up a tremendous howl. Seafaring folk are always superstitious. They were convinced that the presence aboard of a youth convicted of such an unspeakable impiety would bring old Poseidon bellowing up from the ocean floor to loose all the winds of heaven, stir up mountainous waves with his trident, and wreck their frail bark, drowning them all.

Telamon settled that by having an augur called in to read the omens. Or he thought he did. Actually, it was Ariston who settled it. On hearing of his foster-father's intent, he borrowed a whole mina from Telamon on the pretext that he wanted to set up a stele in the temple of Athena of the Brazen Horse in order to induce her to at least refrain from aiding the Athenians, but actually to grease the soothsayer's palm with it, thus inclining that wise old man to charity in his interpretations of the signs and portents.

So they sailed at last, all this having cost them a day's delay. But, as the hawsers were cast off and the three tiers of oarsmen took up the beat, they saw a strange sight: A hoplite in full armor came running down the quay and dived into the sea. They saw him bob to the surface and start swimming strongly after them, despite all the weight he bore. At once Brasidas ordered the trireme stopped.

"I'd have a man of such spirit in my ranks!" he said. "Throw him a rope, you fools!"

And so they drew Orchomenus aboard. Ariston went to him at once and kissed him. Orchomenus grinned at the boy.

"Where you go, little donkey in armor, there go I!" the former ilarch said.

"Still think the Athenians are cowardly dogs?" Orchomenus said.

Ariston looked at Orchomenus, then he looked back out to sea. He didn't even need to answer that question. For it had all gone very badly from the first. And now there wasn't any hope.

When they'd sailed into the Bay of Buphras with the majestic fleet of forty-three triremes under the command of the navarch Thrasymelidas, the whole thing had seemed a lark. Something like sending an elephant to crush a flea.

144

But the Athenians under Demosthenes, outnumbered ten, twenty, even fifty to one, stood on the shore of the one narrow inlet at Pylos where boats from the triremes could land, and where the Spartan superiority in numbers was reduced to its opposite by the simple fact that it was impossible for the Lakedaemonians to put ashore at any one time enough hoplites to match the number of Athenians on the rocky beach. And the Athenians fought like cornered lions.

In the first hour, the Spartan ship captain Brasidas had fallen, covered with blood from a dozen wounds. As he fell back, his shield was torn from him, and the heart went out of the Lakonian attack. For the first time in history, the Athenians had taken a shield from a living Spartan.

Ariston didn't see that first attack or either of two equally futile ones that followed it. For he and Orchomenus were among the four hundred and twenty men commanded by the lochagos Epitades, seconded by the pentecostye Hippagretes, who had been chosen by lot to occupy the island of Sphacteria in order to protect the Spartan fleet from being bottled up in the bay by the Athenian navy, sure to appear any hour now, since Demosthenes had succeeded in getting two of the five triremes he had with him past the Lakonian flotilla and had raced out to sea.

Telamon hadn't been among those chosen, but he begged the privilege of accompanying his son on the suicide mission of occupying that hopelessly untenable island. For though in private life Telamon was not remarkably bright, in his own profession he really wasn't as stupid as people claimed he was. All he suffered from was a certain want of imagination. But his grasp of topography was professional. He saw at once that no four hundred and twenty men on Sphacteria, nor even four hundred twenty thousand—had it been possible to crowd such a host into a splinter of stone no more than twenty stades long by five stades wide at its very broadest point—could hinder the Athenian triremes in any way at all. The only way the Athenians, once they arrived, could conceivably be stopped would be to block both inlets into the Bay of Buphras—the narrow one between Sphacteria and Pylos to the north and the broad one between the southern end of Sphacteria and the mainland to the south—with a wall of ships, thus denying the Athenians the advantage of their specialty, speed of maneuver. If they didn't do that, he pointed out to Ariston privately—for, having stripped himself of his rank, he scrupulously refrained from giving orders or advice—the Spartan fleet had no chance at all.

It wasn't, Telamon reasoned, that the Spartans had lost one iota of their justly celebrated valor or even that they were seriously outnumbered, for the Athenian line numbered fifty sail, all told. It was only that the Spartans were soldiers, the Athenians, sailors; and no amount of bravery could make up for your lack of skill when you had to fight a resolute foe in his native element.

He was so right, Ariston thought. It took Eurymedon one day to sweep us from the ocean, and now the Athenians are free and we, besieged.

"Think anything will come of the truce?" he said to Orchomenus.

"No," Orchomenus said.

"Why not?" Ariston said.

"Because in Athens the power is in the hands of the people. One of their chief men's a tanner. Name of Kleon. And we, when we conquer a polis, what do we do? We throw out the democratic government and set up an oligarchy. We're reactionaries by pure instinct, my boy. So the sweat and garlic crowd in Athens aren't likely to be merciful. See any of them yet?"

"Them" were the Helots who smuggled cheese and bread and wine in to the garrison on the island from the mainland in their crazy little boats—at a price. The price was their freedom. They demanded a signed bill of manumission before they would even hand over the pitifully scant supplies that were all that had kept the Sphacteria garrison from starving. But the Athenians had taken to running down the Helots' boats with their own thirty-oared triaconters, or fifty-oared penteconters, light, swift galleys which fairly flew through the waves. So the Helots had begun to swim in, under water, dragging skins stuffed with poppy seeds mixed with honey and bruised linseed behind them.

Of course now, after the terrible beating the Athenians

had inflicted upon the Spartan fleet, they really didn't need the smuggled supplies so much. For one of the terms of the truce was that the Spartans be allowed to supply their besieged garrison on the island two choinixes of barley meal, one pint of wine, and a piece of meat daily for each man in the garrison, and half that much for the officers' Helots.

"And for such miserable rations we surrendered sixty ships to them!" Ariston said.

"Not 'surrendered,' pledged them, as evidences of good faith," Orchomenus said mockingly, "until our peace commissioners return from Athens with the news the war is over, or—"

"That it isn't. Think they'll give them back?" Ariston said.

"No," Orchomenus said. "Which is why I persuaded Hippagretes not to stop the Helots from smuggling us in a little extra. We're going to need it, Ariston—if I know the Athenians!"

He was right. As right as Telamon had been about the disaster to the fleet. The demagogue Kleon stormed at the Lakedaemonian envoys, demanded the return of territories Athens hadn't held in over a hundred years. So the envoys came back empty-handed. The war went on. The siege was renewed, crueler, more vigilant than ever. Only one Helot smuggler in ten got through now.

And the Athenians refused to give back the ships.

"Told you!" Orchomenus said. "Never trust a Greek, my boy!"

"A Greek?" Ariston said. "What's a Greek, Orchomenus?"

"The Ionians, mostly. And the Aeolians. When they first came into Hellas, the aborigines persuaded them to worship Hecate. And since their name for her was the Gray Goddess, the Aeolians became Graikoi, worshipers of the Gray. So did the Ionians, which is what the Athenians are, you know. And that makes them witch worshipers, or Greeks. Accounts for their double dealing, dirty fighting, and general crookedness. Funny thing, the Italiots call us *all* that. The first Hellenes they ever saw were Ionian Graikoi. So nobody can get through their thick skulls that

147

we aren't all worshipers of the Crone. They even call Hellas, Graikia, the idiots!"

"I see," Ariston said. "What are we going to do now, Orchomenus?"

"Starve," Orchomenus said.

They very nearly did. The siege wore on. It had been late in Thargelion when they arrived. Now Skirophorion had come and gone. It was the beginning of Hectombian now. The heat lay on them like a weight of molten brass. The low trees and brush with which the island was covered were tinder dry.

Then, on the morning of their seventieth day on the island, all the sky to the south of them went black with smoke, shot through with tongues of flame.

"Do you think it'll reach us?" Ariston said.

"No, but as sure as Hades rules Tartarus, I know who started it," Orchomenus said.

"The Athenians?" Ariston said. "Why should they do that? They know the brush doesn't extend this far. So they can't hope to burn us out."

"No. But did you ever see a neater way of clearing the ground for a massive frontal attack, Ariston? And if those aren't sails on the horizon, I'm going blind. We'd better get out of here, retreat to that high ground on the north end of the island, and—By the phallus of Priapus! What luck! What miserable, stinking luck!"

"What do you mean?" Ariston said.

"Both Epitades and Hippagretes are out with scouting parties. So you know who that leaves in command, Ariston? You know?"

"My foster-father, Telamon," Ariston said.

"And the chances of getting an idea through that marble head are nil! By lame Hephaestus, god of all cuckolds, he'll only snort and—"

"Still, you have to try it," Ariston said. "It's your plain duty to convince him of the danger."

"Ha! You think he'd listen to m? A lowly hoplite? Besides, he knows my father. Which means he's probably aware the old man got me a be th in the City Guard to keep my precious hide safe—I m an only son too, you

148

know. I was there all of ten years, Ariston. From seventeen to twenty-seven, and that, in the august Telamon's eyes, adds up to cowardice—"

"And in yours?" Ariston said.

"Intelligence. Though perhaps the two are synonyms; I wouldn't know. Anyhow, you'd better warn him, Ariston."

"*Me?* I'm supposed to have hung a pair on his forehead, remember. With his wife. With—my—own mother, Orchomenus. So he—"

"—will listen to you because he loves you. I don't think he's ever admitted to himself that you're not his son. As for that monstrous fabrication, any man who ever spent five minutes in your mother's company would know better than to believe it! And he lived twenty-seven years with her, Ariston. Why am I so sure? Because I, in the last few weeks before she died, spent some hours with her and with Talos. So I *know* she was incapable of such a thing, Arisbe or twenty thousand Arisbes to the contrary! I even know you're incapable of it. Which doesn't change anything between us. I am both a Hellene and a Spartan. By our code, a man who neglects his plain duty to avenge the fallen is no man at all."

"He was my father, remember," Ariston said.

"And *my* mentor, which is more important. You killed him—or, if you want to split hairs, you caused his death. Anyhow, your loss was slight because you didn't know him. Mine was great. You slammed the door to—beauty, wisdom, knowledge, philosophy, love—the true love of the spirit, not the stink of carnal rutting flesh—in my face. I was getting used to the awful pain of thinking, Ariston! At that, I'll never be the same again. Even in the hour of my bitterest despair, I retained enough of the subtlety *he* taught me not to kill you; I remembered that he said life's the punishment, not death. So live, patricide! Live and remember. But now, for the moment, clank your iron harness, little donkey, over to that graybeard whose want of wit, at least, you share, and warn him that if we don't march away from here to that peak on the north shore, the Athenians will feed the crows with our carcasses before tomorrow. Which is all very well for him, since he promised the ephors not to survive the first battle; and even for you because you, after all, *are* guilty of patricide—though I mean to thwart him in that, my boy! But Hades and Persephone both take me if he has any right to get the lot of us butchered for your sin, especially a sin you didn't even do! So, up on your hind legs, little armored ass, and trot!"

Ariston smiled.

"You put it fairly," he said. "But come with me. I'll do the talking, but I need—moral support, shall we say? For your own sake, do that much. Back me up a little, will you, Orchomenus? He scares me witless. And I—"

"Oh, all right!" Orchomenus said.

Telamon listened to them—because, before the lame halting of Ariston's speech, the feebleness of his arguments, could ruin everything, Orchomenus had to intervene—quietly, and carefully. Orchomenus spoke with considerable fervor, even some degree of heat. Telamon studied the great wall of smoke and flame advancing toward them a long, slow time. What was in his mind at that moment was both a complicated, and a bitter thing. First, he was past caring about anyone's war or what happened to anything, including his beloved Sparta. Second, he resented furiously being put in the position of having to make a decision upon which the lives of so many men depended, when he had no official rank and was left in command only by the younger officers' condescending courtesy toward his gray hairs. Third, if that decision was wrong, although he would surely be dead by then, it would tarnish his reputation forever. And his reputation as a generally successful military commander was the only thing he had left now. He thought about all that. Then he came to a decision: He would evade the matter. He would dump the whole thing into the laps of the gods. He lifted up his head, his voice.

"Call the hpatskopikos!" he said.

Ariston looked at Orchomenus. The former ilarch was shaking all over. There were tears in his eyes. But, Ariston saw at once, they were the tears of a suppressed mirth so great that it was synonymous with rage.

Ariston took his arm.

"May we—retire, fath—my general?" he said.

"Of course, of course," Telamon said. "I say! What ails your friend? Speak, hoplite! What's the matter with you?"

"A touch of—of liver, great Strategos!" Orchomenus said with a straight face. "It will pass!"

"Especially if you forego your wine ration for a week," Telamon said. "See that you do, soldier! I can't have sick men on my hands now. You may retire, both of you!"

"Orchomenus!" Ariston said, "Did you have to say *that*? A touch of liver! Just when he was sending for—"

"The hpatskopikos. The soothsayer. More accurately, the reader of livers. So now the lives of several hundred men depend upon what an old fool sees in some chicken guts! Oh, Ariston, Ariston! It's Aristophanes, not Euripides or Sophokles, who has the right of it! Life is an obscene farce, never a tragedy! So now we sit here and wait while a gray-bearded donkey in armor and a solemn idiot poke and paw into the slimy tripes of a snow-white rooster! Then, upon the divine evidences of divine wisdom—I can hear all Athena's owls hooting now!—we sit on our tails and wait to die!"

"Perhaps not," Ariston said. "Perhaps he'll find the omens unfavorable—"

"No, Ariston. Sweet Ariston. Beautiful Ariston. Beautiful, beautiful father-killer! The gods love—blood. Don't you know that by now?"

"I don't believe in the gods any longer," Ariston said.

"Nor do I. But something—loves blood. Pain's the first principle on which the universe is built. Terror is the second. Lust is third, followed by madness, followed by death. Haven't you demonstrated that to your entire satisfaction? You have to mine! So, long live the wisdom divinely enshrined in chicken guts! O sacred rooster intestines strong enough to choke the life out of four hundred men! Why—"

"You're wrong!" Ariston said; "you must be! For—"

"Am I?" Orchomenus said. "Just you wait!"

He wasn't. Telamon ordered them to stay where they were. His excuse was the necessity of defending the well, the only source of drinking water on the island. The liver reader counseled such a course. So, whatever happened, the august Telamon could blame it on the gods.

Of course, it would have made small difference as far as the outcome was concerned, had they marched away at once. In sober fact, it could be argued that the delay caused by Telamon's superstitions had no bearing upon the battle for Sphacteria at all. Naturally enough, the Athenian commander, Demosthenes, had been quick to gather his forces to take advantage of the visibility and lack of obstacles granted him by the gods—for the brush fire had been a pure accident, set by a spark from the campfire of an Athenian scouting party while they were cooking their soldiers' slops. Demosthenes had a horror of fighting in brush or forest, for once before, in the Aetolian northwest, the Spartans had all but wiped out his forces in just such wooded terrain. So seeing the way clear, he prepared at once to move.

But at the last moment, he was halted by the arrival of the tanner Kleon from Athens, to whom the strategos Nikias had surrendered his own command in order to call that loudmouth's bluff. Kleon, it seemed, had boasted that had he the command, he could take both Pylos and Sphacteria, and return to Athens all within twenty days.

Whereupon the frosty, aristocratic Nikias had taken off the insignia of his rank and handed them over to the tanner.

"Do it then," he said.

Kleon had wasted a whole session of the Ekklesia trying to wiggle out of the noose he had stuck his own head into, but seeing no escape before the populace's obvious enjoyment of his self-inflicted plight, he had rallied, taken over the relief expedition with surprisingly good grace. Now here he was, his arrival causing untold dismay to his thoroughly professional colleague, Demosthenes—at least until the wily Kleon told the strategos flatly that he had no intention of meddling in matters he didn't understand. Propaganda, treaties, and the like, he'd handle gladly; but the ugly business of fighting, with its risk of getting killed, was up to Demosthenes!

So the attack that Ariston and Orchomenus had warned

152

Telamon of did not come that day. Nor the next. For the two Athenian strategoi wasted that much time in sending messengers to the Spartans on the mainland demanding that they order the garrison on Sphacteria to surrender. And even after that, they waited one more day before launching it.

In the meantime, Orchomenus looked on and shook with wild and bitter laughter, as the lochagos Epitades, and the pentecostye Hippagretes listened respectfully to Telamon's solemn councils that they do nothing. The Athenians wouldn't attack, that ex-everything but doddering old fool kept saying. They had only to hold on until the winter gales set in. The Athenians wouldn't dare risk their fleet against the elements in such an exposed position. Besides, the question of logistics entered in. Already now, messengers from the mainland had told them, they should recall that the Athenians were almost as hungry as they were. True, their enemies could prevent sufficient supplies from getting to the Lakedaemonian garrison; but time, distance, the lack of bottoms in which to convey them, the summer heat which spoiled them, made it certain that the Attic forces got precious few rations themselves! There was already sickness in their fleet. And these new arrivals only made the logistics problem worse. Therefore, young officers, listen to a man of experience! Hold on! Hold on!

The morning after Telamon made that particular speech, the Athenians put ashore eight hundred archers, the same number of slingers, two companies of Messenian reinforcements, all the troops on duty on Pylos except the garrison of the fort, all the crews of more than seventy ships, right down to the oarsmen of the top and middle tiers of the triremes, leaving only the bottom tier at their posts to maneuver the now lightened ships—and annihilated the Spartan outpost at the southern end of the island, cutting down the thirty men there as they stumbled out of bed half-dressed, clutching for their weapons.

But, for all that, the Spartan hoplites of the main body around the well in the center of the island marched out in good order, confident that they could drive the Athenians into the sea as usual. Their confidence was not as foolish as it might seem. Sphacteria was one of those places

153

where numbers meant nothing. The island was shaped like a long, bony finger; its topography designed to remind a sinner of Tartarus. Now superior numbers enable a commander to do but two basic things: to outflank his enemy's wings, thus enveloping and crushing him, or to pulverize his center by sheer weight; or, in the rare cases where the superiority is great enough, to do both things at once. But on Sphacteria, the only way to outflank the Spartans would have been to swim, since the sea protected both their flanks; and nobody in the memory of man ever rolled up a Spartan center. And because the island was so narrow, the number of hoplites the Athenians could throw in to charge the Spartans at any one time was never more than the Lakedaemonian spearmen could cut to pieces with professional ease.

What they counted on was inflicting such terrible losses on the Attic forces that the Athenians—nobody's heroes, may the gods witness it!—would give up the attempt. Only they hadn't reckoned with one thing: They were opposed by Demosthenes, a man who not only had brains in his head but who had spent a good many years fighting Spartans.

No troops on earth, that great strategos knew, could stand up to Spartan hoplites. So, why stand up to them? Why not, for once, in this exceedingly favorable terrain, make use of missile troops and cut them down from afar? It would take longer but he wasn't in a hurry. Besides, the traditional commander's contempt for light armed troops made no sense. The future, Demosthenes reasoned, lay in their hands. Why sacrifice good men in the insane business of hacking the enemy to bloody bits with the certainty of getting hacked in turn, when you could murder him with impunity from fifty yards away?

So, by midafternoon, Ariston was raging:

"Dogs! Cowardly dogs! What a bastardly way to fight!"

"Is it?" Orchomenus said coolly, wiping the blood and sweat from his face. "I call it beautiful, Ariston. Intelligence always is. Their object is to beat us, isn't it? And they're doing that."

"But in such a dishonorable way!" the boy wept. "Never charging! Their hoplites standing off there in their heavy armor with their weapons dangling from their hands and grinning at us, while their javelin throwers, archers and slingers pick us off one by one! And when we charge those armorless insects, they—"

"Skip lightly and blithely out of the way, and wait until the load of useless iron we're wearing brings us to a dead stop. Then they start perforating us all over again. Beautiful! In a word, instead of fighting like armored donkeys, they fight like men. Using the intelligence the gods—if there be gods—gave them. While we have only our hooves and harness—There! Looks like a glimmer is penetrating our commander's head. There goes the retreat!"

"Not our commander," Ariston said. "Epitades—is dead, Orchomenus. And Hippagretes is so badly wounded that we —we'll have to leave him if we retreat to the fort. My foster-father told me that when I went to see him a while back, so—"

"Telamon is in command!" Orchomenus whispered. "The gods in their mercy help us!"

"No, he isn't," Ariston said. "He refused it. Said he's too old, and anyhow that he'd brought enough misfortune upon us now by his foolish advice. So a man named Styphon has it. He's the senior enomotarch in years of service, so you can stop worrying, friend."

They closed ranks and marched northward with their rear guard doing what it could to beat off the light-armed troops' attacks. Which wasn't much. Not an instant during that infernal march under a brazen sun, blinded as they were by dust, sweat, the ash of the burned-over brush, tormented by raging thirst, their stiffening wounds, did that murderous rain of arrows, stones, and the leaden bullets from the slings, cease.

They could see the high promontory where the fort was, now. But no one believed they were going to live to reach it. For, as the strength drained out of them and their movements became wooden and slow, it began to dawn on their light-armed adversaries that the Lakedaemonians were, after all, men. So the slingers, the javelin throwers, and the archers crowded in to a range where their weapons were really effective. Besides, at that time the Spartan cuirasses were of felt instead of the stout leather they afterward adopted; and their contempt for their foes had caused them to leave their breastplates at home as a concession to the summer's heat. So the arrows went through the cloth straps as though they weren't there; the points of the javelins broke off and stayed in the wounds they had made.

Ariston caught a leaden bullet on his shield. It had been slung so hard it flattened, made a dent. A rod away, another slung shot caught a hoplite in the forehead, just below his helmet. He dropped like a stone, dead before he struck the ground.

But worst of all were those archers. They were really proving that a bowman could kill people now.

Yet even so Styphon and his Spartans made it up the hill. And now, with the thirty fresh, unwinded men from the garrison of the fort to aid them, and their flank protected by an old Cyclopean wall, they were free of the worrisome attacks of the light-armed troops and could make a stand against the Athenian hoplites with all the advantages on their side.

Or so they thought. What they didn't remember was that the Athenians' Messenian allies knew this part of the Peloponnesian coast far better than even they did. So as they stood there, grimly and confidently watching the Athenian hoplites struggling up the hill toward them, they paid no attention to the frowning, impassable cliff at their backs. Not even a fly could scale such a height, they were sure. Zeus the Averter, witness that!

So, when the first man plunged forward with a javelin through his unprotected back, they couldn't believe it. But there the Messenians were, on the heights behind them, having rounded the island in boats, landed and scaled that impassable cliff with mocking ease. They turned to face them. Then, of course, the Athenians stormed up that hill.

It was a pure, pitiless slaughter. Ariston saw his fosterfather reel back, a feathered shaft protruding from his throat. He got to Telamon's side in two long bounds, but he hadn't even time to draw the arrow out for already, as he eased the ex-strategos down, the Athenians were upon him.

Ariston stood over his foster-father's body and fought

156

like a wounded lion. So did every man at his side. To a Spartan the very idea of surrender was inconceivable.

But it didn't stay inconceivable very long. For the wily Kleon realized that live Spartan prisoners were ever so much more valuable than dead Spartan carcasses. In the first place, to parade them in chains through the streets of Athens would give the disdainful Nikias a belly ache he'd never recover from. In the second, as hostages they were worth their weight in gold, not only from a monetary standpoint, but also as deterrents against future Lakonian attacks on Athens herself. If the Spartans knew it would cost them their noble sons hanging upside down and disemboweled from the long walls, they'd think twice before storming them.

So, suddenly, the Athenian trumpet cried out the retreat, and the victorious Attic hoplites pulled back, to the vast astonishment of their dazed, parched, bleeding, half-dead foes. But a moment later, a herald came out from the Athenian ranks and proclaimed that their lives would be spared, and their treatment as prisoners of war honorable, if they would be wise enough to lay down their arms.

The Lakedaemonians looked at one another. They were Spartans, but they were also men. Young men, for the most part, with life still running strong and the desire for it hot and sweet through their veins. So, one by one, they lowered their shields and waved their hands.

All of them except one. Except Ariston, son of Talos, now of them all, made truly a Spartan by grief, by pain. He lifted his shield before him, thrust out with his sword and charged

The Athenians saw him come with admiration, with regret. In a moment they were going to have to kill him, but his gesture was magnificent; they admitted that. Then they saw another Spartan charge out behind him. Only this one had thrown away helmet, shield, spear, and sword. Burdened by nothing but his cuirass of felt and the greaves on his legs, he gained with every racing stride on the heavily armored boy. Halfway between the lines he caught up with him. The Athenians saw his hand fly out, hook into the horsehair crest on the youth's helmet. With one mighty pull, he tore it off.

157

Ariston felt that jerk, and air flooded over his scalp, cool as a caress amid his sweat-soaked, dark blond hair. He halted, whirled. Saw Orchomenus standing there grinning at him with the helmet in his hand.

"Beautiful fool, beloved enemy," Orchomenus crooned, "I give you—life!"

Then he brought that heavy bronze helmet crashing down on Ariston's unprotected head.

# CHAPTER TEN

FROM WHERE HE STOOD, straining hard against the man-
acles that chained him to the bulkhead, trying thus to
substitute a lesser, for a greater pain, Ariston could see
through the porthole of the Athenian galley's forecastle. In
this he had been doubly favored: first, because Kleon out
of consideration for his prisoners' value had ordered them
confined in the forecastle instead of throwing them into the
reeking bilge, as was usually done with prisoners, where
all they could have stared at was the hindquarters of the
oarsmen on the benches above them; and, second, because
his great beauty, as well as his captors' admiration for his
last, magnificently suicidal charge, had earned him the
privilege of being manacled in that best of all positions,
which allowed him not only to see, but to breathe fresh,
salt-tanged air.

So now he hung against his chains, swaying with the
long slow roll and pitch and creaking shudder of the galley,
and looked downward at the oars walking the great vessel
across the Ho Pontos, the great sea. It was an hypnotic
sight: the long blades biting blue water, lifting, flashing
sunbright, showering silver, feathering edgewise, thrusting
forward, sinking downward, biting again; three rows of
long-beamed, broad-bladed sweeps to a side, working in
perfect unison; for, aboard an Athenian trireme, they were
manned by freemen, not by slaves, so that pride entered
into the Athenians' rowing, making a world of difference
between their smartness, their precision, and the clumsy
way that Lakonian war vessels were handled. But then,
Ariston reflected, pride—at least when it didn't extend to
hubris—was the essence of a man.

Above him, slightly aft, he could see the lateen-rigged

triangular sail swollen like a full wineskin with a stiff wind from only one quarter off dead astern. Even in this the gods he told himself he no longer believed in favored the Athenians. The beaked prow of the trireme turned snowy furrows of foam through the wine dark sea. At this rate they would sight Piraeus by tomorrow's dawn. And then?

That was the question that repeated itself with nagging insistence in the mind of each man chained in the forecastle of the Athenian war galley until it became one with the wooden mallets of the Keleustes, the oarmaster, pounding out the beat for the rowers. The Spartans among the prisoners began to display some of the characteristics for which they were cordially hated throughout Hellas. For while at home, the modesty, dignity, even nobility of bearing that awed visitors to Sparta, making them believe her sons a super race, were every instant everywhere apparent; once a Spartan was removed from his native habitat, these traits vanished as if by magic, and he at once, by some reverse alchemy, became a profane, greedy, obnoxious boor.

And though, among the two hundred and ninety-two Lakonian prisoners, only one hundred and twenty were Spartans—the rest being Helots forced to serve their masters as armor bearers in battle, and some thirty-odd light-armed Perioeci who hadn't run fast enough—their roarings made them seem twice as many as they were. For now, rested, fed, and with the enforced leisure in which to think, the shame of their plight began to come home to them. So, as men always do who know that their own behavior upon a given occasion will not bear close examination, they sought excuses, dug into every detail of the fight to find causes—exterior, of course, to their lordly selves—upon which to fix the blame.

"We should have left these dogs aboard ship and landed more men!" one of their pentecostyes howled. "With a few more fighters, we could have honorably—"

But there are two places on earth where human equality is absolute: in the grave and in a prison cell.

"Honorably?" a Helot jeered suddenly, knowing that his master, chained to a bulkhead just as he himself was, could do nothing to shut his mouth. "What honor is there among

160

Spartans, I ask you, my masters? Orestes, the first of your kings, killed his own mother for horning and murdering his father, Agamemnon; and you lost this battle because you had a pharmakos among you——"

"Dog!" the pentecostye roared; "I'll——"

"Do nothing, chained up as you are, Spartan!" the Helot said. "But, if you want an excuse for your ill luck, I'll give you one! You see that pretty little catamite over there? That dainty little towhead of a pornos, whose lover cracked his pate for him to save his life? He was honorable wasn't he? He was still charging at the end, O my masters! Spartan honor! Spartan valor! I give you this example—brave as a lion, wasn't he?"

All the Spartans were staring at Ariston now. "What are you driving at, dog?" the pentecostye said.

"*I* sailed with him on the trireme of the great Brasidas. So I know that the crew mutinied when he was brought aboard. For he who plugs the same opening out of which he was dropped is——"

"Silence, dog!" Orchomenus cried.

"Ha!" the Helot laughed. "The lover! O most lordly pervert! Tell me, noble pederast, how do you go about it? Among us it is commonly held that *men* lie with women. No matter! Fore or aft, 'tis all the same, O noble practicer of most ignoble vices! But never again, my masters, speak to me of your honor—you who love boys and whose only hero at Sphacteria was charged with the crime of incest— a nice, lordly word, that, but all it means is that he was caught bumping bellies with his own mother, of which most Spartan impiety he was duly convicted before the Ephors' Court!"

"He lies!" Orchomenus roared, but there was a cracked note at the top of his voice, a shake, a falsetto timbre.

"Towhead," one of the Spartans nearest to Ariston said, "golden boy, pursued, no doubt, by all our ancient queers, have you ever known—a woman?"

"Yes," Ariston said.

"And was—such a charge brought against you before the ephors? Speak up, lad; I like your looks. Tell me this foulmouth of a hindleg-lifter lies, and he won't live to reach Athens, I promise you. Were you charged with this impiety?"

"Yes," Ariston said.

"But he wasn't guilty!" Orchomenus got out; "I swear—

"Ask him what decision the court handed down," the Helot said.

So now they had their excuse. The gods had willed their defeat because they had had this pharmakos—this sacrificial goat—among them. This bringer of bad luck. And there was only one way to remove the curse of the gods: The pharmakos had to die.

And I—Zeus, Hades, and Hecate help me!—have to prevent that, Orchomenus thought, prevent it any way I can. But why? Because what that foul-mouthed lump of slave dung bellowed for all the world to hear had truth's own coprolitic smell? Yes. There's that in it, too. In part. In goodly part. The coprophagist got that much right. But not wholly. Nothing is ever wholly, purely, or entirely anything. Not even love. So I love him. Still, I hate him for are not the two but reverse faces of the same coin? And hate's the more honorable face now. This pretty, brainless little swine cost me a brilliant future, caused terrible tragedies. For that he—must live and suffer. The dead, you oafs, are beyond all pain! For that. For—Hades take it!—twenty thousand complicated reasons, I don't want him to die! Because I love him; because I hate him, I don't. For both reasons. And for others I don't even know.

So Orchomenus reasoned worriedly, taking some small comfort from the fact that time for the moment was still on his side. As long as they were aboard the trireme, there was no danger at all; but once they were lodged in an Athenian prison, it was unlikely that their captors would keep them chained to a wall. Ariston, Orchomenus was bitterly sure, would not survive their first night's confinement in a common cell with his fellow Spartans. They would, if his judgment of the trireme's speed was accurate, arrive at Piraeus by dawn tomorrow; therefore, by dusk of that same tomorrow he must have Ariston removed from the group, placed in a separate cell. But how? In the name of all the dark, Chthonic gods, how?

But noon of the next day had come and gone, and that "how" still hadn't occurred to him. He stood there in the common cell and watched Ariston, who sat resting his bandaged head on his arms, totally oblivious both to the Spartans' ferocious glares and to the lisping, lilting Ionic chatter of the Athenian citizens who all morning long had poured through the prison in an endless stream to stare at a sight unique in their history: two hundred and ninety-two Lakedaemonians taken; one hundred and twenty Spartans who had laid down their shields while still alive!

Then, one hour later, at long last Orchomenus saw his chance, for at that moment Kleon himself arrived, surrounded by a party of admirers and dragging the chagrined Nikias along.

"Look, Nikias!" the tanner bellowed. "See for yourself! A fine batch of Spartans delivered within twenty days, exactly as promised! What say you to that, my friend?"

"That you were lucky," Nikias sneered. "A sorry-looking lot, by Ares! Can't be their best fighters. Spartans don't surrender, you know. I'd say that all true Lakedaemonians were left on the field; and only these poor devils without honor—"

"The day the atraktos of your bowmen," Orchomenus said from where he stood beside the iron barred door, "can distinguish the men of honor, it will have become a valuable weapon indeed, great Strategos!"

"Well spoken, Spartan!" Kleon laughed. "I tell you, Nikias, they fought like lions and only gave in when they saw it was hopeless. But if you insist upon having a traditional Spartan, I'll show you one! You see that pretty lad over there all by himself?"

"The injured boy with the bandage around his head?" Nikias said.

"Exactly. He didn't surrender. He charged our whole line alone, after his comrades had lowered their shields. And the only reason we didn't kill him was—Ho!" the tanner roared, "I thought I remembered you! You cracked his pate for him, didn't you?"

"Yes, great Strategos," Orchomenus said. "He's my friend. I didn't want him to die."

"Good for you," Kleon guffawed. "I give you thanks,

Spartan! For surely he's the prize of the lot of you. Highborn from his looks; maybe even a son of one of your two kings—not that you'd admit it, you wily dog!"

"He *is* highborn," Orchomenus said slowly, "but now he's an orphan, with no one to ransom him. His father, one of our noblest polemarchs, fell at Sphacteria, great Kleon."

"Ransom! Ho! What need have we of your rusty iron cartwheels, Spartan? As long as there exist those in Lakonia who don't want to see his carcass hanging head down from our walls and for that reason will keep your hoplites out of Attica, we'll be content enough, I tell you that! Why—"

A roar of laughter from the Spartan prisoners drowned out his words. Zeus bless you, you fools! Orchomenus thought. Witless sots, how beautifully you've played into my hands!

"My lord Kleon," he said quietly, "he—and I—are for that purpose useless. In fact, if you leave us here with these gentle comrades of ours, by tomorrow you'll have to bury whatever they'll leave of us—"

Kleon glared at him.

"Why?" he said.

"They hold he is a pharmakos—that through his impiety the island fell. They plan to kill him tonight. To kill me for saving him."

"Nonsense!" Kleon spluttered. "They'd never—"

"Wouldn't they?" Nikias lisped. "Just look at them!"

"What's this impiety of which he stands accused?" Kleon asked.

"Forgive me, great Strategos," Orchomenus said gravely, "but I'd rather not—"

"Ho!" a Helot roared. "I'll tell you, Leather Aprons! And accused is the wrong word! Convicted before the Ephors' Court, condemned to death! But since his old man was a senator-general, they allowed him to cart the little mother-gripper off to get him done in at the front. Smells better that way, what?"

"*What* smells better, foul mouth?" Kleon bellowed.

"What he did," the Helot bellowed back at him; "The little pornos. The pretty little blond-head catamite. Got tired of being on the receiving end, I guess. So he tried poking his into—"

"Shut up!" Orchomenus said.

"Let him speak." Nikias laughed. "I'm beginning to enjoy this! Of what precisely is this beautiful youth accused? By Eros, I don't think I've ever seen a fairer lad in all my life! What on earth could he have done that—"

"He was convicted of—" the Helot began.

"The crime of Oedipus," Orchomenus cut him off.

"Well, if this Oedipus was a mother-gripper too, that's what the ephors condemned him for," the Helot said. "Caught in the act. Busily trying to get as much of himself as possible back into what he came out of. With the old bitch helping him along, I tell you! They tortured poor Arisbe—the finest piece of hot and wiggling tail this side of Tartarus!—to death, but they couldn't get her to deny that his old lady and him—"

That was as far as he got. Because Ariston was standing before the Helot then. The boy's motions were incredibly graceful and as beautiful as expertness always is, even when destruction is its aim. He brought his knee up between the Helot's thighs while everyone was still watching his hands. The big man's scream went woman-shrill. As he doubled up, Ariston chopped him on the back of the neck with two linked and prayerful hands. The Helot went down on his belly on the floor. The boy leaped high, came down with both feet with all his weight upon the fallen slave. Then, in a roaring avalanche of flesh, all the other Lakonians, Spartans, Perioeci, and Helots were upon him.

"Guards!" Kleon bellowed. "In Zeus' name, bring the guards!"


"Well now, little Oedipus," the tanner said. "What do you think I should do with you?"

Ariston didn't answer the strategos autokrator. He stood there, his blue eyes gazing through Kleon as though the chief politician were not there.

"The boy's mad, Kleon," Nikias said. "Can't you see that? It's useless to question him. I'd suggest you put him to death. Since their own judges convicted him, it seems to me that he—"

"Is innocent in spite of that!" Orchomenus snapped. "You've been a judge, great Nikias. Would you tell me you've never made a mistake?"

"I've made—hundreds of them, Spartan," Nikias said quietly. "As what man has not? Still, in a case of this kind, I can't see how serious error could enter. A thing so—shocking—would be most thoroughly investigated, at least among us. And for a sentence of death to be handed down, the evidence must have been—"

"Overwhelming," Orchomenus said. "It was. And overwhelmingly—wrong. But we couldn't shake the story of the chief witness against my friend, great lords. The trouble was, she wasn't lying. She was mistaken, but she *believed* what she was saying. Besides, she was a Boeotian. Have you ever had dealings with the Boeotians, my lords?"

"Have I!" Kleon roared. "Zeus the Averter save me from them! In all of Hellas there are no duller-witted clods. Every time I go there, I have to remind myself how to distinguish the Boeotians from their cows."

"And how do you, Kleon?" Nikias said. "By the horns?"

"No, by Hades! All Boeotians wear horns, Nikias! Awarded them by their loving wives with every passing stranger. If you ever go there, remember this: If you see a creature with an intelligent look on its face, it's a cow, not a Boeotian! So this wench—"

"Condemned Ariston quite honestly—according to the limits of her Boeotian wit. Though I must say the element of female jealousy entered in. Would you like to hear the story, my lords?"

"Of course, Spartan!" Kleon said.

"Sounds reasonable enough, doesn't it, Kleon?" Nikias said.

"I'll accept it," the tanner said at once. "If you were a hardheaded businessman like me instead of an idle aristocrat, Nikias, you'd learn to judge men accurately, as I have. This Spartan isn't lying. And besides, the lad hasn't an ounce of depravity in him—one can see that—"

"What are you thinking now?" Nikias said rather sharply.

"That what cultured folk like you call intangibles have

their market value. Things like—innocence. Like virginity, say. Like—beauty. And that now I know what to do with the boy—in fact with both of them," Kleon said.

What he did with them proved the essentially mercantile quality of his mind: He took them to the Agora, the marketplace, and turned them over to a trader to be sold as slaves.

Ariston stood on the slave block and looked around him. He was surprised to find that he could feel again, even if the emotion that gripped him was only a kind of pure and childlike wonder. Surely there was no other city like Athens in all the world! A youth spent in the rather squalid dullness that was accepted as dignified austerity in Sparta had left him unprepared for the stunning perfection of the Attic capital's beauty. So impressed was he that he scarcely even listened to Orchomenus, who was exchanging banter with a threadbare, exceedingly ugly Athenian who surely hadn't so much as an obol in his purse, and whose face resembled that of a besotted satyr, except that it was maybe uglier than even a satyr's face was supposed to be.

"And if you could choose your master, whom would you choose?" the ugly Athenian said.

"Myself!" Orchomenus quipped.

"Good. And failing that choice?" the bald, pug-nosed, thick-lipped powerful man with the dark and twinkling eyes persisted.

"The poet Euripides," Orchomenus said.

"An excellent choice. Mind telling me why?" the ugly one said.

Ariston didn't listen any more—at least not to Orchomenus and the ugly Athenian. Instead he fixed his attention on the things the ancient, wizened slave at his side had been telling him, repeating them under his breath until he had the names of all the sights before him graven upon the tablet of his memory. His gaze swept over the Agora from the Cerameicus, the potters' quarter, to the dark and smoky factories of the metalworkers clustered at the foot of the hill of the Colonus Agoraeus, then upward to the great Doric style temple of Hephaestos, the blacksmith god, which crowned it. To his left was a long, covered colonnade decorated with paintings, called the Stoa of Zeus, under which the citizens gathered to gossip, sheltered by it from the sun and rain. Next to it was the temple of Apollo Patroös, Apollo the Patron; a little further south was the Metroön, dedicated to Hera, and guarding the state archives under her watchful eye. Behind it was the Bouleuterion, where the Council of Five Hundred met. Then a circular building called a tholos, used by the prytaneis, or committees of the council. Each committee, the old slave explained, was made up of fifty members from the same tribe; but to prevent any one tribe's entrenching itself in power, they only ruled the Boule, or Council, for thirty-seven days. And to prevent any interested citizen from bribing any member of a prytanei to bring undue influence to bear for or against a piece of legislation in which he was interested due to come up before the Boule, there was no regular order for one prytanei to succeed the next, the succession being decided by lot, so not even the members of any prytanei knew just when they'd be in power. The Athenians, Ariston thought with wry amusement, were true students of human nature!

Behind the wooden and temporary slave block where he, Orchomenus, and the other slaves were exhibited for sale, were two great stoas, one with a nine-spouted fountain called the Enneakrounos, on its western end, while the other faced the Odeon, or music hall. The old slave who'd volunteered all this information pointed out to him, on the northern side of the Agora, the Altar of the Twelve Gods, from which all distances in Attica were measured. A little further off, he told Ariston, was the Stoa Poikile, the painted Stoa, with murals by Polygnôtus showing the battle of Marathon, which included portraits of the notables who had taken part in the fray such as the polemarch Callimachus, as well as Miltiades and the poet Aeschylus, looking as though they were alive, and the whole thing having such a wonderful illusion of depth that—

But here the ugly Athenian cut the garrulous old man off.

"And you, kouros kalon, beautiful youth," he said to Ariston, "What do you want from life?"

Ariston studied that satyr mask of a face. Zeus witness

the man was ugly! He swept the blue flicker of his gaze over that monstrous countenance with something close to repulsion, to contempt.

"To be quit of it," he said.

The ugly Athenian smiled. And suddenly, astonishingly, his ugliness was gone. His humorous little dark eyes poured illumination over his hideously ill-assorted collection of features: nose and lips as thick and flat as an African's, high cheekbones like a Scythian's or a Tartar's, bald head, scraggly beard, until they made no difference at all. This man was beautiful, because something inside him—his pneuma, his spirit, his daimonion—was.

"That's too easy," he said to Ariston gently. "Why don't you try mastering it, beautiful boy?"

Ariston stared at him.

"Master it—how?" he said.

"Maybe—by accepting it. By realizing that pain, horror, suffering, grief—strange that one so young should have these things in his eyes!—are illusions, just as honors, wealth, fame also are. That happiness consists of philosophy, which means the love of wisdom, not the possession of her, my son! For wisdom is like a woman; clasp her to your bosom and she turns out to be as much of a shrew as my Xanthippe is—though Hera and Hestia both witness I've given her cause enough for her sour temper! I know nothing. I am only a midwife like my mother was, except that it is ideas I deliver from the dark prison men keep them locked in, not children. Tell me—why do you want to die?"

Ariston went on staring at the ugly Athenian. What rose to his lips was: "In black Hades' name, what concern is it of yours?" But the bitter question died there on his lips unuttered. In part, his Spartan training, with its emphasis upon respect for age, hadn't allowed him the relief of downright rudeness, but only in part. For somehow he sensed that it *was* this oddly compelling creature's business, that nothing within the whole compass of human experience was beyond his interest, concern, pity, and perhaps even his help. Still feeling that, knowing it, Ariston didn't speak. He didn't because he couldn't, what was in him lay too deep for either voice or tears.

"Tell him!" Orchomenus hissed. "I'd like to hear it, too. *Your* version of it, anyhow. Though maybe I'd better warn him—it's your destiny to murder wisdom—and he seems wise—"

"Speak, kouros kalon," the Athenian said.

"Why should I?" Ariston said. "What good would it do?"

"Ever see a surgeon lance a boil?" the ugly Athenian said.

Ariston laughed. The sound of his laughter was the shattering of icefloes. It took the heat out of the day.

"Would you drown in pus then, stranger?" he said.

"I'm a strong swimmer," the Athenian said. "Speak, my son."

"Very well!" Ariston grated. "I was born a bastard. I lay with my own mother. I murdered my father. I—"

He stopped short. The ugly Athenian was smiling at him.

"I have all day, golden boy," he said. "And more patience than you ever dreamed existed in this world. Still, I'd suggest—that only truth is healing, my son. Ever thought of that?"

"Truth?" Ariston whispered. "What is truth, stranger? Does it exist? Is there anything in this world beside lust and horror? Is life concerned with more than madness, grief, and pain?"

"I don't know," the Athenian said. "But then, I don't know anything. Tell me, kouros—when they brought you here, did you pass through the Akropolis?"

"Yes," Ariston said.

"Is it not—beautiful?"

"Yes," Ariston said.

"Isn't that part of life too? Beauty, I mean? Harmony of line? Order? Proportion? Have you never met a fair maid as she came singing down a country lane, when all the almond trees blew white with spring?"

"Yes," Ariston got out. "God, yes!"

"Start there, then. Tell me about—her."

And suddenly, from somewhere a long way off, Ariston heard a voice whispering:

"Her name was—Phryne. And she was as beautiful as a starry night. The way she walked—was music. Her hands were—tenderness. Her mouth—"

Then, abruptly, incredibly, he realized that the voice speaking was his own.

"Go on, my son," the ugly Athenian said.

And Ariston told him. All of it. It poured out of his throat a grate, a scrape, a tearing. It had the taste of bile and brine and blood. But he couldn't stop it now. He had to get it out of him. All of it.

The Athenian didn't interrupt him, except to say quietly, "Go on, kouros," each time he paused for breath. But when he had finished at last, the man bowed his massive bald head and said, simply:

"I am a fool. To this I have no answers. But, perhaps—"

"Perhaps what?" Orchomenus said.

"I ask questions; I never answer them. For as I said, I'm an ugly old fool who knows nothing. But I ask this—could not so much suffering have been crowded into this brief span of living to make room for much happiness in the long stretch remaining to him? Is it not possible that he may find—love, self-mastery, quietude, peace? Even—wisdom, though that's denied most men? Isn't he more than a pretty boy to be pursued by women and perverts? Isn't that—depth—I see in him—real?"

Then, without waiting for Orchomenus' answer, abruptly the ugly Athenian turned away.

"Wait!" Orchomenus cried out, his voice vibrant with hunger, with pain.

"Yes?" the ugly Athenian said.

"Buy him!" Orchomenus almost wept. "Buy me! To have a master like you would be all I'd ever ask of life!"

The ugly man stood there, and now his face was truly sad.

"My son, I haven't an obol," he said.

"Find a rich friend! Ask it of him as a loan! I'll work—I'll pay back—"

"You honor me, my son, but what rich man would advance a public nuisance like me money to buy slaves with? Especially knowing I'd only free you both since, even stupid as I am, I do know slavery's an indignity and a curse—"

"Please!" Orchomenus *was* crying now.

171

"I thank you for your trust, my sons. Both of you. I go. But I'll come back again. More than that I cannot promise. For to raise false hope is both a cruelty and a wickedness."

And now finally Ariston spoke again.

"What are you called, master?" he said softly.

"Many things, most of them obscene. But my name is Sokrates, the stonecutter," the ugly Athenian said.

But of that, nothing came. It is probable that Sokrates tried to raise the money to buy their freedom, but at that time he was not so well known as he afterward became, which made fund-raising difficult, and in any event he hadn't time enough. For an hour later, Orchomenus was sold to the steward of the strategos Nikias, who greatly admired his rippling muscles, his almost Heraklian build. It so happened that the noble Nikias gained a respectable fortune by renting out a thousand slaves to the mine owners at Laurium for an obol each day. His steward, therefore, was well aware that the general would appreciate a man of Orchomenus' size and strength. It was only good business. A thousand times an obol was a mina and three-quarters daily, one mina seventy drachmas to be more precise, which added up to better than ten talents a year. Which wasn't bad at all.

But the steward rejected Orchomenus' plea that he also buy Ariston, with a knowing shake of his head.

"Your pretty little friend wouldn't last a week in the mines. No profit in having to replace slaves too often at what you fellows cost these days. But I'll do you—and him —a favor: I'll tell Polyxenus, the bathhouse keeper, about him. That's not a bad life, and pretty as he is, he'll soon earn enough to buy his freedom—"

"Earn it how?" Orchomenus asked him.

"Oh—as a bathhouse attendant," the general's steward said.

# CHAPTER ELEVEN

THE ONLY TROUBLE WAS THAT, being Spartans, being relatively straightforward, even in their sins, their vices, they didn't know what a bathhouse attendant was. It is probable that Orchomenus, with his ten additional years of age, his greater experience, his dawning sophistication would have guessed at once, had he been there when the bathhouse keeper, Polyxenus, came. But he wasn't. By then the former ilarch of the Spartan City Guard was already on his way to the sure death by slow daily torture that slavery in the silver mines was.

So the metic Polyxenus—the name being, of course, an alias awarded him by his clients, both because they found his original Syrian one unpronounceable, and to display their wit, since its literal meaning was "many guests"— came, and sickened Ariston into near nausea at the first sight of his obvious, soft, eunuchoid, oily corruption. Polyxenus was no fool. He saw at once that for his purposes here before him was a treasure beyond price. He bought Ariston in five minutes flat for the highest price in the slave dealer's memory. He didn't even haggle, which ruined the dealer's pleasure at this unheard-of coup—fifty whole minae for a beardless, pretty boy!—by burying his triumph under the conviction, realized too late, that he could have asked twice as much and got it from the Syrian without a protesting word.

Polyxenus took Ariston by the arm.

"Come with me, darling," he crooned. "Come home with Papa Polyxenus, my little love."

That same evening Ariston found out what a bathhouse attendant was. And when he did, for the second time in his life he deliberately tried to die.

The fat and perfumed client, who had paid Polyxenus two whole minae for an hour's use of his beautiful new acquisition, ran screaming from the little bedroom. Polyxenus got there in time to cut Ariston down from the chandelier where he swung by his neck, having used his own cord belt as a noose. Fortunately, or unfortunately, depending upon from whose point of view the matter is regarded, the boy was still alive, though his beautiful young face had turned a most unappetizing shade of blue.

Thereafter Polyxenus kept him locked, stark naked, in that little room and increased his asking price to three minae for an hour. Those wealthy Athenians, wholly or partially of the more delicate persuasion, complained that this was quite outrageous; but they paid it just the same.

"My dears!" they twittered and cooed. "He's absolutely the loveliest thing! Stunning. And so—demure. So chaste. Makes one rather pity him."

Next, Ariston tried starvation. But this proved beyond his strength. The Syrian, with all the cunning of his race, put dishes before him that the king of Persia would have rewarded his royal chef with a satrapy for concocting. Now the cooking Ariston was accustomed to, that of his native Sparta, was so bad that the other Hellenes jested that Spartan bravery was due to it, that even death was preferable to a Spartan black pudding, or anything else for that matter served in the men's mess. But if the truth were told, no Hellenic cooking was anything to brag about, being at best austere, while the Oriental viands Polyxenus set before his prized slave would have, by their mere aroma, debauched a saint into gluttony.

So Ariston ate and lived, and by that very act ceased to be a Spartan. He no longer tried to kill himself. By now, he had found another refuge: He conceived the idea that his unspeakable existence was the Erinyes' punishment for his sin of patricide. And there was in this a dim, far off, and subtler glimmer of hope. For if he were so punished, his logical Hellenic mind told him, could not that punishment be considered a form of expiation? Would not one day the gods—

If there were gods. If there were any aspect of life that was not nauseous, vile.

He was, of course, damaged. He knew nightly the kind of Hellenes who weren't supposed, officially, to exist: those who took the poet Thamyris, according to legend the first man to love a member of his own sex, as their patron; worshiped Apollo, the first god to also succumb to deviate passion; wore the hyacinth in memory of the Spartan prince Hyacinthos, whose tragic death was caused by the rivalry of the West Wind and the god for his favors.

He listened, sickened in a new and different way, to their diatribes against women: "So—so shrill, don't you see? So unappetizing. Their—their natural functions—ugh! Beastly —such a mess, my dear! A sack of tripes oozing blood with every changing moon. Too bad there's no other way to preserve the race, or—"

Even in that frankly bisexual age, they were intolerable. Because the one thing a man wasn't ever supposed to be, even in Athens, was exclusively a pederast. For that, his very citizenship could be taken away from him. Of course, to the Hellenic mind the crime was not the pederasty but the exclusivity. The gods had made both sexes compellingly beautiful, and for a man to refuse either of them in favor of the other smacked of hubris, if not worse. A good citizen, therefore, could—and in Athens nearly always did— have all the pretty boys he wanted as long as he also took good care of his wife, his concubines, and his female slaves. The balance, of course, was tilted slightly in favor of those sturdy, reactionary citizens who stoutly held that the only field for a man's labors was the female. Such old-fashioned males, after all, produced sons and Athens needed seamen and soldiers now. But they were looked upon as slightly ridiculous, a bit rustic, something of boors. What on earth was there more beautiful—for the Hellenes had no adjectives of a distinctly masculine or decidedly feminine connotation such as handsome or lovely—than a chaste, well-mannered boy? A fair maid? Perhaps. But who could *talk* to a woman? Once the act of love was over and done with, what congress could a man have with a creature without a mind?

There was, of course, deep hidden in this so very Hellenic attitude toward love, the real reason that Ariston did not go completely mad during the six months his unutterable servitude lasted: Being of his age, his people, his civilization, he could not, naturally, look upon what was done to him, what he was forced to do, with the total horror that a youth of another culture, another epoch, might have. So he endured it, remembering Phryne, remembering—in one dim whitening ember somewhere in his revolted blood —even Arisbe, who had taught him the actuality of normal love.

The one way he could have freed himself—for his hoarding of the extravagant tips his wealthier clients gave him in hopes of buying his freedom was the most futile of all futile dreams—by a violent assault upon one of the purchasers of his favors, never even occurred to him. Of course, at best, that would have insured his being condemned to the living death in the mines. Even so, men had been known to escape from Laurium. In fact, revolts and escapes from the silver pits were becoming so frequent now because of the necessary reduction of the garrison of guards caused by the need to employ them more actively in the war that the very existence of the Lauriot Owls, as the Athenian drachmas were called, was threatened.

He thought often of Orchomenus, wondering if his foe/friend was still alive, for few slaves survived many months in the pits at Laurium. On the other hand, knowing as he did Orchomenus' intelligence, resourcefulness, and courage, it was not beyond reason to hope he had escaped. But what would Orchomenus do in such a case? Go back to Sparta? Or continue somehow to remain in Attica in order to—

Revenge himself upon me for the death of his mentor, my father. I shouldn't be here when and if he comes. I must get out of this, escape—Escape—Ha! From where, into what? Say I were to use that dagger I stole from Hylas, dress myself in that womanish silk chiton that Deion gave me, and flee. How could I escape from a city totally walled? Into what new horror, in a world composed of horrors, would I then fall? Still I have to try it, for—

He was thinking all that when he heard the singing girl. Her voice was utterly lovely: low and crystalline and sweet. The notes she shaped had a flutelike quality; they were so pure, so rippling silver, that they reminded him of spring-water gushing over rocks into a forest pool. And yet there was a timbre behind, below her voice, that was unutterably sad.

A trembling got into him. An ague. He shook like a man with chills and fever. And the name of the sudden malaise that attacked him was hope. This girl, this possessor of such a lovely, angelic voice, surely she would be beautiful! Surely her smile, her touch, would restore to him what nightly, hourly, he was being robbed off: his manhood. And forgetful of his nakedness, of the perfumed oils with which his body reeked, of the paint upon his face, his rouged lips, the dusting of blue seashell powder that shadowed his eyes, making them larger, more brilliant than they actually were, the fact that his burnt-honey-colored hair had been bleached into a startling shade of silvery ash blond, he leaped to his barred window and looked out.

She had already passed, but he could see her body was willow slender. She wore a robe of yellow silk so transparent that she was more than naked. The robe had great sunflowers embroidered on it. Which meant she was a porna, a whore.

Still, there was that voice. And—swift soaring hope, profound compassion, told him—she was very likely no more responsible for her condition than he was for his own.

"Girl!" he called out to her. "One moment, please!"

She turned and he saw her face. But he couldn't tell whether she was beautiful or not. Or whether she had ever been. For her young face was—ravished. Too many things had been done to her. Too many utterly unspeakable things.

And now, looking at him, that stolid, stunned mask—long since trained to avoid the slightest vestige of a thought because, he realized with a poignant winging out to her of his own pity and his pain, to think would be to invite madness—changed. But he couldn't tell what that change was, what it meant. She stared at him a long time. Then she spat copiously upon the ground.

"Catamite!" she said and, turning, went away from there.

Watching her go, her small, straight back bisected vertically by the black plume of her hair, he knew what the expression that had lighted her dead eyes at the last had been. Contempt. This whore had felt contempt for—his mind halted in mid rage-quivering flight, plunged earthward like an arrowed bird—for another whore. For a pornos who hadn't even the excuse, the defense, of being female. Who was sold nightly to creatures not even male.

It wasn't to be borne. He had to find her, show her, convince her—of what he was no longer sure himself. He dreamed of her nightlong, in the intervals when he was not occupied with a client. He decided, against all the evidence, that she was beautiful. He willed her to be lovely, whether she was or not. He endowed her with sensitivity, intelligence, sympathy, humor, wit, compassion. He outdid Pygmalion in the darkness of his mind.

And, on the morrow, he scrubbed the reeking oils from his body, the thick plaster of paint from his face, the red from his lips, the blue seashell from his eyelids, dressed himself in the silk chiton that the sickeningly effeminate Deion had given him—after carefully ripping from borders and hem its heavy freight of gold and silver broideries —and went to work on the bars in his window, digging at their bases with the point of the jeweled dagger he had stolen from Hylas.

Here he had some luck. The cement holding the bars in place was old and crumbling. The bars came loose after less than half an hour's work. He slipped through the window. Outside in the street, he paused long enough to put the bars back in their place so that their absence would not catch Polyxenus' eye. Then he began his search for the singing girl.

But, as he came out of the very first brothel, Polyxenus was waiting for him in the street.

"Look, my boy," the Syrian said in that tone of sorrowful affection he always used toward Ariston, "how was I to know you wanted a woman? I'll bring you dozens! And not one of these cheap pornai, nor even a mere auletride. An etaira, clever and beautiful! Why, heaven help me! Haven't I always treated you well? Have I ever been harsh with you? And now you run away like—"

"I wasn't running away, master," Ariston said gravely. "You had it right the first time. I was looking for a girl."

"But you mustn't go into *these* places!" Polyxenus said. "Look, darling, these whores are absolutely filthy! You'll catch a disease that'll ruin you forever. Leave it up to Papa Polyxenus—I'll bring you a fine etaira, guaranteed so clean you can drink wine out of her navel, and—"

"But I don't want an etaira," Ariston said. "They're too old. I want a girl. And not any girl. This one girl."

"What's her name?" the Syrian said.

"I don't know. All I know about her is that she's beautiful, and that she sings."

"Humphf!" Polyxenus snorted. "All pornai sing, especially when they see money. Come along home with me now, sweetheart. Tomorrow I'll bring you a little tit-and-tail-wiggler, who'll make you forget—"

"No," Ariston said. "Master, let me look for her! Besides, I need air. Without exercise, without sunlight on my skin, I'll get fat and ugly. Then I'd be of no use to you. Give me my days free! I'll come back, I promise you! Or—send an armed slave along with me! I'm not trying to escape! Where could I go? You know perfectly well I'm under a death sentence in Sparta. And who could escape from a city surrounded by the greatest walls in the world without being taken by the guards?"

Polyxenus thought about that. The brothel keeper was not an unreasonable man. It wouldn't hurt to let the boy wander about a bit. Even this one morning in the open had improved his color. And this business about the girl was all to the good to the Syrian's way of thinking. It wouldn't do to let the boy become too effeminate. With the kind of clients that frequented the "bathhouse," Ariston's fine tempered masculinity, half hidden under his matchless beauty, was, after all, the basis of his charm.

"All right," the Syrian said slowly. "Come along home now. This afternoon you can go out again. I'll send Velchanos along with you—to—to keep you safe from inflamed pederasts. But you mustn't lie with whores. Promise me?"

"Except that *one,* I promise," Ariston said.

So he found himself free to pursue his quest. After the fifth day, when he'd twice lost Velchanos in the crowds and returned to the bathhouse of his own free will, Polyxenus let him go out alone. But it took him all of fifteen days to find her. She was in the pornoboskieon of The Three Fishes, in the port of Piraeus, which was the lowest level to which any porna could descend. Because The Three Fishes was the kind of establishment that hung a huge carved emblem of Priapus over the door so that its clients might not mistake it for a temple dedicated to Artemis, goddess of chastity; the sort where the girls were called gymnai, naked ones, for the very explicit reason that that was exactly how they were kept; the type of flesh market whose clients were every species of drunken brute, roaring lout, and Panhellenic oaf whose wit extended at least to begging, borrowing, or stealing the admission price, which was one beggarly obol.

She recognized him at once, but only her eyes gave any hint of that. And she was nothing like any of the dreams into which he had distorted her. She wasn't even pretty. She was, rather, a thin, sinewy, tormented animal with fallen breasts, a coarse face, and dead, utterly lightless eyes. But having gone to so much trouble to find her, Ariston went upstairs with her just the same. It went wrong from the first for, just before they reached her cubbyhole, reeking with the stench of her and all her predecessor's former guests, a girl screamed shrilly, terribly, from another room. Again. Again. And between her anguished shrieks, Ariston heard the singing whine of the lash.

He turned startled blue eyes toward the girl.

She shrugged.

"We get all kinds here," she said. "The ones they won't even let inside a decent house in Athens any more. What's *your* specialty, friend?"

Twenty minutes later, he himself was crying like a whipped child in her arms.

"Don't," she said, her voice rough with pity. "I won't tell anybody, pretty boy. So you can't. That's not so awful. What'd you expect? Boys who go into the bathhouse trade always end up useless. There're other ways to geld a fellow besides using a knife on him. All those filthy queers! You should have thought about that before you—"

"I didn't go into it!" Ariston raged. "I was captured, sold! I'm not a—a catamite, Diotima! I'm not! It's just that—"

"Hush, lamb," she said, "or you'll have me crying next. And I forgot how years ago. You want me to bring you around by—" She used the then current euphemism for one of the more esoteric methods of making love.

He looked at her in horror.

"God, no!" he said.

"All right. Just thought maybe you needed relief. You do, but not that kind." She stared at him speculatively. "Tell you what, pretty boy. You go to this address I'm going to give you. House of a friend of mine. Name of Parthenope —most beautiful woman you ever did see. She's a graduate of this place. Fact is, she wasn't here but two weeks before a rich fellow bought her out. So she didn't get ruined. That was long before my time. I met her because she comes back to visit old Oreithyia who was in with her. Funny thing—they're exactly the same age, but Parthenope looks like old Oreithyia's granddaughter."

"Why should I visit her?" Ariston said sullenly. "What good could she do?"

"A lot. Look, kalon, I'm not your style. Used-up old sack of tripes like me. Parthenope can cure what's ailing you. She's gentle, refined. Reads writing. Makes poetry. All the wise men and philosophers are mad over her. She's high class. A real etaira, not a porna. And she's unoccupied right now because her protector lost his son—a good-for-nothing who got himself killed in a chariot race. Seems the young idiot lost a bet to that wild Alkibiades and couldn't pay. So to settle up, Alkibiades made him take the place of one of his slaves driving a four-horse chariot in last month's games. Him who couldn't properly manage a two-horse rig—the effeminate little fop!"

"How do you know so much about him?" Ariston said.

"Seen enough of him, the swishy little bastard! Used to show up at Parthenope's every time he ran out of money and his old man wouldn't give him any, to beg her for a mina or two. She's got a weakness for pretty boys, the fool. 'Specially when they're young enough to be her own sons. But then nobody's perfect and—"

"*You* go to Parthenope's?" Ariston said. "Why, Diotima?"

Her head came up. She stared at him defiantly.

"I—I'm in love with her. Don't look at me like that! You ought to be able to understand. D'you think that any girl who's been in *this* business five years the way I have could love a *man?*"

"Does she—reciprocate?" Ariston said.

"If by that jawbreaker you mean does she let me have her, the answer's yes—sometimes. Once in a great, great while. Out of pity, mostly, I guess. I can tell that because, although with her, I can *always* get there, which is a thing no man can make me do, she very seldom can with me. If she ever does. If she's not just pretending, to be polite. Anyhow—"

"Anyhow, I'll have nothing to do with her," Ariston said. "I've seen enough of male perverts not to be interested in a female one."

"Sweetie, you're a fool. Parthenope's nobody's flat-chested half-male queer. She *likes* men. Adores 'em, in fact. Every obol she gets out of rich old types with bald heads she spends on pretty young ones like you. She could really straighten you out. She did as much for the little Oebalides, or she would have, if that lisping swine Alkibiades hadn't—Saaaaay!"

"Say what?" Ariston said.

"You look like him! You look just like him! Enough to be twins maybe! By Priapus, anybody'd swear that—"

"I look like whom?" Ariston said.

"Oebalides. The boy who got himself killed. The son of Timosthenes, Parthenope's chief protector. Of course, she has a few other lovers on the sly, but—"

"So," Ariston said quietly, "I look like the late Oebalides, whom you yourself called an effeminate little fop. Goodbye, Diotima—and thanks—"

"Wait! I didn't mean to hurt your feelings. You *do* look like him. Just like him except his hair is darker, about like yours really is, to judge by the color at the roots. Only you don't *act* like him, honey lamb. He'd *never* have come here looking for a girl. Not even to prove to himself that he hadn't lost his arete, his manhood, which is why you came.

182

And you *haven't*, sweetie. You're just mixed up and hurt and confused. That's why you ought to go to see Parthenope; especially now that poor old Timosthenes is so bowed down with grief that he doesn't come around anymore, because she—"

"No," Ariston said, and started toward the door.

"Lambie," Diotima said, "don't go. Not yet. Stay at least an hour. No, two. Please."

Ariston stared at her.

"Why?" he said. "You said yourself that you don't like men."

"I don't; they make my big gut sick, the brutes. But— you're prettier than any girl. That's one thing. And another is you're building my reputation up higher than Olympus. I'll make that old Hecate who runs this place increase my share of the take because of this!"

Ariston went on staring at her.

"Don't you see, honey lamb? You look like a young prince—no, like a god. Every girl on the line was wild to go upstairs with you. Some of 'em nearly died when you chose me. They'd have done it for nothing to have a beautiful boy like you for a change. So now I've bested them all—even the younger, prettier ones. And the longer you stay, the better it looks. You don't have to try anything any more. Of course, if you want to, I'll oblige you. That's what I'm here for, isn't it? But—"

"No," Ariston said. "I don't want to. Not anymore."

"But you will stay, won't you, honey?"

"All right," Ariston said, "but on one condition—"

"Which is?"

"That you sing for me," Ariston said.

But he didn't visit the etaira Parthenope as Diotima had suggested. Instead, he used his new privilege of daytime liberty in a curious way: He wandered about the streets until he came upon a crowd being lectured to by one of the Sophists. Then he'd stop and listen because the most dreadful hunger in him was to understand, to know. In a curious way, he had an Athenian's mind in a Spartan's body. And he must have hoped that from these wise men he'd get some clue that would solve the mystery of his terrible life.

183

Why had such awful things happened to him and not to another? Why were they happening still? Why did everything he touched become blighted? Why must everyone he loved suffer and die? Did not the gods have mercy? Were there gods? How could one account for the prevalence of evil in this world?

When the lecturer was the ugly philosopher Sokrates—though, truth to tell, Sokrates didn't lecture; he only asked questions which bitingly revealed the emptiness of his interlocutors' heads, the windy vacuity of their concepts, the ridiculousness of their most cherished beliefs, maddening them to the point that quite often the younger and more vigorous of his disciples (such youths as the gilded Alkibiades, nephew of the late, great strategos autokrator Perikles, and brave as a lion despite his seemingly effeminate ways, or the even braver Xenophon, who afterward became a famous soldier), had to intervene to save him from bodily harm—Ariston hung far back for fear the philosopher might see and recognize him, for the greatest of his destructions was his shame. Which was a pity in two ways: first, because it made him miss a large part of the discourses, often losing the thread of Sokrates' intricate arguments; and second, because almost surely Sokrates would have done for him what he afterward did for the beautiful young Phaedon, that is, to persuade some rich man like Kriton to buy his freedom.

He was returning from one of Sokrates' discourses, saddened at the fact that he hadn't been able to follow the half of it; and puzzling out what he could of it, when the event occurred that afterward with much justice he considered the turning point of his life.

A little slave girl no more than twelve years old came up to him and touched his arm. He looked down into her face and was outraged, for this little minx wore more paint on her face than any porna. Then it came to him that that was what she probably was, and he shook off her hand. It was then that he heard the woman's voice say: "Stop!" and that one word pierced him like a host of swords. Because it was his mother's voice speaking—as lilting, as serene. Except, of course, the accent was Ionic, not Doric, and therefore even more musical.

She lowered the veil she wore and stared at him without shame. He stared back and decided she was a goddess. Nothing human could be so beautiful.

"You're—Ariston, aren't you?" she said. And her voice, shaping his name, made of it a bar of music, the opening strophe of an erotika, a long and lingering caress.

"Yes," he said woodenly. The way she looked at him made him ashamed.

"Diotima didn't lie," she said. "You're the most beautiful boy in all the world. So come on. Take my arm, kalon."

"But—" he protested.

"The spectacle of a man fighting off a woman is—ridiculous," she purred. "As well as damaging to his reputation for masculinity, shall we say? And that's what you're going to have to do in about a minute—because *never* will I let a gorgeous thing like you escape me. You heard me, Ariston. Come along!"

Sheepishly Ariston took her arm. She paused long enough to cover her face again with her veil. "Lead on, Phyllis!" she said to the painted little slave girl. Then, clinging to him like a lover, she walked beside him through the dusty street.

"You see!" Parthenope laughed. "There's nothing wrong with you at all! Zeus witness that! By the girdle of Aphrodite, I feel like—"

"Leda?" Ariston suggested.

"No! Like Europa! Like Pasiphaë! Come, my beautiful, golden Zeus-Taurus, let's go have a bath!"

"Together?" Ariston said.

"Of course. If *this* didn't shock you, why should that?"

Ariston considered the question gravely.

"It doesn't, I suppose," he said. "Tell me, who was Pasiphaë?"

"Come, I'll tell you in the bath," Parthenope said.

Lying in the bath—a marble pool big enough to wash Zeus in his taurine metamorphosis, into which hot and perfumed water was piped—Ariston studied her curiously. Her body was absolutely perfect. And yet—

For one thing, she wasn't really blonde. He was still so

185

naive that he didn't know nearly all the etairai dyed their hair in the not so silly belief that the unusual attracts. Since in Hellas blondes were very rare, that belief had had to meet the test of commercial success, and had thereby been fully proved. So Parthenope, like most of her colleagues in the luxurious upper ranks of her delicate trade, bleached her long, dark-brown tresses into a rather ugly and uneven pseudo-blondness varying from yellow gold to white. The reason he was able to tell this coloring was not natural was, in a way, his own fault. So excited had Parthenope been by Diotima's glowing description of him that she had left the house far too early in the morning for her slave girl to complete all the refined elaborations of her toilette, which, of course, in classical Hellas included the total depilation of arms, legs, and everywhere else the human body stubbornly retains its ancestral animal hair. The resultant overnight growth of stubble that shadowed her here and there, was much too dark.

But it wasn't that. He had the feeling that this good, beautiful, perfect, wonderfully expert and useful body wasn't—young. He wanted to ask her how old she was; but as scanty as his experience with women was, he knew better than that. So he limited himself to guessing. Twenty-five, he thought, naming a figure which to his eighteen-year-old mind seemed near senility. The truth would have shocked him speechless: Actually, he had cut a flattering ten years from her age.

"Lamb," she purred now, "haven't you *ever* seen a naked woman before?"

"Hundreds of them," he said truthfully, "but none so lovely as you are, Parthenope. Now tell me: Who was this Pasiphaë you said I made you feel like?"

Thereupon she repeated in her lilting, perfect, cultivated Ionian the absolutely outrageous story of how the Cretan princess Pasiphaë managed to become the mother of the monstrous Minotaur.

"She had the great craftsman Daedalus—who afterward became the first man to fly like a bird with artificial wings —make her a hollow wooden cow covered with natural cowskin and with, of course, openings in certain strategic

186

places. Then she took off her clothes and got inside the cow with her arms down inside the forelegs and her legs inside the hind ones, which had been carved conveniently apart, lambie. Then they pushed her out to where this pure white bull, sacred to Poseidon, waited, and—"

Ariston stared at her. Then he said.

"I'm sorry, Parthenope. Forgive me. . . ."

"In the name of Eros and Aphrodite both, lambie, for what?"

"For making you feel like her. Though you're only teasing me, aren't you? My uncle Hippolytus always scoffed at those legends. He says that physical love between a woman and a great creature like a bull would be impossible. Or—disastrous." Then he repeated Hippolytus' mocking quip, mimicking the fat little sybarite's words and gestures.

Parthenope laughed until the tears ran down her face and mingled with the bath water.

"Impossible, no," she said, "but—disastrous, very nearly. But—such a renewing disaster, kalon mine, resembling that of the first night. So now, come on!"

"Come on where?" Ariston said.

"Back to bed, my little minotaur! And long live disaster!"

"Diotima says you look like someone I know," Parthenope said as she lay beside him, stuffing little cakes into his mouth. "And she swore I'd see the resemblance at once, without her having to tell me. But Athena help me if I do! I've never seen anyone half so beautiful as you are, my little maker of disasters. No, of catastrophes—for that was what that last bout was! Let me think, let me think—who this side of Tartarus do you—"

"Not this side of Tartarus," Ariston said.

Parthenope sat bolt upright in bed, staring at him.

"You do!" she whispered, "Zeus help me, but you do! Of course, you're ever so much more beautiful, mainly because you've somehow managed to keep your manhood intact—Ohhhh! great Athena, I thank you! And you divine Hera, mother of the gods!"

"I don't believe in the gods," Ariston said stiffly. "But

187

would you mind telling me what you're thanking them for?"

"For—showing me a way to save you from that infamy," Parthenope whispered. "To rescue you from that utter vileness that you've gone through and yet stayed— clean. Get up!"

"Get up?" Ariston said.

"Yes! Get up and go back to your den of perverts! I have things to do! Oh, lambie, don't look so hurt! They're for you, these things. By tomorrow night you'll be out of there forever!"

She was as good as her word. For at noon of the next day, as Ariston half-ran through the crowded streets toward the place where, according to the news he'd had of a client last night, Sokrates was going to discuss the question of the existence of the gods, he saw, with the petulant annoyance of the sexually satisfied, her coming toward him.

He swore profanely under his breath and stopped because he was sure that she had seen him. But she went by without pausing; and he saw then the tall, bald man of some sixty years of age, lean and sinewy, with a high beaked nose, hollowed cheeks, and an expression of ascetic severity that belied his present mission, riding along on a magnificent horse behind her.

At that instant, Ariston's petulance vanished and an icy pang of jealousy cut off his breath. The pain of it was terrible. He had told himself that Parthenope didn't matter to him, that she was much too old, that he was only using her to make sure his perverted clients wouldn't force him into their ranks, that—

"Hades take her!" he raged. "Why should I care? She's nothing but a whore! As all women are at heart! Even my mother—"

He stopped then, an instant short of repeating that outrageous blasphemy, dashed an angry hand across his eyes, and loped on toward where Sokrates was debating with the crowd.

An hour later, he returned through that same street. He

188

felt angry and hurt and more than a little disappointed. All Sokrates had said was: "Of the gods we know nothing. So why dispute about matters which by their very nature are unknowable? Have any of you mastered the management of human affairs well enough to set yourself up as an authority on those of heaven? The best thing to do, friends, is to acknowledge your ignorance, obey the Delphian Oracle, make the proper sacrifices, and forget the matter." And, on being asked by an obvious foreigner how the gods should be worshiped, the ugly old mocker quipped: "According to the customs of your country."

Not very satisfactory, damn him! Ariston thought. He's as slippery as an eel. Nobody can pin him down on any principle. Why Hades and Persephone both take him, he—

Ariston stopped short for he had become aware suddenly that a man was blocking his path. Deliberately. He opened his mouth to swear at the man, but then he swallowed his oaths unuttered. For one thing, he had recognized the Athenian as the rider who had been following Parthenope an hour before. And for another, this tall, proud patrician was staring at him with a look he had seen upon but one other face before in his life: that of his own father, the Helot Talos.

He peered closer, his astonishment growing. This old eagle beak had tears in his eyes! And then he saw with something surer than thought, closer in fact to instinct, that the fine chiseled lines of sternness, of aristocratic hauteur on that face were but a sham, a fraud—that this old man was endlessly kind.

"Sir," he said, "are you ill? Or—is there something about me that—that offends you? I assure you it's not intentional. For I—"

"Ariston—" the man said, and his voice was as deep as the sea and as sad. Then, wordlessly, he drew the boy into his arms.

Ariston made no resistance. He let the man hold him, kiss him, wet his young cheeks with his tears.

"You," he said, "are the—Lord Chief of the Hellenotamiae, are you not, sir? The noble knight Timosthenes? And I—look like the son you lost. That's it, isn't it, sir? If so, I'm sorry. I'm sorry. I don't like causing pain."

"What you cause, my son, is joy," Timosthenes said. "Or you will, if—"

He stopped short, pushed Ariston away from him until he was holding the boy at arm's length and staring into that young face.

"Ariston," he said, "would you like to be—my son?"

Ariston considered that. He didn't know whether he'd like to be the son of anybody now. What he wanted to be was free. But how many times had he heard Sokrates arguing that freedom was relative? And even as this man's slave, he'd be freer than he was in the bathhouse. At least no one would be allowed to perform nameless vilenesses upon his helpless and revolted body any more.

"Yes, sir," he said.

"Good!" Timosthenes said. "Let's go to the establishment of that oily Syrian swine. I'll offer him what he wills for your freedom, and—"

Ariston frowned. What his newfound benefactor proposed to do was the worst possible tactic, and he knew it. Given a proposition like this one, such a past master at deceit and guile as Polyxenus would gleefully proceed to bleed this sentimental old nobleman white. That must be prevented at any cost. But how? In the name of Hermes, god of tricksters, cheats, and thieves—how?

Then it came to him. He looked up the street, then down it. Crowded as besieged Athens was, to talk thus in the open without being overheard was next to impossible. And there were a good many people who made a comfortable living by repeating the conversations of rich and important men like Timosthenes to those who had something to gain by the knowledge. For since his own contact with Athens' underworld had necessarily been profound, among the things he'd learned was that no city in Hellas was more plagued by the nefarious tribe of sykophantos, or extortionists, than was the capital of Attica. So now, seeing that no one was within a rod of the spot where they stood, Ariston leaned swiftly close to the lordly hippêus' ear, whispered a rapid phrase so low that only Timosthenes could hear it.

The knight listened, his finely chiseled, patrician's face set in lines so stern, so forbidding, that, seeing his expression, Ariston faltered, came to a halt.

"Go on!" Timosthenes said.

"Forgive me, noble Timosthenes," Ariston said quietly, "but truly there is no other way. Now here's what I'd suggest you do—"

The knight listened quietly. Little by little the iron cast of disapproval left his face. But what replaced it was the flush of a deep and abiding anger.

"The son of a man whose lands are rich and extensive enough to produce five hundred bushels a year, you say?" he growled.

"Yes," Ariston whispered, "and the other one's the one of a hippêus like yourself, sir."

"Zeus Thunderer!" Timosthenes swore. "What's Athens coming to?"

"To no good at all, unless—" Ariston let his voice trail off in midphrase, deliberately.

A slow smile lighted Timosthenes' small blue eyes. He brought his hand down on Ariston's shoulder, hard.

"I'll do it!" he said. "What use is nicety of scruple in a case like this? After all, it's scarcely customary to use a jeweled dagger to stick a pig, is it?"

Ariston let his breath out slowly in a long, relief-filled sigh. Then he too smiled.

"Whatever you stick him with, be sure your thrust strikes home, my lord," he said.

When Polyxenus saw the bearing and the dress of the three strangers who stood in the opened doorway of the bathhouse that same night, he almost bumped his forehead against the floor, so sweepingly low did he bow. Then he straightened up, rubbing his pudgy little hands together as though he would remove the skin from them.

"My lords!" he murmured. "Noble knights! Truly my poor house is honored—"

Then he stopped short, and his swart complexion grayed a little. He ceased rubbing his hands together. His thick underlip dropped down. A whitish trickle of saliva stole down from one corner of his mouth into his inky beard.

"The noble Timosthenes!" he got out. "But—but—"

Timosthenes smiled at him. That smile was wintery with contempt.

"You've been told that I have no taste for deviate play, have you not, O Syrian?" he said.

"Precisely, my lord," Polyxenus said. "More than that, I've heard that you actively oppose—"

"Ah, there you've heard too much!" Timosthenes cut him short. "I hold that a man's freedom includes the right to debase himself if he so desires. These kalokagathoi, these gentlemen from Argos, would like a bit of sport after the curious manner you provide, Syrian. They're fully aware that I don't approve of such twisting of nature's ways, but hospitality is a higher duty than the maintenance of scruple, especially since I've no intention to sully my own flesh in this odious fashion. So, to it, Syrian! See to their wants. I'll sit and wait."

Polyxenus looked uneasily at the two Argive knights. Then he relaxed a little. Long practice at his trade reassured him. These two were the sturdy masculine type, fathers of families, stern husbands who loudly sneered at effeminates in public, made great capital of their obvious maleness—at home. But, once out of their native polis, beyond the hard gaze and wagging tongue of scandal, they had as lively an eye for a pretty boy as any other Hellene. Oh, he'd seen many such!

"Have you anything special in mind, my lords?" he said.

"Well," one of the Argive hippêis said slowly, "a visitor from Athens told us that you have a pair of dainty lads who are extraordinarily fine. Called—I say, Temos, what are those little beggars called?"

"Diomedes, and—and Iphiklos, I think it was," the other hippêus said.

"Your friend has taste!" the Syrian said. "Those two are my very finest boys, except—"

"Except who—or rather—what?" Timosthenes said mockingly.

"A Spartan boy called Ariston," Polyxenus said boldly, "a youth whose beauty is almost godlike. So lovely is he, my lord, that did I not know how unshakable your virtue is in this regard—"

Timosthenes' gaze rested upon the Syrian's face like frost and flint. Then he smiled, but his smile was more than half a sneer.

"Have him in then, and put the matter to the test, O Syrian!" he said.

When the Argive hippêis had gone into the bedrooms with the two perfumed and lisping catamites, Timosthenes sat in the sitting room with Ariston and the bathhouse keeper, and talked. Polyxenus' fears vanished before this convincing proof that no trickery was involved, that the two big, muscular men had actually come to enjoy his delicate wares. He quickly let the Athenian hippêus know that he was free to converse with the boy as long as he liked, that is, if no client whose needs were more basic and more pressing appeared.

"I'll pay you your usual rates for the time we spend in talk, Syrian," Timosthenes said flatly. "See that we're not disturbed, will you?"

"Of course, my lord!" Polyxenus said with practiced servility. "But don't you think you'd be more comfortable, as well as having greater privacy for your—chat—if you retired to his bedroom, say?"

"Don't be an utter ass, Syrian," Timosthenes said. "When I say talk, I mean talk. And for that, this sitting room will do perfectly well. Besides, I want you to stay with us. I've a feeling that this conversation might be profitable to us both."

"As you will, noble hippêus," Polyxenus said.

Timosthenes turned to Ariston.

"Tell me, my boy," he said flatly, "do you *like* this life?"

"No, sir, I hate it," Ariston said.

"Then why do you engage in it?" Timosthenes said.

"Because I—I'm a slave, sir," Ariston said sadly. "He, my master, Polyxenus, bought me—for this."

"And for your beauty, which is great," Timosthenes said. "And which pleases me, though for no unmanly reason. But rather because you remind me of the son I lost, whom greatly you resemble. So I, in my turn, propose to buy you out of this infamy. Well, Syrian, how much will you take for him?"

Polyxenus stiffened. Then he smiled a little.

"Your entire fortune, sir," he said mockingly, "plus the

193

fortunes of your two friends within, plus the treasury of your dene, your tribe, plus—"

Calmly Timosthenes shook his head.

"No, Syrian," he said, "you'll take far less than that. In fact, you'll take—No, wait. Let's put it to the boy. Ariston, my son, how much should I offer him?"

"One mina," Ariston said, "and not one obol more. He paid fifty minae for me. But considering the use he's had of me, the price is just. Don't you agree, my lord?"

"Perfectly," Timosthenes said and took the silver coin from his purse.

Polyxenus stared from one of them to the other. He was no fool. He knew that something was afoot now, but for the life of him he couldn't tell what that something was.

"You jest, my lord," he began. "Surely you cannot think that I'd accept—"

"I never jest," Timosthenes said sternly, "and what you'll accept, I don't have to think about for I know it already." Then he lifted his big voice, called:

"Temos! Miltrades! Come out of there and bring those mincing little lapdogs with you!"

The hippêis came out of the cubbyholes with the boys. Timosthenes glared at the two perfumed and painted little demi-males.

"Diomedes," he spat. "Son of Thenelaides, of the dene Lapodia, freeborn and son of a citizen, what have you to say for yourself?"

"My lord!" the boy got out. "You—you won't tell my father, will you? For he—for he—"

Timosthenes' frosty glare halted his words. Diomedes searched the hippêus' face for a sign of mercy. He didn't find it. Then suddenly, appallingly, he began to cry.

Timosthenes ignored him.

"Iphiklos," he said sternly, "son of the noble hippêus Thessalos, of the dene Scambonidae, freeborn and son, not of a mere citizen, but of a noble—what have you to say for yourself?"

Iphiklos opened his mouth. What came out of it was a high-pitched female wail. He fell to his knees, groveling before Timosthenes.

194

"My father will kill me!" he shrieked, "and, oh, my lord, I am too young to die!"

Ariston looked away from them. The sight of their shame was too—lacerating somehow, too hurtful. Instead, he looked at the bathhouse keeper. Slowly the Syrian sank to his knees in his turn, his face purplish gray and working. His mouth opened but no sound came out of it, no sound at all. His lips made a bluish blur as they fluttered wildly, trying to form words, seeking sound.

"Polyxenus, Syrian swine," Timosthenes said quietly, "what will you say when these gentlemen, my friends, appear before the Heliaea, the Popular Court, to testify that they have lain, in *your* establishment, with these two boys, both sons of citizens? Will you pretend to the Court that you didn't *know* that inducing a freeborn Athenian to prostitute his body is a crime punishable by imprisonment, confiscation of all your goods, and perpetual exile from Attica once your sentence is served? Tell me, Eastern dog, what will you say?"

"Mercy, noble lord!" Polyxenus all but wept.

"Mercy?" Timosthenes said. "I should show mercy to you, who wouldn't free this chaste and noble lad from the vileness you bought him for, forced him into? You who demanded my fortune and the fortunes of these my friends as your price for—"

"Father," Ariston said suddenly.

"Yes, my son?" Timosthenes said right tenderly.

"Show him mercy. You can afford it. He didn't force these two effeminate little fops to come to his place. And—in his way, according to his lights—he has been kind to me. Make him take one mina for me, in the presence of these kalokagathoi as witnesses, sign a bill of sale. That—and the loss of my services—will be punishment enough—"

Timosthenes stared at the boy.

"You're a noble lad," he said. "I think, the gods willing, you'll make me a better son than the one I lost. Well, Syrian! What will it be? Will you sell me this boy, or—"

"Oh, take him!" Polyxenus shrilled. "In Zeus's name, take all three of them!"

"No," Timosthenes said. "This one is enough. These

mincing little swine, you can keep. Well, Ariston, do you think you can endure existence as my son?"

Wordlessly Ariston knelt before the stern old knight, bent and kissed his hands.

"May the gods grant me no greater blessing, sir," he said.

So it was that Ariston, a bathhouse slave at sunset, was by sunrise a freedman and the adopted son of the richest man in all Athens. The Fates had smiled upon him at last.

That is, if the Fates know how to smile.

Or if the Furies ever sleep.

# CHAPTER TWELVE

THE SUPERINTENDENT OF THE slaves read the bill of sale and handed it back to Timosthenes.

"You realize it will be difficult, noble Timosthenes," he said. "We have close to twenty thousand men in the mines. But the general's word is law, of course. It shall be done. Only it will take some time. First we'll see the foremen of the night shifts—those men are sleeping now, so locating one of them will be far easier. And if, luckily, your son's friend is among them—"

"All right," Timosthenes said.

The superintendent turned to Ariston.

"Would you be so kind as to describe your friend, young lord?" he said.

"Why?" Ariston said. "He's been here seven months. What good would any description I could give of him do now?"

"True—" The superintendent sighed. "It's a hard life—and it does change men; but—"

"It is murder," Ariston said. "Assassination. And more of the soul than of the body. All slavery is."

The superintendent stared at this boy whose eyes didn't match his youth or his beauty. The superintendent had seen eyes like these many times, and he knew what they meant, usually. It paid to know. Sometimes, if you were quick enough, you could prevent a slave with eyes like these from throwing himself into the smelting cauldrons or piercing his own chest with an ore chisel or knocking out his brains with a sledgehammer. Sometimes. But such a one usually died anyhow, a little later. Men cannot live without hope.

"Oh, come now, Ariston!" Timosthenes said. "All slavery isn't bad. My household slaves now—"

"Are owned things, Father. You don't mistreat your horses, mules, donkeys, goats, and other livestock either. But they're still—cattle. Tell me: Does man have—a soul?"

Timosthenes looked upon this strange and troubling adopted son of his.

"Yes," he said.

"Then answer me this: What do you think it does to that alleged soul we're suppose to have to *know* you're another man's creature? That you can be beaten, tortured, killed—"

"Ariston—" Timosthenes said.

"Hear me out, Father! On the one hand, kissed, fondled, petted, used for pleasure, committed sodomy upon—on the other? Say you're nothing more awful than a paidaigogos, your task no more hateful than accompanying boys to school and bringing them back again; or a man of great learning such as the wealthy sometimes buy to tutor their sons at home—don't you know, my loved and respected father, that even so you must lift your eyes toward a bird beating across vast heaven on free wings—and weep?"

"Aye," the superintendent said, "that's true. I—"

Ariston turned upon him.

"How would *you* know?" he said.

The superintendent smiled at him, a little sadly.

"Because *I* am a slave, my lord," he said.

Ariston stood there. Then he put his hand out and let it rest upon the superintendent's shoulder.

"I apologize," he said. "I didn't know."

"No apology is necessary," the superintendent said. "Except for the guards, no man here is free. My engineers, my foremen, all are slaves. Free men never stay at Laurium, my lords. They can't. It is one thing to receive one mina, seventy drachmas a day, as the great, noble, and pious Nikias does for the use of his thousand slaves; and quite another to have to witness men being broken, reduced to animals, tortured to death by inches to produce that wealth. We have to stay. We can't turn away our eyes. Some of us are forced to act as torturers. And let me admit it at once, the ones who are, quickly learn to enjoy inflicting pain. There are depths and twistings in the human soul that—"

"I," Timosthenes said sternly, "find this conversation unseemly. Let us, therefore, end it. But before we do, I'd leave a thought in both your heads: What man—what man above ground, treading earth and breathing air—is free?"

Ariston stared at his adoptive father. Then he went to him and kissed his cheek.

"Forgive me, Father," he said.

"It's all right," Timosthenes said gruffly. "Well, superintendent, shall we begin to look for this Orchomenus my son insisted upon my buying out of here?"

"That is already being done, my lord," the superintendent said. "In the meantime, would it please my lords to be shown about the mines?"

"Gladly," Timosthenes said.

Afterward, Ariston realized the subtle malice behind the suggestion, for Pantarkes, the superintendent, spared them nothing. He took them down the long, slanting main shaft until they could peer into the galleries. Those galleries were so small that even in the biggest of them a man had to work on his knees, while in the usual one, the slaves lay on their bellies, or on their backs, prying the ore loose with hammer and chisel, keeping their eyes closed to avoid being blinded by the down-showering rock dust, then handing the ore out from man to man in baskets, because no two men could pass abreast in those tunnels. The only advantage that their position had was that the narrowness of the tunnels also made it difficult for the foremen to swing their lead-tipped bullwhips effectively. But they managed to draw blood now and again, when a slave paused for a moment's rest.

The smell was awful: sweat and human offal and urine and dust and blood, and even now and again putrefaction where some slave had been pinned down by falling rock, and it hadn't been possible—or even worth the bother—to dig his useless carcass out. If, Ariston thought, there is a Tartarus, this is it.

They moved into the crushing room. Here slaves walked endlessly in a circle pushing huge beams which worked the heavy iron pestles in the enormous mortars. And here the foremen had full space to swing their whips. The slaves' backs were dreadful to see. In the mills, water power and man power both turned the great millstones of diamond-hard trachyte, grinding the crushed ore fine enough to be screened. Slaves shoveled it against the screens; the particles that passed through went to the washer, where they were thrown upon the inclined tables of stone, washed through with jets of water from the cisterns; the flowing current turned again and again at sharp angles, until the heavier particles of metal settled out and the stone dust floated free. Then the smelting hall, that perfect image of hell, with its hundreds of small furnaces attended by slaves, all of whom were en route to death from lung sickness caused by the fumes. Beyond that, the separation room, where the silver was freed of its mixture of lead by reheating it on cupels of porous stone exposed to air. The lead combined with the air, becoming litharge; and the silver, now 99 percent pure, floated on the surface to be skimmed off, while the slaves who did the skimming spat blood and coughed up shreds of their lungs.

I, Ariston thought, will never touch a drachma again without feeling pain.

But when they got back to the main office, Orchomenus was there waiting for them. Or what was left of him was. A bearded, filthy animal, whose gigantic muscles seemed to weigh his body down so that he couldn't straighten up, glared at them from wild beast's eyes. His nose had been broken. There was a brand burned into his forehead. His hands and feet were manacled. The stench of his body was overpowering.

Then he recognized Ariston and grinned at him like a wolf.

"You," he said, "who always manage to escape everything—"

"Except maybe you," Ariston said and kissed him despite his smell. Then the boy turned to the guards.

"Strike off those fetters," he said.

That night, bathed, well fed, full of wine, his hair cut, his beard trimmed and perfumed, Orchomenus looked almost human again. He discussed gravely and politely with

Timosthenes the possibility of having a surgeon remove the ugly, puckered brand from his forehead—inflicted upon him for his many attempts to run away from the mines.

"Of course," Timosthenes said, "you'll be left with a scar, but it will appear an accidental or a military wound. That way, no one will know—"

"Good," Orchomenus said. "I'll submit to it then, noble Timosthenes. Zeus witness I can bear pain. But what troubles me more is how I am going to live. We Spartans have no skills beyond killing people. You know our system, sir? Inviolate tenure of land, worked by Helots, which frees us to—"

"Be slaves of duty, discipline, and the necessity of guarding an overwhelming and rebellious slave population," Timosthenes said dryly. "I shouldn't like to be a Spartan, friend."

"Nor I, anymore," Orchomenus said quietly. "I have no intention of going back to Sparta, sir. Besides, my life is linked to Ariston's—by destiny, by fate—"

"And not by—love?" Timosthenes said.

"That too I suppose, though much of the time I'm strongly tempted to wring his neck," Orchomenus said. "He's an irritating little bastard—or hadn't you noticed that, sir?"

"I have." Timosthenes smiled. "But then, he has had reasons enough to make him so. As for work, I'll provide you with it. Next week, after you've rested and enjoyed a short holiday, I'll make you superintendent of one of my ergasteriae—"

"Your factories? What sort of factories, sir?"

"Metalworking, mostly. Shields, armor, weapons. It's simple enough. You merely take note of the amount of crude metal delivered to the shops—its weight, its quality —no blowholes or sandpits, mind you!—and the weight and numbers of the output, in shields, breastplates, greaves, swords, daggers, spear points, and the like. There's a certain amount of inevitable loss in production, of course, but one of your duties will be to keep it small. Clumsiness, poor workmanship is one of the causes of losses. Another is petty thievery. Still another, less apparent,

201

is laziness, slackness, which causes the time it ought to take to make two shields to be spent on one. But you'll catch on quickly. You're very intelligent, that I can see."

"Father," Ariston said. "Why don't you give *me* a factory to manage? I'd like that very much. I hate being an idler and a parasite. Why——"

Timosthenes shook his head.

"No, Son," he said kindly. "You've got to complete your studies, which are woefully inadequate. After that, we'll see."

That night Orchomenus came into Ariston's room and got into bed with the boy. He put his arms around Ariston and began to kiss him passionately.

Ariston shuddered.

"Orchomenus—no," he said.

Orchomenus grinned at him mockingly.

"Why not?" he said. "You were in love with Lysander. When he died, you kissed his dead mouth for half an hour. What's the matter? You find me too ugly now, or——"

"No. It's just that I—I can't. Your scars show. Mine don't. I've seen the mines. But believe me, given my choice, I'd take them any day in preference to what happened to me. I'd take death first. And that's no idle phrase, Orchomenus. I mean it."

"Why?" Orchomenus said.

Then Ariston told him. All of it, without omitting the smallest detail. His voice was low, flat, almost expressionless. Which made his tale all the more effective. Nothing deepens horror more than its being related with quietude.

"I see," Orchomenus said. "You want me to kill the Syrian for you? Or that swine of a steward of Nikias' who told him about you?"

"I don't want you to kill anybody. I don't want ever again as long as I live to inflict a scratch on anyone's little finger. Or to be the cause of any man's humiliation—or any woman's. There is nothing worse, my friend. I'd like to devote my life to them—to the offended, the humiliated, the people denied human dignity, denied——"

"Even humanity," Orchomenus said.

"You understand. Now get up."

"Get up?" Orchomenus said.

"Yes. I'll find you a woman. You need that—after so long. Maybe I need one too, but I don't think so. I'm past that—I hope—"

"You're past *what*, you hope?"

"Having to prove to myself I'm still—male," Ariston said.

"All right," Orchomenus said. "I've probably lost all desire for females, after so long. When there's nothing else but hairy, stinking crow bait available, you acquire a taste—"

"I didn't," Ariston said. "Now come on. . . ."

He didn't take Orchomenus to a pornoboskieon, or porneia, or any of the other varieties of brothels. Nor did he take him to Parthenope's. He suspected that she might find Orchomenus' size and strength too attractive. And he was afraid of losing her. Dreadfully afraid.

Instead he led his friend, foe, would-be lover to a quarter of the city where the auletrides, flute girls, and even some of the lesser etairai were to be found. He took all the precautions, providing Orchomenus and himself with walking sticks, without which a man was subject to arrest for drunkenness for in that quarter, the magistrates concerned with flute girls, dancers, and scavengers were very strict. They were both richly dressed, and Ariston's air of gentlemanliness, good breeding, would protect them from interference if they didn't have to open their mouths. If they did, their thick Doric accents would ruin them, for the magistrates had no patience with metics—resident aliens—at all.

It proved easy. Too easy. As soon as they got there, a spritely little creature with bleached-blond hair tripped along ahead of them, looking mockingly back over her shoulder. As she passed under a street lamp, they saw that her gilt sandals had nails in their soles arranged to spell out "FOLLOW ME!" on the dusty street.

Ariston caught up with her.

"Have you a friend?" he said.

"For who?" she whispered.

"For me," he said.

*"I'm* for you, honey lamb," she said. "Even free, if you haven't any money. A girl doesn't get this kind of a chance to combine pleasure with business very often. And a boy like *you,* kalon—"

"Then for my friend?" Ariston said.

She looked over his shoulder at Orchomenus and shuddered.

"That ugly brute?" she whispered. "Ugh! What're you doing with the likes of him, honey?"

"He's my friend. Saved my life in battle. He only looks like that because he was taken prisoner and enslaved. He's really quite gentle."

"Well—I'll try. But he'll have to be content with a porna. Good girl. Clean. Her name's Thargelia, if you're interested. I let her stay at my place on her free nights to earn the money to buy herself out. She's pretty enough. Too good for that life."

"All right," Ariston said. "But I only hope she's strong! My friend hasn't touched a woman in over seven months, so—"

"Eros save us!" the little etaira said.

When Orchomenus and the girl called Thargelia had left the room, the little etaira, Theoris, who in sober truth was not a day over fifteen years old, came over and sat in Ariston's lap. Then she began to kiss him very expertly.

He pushed her away.

"No," he said.

She stared at him.

"Why not?" she said.

"Don't know. Not in the mood, I guess. Which shouldn't worry you. You'll get paid just the same."

She studied him with some care.

"Honey—are you a queer?" she said.

Ariston smiled at her, completely at ease.

"No," he said.

"Prove it to me."

"If I were an extreme case, I wouldn't be here. And if I were the kind who was wavering, I'd have made a great show already to convince you, convince myself. But since I'm neither, I don't have to prove anything to either of us.

204

All I am, Theoris, is bored. And a little sad. What I want you haven't got—"

She said a short, expressive word that was very Attic, very profane.

He grinned at her.

"Sorry. I didn't mean to offend you. You're beautiful enough, Aphrodite witness it, Theoris. Only—"

"Only what, kalon?"

"I don't suppose I'm looking for beauty, really—"

"Then what in black Hades' name *are* you looking for?" Theoris said.

Ariston smiled at her.

"You could call it—love," he said. "The one thing that's not for sale. That can't be bought, faked, or counterfeited. And is priceless—when you find it. That is, if you ever do."

She went on studying him.

"Honey, you mean to tell me that nobody's *ever* loved you?"

He shook his head.

"Once," he said.

"What happened to her?"

"She died. No, that's not right. She was murdered."

"Because—of you?"

"Because of me."

"Tell me about it?"

"No," Ariston said.

"Oh," Theoris whispered, "and ever since, you've been looking for—"

"No. Ever since I haven't been looking for anything or anybody. Except maybe the ferryman, the black river. I went to her once—down to Tartarus. Only, my father came after me and brought me back. I remember how she looked kneeling between Hades and Persephone with her arms outstretched to me and crying. But life was too strong in me. I couldn't die. I wanted to, but I couldn't—"

"Honey, anybody ever tell you you're a little crazy?"

He smiled at her gently.

"Only a little, Theoris?" he said.

"More than a little. You're crazier than a lotus-eater. But it's a nice craziness. I like it. I—like you. Do me a favor will you, kalon?"

"What favor?" Ariston said.

"Come to bed with me. I'll make love to you as though I'd just found out what it was. As though we'd invented it. Like—like a bride. Timid and shy and gentle—and—and tender—"

"No," Ariston said. "I'm sorry, Theoris."

"*You're* sorry. Tell me, kalon, how much are you going to give me for *not* doing it?"

"Whatever you like. Fifty drachmae. A mina. Two."

"Two minae. All right. Let me see 'em."

Ariston took the two heavy silver coins out of his purse. They were worth a hundred drachmae apiece. He held them out to her.

But suddenly, wildly, Theoris shook her head.

"No. Keep them. Take them and perform the act of sodomy on yourself with them! No—take them and—and buy a sacrifice—for her. On the high altar before the Parthenon. For the gods' mercy upon her shade, her pneuma. In my name. Will you do that, kalon?"

And then he saw she was crying.

"Theoris!" he said.

"So now you can say there were—two of us. Who loved you, I mean. Because I do. And it's awful. I think I'm going to die of it. In this business we can't afford falling in love. Only—I have. Tantalus' fruits. Sisyphus' stone. That's what it feels like. Tell me—she—was—a—a virgin, wasn't she?"

"Yes," Ariston said. "She was pledged to Artemis."

"Go!" Theoris said. "Get out of here, kalon!"

"But, Theoris—"

"That big ugly ox can find his way home alone. And I can't stand this any more. Looking at you, wanting you so, I mean. Only what have I got to offer? Used, dirty thing like me? By Aphrodite, I've had a hundred men. No, more. And now I—I want—"

"What, Theoris?"

"To be clean again. To be pure. To be yours. Your first girl. And you, my first boy. And my last. Forever. So get out of here, kalon! Go! And don't come back!"

"Theoris—" he began.

And it was then that they heard Thargelia scream. They stared at each other, turned at the same time toward the door. The girl, Thargelia, burst through it. She was naked, and bleeding from cuts on her shoulders, her breasts, her stomach, her thighs. There were teeth marks on her throat, her upper arm. One of her eyes was swollen shut and was turning purple.

"Save me!" she screamed. "He—he's gone mad!"

Ariston caught her by the arm, and put her behind him, just as Orchomenus came through the doorway with a knife in his hand. He was grinning with pure, diabolical joy. His eyes were glaring, wild. Something like silent laughter shook his mighty body.

"Where is she?" he bellowed. "Let me at her, boy! I'm going to carve her up slice by slice and eat her, raw! Sweetest tasting little she-goat I ever—"

Ariston didn't hesitate. He drew back his hand and slapped Orchomenus across the face. The sound of it was loud in that little room.

Orchomenus shook his head like a bull about to charge. Then his eyes cleared. He stared at Ariston, at the two girls, at the knife in his hands. Opened his brawny fist and let it drop.

"Too much wine—" he muttered. "No. That's not it. I tried to get away from the mines. They—they hit me over the head with a club. Ever since—"

"Nor that," Ariston said.

"I guess not. The heat. The fumes. The darkness. Too much pain. Or—something in me maybe. Something rotten. I—I killed a boy there. I made love to him first. Then I killed him. I don't know why. Talos is gone. *You* killed him, you pretty little patricidal bastard! Nobody to explain—"

"What?" Ariston said.

Orchomenus looked at him. Grinned like an outcast dog, a rabid wolf.

"Evil," he said.

"Come on, Orchomenus," Ariston said. "Let's go home now. You'd better lie down, rest—"

"No," Orchomenus said thickly. "I want to apologize. To this little dryad, this wood nymph. I abused her. Bad. And I'm sorry. Going to prove how sorry I am. Thargelia!"

"Yes—yes, Orchomenus?" the girl quavered.

"Get up from there. Stand up like a queen. That's it!"

Then Orchomenus knelt down and kissed her feet. Both of them. Lifted the right one and placed it on his thick, muscular neck. Turned his big head sidewise and gazed owlishly up her naked leg.

"Now I'm your slave," he said.

"Oh, get up from there, you fool!" Ariston said.

But Thargelia was staring at the big Spartan. With awe, with pride. With something very like tenderness.

"Let him stay, my lord," she whispered. "He—he won't hurt me anymore. Will you—lover?"

"On the grave of my mentor, Talos, I swear it!" Orchomenus said.

Theoris looked at Ariston wonderingly.

"He won't hurt her," Ariston said. "Before he'd break that particular oath, he'd die."

Two months from that day, Orchomenus married Thargelia. He could do that because she too was a metic, an alien resident, like himself.

Sitting next to his adoptive father at the wedding symposium, which was not the banquet itself but rather the wine drinking and general revelry that followed it, Ariston fairly seethed with helpless rage. He had been astonished at first that Timosthenes had accepted the invitation, but after that, when it came to him *why* his foster father had accepted it—largely for his, Ariston's, sake—for was not Orchomenus his best friend?—he was more than a little sick. Because the symposium was being held at the house of Alkibiades, by whose most grievous fault Oebalides had been killed. Surely Timosthenes did not know the details of that monstrous affair. He must have believed, must believe still, that his son had volunteered to drive one of Alkibiades' chariots in that fatal race. That was not unheard of, Ariston knew. Quite often the more sporting of the young Athenian aristocrats drove their own rigs, or the chariots of a friend, in the ceremonial races. One or two of them had even been known to win, though that was rare.

But the cause of Ariston's present and towering anger was a more immediate thing. He looked toward where

Orchomenus sat beside his bride. Orchomenus had a sheepish look on his face, Ariston thought. "He should!" Ariston muttered under his breath. "To lend himself to this! I wonder how in black Hades' name he met this two-faced swine?"

Timosthenes leaned toward his adopted son, his noble and stately countenance filled with concern.

"What ails you, Son?" he said.

"Nothing, Father," Ariston said.

But Alkibiades saw their heads bent together and leaped to his feet like a dancer. He came over to where Ariston and Timosthenes sat and stood there before them, swaying a little on his feet, his handsomely dissipated face wearing a bright and mocking smile.

"Is she not lovely, my little cousin?" he lisped. Alkibiades always lisped.

"Very," Ariston said dryly.

"You understand the circumstances, don't you, noble Timosthenes?" Alkibiades said. "My little cousin Thargelia is an orphan—of that branch of our family who lives on the Island of Lesbos. So it seemed to me fitting, as her kinsman, to provide this banquet and symposium in public recognition of her lineage and her chastity—"

"Generous of you, I'm sure," Timosthenes said stiffly. He didn't like Alkibiades. Although, not knowing the depth of his responsibility in the matter, Timosthenes had absolved his host of the death of Oebalides, it was hard to stomach a man who'd had anything to do with it. But the painful matter of his only son's death set aside, he'd heard too much of Alkibiades, of his perversions, his vices, his sins to be able to like him. For one thing, a man who was the nephew of the immortal statesman Perikles owed it to his rank, his position, his family's honor to behave better. For another, from Timosthenes' somewhat old-fashioned point of view, a man who'd sired as many bastards as Alkibiades was reputed to have done should be able to let boys alone.

"No more generous than you're being, sir," Alkibiades said solemnly, "for if I'm taking the place of the father poor Thargelia lost in early childhood, you, sir—"

"I am allowing Orchomenus to bring his bride to my

209

home. A gesture, merely. Call it good business. In the less than a month he has been working for me, he has produced more revenues than any other factory manager I have ever had. Besides, his bride seems a sweet child—"

"Oh, she is! She is!" Alkibiades said. "She'll be able to hang her nightdress from your window this very evening without fear or shame—"

"Alkibiades, please!" Ariston said.

"Forgive me, beautiful Ariston! For, by Eros, I love you! I didn't mean to shock you. All the world knows—"

"That it is our barbaric custom to hang the bride's nightdress from the window with the bloody stains of her lost virginity upon it in proof of her chastity. All right. But do you have to talk about it beforehand?"

"How delicate you are, kalon!" Alkibiades said. "Ah me! It's part of your charm, I suppose. More wine? Another piece of wedding cake?"

"Nothing, thank you," Ariston said.

"Then I'll leave you, especially since my company seems to please you but little."

"Do," Ariston said.

"Son," Timosthenes said after Alkibiades had sauntered away, "I know he's a monster of impiety, but did you have to be so rude to him?"

"Yes, Father, I did," Ariston said. "He's always after me to—to sleep with him. He who is married and has a child. He boasts that he lies with Sokrates, which is a dirty lie! Sokrates doesn't lie with men. He cut the tail off that beautiful dog of his because people remarked on its beauty —and he'd rather be cursed for his cruelty than ignored. His wife left him—"

"And he took her out of the divorce court in his arms, and she bides with him still. All that I know. Don't repeat gossip to me, my son; it's unmanly. What I don't understand is why you're so angry now."

"Father," Ariston said, "if I tell you—you won't spoil Orchomenus' wedding?"

"Of course not," Timosthenes said.

"Then I'll tell you! It's all a lie! She's not Alkibiades' cousin. She's nothing but a whore. All those women over there, playing the parts of relatives and friends, are either pornai, auletrides, or lesser etairai. He didn't dare invite the better-known ones like Parthenope for fear—"

He stopped suddenly, aware that Timosthenes was chuckling quietly to himself.

"A good joke!" his foster father said. "And a rich one! And I'm the butt of it, am I not? The wedding procession led by the flute players and the torch bearers, conveying this poor little refugee from a porneia to my house! The noble knight Timosthenes granting solemn honors to a whore! Ha! Took brains to think of this one, Son. Rich! Tell me, does Orchomenus know? That she's a porna, I mean?"

"Yes, Father," Ariston said. "He—he loves her sincerely. He thinks that his love will redeem her, and—"

"Then it's all right. I'll go through with it," Timosthenes said. "I do wish he had waited, though. Even among the metics there are fair maids and chaste."

"You'll have to find me such a one when it's time for me to wed," Ariston said. "I can't marry a citizeness either, you know."

"That fool law!" Timosthenes snorted. "The most idiotic thing Perikles ever did! Proved it himself, when he met Aspasia. Divorced his wife, went to live with that dyed-blonde hussie, in spite—"

"Father," Ariston said, "didn't you just tell me that gossip's unmanly?"

"True. But the point worries me. I've tried every way I know to obtain Athenian citizenship for you—"

"Except to let me go to war," Ariston said.

"I'd do that if it would do any good. But since so many metics have grown wealthy and influential, envy has her say! Even if you captured Sparta single-handed, the Assembly wouldn't grant you citizenship. Besides, the risk's too great. You're Lakedaemonian. If they took you prisoner, they'd consider you a traitor and torture you to death. So, forget your warlike valor! But this law *is* a sore spot with me. I want no Syrian slut's blood flowing through the veins of my grandsons!"

"Would you settle for an Egyptian, Father?" Ariston said

solemnly. "I like their swart skins. Or an Ethiopian? So velvety black and glistening, like splendid mares. Or a Scythian? I love the way their eyes slant—"

"Oh, stop plaguing me, Boy! You can find Hellenic maids from every other polis in Hellas among the metics. Only, who knows anything about their backgrounds?"

"What do you know of mine, Father?" Ariston said.

"Enough. Tell me—do you have lovers among this rabble? *That* lissome little creature who's devouring you with her eyes, for instance?"

"I know her," Ariston said quietly. "Her name is Theoris. But I'm not her lover. I made the mistake of refusing her, so now she fancies she's in love with me. She comes to Parthenope for lessons twice a week to make herself more cultured. She thinks I don't like her because she's ignorant."

"Is that why?" Timosthenes said.

"No. She just doesn't interest me. None of them do—not even Parthenope really. It's strange. I keep looking for a girl—who's dead, someone like the Phryne I lost. But there's no hope for that, I suppose—"

"None. I adopted you because you looked like Oebalides. And it turns out that you're nothing like him. Nothing at all, Zeus be praised. Ariston—that boy. Who is he?"

"I don't know. I've never seen him before."

"The way he's looking at you, anyone would think—"

"He might as well stop it then," Ariston said. "You know how I feel about that."

"Strange your beloved Sokrates isn't here," Timosthenes said.

"No, it isn't. He's away—at the front, Father. I pray Zeus that his life be spared!"

"Humphf! Fine soldier that windy old fool will make!"

Ariston whirled upon his foster father.

"The best. Absolutely the best. Didn't you know that, Father? At Potidaea, in the fifty-eighth year after Marathon, he saved Alkibiades' life and took back the shield the Spartans had wrested from him. Ask Alkibiades, if you don't believe me! All night long he alone of the whole Athenian army held his position against a host of foes. He was awarded the prize for valor, but he surrendered it to Alkibiades to encourage our swinish host to virtue."

"Fat lot of good it did, then. Although people say they're lovers—"

"Lies! Gossip! Sokrates doesn't lie with men! And last month, at Delium, he saved Xenophon's life too when he fell from his horse—and you know what a hero Xenophon is. Ask him when he gets back. Sokrates was the last Athenian to quit the field. And when they praised him for it, he made a jest of his valor, saying that it was his ugly face that turned the Lakedaemonian hearts to stone."

"All right, all right. I know how devoted you are to your mentor. Maybe he's not the pernicious teacher of atheism men say he is. I myself have seen him sacrificing upon the high altars. Still—"

He stopped short for Theoris stood before them. She was lovely. The more so because she wore almost no paint or rouge.

"Ariston—" she breathed.

"This is my father, Theoris. Don't shame me before him," Ariston said.

The wedding procession wound its way through the streets toward Timosthenes' house, making all the night loud with revelry. In the midst of it all, Ariston felt someone touch his arm and whirled.

"I told you, Theor—"

But it wasn't Theoris. It was the handsome boy who had been staring at him at the banquet in Alkibiades' house.

"My name is Danaus, son of Pandoros, and I should like to be your friend. In fact, I'm afraid I've fallen in love with you, Ariston," he said.

Ariston started to say something sharp, cutting, and cruel, but suddenly he couldn't. The boy, Danaus, was too —open. Too innocent really. There was something frank about him, an air of true arete, of nobility even.

Ariston put his hand on his shoulder.

"My friend you can be, I think," he said slowly, "but my lover, never."

"Why not?" Danaus said.

"Call upon me at noon tomorrow, and I'll explain it to you," Ariston said.

That next morning, when he arose and left the house for the palaestra—where he practiced the heaviest kind of wrestling, and even lifted great stones in an effort to destroy his body's beauty by weighting it with bulging muscle, thus making it both repulsive and a little clownish to the refined Athenian taste, since a gentleman should never have the gross thews of a brute slave—Ariston saw something fluttering from an upper window. He stopped and stared at it.

It was Thargelia's nightdress, stained with enough gore to drown the Trojan hosts. Alkibiades had thoughtfully provided the happy couple with a live chicken from which Orchomenus had been able to draw most convincing evidences of virginity.

What in our lives is not farce? Ariston thought, and fled.

# CHAPTER THIRTEEN

ARISTON FELT DANAUS' HARD YOUNG HAND slow suddenly, then stop just between his shoulder blades in the act of rubbing in the oil. He frowned. Hadn't he cured Danaus of those tendencies after all? Couldn't his new young friend be trusted to give him a rubdown before a wrestling match without—

He turned and looked at Danaus. But the boy wasn't looking at Ariston's naked body. Instead, he was gazing across the palaestra. Ariston followed his gaze and saw Theoris standing there. Even from that distance, he could see that her eyes were sick with longing. He didn't like the way she was looking at him. It made him conscious that he was naked. She shouldn't have looked at his body like that in public. It was a shameful thing to so openly show desire.

Then he became conscious of the look in Danaus' eyes, as the handsome boy watched Theoris. But he couldn't decipher Dan's look either, at least not at first. It wasn't anything so simple as lust. No—it was rather like confusion, compounded by shame. Then he knew. Quite suddenly, he knew.

"Want to tell me about it, Dan?" he said.

"Ariston I—Charon drown my wicked soul in the Black Waters—I've—"

"You've what?" Ariston said.

"I—I've betrayed you. With—her," Danaus said.

Ariston threw back his head and laughed. The pure, delighted sound of it caused his opponent in the pankratieon that was about to begin to lift his head from where he lay face down on another rubbing table and to stare at him. Ariston was very fond of his friendly foeman, especially since he, Autolykos, son of Lykon, had no trace of

215

effeminacy about him at all despite his great beauty, fully equal to Ariston's own.

Autolykos turned away from his trainer—the famous professional wrestler who, by a simple coincidence, was also named Ariston, so that when he deigned to show Ariston a fall or two, the resulting confusion delighted the wits, who roared out: "Look! Ariston's breaking Ariston's legs!" and other such nonsense—and started across the palaestra.

Then he grinned mockingly.

"I say—Ariston, how about making little Theoris the prize, winner take all?" he said.

"Can't. She's not mine—not that she ever was," Ariston said. "You'd have to fight Dan, here, in that case."

"Dan's no good in a bout," Autolykos yawned. "He'd have to bring his brother Brimos along. Or Chalcodon. I say, Ariston, did you ever wrestle Chalcodon? He just loves to be hurt. Every time you hit him, he squeals: 'Oh, darling, do that again!'"

Ariston looked at Danaus then.

"You were right," Danaus said sadly. "There's nothing worse. I guess I couldn't see it because both my father and my brother Chalcodon are that way. Thank Zeus, Brimos isn't. But even so, he's a filthy swine. Ariston, about Theoris—"

"Forget it. You know she's nothing to me. For Herakles' sake, Dan, rub in that oil!"

After Danaus had finished rubbing him down, and the second Ariston had done the same for Autolykos, the two young athletes strolled together to the sand pit. There they lay down in the warm sand and rolled. Afterward they powdered each other's bodies with the sand, for the purpose of oiling was to make the muscles supple rather than the skin slippery, though of course oiling incidentally did that too. But it was considered a point of honor to sand one's self after oiling and thus afford one's opponent a decent grip.

As they walked back together to the wrestling ground, Ariston saw two new spectators had arrived.

"Oh, Hades!" he said with feeling.

Autolykos grinned at him.

"So you know Kritias too?" he said.

"No," Ariston said, "it was Alkibiades I was swearing at. The other one's Kritias then? Who's he?"

"Charmides' uncle. We call him old Hot Hands. Always feeling a fellow up. Ugh! Beastly creature. Know what Alkibiades did to him?"

"Obliged him, I'd imagine," Ariston said drily.

"No. Alkibiades isn't queer. He only pretends to be— Athena in her wisdom alone knows why. It was the richest joke of the year. He promised Kritias an assignation with me, and arranged it so Kritias had to come into the room without lighting a candle. But he'd brought the etaira Laïs there first, and had her there waiting stark naked in the bed. And when old Hot Hands' tactile sense showed him she was female, you know what he did?"

"No, what?" Ariston said.

"Puked his guts up," Autolykos said.

"He's *that* bad?" Ariston said wonderingly.

"Worse than that. He's queerer than a lead obol. Are you ready now?" Autolykos said.

Autolykos won the first fall; Ariston, the second. Autolykos was much more skillful than he was; but, Ariston felt now, he was catching up. Neither of them tried to hurt the other; or rather, more exactly, they did their best not to. For the pankratieon, when seriously engaged in, was absolutely murderous. Unlike simple wrestling, one was allowed to use one's fists, one's feet, the edges of one's hands; and at least a dozen of a trained pankratist's blows were instantly lethal, if struck home. Both of them had witnessed the tragic occasion when a slave in the house of Charmides, son of Glaucon, had suddenly gone mad and run amok with a meat cleaver in his hands. On that occasion, the trainer and professional pankratist, Ariston, who had been for many years in the employ of that great house, leaped upon the poor deranged devil from behind and killed him with his bare hands.

So their caution was necessary, for a small error of judgment could have been the cause of a crippling injury, or even death, to one or the other of them. The professional wrestler, Ariston, watched both Autolykos and the boy Ariston worriedly. Of all the spectators, only he knew how truly dangerous the pankratieon was.

To the others, it was oddly like a Dionysian dance, wild and free and stunningly graceful. Autolykos would aim a seemingly murderous blow with his fist, and Ariston would catch it on his forearm, flick it aside, its power gone. Or Ariston would lash out with a kick sure to disembowel Lykon's son; and Autolykos would leap away, seize Ariston's ankle, jerk his leg high, and tumble him unceremoniously upon his back. Every time Ariston won a round, as he did about once out of every three falls, Kritias cheered and clapped his hands. So did Alkibiades, but with more restraint.

Then it happened: Ariston failed to twist his head aside in time, and a grazing blow from Autolykos' iron fist opened a cut above his eyes. It was of no importance, but it bled freely. Ariston leaped in, shaking his head to clear it, but as he did so Theoris saw the blood upon his face.

She screamed wildly, terribly. At the sound of it Ariston half-turned, so that the second blow that Autolykos had aimed with terrific force, sure that as always Ariston would duck under it, or block it with his forearm, landed flush upon his unprotected jaw. His knees buckled under him; he sprawled out unconscious upon the ground.

At once Theoris was upon him, her anguished terror lending her feet the winged sandals of Hermes. She hurled herself down beside him, lifted his inert head in her arms, covering his dirty, oily, sweaty, bloody face with open-mouthed kisses, so that only the contact of his flesh against her lips muffled momentarily her demented screaming.

Kritias was but a step behind her. He stood there above them glaring down at that pitiful sight. He opened his mouth, and his words hissed out like serpents striking.

"Let go of him, whore!" he spat. "You'll strangle him or poison him with your filthy mouth!"

Danaus stared at Kritias. Unlike Ariston, he knew him well, for Kritias was of his father Pandoros' and his brother Chalcodon's circle. Before, he had admired Kritias for the brilliant poet, playwright, intellectual, icily resolute politician that the tall homosexual was. But now he saw only the ugliness of deviate passion, saw the bitter, bottomless hatred that Kritias felt for every woman born.

218

Felt even for poor tender Theoris, whom he, Danaus, loved.

Then he leaped in and shouldered Kritias aside. He, Alkibiades, and the second Ariston bore Ariston into the gymnasium. Autolykos walked beside them, white and shaking, great tears penciling the dirt on his face.

"If I've killed him," he wept, "I'll open my veins! By Hera, I swear it!"

"You did nothing, beautiful boy," Kritias said. "It was that filthy little whore who—"

Danaus looked at Kritias then.

"You say that just once more, and I'll kill you," he said.

So it was that Ariston came back to consciousness with five heads bent worriedly above him, for naturally they hadn't let Theoris come into the gymnasium. His namesake, the trainer, was massaging the back of his neck with huge and powerful hands. Ariston's head ached dully, but under the skillful manipulation of the pankratist, the pain was rapidly going away. He smiled up at them.

"I'm all right now," he said.

"Zeus, boy! Did you give me a scare!" Autolykos said. "Thought I'd done for you!"

"Hitting me on the head?" Ariston said. "The wonder is you didn't break your hand. I say, Dan, scrape me down, will you?"

The others went out into the palaestra and waited there while Danaus and the trainer scraped the dirty oil and sand from Autolykos' and Ariston's bodies with the crescent-shaped strigils, and reoiled them with a lighter, more fragrant oil. By the time they'd done, Ariston felt very nearly all right again, except for a sore and swollen jaw and a lingering dull headache. He and Autolykos dressed, which was a matter of pulling on their chitons and looping a length of cord about their waists. Then they came back out into the exercise grounds, Autolykos keeping a worried grip on Ariston's arm.

"I'm all right, truly, Autolykos," Ariston said, "so turn me loose. I'm to lunch with Dan, and after that I have a thousand things to do. Say, why don't you come and eat with us?"

"Can't," the young wrestler said. "I have to break bread with Kleinas—Alkibiades' cousin, you know. He's sticky enough, but at least he keeps his hands to himself. I say, you do look all right now. Solid marble, that dome of yours, thank Zeus! Chaire, Ariston, Dan. Tumble Theoris for me, whichever one of you is at her now. And when you're both sick of her, just let me know."

"The brute!" Danaus almost wept. "He doesn't know, can't understand—"

Ariston stared at him.

"Why Dan, you're in love with her!" he said.

"Yes I am," Danaus said miserably. "Fat lot of good that does me!"

"I'll talk to her," Ariston said. "I'll tell her—"

But that was as far as he got, because both Alkibiades and Kritias were blocking his path.

"Will you have lunch with me, beautiful Ariston?" Kritias said. "I'll order a beaker of Diapras to cool your aching head—"

"No, thank you," Ariston said.

"Why not?" Kritias said.

"I'm otherwise engaged," Ariston said.

"With that little wench?" Kritias said, jerking his head to where poor Theoris still stood, a little way off, devouring Ariston with her eyes.

"Perhaps," Ariston said coldly.

"I just don't understand it!" Kritias said. "Women! With their smell of curdled goat's cheese and spoiled sardines, how you young fellows can—"

"No, you couldn't understand it, could you?" Ariston said. "And you never will, the gods pity you!"

"I'd rather that you pitied me, beautiful Ariston," Kritias said, "enough, say, to sup with me one night—alone."

Then he put out his arm and let it fall languidly across Ariston's shoulder.

Which was a mistake. Ariston had undergone six months of utter revolting hell at the hands of creatures such as this. Blind, unthinking rage flamed behind his eyes. He caught Kritias' wrists and whirled. Using his hard, well-muscled young body as a fulcrum, he sent the poet, playwright, brilliant intellectual, total homosexual cartwheeling

220

through the air to measure his length five rods away upon the ground.

Kritias got to his feet without a word and scuttled away with a noticeable limp. Then for the first time, Alkibiades spoke.

"You shouldn't have done that, Ariston," he said.

"Why not?" Ariston snapped.

"Because Kritias never forgets an insult or an injury," Alkibiades said.

"So?" Ariston said.

"You underestimate him," Perikles' nephew said, "just as you underestimate me." He looked around him, his dark eyes somber. "I'm going to rule this polis one day," he said.

"As strategos autokrator as your uncle Perikles did?" Ariston said.

"If you Athenians know what's good for you—yes. If not, as tyrannos!" Alkibiades said and, turning on his heel, he left them there.

Ariston stood there, staring after the gilded youth.

"I think he means that," he mused. "Strange—I've never seen him serious before—"

"Alkibiades is a man of many parts," Danaus said slowly, "and that he chooses to show the world a clown, an effeminate fop, a lisping fool is—perhaps—strategy. He'll do what he said. And you *have* underestimated him. You and I and all the world."

"Ariston—" Theoris whispered suddenly.

"Yes, Theo?" Ariston said, not unkindly.

"If—if he'd killed you, it would have been my fault!" she said, her voice thick with horror. "I attracted your attention so that you—"

"Forget it, Theo," Ariston said.

"May I—walk with you a little?" Theoris said.

"Walk with Dan," Ariston said. "Aren't you lovers now?"

"No!" Theoris spat. "He—bought an hour of my time. The use of—of this mindless carcass that had neither my heart nor my spirit in it on the occasion. Why not? That's my trade. You should understand how little it means—who escaped from it yourself!"

"As you'll escape one day," Ariston said.

"No. Never. There was only one door out, and you slammed it in my face," Theoris said. "So I must be a whore forever—"

"You're not!" Danaus said. "You're—"

"An etaira. A high-class whore, instead of a cheap, pawed-over porna. A difference of degree, my dear Danaus! In any event, never a chaste, respected wife. Or would *you* care to marry me?"

"Yes," Danaus said. "Now. This minute."

"Don't be a fool, Dan!" Ariston said.

"No, Dan," Theoris whispered. "Darling, darling Dan; don't be a fool! Never, as I do, love where love isn't given back. Don't marry a whore. Don't marry this cheap little slut your best friend despises! Don't marry this mangy little bitch groveling on her belly at his feet, licking the buskin that kicks her! Oh, no! That never!"

"Theo," Ariston said reproachfully, "that's not why."

"Then why?" Theoris said.

"My heart was—butchered, a long time ago," Ariston said, "hacked into pieces, torn—"

"To bits by a pack of mountain she-wolves. Along with your love. Along with—Phryne. The guts pulled out of her ripped belly by the dogs, her legs lopped off, her—"

"Theo!" Ariston said. "In Artemis' name, who told you that?"

"Orchomenus. Or rather he told it to Thargelia—in between spells of beating her almost to death, coming home drunk and burning her with hot pokers, slicing cuts into her everywhere he can reach. He's mad, of course. But then, who isn't? I am—over you. Ariston, tell me—swear by —by her! By Phryne—swear on her tomb that it's not— this life I was forced into that makes you not love me! Tell me that if your heart could forget—that—that horror, you'd love me a little! Tell me that, Ariston. Swear it, though you lie!"

"I don't have to lie. I do love you, Theo—as much as I'm capable of love, which is very little. And I don't despise your life or blame you for it. Upon what grounds could an ex-pornos look down upon an etaira? Believe me, as much love as I've got in me, you already have."

"Fat lot that is! And I don't believe you! After all, you—"

222

you lie with that ancient chemist's shop counterfeit of youth, that old witch Parthenope!" Theoris said.

"Because I don't love her," Ariston said softly, "and because it's meaningless, even to her. A convenience, Theo. With you, it wouldn't be—for either of us. I couldn't make use of you, dear girl. Not ever. To me, you're far too real."

"I thank you for that, at least," Theoris said. "Then it isn't true that you're going to marry Dan's little sister, when she's old enough?"

"Chryseis?" Ariston said. "Would you believe that I've never so much as even seen her, Theoris, as often as I've been in Dan's house?"

"It's the custom here," Danaus said stiffly. "I've explained it to you a dozen times, Ariston! It's nothing against you. An unmarried girl can never receive male guests— only her betrothed, under supervision, once her father has seen fit to find a worthy husband for her."

"Which is why so many of us drift into the street, the way you treat us!" Theoris said. "But, even so, whether you've seen her or not, Ariston, my love, I was told that the noble Timosthenes actually got Dan's simpering old pervert of a father out of the bathhouses long enough to—Say, Dan, I've been meaning to ask you! How'd your mother ever get children: tie him down? Or did she just hang the keroesses on him?"

"Theo!" Ariston said.

"Zeus' own truth! Next to him, Kritias looks like Herakles. As I was saying, with no apologies to your alleged father, Danaus, the talk is that the betrothal's already arranged. Everyone knows old Pandoros has spent his last obol on the boys in Gourgos' and Polyxenus' places; and your adoptive father is awfully rich, Ariston, so—"

"So," Ariston said gravely, "Chryseis, by my reckoning, is not quite twelve years old."

"Which means she has a year to go. Athenian girls are always wed at thirteen, Ariston—for the very simple reason that nobody ever figured out a way to keep them virgins after that—"

"You've a spiteful tongue, Theoris!" Danaus said. "Don't judge every girl by yourself. I—for one—would be happy

223

to have Ariston as a brother-in-law. The real question is whether he'd be happy, married to Chrys—"

"Why not?" Ariston said.

"She has a temper like all the fiends in Tartarus," Danaus said ruefully, "and, if you're being most indulgent, you could call her plain. Actually she looks like Hecate's great-granddaughter. None of us is much for looks, but poor Chrys—"

"Now you interest me," Ariston said. "Have you ever thought of all the things my so-called beauty has cost me? If I ever marry, I'm going to take such a bride as will make it impossible to inflict upon my son the kind of looks I have, the kind that all my life has kept a pack of panting perverts baying at my heels. And anyhow, I've never seen why a man should give a fig for a woman's looks, as long as her mind's alert, and her heart is kind."

"Great Hera, save us!" Theoris said. "I knew it! I knew it! All you need is family, a good name, and never to have let some winged foot pry your knees apart! So now—"

"So now, nothing," Ariston said.

"What do you mean—nothing?" Theoris moaned. "This time next year—"

"I'll attend dear little Chryseis' wedding—to someone else," Ariston said. "You're forgetting one vital detail, Theo—"

"Which is?"

"I'm a metic. A wealthy metic, if you please, but still—an alien. And you know what the law says."

"Oh!" Theoris breathed. "You can *never* marry a citizeness! I hadn't thought of that! O great Hera, I thank you!"

"You're a citizeness," Danaus pointed out wrily.

"He doesn't *have* to marry me!" Theoris said. "All he has to do is to climb into bed with me, and stay there—all the rest of my life. Acknowledge our brats, of course. Legitimize them. But apart from that—Ariston! Where are you going?"

"Into this house. You both can come in too, if you like. Aristophanes won't mind."

"The comic poet?" Danaus said. "Is *he* a friend of yours?"

"Sort of. In a way. Of my adoptive father—yes. They

both hold the same ultraconservative views. But at the moment, I need Aristophanes' help. I'm going to ask him for a part in his next comedy. He pays well, and I could use the money. . . ."

"You!" Dan hooted. "You need money! Badly enough to become a comic hypokritos—an actor. By Pluto, Ariston! I don't believe that! All you have to do is ask Timosthenes for anything up to a whole talent and he'll—"

"Refuse me—for this. I want to open a factory of my own. And that he's dead set against. Says it's no work for a gentleman. To own them, as he does—fine. But to run one myself? Never! I'm sick of this parasite's life. Tutors and fine horses and idleness and pleasure, while beyond the long walls men are dying. I've had to watch Sokrates march away to war, risk the finest mind the ages have ever seen against idiot Spartan brutes—like I was before the gods granted me the boon of being captured and brought to Athens. I can't stand being useless, Dan! And yet, being precisely and exquisitely useless is the noble Timosthenes' idea of a gentleman! Not even his experience with Oebalides taught him how wrong that is! And it isn't enough to defend all Athens stands for with my body—what one hoplite can do in the ranks is little enough, Zeus knows—what I want to do is a greater thing: to help forge the weapons that will defend civilization against barbarism!"

"Civilization?" Danaus said mockingly. "You call *us* civilized?"

"Yes. With all your faults, yes. The day I met Euripides, I found that out. There's intelligence for you! His mind's as keen as Sokrates', and his verse! I've been more drunken upon it than from any wine! I tell you—"

"He's a misogynist. He hates women," Theoris said.

"And you, my sweet, if you really think that, are a fool. Now come in, will you?" Ariston said.

Aristophanes greeted them kindly. He was a small dark man, with somber, haunted eyes, and a face that smiled but with great difficulty. Ariston wondered why that was. On the many occasions that he'd rowed out to the island of Salamis in the harbor, where Euripides lived in a huge cave as well and comfortably furnished as any house, he'd always found the great tragic poet full of restrained mischief, his small eyes twinkling with fun, and displaying in his talk a dry and mordant wit that never appeared in his tragedies. While this little man, who wrote the most outrageously funny pieces the world had ever seen, was sad. Truly sad.

"I've a treat for you, Ariston, my boy," he said. "I've just finished some lines for my new comedy, *The Clouds.* I'd like you to read them for my guests. You read so well, you know. I've a part for you in it. The student. It's only a denteragoites, a bit player's kind of part; but it does have some good lines. By the way, who're these friends of yours? Danaus, son of Pandoros? Yes, I know your father. I once made a comic sketch of him—a spicy bit I've never dared to use on the stage for fear he'd sue me. And this little lady?"

"Theoris," Ariston said gravely, "who, if I ever decide to marry, will be my intended."

"I don't need to write good lines for you," Aristophanes mocked. "You make them up yourself! By the way, Sophokles is here—the lordly tragedians condescend to visit us lowly jokesmiths from time to time. And you, my child"— Aristophanes bowed ironically to Theoris—"will please him. He refuses to admit he's older than Night and Chaos, both of whom existed before Zeus was. Come in, come in! O Sophokles—look upon this fair child! A feast for your lecherous old eyes, isn't she?"

Theoris stood there, staring at the great tragic poet. Sophokles sighed a little.

"It's a pity that this maker of bawdy jests doesn't lie," he said, "for seeing you, child, I could pray to the gods to remove twenty years from my age."

"You—you don't need to cut anything, sir," Theoris whispered. "You're old, but that doesn't matter. In all my life, I've never seen so beautiful a man! Not even Ariston, though maybe he will be when the years have rubbed him smooth and polished him like you."

And looking at Sophokles, seeing his high-piled snowy ringlets, the great white cascade of his beard, his lofty forehead, his fine, high-colored, totally unlined face of a benevolent Zeus, Ariston realized that the little etaira spoke the simple truth. No man in all Athens, of any age whatsoever, was physically more beautiful than Sophokles was.

"Thank you, child," the poet said. "Come, sit here at my feet. I adore youth—because I've lost it. And you—you're like Antigone—"

"Antigone?" Theoris said wonderingly. "Who was she, sir?"

"Why," Sophokles said, "she was love—the thing itself, I mean. As you are, child. For

> Surely you swerve from its even course
> To crash headlong into ruin
> The just man's consenting heart;
> And here you've made anger
> Flash like a blade
> Between a father and his son.
> Because no one wins at the last of it,
> But you, Love.
> Your girl child's glance works
> The will of heaven,
> Granting the final joy only to her
> Who forever mocks us,
> Aphrodite, the goddess
> Immune to pity. . . .

"And I—I'm all that?" Theoris said. "All those beautiful, terrible things?"

"Yes, child, you are," the poet said.

Of course Ariston had no way of knowing what the consequences of that meeting between Theoris and Sophokles were going to be, but he found it strange and troubling even then. So much so that as he read Aristophanes' bawdy verses, the comic poet's merciless attack upon poor defenseless Sokrates, in which he accused the philosopher of running a hard-thinking shop where his students buried their noses in the mud to study secrets deep as Tartarus while their buttocks, waving in the air, busily engaged in deciphering the mysteries of astronomy, his anger at Aristophanes' cruelty—for it is the comic poet who is truly cruel, while the tragic one is kind—was muted by it.

"You see?" Aristophanes said. "You do the student wondrously well. You'll take the part, won't you? Ever since I saw you play the role of Hektor in old poison-pen Euripides' *Hecuba*—your father was choregos that year, wasn't he? Only reason old Vinegar-and-Bitters let you have the part—I realized what a fine hypokritos you naturally are. Of course, you don't need the money, but that doesn't matter. You can always spend it on little dolls like this one and—"

"But I *do* need the money," Ariston said.

Sophokles looked up from where he was stroking Theoris' dark hair, for she had let it go back to its natural shade ever since Ariston had told her he hated the lie implicit in her bleaching it.

"In Zeus's name, why?" he said.

Then Ariston told them. He spoke slowly at first, but with growing verve and fire, shaping his dream into words: that somehow he should become worthy of the great polis he'd come to love, this Athens—broad of mind and spirit enough to let Aristophanes call her citizens blackguards to their faces and have them take it in good part, where Euripides could defy and deny the very gods and enjoy a respectful hearing, where Sophokles could chant the old, dark-haunted terrors of Oedipus' line and gain the Dionysian prize time and again—where genius was honored, respected, loved, instead of silenced, murdered, crushed as it was in his native Sparta.

"Only," he said at last, "I can't make my father see what I mean. He wants me to be a fashionable young gentleman, not knowing his terms are synonymous with an idle, effeminate fop. So I have to get around him. I have to demonstrate to him that I can. The gods witness that I've tried everything. I've posed naked for Alkamenes, the sculptor. Painted scenery for both of you. Teetered around the stage on high boots, those kothornoi built up in the soles to make a hypokritos look taller, with a mask uglier than Hades on my face, and a brass mouthpiece in my mouth so that even the plebeians in obol seats could hear me—though both of you said you hired me for my beauty! Fat lot of it showed, with the onkos projecting from the top of my head, and the tragic mask covering my face."

228

"You're a good actor for all that, my boy," Sophokles said.

"I hope so. I should like to be good at something. I've even tried my hand at mechanics. I designed new periaktoi for Euripides—triangles with different scenes painted on each face that can be turned to shift the action half around the world in a trice. I also made him a new kind of ekklema, lighter and easier to roll out, to show the tableaux of what has gone before, or what the law won't permit shown on the stage—"

"Murder and incest and torture. The stuff of life," Sophokles said. "Go on, my boy."

"I even tried to make a new kind of mechane—"

"To let the god down on ropes to arrange everything?" Aristophanes quipped. "Athena witness how old Euripides loves that lame trick!"

"He doesn't need it," Ariston said. "He's a great poet—as great as either of you. Only all my efforts weren't—and aren't—enough. I need more than a talent to start the smallest kind of metalworking shop. And I can't earn that much money, no matter what I do."

Then it was that Aristophanes made his calm, considered, perfectly logical suggestion:

"Why don't you borrow it from your friend Orchomenus? Men say he's as rich as Croesus now."

Ariston stared at the poet.

"Why—why I never thought of that!" he said. "I'll do it! I'll ask him tomorrow! Pay him what interest he will—"

Hearing his voice, Theoris shuddered suddenly. There was a sound behind it—like the beat of ominous wings, like the whir of a hard-spun wheel.

Furies' wings.

Fates' wheel.

But none of them knew that then. Mere mortals never do.

# CHAPTER FOURTEEN

BEFORE HE HAD GOTTEN HALFWAY up the little rise leading to the metalworkers' quarter at the foot of the hill of the Kolonos Agoraios, beneath the soaring temple of the blacksmith god, Orchomenus came down to meet him. Which was odd. No, it was more than odd. There was no way on earth that his former comrade-in-arms could have seen him coming up the rise from the office at the back of the ergasteria, or, for that matter, even from the doorway of the factory. It wasn't the first one in that street, and its view downward toward the residential districts was blocked by the other shops before it.

A coincidence? Ariston didn't believe it. He knew Orchomenus far too well by then.

"How did you know I was going to visit you today?" he said.

Orchomenus grinned at him like a shaggy wolf.

"Oh, I'm a soothsayer!" he said.

"And I'm Dionysus. Come on, Orchomenus, how did you?"

"Spies," Orchomenus said calmly. "I keep all the ways leading to the shops infested with them, to warn me when the tax gatherer's coming. Or, for that matter, when Old Eagle Beak is—"

"Or when I am," Ariston said.

"Right. So that I can receive my lords and masters with the proper unctuousness and fawning, doglike servility. After all, you've made a rich man of me, chiefly by not watching me too closely."

"By which you mean you rob us blind," Ariston said.

"Of course! With all the opportunities you give me, my sterling honesty rather bends under the strain. By Eros,

230

you're a lovely! Did I ever tell you that you get prettier every day? Brings out all the ancient pederast in me."

"Oh, Orchomenus, for Zeus' sake! Look, let's go up to the factory and—"

"No. Too noisy. I'm used to it, but you couldn't even hear yourself think. What brings you up here? Don't tell me you were filled with a sudden yearning for the sight of my manly beauty!"

Ariston stared at him. Then he said it flatly:

"I need money. A great deal of money. A whole talent. No, two."

Orchomenus' wonderfully ugly face was filled suddenly with real concern.

"You're in trouble, boy? Done something that let the sykophantos get their hooks into you? Had yourself delivered into some married woman's bed, sewn up in a new mattress? Alkibiades did that once. Nearly suffocated, he says."

"Pity he didn't," Ariston said. "Besides, you know well I'm not fool enough to get my throat cut over used goods!"

"Well, it can't be a boy. Even if you seduced a knight's son, easing the old man's bruised feelings wouldn't cost *that* much. And you don't even like boys—except maybe Danaus. And him you can have for nothing."

"Orchomenus, for the love of Artemis!"

"Meaning I've a filthy mind? That's what makes it so accurate. Anyhow, tell old Uncle Orchomenus what in black Hades' name you have done that it's going to cost you two whole talents to get out of?"

"It isn't anything I've done. Rather, it's what I want to do," Ariston said.

Orchomenus stared at him.

"Tell me about it," he said.

"Hmmnn," Orchomenus said. "So you want to open an ergasteria of your own, because you're sick of living like a Persian prince, having gorgeous things like Parthenope and Theoris lie down for you every time you snap your fingers, being waited on hand and foot, having the blessed boon of idleness, your lovely hide carefully kept unperforated by attrakos, javelin, sword, and spear—because, I

231

repeat, of this absolutely miserable existence you're forced to endure, you—"

"I don't think you ever really listened to Talos, my father, not to mention Sokrates," Ariston said. "And my existence *is* miserable. The life of a parasite always is. You, at least, are doing something useful. You're furnishing Athens with the sinews of war. A man has to live with himself, Orchomenus. And I can't. Not like this. I simply can't."

"Look, Ariston, this is hardly the time to start an arms factory. Why, the peace negotiations are going full tilt! I wouldn't be surprised if any day now—"

"Even if it comes, the peace won't last," Ariston said. "It cannot. There's no sound basis for it."

"There you're right. This miserable war has been going on for nine full years now; and the only thing that would truly end it would be for Athens or Sparta to be taken and destroyed. Which isn't bloody likely in either case. Well, I don't have to tell you that an ergasteria's a manmade imitation of Tartarus; you've seen them often enough. And this idea of yours of using the new metalworking techniques invented by your friend Alkamenes, the sculptor, has merit. Your little shop could be the experimental branch for the whole combine. Hades take me, I like the idea! Two talents? That's the rub. I'm richer in debts than in cash, as always. But I'll raise them somehow. Give me two weeks, say?"

"All right. I'll come back in two weeks then," Ariston said.

"Not here. Come to my house," Orchomenus said.

The night the two weeks were up, Ariston went to Orchomenus' new and pretty little house. But Orchomenus wasn't there. Only Thargelia was. Even by lamplight, Ariston could see the mottled bruises on her arms, the scars of old cuts, whip marks, burns. She was great with child, and her eyes were animal-like and dull. She didn't even seem to remember who Ariston was.

"He's not here," she said tiredly. "But then, he never is. Try the house of Kritias, son of Kallaeschros, or Alkibiades'. He'll be at one or the other. If he isn't in a porneia, or a bathhouse. That's all he ever does—spend his money on whores and boys. People think we're rich, but we're not. And I'm pregnant again. Lost the other two. He got drunk and beat me, so I lost them."

"I'm sorry," Ariston whispered. The phrase was lame, but he couldn't think of a better one. In Hera's name, why was Orchomenus the way he was? Because he'd suffered in the mines? Other men had been enslaved, suffered. Talos had. I have, Ariston thought. And yet—

He left the house, and mounting his horse, rode through the quiet streets. When he got to Kritias' house, he was confronted by a strange sight: The tall, icy homosexual stood in the street surrounded by armed guards. With him were servants bearing baggage. He smiled at Ariston mockingly, his face vulturelike in the light of the torches.

"You come too late, beautiful Ariston!" he said. "If, indeed, you've decided at long last to be kind. I go into exile —at the command of the polis. My name has been written on the ostraka, the broken pot shards—there's irony in our use of them, I think! We say this to a man that he's just as useless as a smashed pot, unfit even to be urinated into, or upon—it would seem! In other words, if I may coin a phrase, I've been ostracized!"

"Why, Kritias?" Ariston said.

"My play. The pious took it ill that I openly hold the gods but the invention of shrewd politicians, to be used as bogymen to frighten the stupid into virtue. But people always take the truth ill, don't they? Come, kalon! Get down from there and kiss me good-bye. Do that, and I'll forgive you for having tumbled me into the dirt the last time we met."

Slowly Ariston shook his head.

"I couldn't, Kritias," he said quietly. "Believe me, it isn't personal, but I simply couldn't."

"Why not?" Kritias said sharply.

Ariston smiled.

"Remember what happened when Alkibiades tricked you into lying with the courtesan Laïs?" he said.

"Ugh! Rather! I threw up. Never could stand the smell of women. Even when they're clean—as Laïs was—that lingering fishy odor of theirs strikes through all their perfumes. A peculiarity of mine, I'll admit. I was born with too keen an olfactory sense."

"A defect I share," Ariston said.

"Then?" Kritias said delightedly.

"Only it's the coprolitic smell of sodomites that offends my nostrils," Ariston said. "Were I to kiss you, I'd respond exactly as you did to Laïs. In short, I'd heave."

Kritias stood there in the light of the torches, surrounded by his guards.

"This makes twice you've offended me, Ariston," he said quietly. "I pray you remember that."

"Why?" Ariston said, "Why should I bother?"

"Because one day your life may hang upon my favor," Kritias said.


Before he even knocked upon the door of Alkibiades' house, Ariston could hear the noise of the revelry within. He stopped short, his temples throbbing with outrage for it was no more than a little month ago that the chaste and pious Hipparete, Alkibiades' wife, had died.

Of a broken heart, surely, Ariston thought, of the starvation diet of even such scant crumbs of his affection as he granted her.

Then he brought the huge bronze knocker down against its plate, hard.

A slave opened the door for him. The man's face was ghastly in the lamplight. He was shaking with what obviously was terror.

"Your—your name, my lord?" he quavered.

"Ariston, son of Timosthenes," Ariston said.

The slave bowed, scurried away. But he did not come back again. Instead, it was Alkibiades himself who came.

"Ariston!" he boomed out. "My poor house is honored! You haven't crossed my threshold since—since Orchomenus married that poor little slut. Come in! Come in! By Eros, you're as beautiful as ever! Not even that wispy little beard spoils you!"

Ariston hung there, rigid with shock. For Alkibiades was dressed as a woman. His face was painted; his lips, rouged. There was blue seashell powder shadowing his eyes. And there was something about the robe he wore—

Then Ariston saw what it was. The feminine dress the burly mocker had on was no ordinary woman's robe. Instead, it was the dress of an hierophant, the sacred robes of a priestess of the awful Eleusinian mysteries, those secret, unmentionable rites, sacred to the goddesses Demeter and Kore. Ariston was not a believer, but the sight offended him. As a matter of basic principle, he held that other peoples' religious beliefs had to be scrupulously respected, whether one shared them or not. And now—

Alkibiades took him by the arm. To his surprise, Ariston found that his host had a grip like iron. They went into the dining room. Upon a high throne, Orchomenus was seated, clad like Alkibiades in woman's dress. He had two pretty, effeminate boys on his right hand and his left, whose mission seemed to be to help him balance a silver basin held on his knees.

Nearly all the guests were dressed as women, except the actual women—auletrides who had been hired to enliven the banquet with their flute playing and who, unless one considered their long double flutes as sort of covering, were stark naked. Some of the guests were busy with these lissome female musicians at activities remarkably remote from flute playing, beneath the banquet tables. Others were occupied with perfumed and painted boys. But most of the guests were engaged in the game of kottabos, which consisted in draining a huge silver cup of wine to the dregs and then flinging the last drop from a considerable distance in an effort to make it fall precisely into the silver basin that Orchomenus held. That meant that Orchomenus had been chosen symposiarch, banquet master. When one of the drunken roisterers hit the basin, he would roar out the name and a wish—usually obscene—to his dearest love. The names, Ariston noted, were about equally divided between the genders.

Alkibiades pressed an enormous cup into his hand, but Ariston didn't even taste the wine. He felt a slow green surge of nausea rising to the back of his throat. Was *this* the civilization he was moving heaven and earth for a chance to defend? This riot of lust and decadence? Of course, Athens had produced great art, music, drama, poetry, beauty, was producing them still, but—

235

But who was the most popular man in Athens if not his host? Every gilded youth in town imitated Alkibiades' languid walk, his effeminate lisp. Let this high-born prince of roisterers but wear a new kind of sandal, and the first shoemaker to copy it had his fortune made. This house, which he had with false, ironic modesty called "poor" when he'd greeted Ariston, was actually a showplace, its costly luxury so ornate, so ostentatious as to violate every canon of the rather austere Hellenic taste. He kept a racing stable and when his chariots won—as they quite often did—he feasted the whole Assembly out of his personal purse. He wore the device of Eros hurling a thunderbolt on his shield, thus mockingly boasting of his victories in bisexual—or wasn't it really trisexual?—love. He outfitted triremes, served repeatedly as choregos, bearing the expenses of the drama festivals. He was the center of men's eyes to the extent that indifference toward him wasn't possible. All Athens either loved or hated him.

And yet Ariston mused now, looking at him in that outlandish, outrageous costume, at the battles of Potidaea and at Delium, his valor amounted to rashness. What's more, Sokrates loves him, so there must be some good in him, though I'll be blasted to Tartarus if I can see—

At his side, Alkibiades stood up suddenly, clapped his hands.

"Friends!" he called out. "Lovers! Let us, in honor of our new and unexpected guest, the beautiful Ariston, perform the mysteries once again!"

Ariston got up then. He couldn't be a party to blasphemy. He couldn't. Out of respect to his adoptive father, whose beliefs were very simple and very pure, he couldn't take part in this profanation of the goddesses or their mysteries.

Alkibiades clutched at his hand, but Ariston threw off his host's grip with a wrestler's practiced skill. He reached the door, plunged out into the night. But as he started to mount his horse, he heard Orchomenus bellowing his name.

He stopped, waited, trembling a little as his former comrade-in-arms came up to him.

"You're right!" Orchomenus muttered. "Get away from

here! Thessalos is going to denounce him for blasphemy. It was only a joke at first, but now it's gone too far. And kalon—"

"Yes, Orchomenus?" Ariston said sadly, seeing the paint on his friend's face, the trailing woman's dress, the rouged lips, the grotesque shadowing of his shaven beard through all the cosmetics he wore.

"Here're your two talents. Told you I'd dig them up, didn't I?" Orchomenus said.

In the three long months it took him to set up his model ergasteria, Ariston had the conviction forced upon him that there was more to Orchomenus' commercial activities than met the naked eye. During that period he was an almost daily visitor to his adoptive father's factories, seeking ideas and advice from the managers and foremen who ran them. Many of them had worked for Timosthenes for more than twenty years; yet Orchomenus, in the not quite two he had been in the noble hippêus' employ, had so won Timosthenes' confidence that he had been promoted over the heads of all of them and was now general manager of the whole combine.

Judged by the results delivered by the Spartan, he clearly deserved the promotion. Not since Timosthenes' father, the eurapatridos Telephanes, had bought three metalworking shops as an interesting speculation more than seventy years before had the concern—a whole group of eight scattered shops, employing from twenty to one hundred slaves in each, and complementing one another by the manufacture of the smaller pieces, which were assembled in the largest shop over which Orchomenus directly presided—showed such profits.

"But how does he do it, Father?" Ariston asked. "He knows nothing about metalworking except what he's learned since he came here. And yet under his management, the ergasteriae are making more money than any other shops in Athens, including those twice their size!"

Timosthenes shrugged.

"Athena in her divine wisdom alone knows, Son," he said. "Nor do I care. He delivers me my profits, which, even with what he's obviously stealing taken out, are huge.

That's good enough. No, better than good; it's excellent."

There was in this reply of Timosthenes' a whole compendium of knightly attitudes that Ariston knew better than to question by now. Aristocrats like Timosthenes gained their wealth by *owning* things: farms, factories, mines, ships, slaves; never by anything so unknightly as working personally. Even the management of the things they owned was delegated to other men. Just as the strategos Nikias earned a fortune by farming out his thousand slaves to the silver mine owners, without ever in his life so much as having visited the mines, so the noble knight Timosthenes lived in luxury on the monies paid him by other men for the use of things he owned, without troubling his head in the slightest over how, in what manner, by what procedure, his factories were run. To him, his very profitable possessions were a row of figures on parchment, delivered to his home from time to time by his managers and foremen, for in the two years Ariston had known his adoptive father, Timosthenes had not once visited the shops themselves.

For to take too obvious an interest in them would have been demeaning to a knight. It would have smacked of commercialism, mercantilism, greed—for which his lordly friends would have despised him.

But I'm nobody's hippêus! Ariston thought grimly. As a metic, no one can look down upon me for engaging in manufacturing or trade. Those are the only roads open to us. So for my own good I'd better find out how Orchomenus does it.

Which proved impossible. The other managers, hearing the Spartan's name mentioned, clamped their bearded jaws shut, and a hard look came into their eyes. Orchomenus himself parried all Ariston's questions with easy, jesting skill. And always, before he entered the shops, Ariston was met in the road before he got there, talked to, delayed. Still, when he entered them, he couldn't put his finger on anything wrong. Except, perhaps—

An ambiance. An atmosphere somehow menacing, brooding, grim. But he couldn't fathom what gave him that sensation about the shops. He couldn't at all.

In those two months, Ariston learned many things, the

most valuable of them, curiously enough, negative. Being quite remarkably intelligent, he asked a number of troublesome why's: Why do the shops have to be so small? Why must the work benches be so crowded? Wouldn't one or two large smelting furnaces be better than so many small ones? Why are the shops so dark, so poorly ventilated? Couldn't the smoke and fumes be vented out some way so that replacing the entire work force every four years because of the deaths from lung sickness might be avoided?

Whenever the answer was: "That's the way it's always been done" he rejected it out of hand. His own ergasteria grew up, large, airy, light-filled, the furnaces, the pouring molds, the tempering baths all grouped together in the center, with the work benches forming the perimeter around them next to the biggest windows Athens had ever seen. All the other shop managers and some owners too—for quite a few metics ran their own factories—came to see it. "Daft!" most of them muttered. "The boy's mad!" But one or two of the metics were open-minded enough to see the advantages of such a layout. They kept their mouths shut, resolved to copy it as soon as they could.

Ariston then began to gather his work force. He gave preference to those workers in bronze who had cast pieces for sculptors and therefore knew the lost-wax process. His next preference was for skilled freemen, whether freeborn or freed from slavery. Last of all, he bought a few highly skilled slaves. To the slaves he made the following offer:

"I will pay you the same wages as the freeman; but from those wages I will hold back the tenth part in a common fund. When, from those monies, one half of your purchase price has been accumulated, I will pardon the other half, and free you. But, on that date, I shall also dismiss those of you who have been poor workers from my employ—so see that you serve me well!"

This idea, be it said at once, wasn't Ariston's but Sokrates'. Ariston, with the memory of his own and Orchomenus' slavery burdening his heart still, would have freed his slaves at once, influenced all the more by the sullen, dull, fear- and hate-filled faces of those in his father's shops. But the ugly old philosopher, who knew men only too well, counseled him against too much generosity.

"Look you, kalon," Sokrates said. "The worst thing about slavery is the way it undermines a man's sense of personal responsibility. Free them at once, and you do them a disservice. First you've got to restore dignity to them, teach them to act wisely, dominate their passions, think for themselves. Therefore, make their freedom a goal to be earned. By the time they've earned it, they will have become once again—men."

So it was done. And on that basis it was hardly surprising that Ariston's ergasteria was successful from the first. Of course, with the fratricidal war between the city-states still smoking the skies of all Hellas with dull misery, the possibility of any arms manufactory's failing was exceedingly remote, but Ariston's enjoyed unusual success. In the first place, as an ex-Lakedaemonian hoplite, he knew arms very well indeed, so that the weapons produced under his personal supervision were of a quality that excited universal admiration. In the second, using the sculptor's lost-wax method to produce figures in low relief upon the breastplates and shields of defensive armor, he turned out not only these pieces, but also helmets, cuirasses, and greaves of such stunning beauty that all the younger hippêis, and many of the older ones as well, descended in person upon his shop loudly demanding that he outfit them completely and at once.

The very first suit of armor he made was upon Alkibiades' order. The second was for his friend Danaus.

Three months to the day after the opening of the factory, Timosthenes accepted his adopted son's invitation to visit it. Considering the fact that he hadn't visited his own in years, this was a measure of the love he bore the youth. He really didn't want to, lest it be said that he was becoming "merchantile"; but by then it was known—or at least believed—all over Athens that not one obol of his money was invested in the venture. Alkibiades hadn't scrupled to let it slip that the two talents spent in setting up the splendid new ergasteria had been loaned to Ariston by himself. And when the outraged youth descended upon Orchomenus, he found out that the nephew of Perikles hadn't lied.

"Where else could I have got two whole talents on such short notice, kalon?" Orchomenus said calmly.

"You should have had them yourself!" Ariston raged. "You've earned enough, and stolen enough on top of that to be worth ten talents by now! Why—"

"I am—in debt." Orchomenus grinned. "Look, beautiful boy, to become rich a man must possess two characteristics: the ability to earn money *and* the ability to keep it. The first I've got, as I've proved. But the second? Hades take me, boy. At picking the greediest wenches—"

"And boys!" Ariston snapped.

"And boys, my fine puritan. What's wrong with boys? As your uncle Hippolytus used to say, they never come home with a swollen belly ready to present you with a crop you never sowed. What was I saying? Oh yes, at picking the greediest wenches, the most demanding little effeminates, and the slowest horses, I'm a genius. It's all a matter of addition and subtraction. I make a lot of money, true, but granted the fact that I spend twice what I make—"

"You should stay home with Thargelia!" Ariston said.

"Ah, true. But you see, she bores me. She bores me past endurance. And when I get too bored, I can't resist tormenting her. Therefore, to avoid killing her, as I probably would if I had to put up with her whining, her hangdog expression, and her sheepdog's eyes two nights in a row, I stay away from her. But staying away is expensive. My tastes are so very refined!"

Whereupon Ariston had done the only thing he could: He went to Timosthenes and told him how he'd been tricked into taking Alkibiades' money. Even at the risk of being called mercantile, Timosthenes couldn't permit his adopted son to remain in debt to the man responsible for Oebalides' death. That same night he sent a trusted messenger with the two talents, plus the accumulated interest, to Alkibiades' house. And Alkibiades, who had been very quick at letting his own generosity be known, was very slow indeed at admitting he had been repaid. In fact, by the time Athens learned that Ariston's establishment was free and clear, Alkibiades was in exile in Sparta.

As they rode along that day through the streets of Athens on their way to Ariston's ergasteria, neither Timosthenes nor Ariston talked about shops, factories, or metalworking at all. What they were talking about, curiously enough, was girls.

For now that Ariston had clearly established himself, it occurred to Timosthenes that the next step was to find his adopted son a bride. Of course, by Athenian standards, at twenty-one, Ariston was still far too young, for the Athenians, having all the pleasures of the flesh readily available, put off marrying as long as they could and complained of matrimony's burdens ever after. But Timosthenes was oppressed by the memory of Oebalides' death. He wanted to have the reassurance of grandchildren to carry on his line as soon as possible. Therefore he determined to see Ariston wed.

But the problem itself was hellishly difficult. Under a law written by the great Perikles himself, aliens couldn't marry Athenian citizens. The ironical fact that Perikles had had to ram through the Assembly an exempting clause legitimizing his own son, Perikles II, by his union with the foreign etaira, Aspasia, helped matters not at all. The exemption was granted the great Athenian for his services to the polis and applied only to that one case.

What was worse, naturalization didn't exist. Adopting an alien was permitted, but it didn't convey citizenship. Such a one as, for example, Ariston, might thereby be catapulted into the very top ranks of society, be received everywhere, accepted as friend by the most glittering aristocrats. But he could never be presented to their sisters—not even on those very, very rare occasions—weddings, funerals, and certain religious festivals—at which Athens relaxed her stern prohibition of social mingling by the two sexes. Although many Athenian citizens, such as Danaus, would have been delighted to wed their sisters to men as rich, brilliant, and handsome as Ariston, with that ironclad law on the statute books, nothing was to be gained by such an introduction except the risk of said sisters' disgracing themselves for love of a man they couldn't lawfully wed.

The only legal way by which Ariston could have obtained Athenian citizenship remained theoretically open to him:

That is, an alien who performed at the risk of his life a feat of singular heroism in behalf of the polis might, at the discretion of the Assembly, be granted citizenship as a reward. But actually, the growing wealth of the industrious metics had by then so excited the envy of the commoners that the standards of what constituted a feat of singular heroism on an alien's part had been raised and raised again until said feat had become tantamount to suicide. In the very few cases that citizenship had been so awarded in the last few years, it had always gone to a surviving son, in honor of the memory of his father's heroic death.

Ariston had had, of course, to go to war. Like any other Athenian, he could be called up until he was sixty years of age. But after two hard-fought campaigns, he had simply taken up Timosthenes' custom of bribing his way out of the ranks. He did this for two reasons: He hated warfare in general, especially the iron necessity it imposed upon a man of having to kill other men for whom he felt no hatred at all. Also, he faced the absolute certainty that, were he to be captured by his own ex-countrymen, the Lakedaemonians, he would not only be killed—which worried him little; both sides quite commonly massacred their prisoners—but slowly tortured to death for the high crime of treason against his native Sparta.

Being a logical Hellene, Ariston saw no reason to run this awful risk in view of the fact that actually he could serve his adopted polis far better by staying at home and making arms for her than by getting his guts hacked out of him as a hoplite—to which consideration he was forced to add the singularly unappealing circumstance that, in all likelihood, he could only gain his citizenship posthumously. Since he had a shrewd suspicion that Athenian citizenship would serve for very little in Tartarus, he calmly decided to forego useless heroism.

So therefore, barring some exceedingly unlikely change in affairs, Ariston could never marry the daughter of a knight, nor of a five-hundred-bushel man, nor even of the lowliest freeborn workman. Conceivably he couldn't so much as take to wife the daughter of an Athenian enslaved for debt, or of a criminal convicted of a crime which did not involve the loss of citizenship.

All of which, be it said at once, troubled Ariston not even slightly. In the first place, he was in no hurry to wed for in Athens the prime motive impelling men to the nuptial altar, sexual starvation, was unheard of. In the second, he was well aware what chaste, fair, lovely maids existed among the better class metics. The real problem lay in the fact that Timosthenes—who was also aware that there were among the resident aliens girls equal in culture, virtue, and beauty to the best the citizen class of Athens had to offer— was handicapped by his total lack of any social contact with metics. And since one of the most rigid Athenian conventions was that a father had to find a bride for his son instead of permitting the youth—impelled by such ridiculous considerations as his own personal tastes, hot blood, and lack of experience—to choose a wife for himself, the handicap was serious indeed. But so great was Timosthenes' love for his adopted son that he was beginning to form such contacts as best he could.

At first the metics politely rebuffed him, out of the wry certainty that the only time a knight sought their friendship was when he needed to borrow money, but Timosthenes got around that difficulty by frankly discussing the matter with his banker, Paris. Now all Athenian bankers and moneylenders were aliens, the profession being considered beneath the citizen class. When Paris learned that all the noble hippêus was seeking was a wife for his adopted son, he at once put himself at Timosthenes' disposal, beginning, of course, by inviting the knight to his own palatial mansion and parading his own three unmarried daughters before him. One of them, the youngest, named Thetis, had pleased Timosthenes immensely both for her quiet beauty and her chaste, demure ways. It was of her that the noble knight was speaking to his adopted son now as they rode toward the ergasteria, and rather reproachfully at that.

"The little Thetis—you know, Paris' daughter—I found her a lovely child, Ariston. And yet you haven't been back to call since I took you there."

"I don't like lovely children, Father," Ariston said gravely. "I prefer a woman—a person with intelligence, spirit, fire. A mind and a will of her own. And I'm not interested in beauty. In fact, it rather repels me somehow.

It's a curse. At least it has been for me. What has it contributed to my life except horror? If I ever do wed, which I tell you now is extremely doubtful, for nothing I've seen of this world would incline me to bring children into it, you may rest assured that my bride will be plain. Or better still—ugly."

Timosthenes stared at his adopted son.

"In Aphrodite's name," he said, "will you—even can you —tell me why?"

Ariston smiled.

"It's very simple, Father. Beauty is a career in itself. I've never seen a beautiful woman—and at Parthenope's, I've seen a good many—whose interests were not totally centered upon her sweet self. Every really pretty woman I know accepts, rather grandly at that, homage from men —as well as flowers, gifts, jewelry, gowns, and hard cash. Call it selfish of me, but when I found a household, I want to be lord and master of it. I want to convey favor, not beseech it. I want my word to be law, my lightest whim an august command. For that, what's better than a woman who's taught humility every time she looks in a mirror? What more keenly instructs the female heart to sweet submissiveness than the knowledge that her lord can walk out the door and find a more lissome form and a prettier face on any street corner? And what greater inducement is there to absolute fidelity than a countenance and a sil-houette which incline a would-be seducer to yawn?"

"You've got it all worked out, haven't you?" Timos-thenes said.

"I have—even to a candidate, a maid I've no hope of ever marrying, which makes the whole thing rather fun."

"And she is?"

"Danaus' sister, Chryseis. Don't worry! I know how unsavory that family is! Pandoros and his younger son Chalcodon are total deviates, while Brimos is a roaring brute. Only my respect for Dan restrains me from point-ing out to him what is obvious: that his lady mother horned that mincing old la-di-da at least twice: once with the butcher boy, thus producing Brimos; and once with a prince, achieving Dan, the only decent human being—with the possible exception of Chryseis—in the household."

245

"Why do you say 'possible exception' if you're in love with her?" Timosthenes said.

Ariston laughed then, freely, gaily.

"But I'm *not* in love with her!" he said. "How can one love a girl one has never seen?"

"You haven't seen her? Oh, come now, Ariston! Even in my day there were ways—slave girls to be bribed, seats at the theatre arranged in proximity, a vigil kept on a street corner during the festivals of women, such as that of Artemis, the Pan Athena, the—"

"Of course! But the whole point is I don't *want* to see her. I can't marry her anyhow, since she's a citizeness; and what would it serve to seduce her? Thanks to Parthenope and her little nymphs, I've no pressing need of another female. As it is, it's a game. I tell Dan to assure her of my entire devotion, which I'm quite sure he doesn't, for he rather disapproves of the whole thing; while to anxious metic mammas and unctuous metic papas, already counting the money I'll inherit from you, Father, she serves to explain my indifference."

"Only she doesn't explain it," Timosthenes said.

"No. Two other women do," Ariston said quietly.

"And they are?"

"Physically, Parthenope, who lends me the satiation that makes me proof against folly, and spiritually—Phryne."

"You're a strange lad," Timosthenes said. "I confess I don't unders—"

That was as far as he got, for at that moment his horse reared, neighing shrilly. Like all Athenian hippêis, Timosthenes was a superb horseman. He fought the plunging, whinnying, maddened beast down again, but the horse went back on his haunches once more, his forefeet pawing the sky; and this time Ariston saw the hard-flung stone that had struck the gray gelding in the flank, rolling along the cobblestones. Turning his head a little, his gaze locked with that of the short, broad, heraklian man whose face above his bushy black beard was absolutely venomous with hatred and whose burly fist held still another stone.

"Look out, Father!" Ariston cried—too late, for the stone was already a whitish blur upon the golden afternoon air. Ariston saw it strike his adoptive father full on the forehead, saw the sudden, savage spurt of blood; but by that time he was already in midair, plunging like a slim, swift gyrfalcon upon Timosthenes' assailant.

The man was at least twice as strong as he, but he had never been trained. Skilled pankratist that he was, Ariston threw his burly, bearded foe at once, dropped him again with a kick to the point of his chin as soon as he got up, chopped him across the side of the neck with the edge of his hand—a blow that would have killed a lesser man—broke the cartilage in the bridge of his nose with a second horizontal chop, causing it to bleed frightfully, and was preparing to finish him off when the Scythian mercenaries who served Athens as the only police force she had, their attention attracted by the outcries of the people who had witnessed the attack, came clanking around the corner and took the man into custody.

Only then did Ariston do what he should have done in the first place: that is, he went to Timosthenes' aid.

The hippêus was badly hurt. His face was covered with blood. So covered, in fact, that not until they had gathered him up and borne him to the iatrieon of the physician Ophion was it discovered that his right femur was smashed in at least three places, so that the jagged splinters of bone had penetrated the muscles of his thigh like so many daggers. And what was even worse, the ball-and-socket joint of his hip was crushed beyond hope of repair.

"Well?" Ariston said to Ophion, once the iatros had finished the examination.

The iatros shook his head.

"He'll die," he said sadly. "The pity is that he won't die at once. But he won't for he is very strong. You see, at his age this kind of injury to the hip bones doesn't heal. The leg, I can set; and that will leave him merely crippled. But there's no way to set a broken hip that I know of. Eventually a mortification will set in, and he'll die. If not from that, from weariness, from too many sleepless nights, too long enduring of unceasing pain. After a time, not even opium will be effective against it. The gash on his forehead is nothing. A slight concussion, that's all."

Ariston looked at the iatros and passed his tongue over bone-dry lips, said: "How long?"

"Six months. A year. Maybe two. But pray the gods for the shortest term. It won't be pleasant, Ariston. Stay with him, give him what comfort you can."

"I'll never leave his side, Iatros!" Ariston said, and turning, went back into the room where Timosthenes lay.

But he did leave Timosthenes' bedside, necessarily, for the whole of a day and night, while his adoptive father lay quietly under the influence of a sleeping potion the physician had given him. The first place Ariston went was to the prison where the slave, Pactolos, was locked up, awaiting the charges of attempted murder to be brought against him before the Helikae, the People's Court. He went there because, on the very face of things, Pactolos' terrible act was totally incomprehensible. Any slave would know that to kill or even attempt to kill a member of the hippàs class would be to seek his own death at the hands of the public torturers. A citizen, in desperation or in rage, might well be willing to risk his own doom, knowing that his execution would be carried out by forcing him to drink a cup of poisonous hemlock, and thus be relatively painless. But to risk the fiendish ingenuity of the public torturers, a slave must have motives terrible beyond belief. And what motives could any servant have against so kindly a man as Timosthenes, who never so much as spoke harshly to, not to mention beat, his slaves?

Therefore Pactolos had to be a hired assassin. But hired by whom? To the best of Ariston's knowledge, his adoptive father had no serious enemies at all. And would a hired murderer choose so clumsy a method as throwing stones? Wouldn't he use a dagger in a crowded street? An arrow, shot from afar? Poison slipped into a cup in a public tavern?

The thing made no sense. And because it didn't Ariston went to see the murderous slave.

Seen close at hand, despite the fact that both his eyes were blackened, and his nose grossly swollen by the blow Ariston had dealt him, the great-thewed slave had a singularly human face. Something about it was even—noble. Ariston went on staring at him a long, long time. Then he said one word, and that one quietly:

"Why?"

In answer, Pactolos silently turned his back.

Ariston's breath caught in his throat. He had seen men beaten, but never before had he seen a human back whip-shredded to the extent that Pactolos' was. It was literally in ribbons. A whipping like this one would surely have killed a less heraklian man. But, again, when he spoke his voice was as quiet, his question as laconic, as was proper to a Lakonian. He said but one word, more quietly still: "Who?"

"Orchomenus!" Pactolos snarled, "but at your knightly father's orders!"

Slowly Ariston shook his head. He said flatly, calmly, but with utter conviction: "No."

"No, what?" Pactolos raged. "You mean to tell me that your father—"

"Knew nothing about it. I do tell you that. My father hasn't entered the shops in years. What Orchomenus does, he does on his own. Now tell me, why did he have you whipped?"

"My little son was dying. My little Zenon. And he was all I had left. My woman died a month ago—of hunger, lordly Ariston! I know, I know! You personally ordered that we slaves be paid a living wage, even though we're owned beasts of burden, and you didn't have to. That's why I didn't aim that stone at your fair head—"

"Go on, Pactolos," Ariston whispered.

"But Orchomenus pockets that money—those miserable few obols that would have saved my wife, my son. In your other shops, the slaves are better off; the managers only steal *part* of their wages. . . ."

"I'm listening," Ariston said.

"I stole some silver—in an attempt to save my Zenon's life. A vain attempt because he died the night before I tried to—kill your father. A few pitiful ounces that were to be used to ornament General Nikias' dress armor—after I'd asked Orchomenus for the money to pay for the medicines to save my son. He refused me, kicked me back to work—"

Pactolos stopped, looked at the elegantly dressed young man. Said angrily: "I suppose you're going to tell me that you don't *know* he has taskmasters armed with leaded whips in every shop of yours! I'll wager that all the times you visited us, you never—"

"Saw them? No. Let me ask you this, Pactolos: On all my visits to the shop where you worked, did I *ever* enter it unescorted? Was I not always met halfway down the street, talked to, detained?"

The slave bowed his head slowly. Looked up again.

"True, young master," he said. "And those assassins with their bull whips always scurried out the back door before you came in the front. I'd noticed that. Even conceded that you didn't know. But that your father didn't was too much to believe! Men say you're kind. Your slaves laud you as though you were—a god. They swear they're to be freed—"

"They are. And so are you now," Ariston said.

Pactolos looked at him, his eyes afire beneath his great shaggy brows.

"In spite of what I've done?" he whispered.

"In spite of what you've done. I'll withdraw all charges against you before the archon Basileos today. And I offer you a post in my household as my father's bodyguard, or as mine if he doesn't live."

Big as he was, as great-thewed, as heraklian, Pactolos bowed his shaggy head and wept.

"Master," he said brokenly, "push your foot through the bars—that I may kiss it—that—"

"No. My hand. That you may take it—as an equal, and a man," Ariston said.

That same afternoon, Ariston went to the Bouleuterion and presented a paper signed by Timosthenes himself, who was conscious by then, though in great pain, asking that Pactolos be freed of all charges and explaining why. The archon Basileos hemmed and hawed over this unheard-of request for half an hour, but he gave in at last, overwhelmed by the fire and eloquence with which the son of the victim pleaded the case of the offending slave.

That done, Ariston went up the far side of the hill of the Kolonos Agoraios, crossed the courtyard of the temple of Hephaestos, and came down to the main shop by the back way. Therefore, he was not intercepted nor detained.

He came into the shop in time to see the three taskmasters flaying the back of a slave with their whips. He didn't

250

say anything. He simply caught the backswing of one lash, and jerked its wielder off his feet so hard that the man's head collided with a leg of a workbench hard enough to put him out of the fight for good; the second taskmaster he flattened with a merciless kick to the groin; the third he caught by the wrist, and broke his forearm over his own upraised knee.

Then he said, his voice flat, deadly, cold:

"Get out. All of you. And don't come back."

By then Orchomenus was running toward him, his big mouth opened to roar. But what he saw in Ariston's face silenced even him.

Ariston stood there, looking at his former comrade-in-arms a long, slow, awful time. Then: "You may accompany your friends, Orchomenus," he said.

That same night Orchomenus came home roaring drunk and proceeded to beat his wife, Thargelia, unmercifully. He continued beating her until even this sport palled upon him. So with the tender gesture of a parting kick full in her swollen belly, he lurched out into the night.

But poor Thargelia was by then eight months with child. Orchomenus' kick caused her both to abort and to hemorrhage. And she was alone. No one at all heard her feeble cries.

When, two days later, his last obol gone, spent as usual on wine, whores, and boys, Orchomenus came home again, the only thing he could do was to bury Thargelia and the little blue, bloody corpse that would have been his son.

The noble knight Timosthenes had occasion to prove both his nobility and his knighthood. Which, be it said, for ten of the thirteen months he continued to live, he did magnificently. But there are limits to human endurance; by the end of the year, his fine old body covered with bedsores, his swollen hip breaking open and leaking pus, his form reduced to a heap of bones straining to burst through the thin parchment of his flesh, Timosthenes was screaming himself into unconsciousness every night.

Ariston never left his side during all that time, nor did the freedman, Pactolos, who had volunteered to expiate his fault by thus serving as nurse, body servant, faithful slave to the man he had injured unto death. Pactolos did all things for his master: bathed him, fed him, shifted his skeletal body about in a vain effort to find a comfortable position, performed even those most repugnant duties that must be done for a man bedridden and unable to move. And, in the end, he did one last great and matchlessly tender thing for Timosthenes:

Sometime during that final night, Timosthenes woke up and saw Ariston sprawled out in the great chair beside his bed, sleeping as only a man who has not closed an eye for over a week can sleep. But Pactolos was awake, his eyes like coals of fire in his dark face, burning with absolute grief for the master he had come to love.

"Pactolos—" Timosthenes whispered, his voice dead leaves drifting down an empty street, a brief rattle, just above the threshold of sound.

"Yes, master?" the freedman said.

"What I told you. If—I start to scream. I can't—I can't —anymore—I can't—bear—I—"

"Master!" Pactolos wept.

"Your promise, Pactolos! You—you owe me—this. I—I command you to—So—" His mouth came open. His head arched back, back, back—

Pactolos got up. Came to the bedside. He took the pillow from beneath the old man's emaciated head. Then, with the great tears dripping down into his inky beard, very quietly and tenderly, he smothered Timosthenes to death.

It took a matter of minutes merely, in the hippêus' weakened state. Pactolos took the pillow away from that kind old face, put it back beneath the dead man's head. Closed those glaring eyes with his own blunt, work-callused fingers. Then he went over to where Ariston slept and shook the young man awake.

"Wha—what?" Ariston mumbled.

"He's gone," Pactolos said.

Then, leaving the youth kneeling beside that bier and weeping as only the truly disconsolate can weep, Pactolos went outside into the garden and hanged himself upon the great branch of an ancient olive tree.

# CHAPTER FIFTEEN

"OH, LAMBIE!" PARTHENOPE SAID. "I'm so glad you came to see me!"

"I'm not," Ariston said morosely. "In fact, I don't know why I did. Certainly not in search of a bedfellow, so don't go parading your latest crop of pupils before me!"

Parthenope smiled. On the occasion of her fortieth birthday, four years ago now—a date which ironically enough happened to have coincided with the termination of Ariston's self-imposed two years of strict mourning for his beloved adoptive father—she had announced her own retirement from active participation in her delicate trade. Instead, she had opened a training school for etairai and auletrides in her home. There she taught the very many young women of Athens who found the career of discreetly commercialized vice infinitely preferable to the life of grinding poverty out of which most of them came how to walk gracefully, sing, dance, adorn themselves, and gave them a shallow but showy smattering of culture. One of her most notable and most apt pupils, who had gone far beyond Parthenope's rather superficial teachings to become something very fine, had been Theoris, who, Ariston had been relieved to learn, had become the poet Sophokles' mistress and had had the idea of putting herself under Parthenope's supervision in an effort to make herself worthy of the lofty wisdom of so great a man.

"Don't be too sure I couldn't show you more than one who could interest you, lambie," Parthenope purred. "They're a vast improvement over last year's group. I have two knights' daughters, one sweet little escapee from a pentakosiomedinos' house, and *four* daughters of zeugitae. Not one splay-footed little thêtes! What do you think of that?"

Ariston stared at her. What she was saying was preposterous any way you considered it. For the pentakosiomedini were the wealthiest of the classes of Athens established by Solon's laws. Literally, the word meant five-hundred-bushel men, in Solon's day an indication of vast wealth, for only a huge estate could produce that much in stony, barren Attica. Of course now, admission to the wealthy classes was measured in money—talents, minae, drachmae, obols, rather than in produce; but the ancient name remained. After them in wealth, but quite often above them in family pride and prestige, came the hippêis, or knights, whose lands produced more than three hundred bushels but less than five hundred, or enough to afford their owners the considerable expense of owning a riding horse and outfitting themselves with a suit of armor. Again, these ancient terms had been largely replaced by the coin of the realm, though many hippêis—especially those who were eupatridae, or nobles, as Timosthenes had been—out of their ancient conservatism clung stubbornly to the land. Next came the two-hundred- to three-hundred-bushel men, whose name, the zeugitae, the teamsters, indicated that they were wealthy enough to afford a high-wheeled cart drawn by a brace of oxen. And last of all were the thêtes, small farmers whose produce didn't even reach two hundred bushels.

In Solon's time, when all Athenians had been georgi, farmers great or small, these names had made sense. Now, in the post-Periklean epoch, more often than not they didn't. A five-hundred-bushel man today nearly always produced his monetary equivalent of bushels of wheat, barley, olives, wine, by owning a shipyard, various factories, or farming out to the mines and shops the labor of his hundreds of slaves. The knights, become city dwellers, did the same, though they retained the privilege of fighting as cavalry instead of slogging through the mud afoot. And most zeugitae only saw an oxcart when it was being loaded with the vases from their potteries or the cloth from their looms or the furniture from their shops, to transport these most urban products to the dock for shipping or to the market for sale—while nearly all thêtes supplied the labor of their brawny arms in the factories and shops of the other three classes.

But what held Ariston there staring speechlessly at Parthenope was his astonished realization of the fact that no daughter of any of these classes, down to and including the skilled workers among the thêtes, or laborers, had any economic need to enter into what, however you disguised it with euphemisms and distinguished among its branches— porna, auletride, etaira—was essentially the world's oldest profession. In Solon's time, and even as recently as Perikles', all etairai, and even most auletrides and pornai, had been foreign born; but now, having been forced to think about it by Parthenope's astonishing claim, he realized that a good many of them were actually native Athenians.

"Why?" he said. "In Hestia's name, Parthenope, why should a girl of a good family, wealthy, protected—"

"Ah!" Parthenope said. "There you've put your finger on it, Iambie! That 'protection' business! How'd you like to spend your life in jail? For no matter how comfortable, beautiful, or luxurious they may be, that's exactly what your Athenian gynaekeia are! Suppose you were an Athenian lady, and hence could never attend a party or a banquet or any other social gathering unless it happened to be the wedding or the funeral of some member of your immediate family? Suppose that even your festivals and religious rites were separate and distinct from the other sex's; that you had to sit apart even in the theater; were forbidden to even so much as go shopping; were unable to walk the streets even at high noon unescorted; had to leave the room the moment a friend—a male friend, of course—of your brother's, or your father's or your husband's entered it, even if you were eating your favorite dish at dinner? How'd you like *that*, Iambie?"

"I wouldn't," Ariston said.

"And they don't either, your highborn Athenian dames. Look, Iambie, you ought to know a good bit about women by now. We, with rare exceptions, simply aren't lustful they way men are. Oh, I don't mean our blood can't flame with a passion few of you can satisfy once it's aroused! But it has to be aroused. And arousing the average woman is

255

nobody's easy task, I can tell you. Put it this way, I have never known a woman to become a whore because she burned with lust. Never."

"Then why do they?" Ariston said.

"Setting aside being sold into a porneia as a slave, which is how most girls get there—hunger, first. When you haven't eaten in a week, letting a brute pry your knees apart doesn't seem so all-fired important, especially since the drachma he's giving you for the privilege will buy you food for the next four or five days, during which, you fondly hope, something will turn up to save you from starvation and that life both. Only it never does, so you find yourself in a 'house' with your delicate charms being advertised in the pornagraphia over the door. That's what happened to me when the plague carried both my parents off in a single night. The second reason's love. Misdirected love. A good many girls find themselves with a rapidly expanding tummy left them by some winged-foot who has already departed for parts unknown. Their fathers toss them out into the streets. Whereupon they procure an abortion, or have the brat and are forced to support it; but in all cases, they have to support themselves. And being women, *what,* I ask you, *what* are they taught to do that they could earn a living by? Rich people don't hire domestic servants; they buy slaves, lambie. And what is an Athenian wife or daughter but a superior sort of domestic servant to her husband or her father? What does she know, beyond the household arts? So, having found out what store men put upon that curious act or even, in rare cases, having rather enjoyed it themselves, it's that or starve."

"All right. But you haven't convinced me—beyond a thêtes' or a zeugitos' daughter, say. The chances of an unlawful pregnancy happening to a pentakosiomedinos' daughter or a hippêus' is nil. Absolutely nil."

"Right, lambie! Quite, quite right! As long as she's under the paternal roof and enjoying that famous protection you mentioned."

"But she always is," Ariston said.

"No. Not now. Not anymore. Increasingly girls who have brains in their heads and blood in their veins rebel, blow up. At first that only means quarreling with Papa, or, in extreme cases, a whipping from his august hand. But later on, quite often after that quarrel or a whole series of them, and especially after that beating, she finds a way to slip out at night, after the old man's snoring the roof down, usually with the help of a female slave as fed to the eyeteeth with an Athenian woman's existence as she is. That's it. She's had it. She doesn't have to *do* anything, lambie. Just be seen out alone or in some tavern with a boy at night. She can be virgin and intact, but she's already a whore in the eyes of the world. And Papa throws her out—when he doesn't kill her, as some old mossyback reactionaries still do. He has to. What else can he do?"

"Forgive her," Ariston said.

"Yes. Only to have her repeat the offense a year or two later when she can't stand her loneliness anymore, knowing as she does by then with absolute certainty she can *never* marry, since no Athenian will wed a girl of dubious reputation."

"So that's how you get your delicate highborn beauties!" Ariston said.

"Yes. That is, if you also include a few wives who've left their husbands, or have been divorced, or who've been caught in flagrante by types too kind-hearted or too weak to kill them, and not kind-hearted enough, or strong enough, to forgive. I don't like divorcees, though. Too bitter. When they find out that the type who caused them to be put aside by friend husband in the first place inevitably develops a sudden yen for travel the minute they're free and he can do something serious about them like marriage, they sour on men. I prefer girls who *like* men. They're more profitable. Insincerity shows."

"Parthenope the philosopher!" Ariston laughed. Then he looked her straight in the eye, still smiling at her a little mockingly. "Now tell me something else," he said.

"Such as?" she said. Her tone was a little startled, he thought.

"Such as the reason behind this—this lecture. Dear Parthenope, I do know women. More especially, I know *you*. You're not an idle chatterbox. You chose this rather odd theme—'The How's and Why's of Becoming a Whore,' shall we call it?—deliberately. You're building up to something. Which rather offends me. After all these years you should know me well enough to realize that if there's something you want to tell me, you can—straight out, just like that. But no matter. Out with it! I confess I'm intrigued. What in the names of Eros and Aphrodite both is there related to *that* theme that could possibly be of interest to me?"

"You know, Ariston," she whispered, "that's why I love you. Truly. You're the only man I ever met who was both sensitive and not a queer. That is, if you still aren't—"

"If I'm still not what?"

"A queer. You seldom come around anymore. And half the time—no, three-quarters—you don't even want a girl, when you do. And Danaus—is an awfully beautiful boy."

"You want me to hit you?" Ariston said.

"No. I want you to reassure me. You don't lie with him, do you, Ariston? I should hate it if you did."

"I don't lie with him. Nor with any man. After six months as a guest of Polyxenus', the only effect that being kissed or caressed by a member of my own sex has upon me is to make me want to throw up. Feel better now?"

"About *that*, yes."

"Aha! So we're getting there! The subject that required so long and so elaborate a preamble, right?"

"Right. O Ariston, lambie, I'm so awfully afraid! *Nothing* like this has ever happened before!"

"Nothing like what has ever happened before?"

"His sister. Danaus'. Chryseis. She—she comes *here!*"

"Zeus Thunderer!" Ariston said.

"And great Hera, mother of the gods!" Parthenope whispered.

"How? How could she? There's no way on earth—" He stopped short, frowning. "No," he said, "she can quite easily, can't she? With Pandoros and Chalcodon always in Polyxenus' or Gourgos' bathhouses, committing sodomy or worse upon helpless boys; Brimos making all the brothel keepers of Piraeus rich, the only one she has to seriously avoid is Danaus—"

"Who is always with you," Parthenope said tartly.

"Not always. Not even frequently, these days. But he is in training for the coming expedition against Syrakuse, which means he probably sleeps in his company's barracks. So there's no one at all to prevent—"

"Except you. You could tell Danaus. Get him word that—"

"No, Parthenope. Danaus is very conservative. Reaction against his father's and his brother's behavior, likely. He'd probably beat her, and then—Tell me, Parthenope, why does she come here? To meet a lover? Or to sell herself for the joy of it?"

"Neither, by Artemis! I'd stake my head that the girl's as pure as the drifting snow. Fat chance *she* has of being relieved of the burden of her virtue, even if she wanted to, which she doesn't. She's as scrawny as a crow, and uglier than Hecate's daughter. Her breasts are about the size of limes and her hips—"

"Don't run her down, Parthenope," Ariston said.

"I'm not, lambie! I like her! She's got a brain in that odd little head of hers. She only comes—swathed in veils like an Egyptian mummy—long after midnight, entering by the tradesmen's and servants' entrance. I made her do that, after the first time, after I got my breath back from pure shock at finding out who she was, and relief at the pure miracle that she hadn't run into anybody at all in the foyer. Her reasons? That I may teach her the charm she thinks she lacks. Not that she hopes to gain a dishonest living thereby. Her object's a perfectly conventional marriage—to somebody like you. That's why she came here. Her brother let slip that this is your hangout. She has a good bit of curiosity about you, you know, mingled with some hostility. She thinks you indulge in dirty effeminate tricks with her brother, and you can't call her illogical on that score, considering what goes on every day in Athens. Only I don't know what to do about her. Her case is unique. Every other highborn girl who comes here has already been expelled from her home, lost her reputation, fallen from virtue. Chryseis hasn't. She maneuvers dangerously between two worlds and seems to enjoy the danger. But if she's ever caught, I'm ruined. That old——"
Parthenope used a very obscene Attic expression whose meaning was "practicer of fellatio"—Pandoros would sue

259

me for my last obol for the crime of corrupting his daughter. And he'd win his case, too."

"Have you told her that?"

"Of course. She laughs at me. Says that there's not the slightest danger. Swears all she'd have to do, if such a case were ever brought against me—and considering the laxness of that household she's right in her contention that the chances of that ancient queer's finding out are slight— would be to unveil her face, let her robe slip from her shoulders—'I have no hips to detain it,' says she—and stand there naked before the Helliaea. 'Then,' says she, 'the case would collapse of its own weight, and my lack of it. For who, having seen me naked and amused himself counting every bone I have, all plainly visible under this sallow skin that has only them and nothing else beneath it, would believe that corrupting me would be of sufficient interest to anyone that she should run the slightest risk attempting it?' "

"She has wit!" Ariston said.

"Of a most mordant variety. Oh, lambie, lambie, what shall I do?"

"Leave it to me. When is she supposed to come here again?"

"Don't know. Not soon, though. She was here last night, which means she probably won't appear again for another two weeks. She *is* careful, you know."

"When she comes again, detain her. Then send a slave to my house."

"And you'll—?"

"Fly over here, my eyes glittering with lust, my lips afoam with mad desire, and make a wild and clumsy attempt to ravish her. Scare her so that—"

"Lambie—" Parthenope said.

"What now?" Ariston said.

"You're an awfully good-looking man, y'know."

"Meaning?"

"Suppose she doesn't scare? Suppose she just says, 'Wait a second, darling!' flips her peplos over her head and lies there all agape with delighted anticipation?"

"No, she won't. But if she does, I'll instantly be overcome with remorse, remember suddenly that she's Dan's

260

sister, threaten to open my veins in expiation of the insult and—"

"And thereby *insure* that she falls madly in love with you!"

"Well—" Ariston groaned. "Have you any better idea?"

"Yes. I'll send for you; but when you come, you talk to her gravely and kindly, like a brother. Make her see how terribly Danaus would be hurt—she adores him as much as she despises those other two—by her being accidentally disgraced. I think she'd listen to you. With your manly beauty lending weight to your words, you'd have much more effect on her than any mere female could. Oh, lambie, will you do that for me—before this clever little witch ruins me forever?"

"Why, of course, Parthenope," Ariston said.

But, before either of them got a chance to put the plan into effect, a whole series of minor disasters occurred. The first of them was that Ariston received a note from Danaus telling him that the fleet under the strategoi Nikias and Alkibiades sailed on the morrow to carry the war to Syrakuse. It so happened that Danaus was mistaken or had been misinformed, but that made little difference. Ariston, naturally enough, started out at once to bid farewell to his dearest friend. But as he was leaving his office at the factory, where he had gone to give his daily orders to the foremen, he saw Sokrates coming up the street.

He stopped where he was. The visit to Dan could wait an hour or two. Nothing, in Ariston's mind, took precedence over the high intellectual delight of the ugly old wise man's company.

And anyhow, how could he know, as he watched that portly figure toiling up the rise toward the ergasteria, that the delay Sokrates' visit was going to cause would have its rarely awful consequences?

# CHAPTER SIXTEEN

SOKRATES PICKED UP THE SHIELD and carried it through the door of the ergasteria, or factory, into the sunlight. There he proceeded to examine it carefully.

Ariston smiled. Of course it was very dim and smoky inside the factory, but that wasn't the trouble. The philosopher could have seen the figures on the shield very well by walking over to one of the furnaces and examining it by the light of the molten bronze. In fact, every few minutes, when a worker tilted a ladle to pour the liquid metal into one of the molds, the whole foundry floor was illuminated with what looked like a stream of melted sunlight, so that Sokrates could have seen anything he wanted to. The real trouble was the noise.

When you came here every day, as Ariston had for nearly eight years now, you got used to the infernal din of the furnaces working under forced draft, air rammed into them by huge bellows, pumped by the brawny arms of his strongest men. And the incessant banging of the hammers, pounding the sheet metal over the carved hardwood dies to form the insignia and the decorative figures in low reliefs; the hiss of the tempering baths into which the sword blades and spear points were plunged; the heavy clangor of the sledges pounding the metal against anvils— all these hideous noises became almost soundless to an ear grown accustomed to them, went unregistered by a mind that fixed itself, as Ariston's did, on other questions, such as: At what point did defense of freedom stop and unbridled aggression begin? And: Rightly considered, could the manufacture of weapons ever be truly justified, for however noble the motives men claimed as impelling them to it, was not war, the thing itself, irrefutably—murder?

But Sokrates wasn't used to the deafening clangor of an arms factory. It set his head reeling. And as always, the old man wanted to talk. Talk—the meeting of minds, the exploration of motives, thoughts, the sounding of the usually disappointing depths of human souls—was his very life.

"It's beautiful," he said. "In fact, it's the most beautiful shield I've ever seen. How did you come to think of this process, Ariston?"

"Of the lost wax? I didn't think of it, Sokrates," Ariston said. "I learned it from Alkamenes, the sculptor. You see, he paid me to pose for him, and—"

"During the time you were so poverty-stricken that you couldn't raise the money to open this shop!" Sokrates quipped. "Despite the fact that your late father was the richest man in Athens!"

Ariston stood there. It hurt still to think of the cruelly slow and bitter declension into death of his beloved adoptive father. Say what men would, dying was always—horrible. A violation of all a man was. The ultimate violation.

"You know why," he said to Sokrates.

"Aye. I do. And Timosthenes was wrong. You, for all your lack of years, were right. Being given everything doesn't strengthen character. Being forced to earn them does."

Ariston smiled a little sadly.

"I didn't earn this, really," he said. "I got the money from Orchomenus. Who, in turn, borrowed it from your beloved Alkibiades!"

Sokrates bowed his head.

"That was one of my failures, son Ariston," he said. "I sometimes fail. Alkibiades is proof of that."

Ariston stared at him.

"You say that *now?* After they've made him strategos, given him joint command along with Nikias of the expedition against Syrakuse?"

"I say it," Sokrates said. "What is success and what failure, Ariston? Air. Nothing. What think you of Thukydides, son of Olorus?"

"I think he was badly treated! After all, he had the whole coast of Chalkidike and Thrace to defend with only seven triremes. How could he know where precisely, along that shore from Potidaea to the Chersonese, Brasidas was going to strike? So he failed at Amphipolis—and you Athenians exiled him—"

"To write the greatest military history the world has ever seen. I've read all he's finished to date. He sends copies to Xenophon. He lost a battle—by being late. I'd venture that his tardiness on that totally unimportant occasion will ensure his immortality. But to pursue the matter further: Who won at Amphipolis?"

"Brasidas," Ariston said.

"And who lost?"

"Kleon."

"And what happened to them that day? To both of them?"

"Brasidas died of wounds received while charging at the head of his hoplites. Kleon was shot down by a peltast while flying the field."

"But both of them are dead, aren't they? The victor and the vanquished? The hero and the coward?"

Ariston stood there, staring at his mentor. Then, very slowly, he smiled.

"You win, Sokrates! But then, you always do. I should know better than to debate with you. After all, it's been not quite ten years since I've been your pupil."

"Yes. A long ten years, son Ariston! When first I knew you, you were a beardless boy, more beautiful than a god. You're still beautiful, but in a different way."

"At least I have a beard!" Ariston laughed.

"And shoulders as great as Orchomenus'. You're overdeveloped, which I suspect you did on purpose, so no man would be tempted again to—But I see this line of talk is still painful to you. Here, take this shield of yours. I'm going to dance."

"To dance?" Ariston said.

"Yes. For exercise. I always do. How else would I keep this gross belly of mine down to at least reasonable size?"

"May I suggest an alternative?" Ariston said.

"Of course! But if you're going to challenge me to a wrestling match, don't be too sure of yourself, my boy!"

"No. I know how strong you are, Sokrates. What I suggest is nothing more violent than a long walk. I propose that you come with me to Danaus' house. I must bid him farewell. He sails with the expedition."

"Gladly. But might he not take it ill? On such a tender occasion, he'd most likely prefer to be alone with you, wouldn't he?" Sokrates said.

"No," Ariston said, "that is, I don't think so. He knows and respects my aversion to carnal love between man and man. I've served him as sort of secondhand mentor, by relaying all you've taught me to him. He'd be honored by your visit, Sokrates, so come."

They set out through the streets of Athens together, the tall young man, all of twenty-eight now, broad of shoulder, brawny—in fact too muscular for the Hellenic taste, to which *meden agan,* "nothing in excess," was inviolable law —his thick, curly blond beard framing a grave and thoughtful face that had not so much lost the stunning beauty of his early youth as transmuted it into a different kind of beauty, having a quality of andreia, manliness, about it that formerly it had lacked—towering above the short, stocky, almost equally brawny philosopher, whose face of Goat-Pan, of satyr, of Silenus, belied the lofty nobility of his mind, his thought.

As they walked, they amused themselves by debating certain propositions of the Sophists: Parmenides' that thinking and being are the same thing, so that things have no independent existence beyond the perception of an intelligent observer; Zeno's paradoxes: that the motion of any person to any point is impossible in finite time, since, in moving, he is always dividing the remaining distance into an infinite number of subdivisions, making his ever arriving anywhere beyond all possibility; Achilles can never catch the tortoise, because as often as Achilles reaches the point the tortoise occupied, in that same instant the tortoise has moved beyond that point; that a flying arrow is really at rest, for at any moment of its flight it is at only one point in space, that is, motionless, thus making its apparent motion metaphysically unreal.

"Would you stand there against that wall," Ariston said, "and let me shoot Zeno's metaphysically motionless arrow at you?"

"Gladly!" Sokrates laughed. "For my own lack of motion would be just as metaphysically unreal; and my fat paunch, which is most unmetaphysical, wouldn't be there when your arrow arrived, since my un-sophistical nerves and muscles, being unacquainted with the metaphysics of Zeno of Eleas, would have twitched it aside!"

With such intellectual foolery they occupied themselves on that long walk. Only once was Sokrates, usually the merriest of men, serious. Seeing the vast display of articles on sale in the market place, he remarked with grave contentment:

"What a number of things there are I neither need nor want!"

The house of Pandoros, like all the houses of Athens, displayed a blank and windowless wall to the street. All its doors and windows except, of course, the entrance, faced a lovely inner court. And once the old slave had led them into the foyer, Ariston saw at once that the wealth of Pandoros must indeed—as Athenian gossip had it—be slipping away from him, being wasted by his two elder sons, and by himself, in riotous living; because the foyer was sadly in need of repairs and repainting. No one accused Danaus, the youngest, of any such folly. Instead, the Athenian wits quipped: "Wisest thing he ever did, becoming the lover of that rich metic, Ariston!" Which, in the precise, scandalous sense they meant it, wasn't true at all; but who could convince any Athenian of that?

But the damage had already been done. The delay occasioned by Sokrates' visit caused them to arrive at the hour of the noon meal, which meant that Danaus was no longer alone. They waited there while the old slave went into the dining room, where, he'd already told them, Danaus dined alone with his sister, Chryseis. For not even their brother's imminent departure on the dangerous expedition against Syrakuse led by Alkibiades and Nikias had sufficed to interrupt Brimos' savage day-long, night-long bouts of revelry, nor Chalcodon's and their father's endless pursuit of adolescent boys. Had Danaus been eating alone, or only with his father and his brothers, the old slave would have ushered Ariston and Sokrates into the dining room without further delay, for in democratic

Athens, people didn't stand on ceremony. But now they had to wait until Chryseis retired to the gynaekeia, because for a highborn Athenian maid to even remain in the same room with male guests—except on certain rare occasions such as weddings and funerals—was absolutely unthinkable.

Unthinkable, Ariston and Sokrates saw or rather heard, to any maid but Chryseis. Her voice came over to them, reedy and shrill with anger:

"I will not! I've waited half my life for a chance to meet Sokrates! The gynaekeia? Pah! Tell me, in what way is my virtue in danger, Danaus? Does Sokrates go around raping girls? In my case, he won't have to; for if he's as wise as men say he is, I—I'll cooperate!"

Ariston brought his hand down on Sokrates' shoulder.

"Shall I leave you?" he whispered. "Such an opportuni-y's priceless!"

Sokrates shook his head.

"She hasn't seen me," he whispered back. "Generally, when girls do, they run away screaming."

Within, Ariston guessed, Danaus was making a valiant effort to maintain his self-control, because the male rumble of his young voice wasn't loud enough for them to hear precisely what he said. But Chryseis' high-pitched tones immediately enlightened them:

"Ariston? Ha! I want to meet him even more! I've been longing to give him a piece of my mind, the filthy old pederast!"

Now it was Sokrates' turn to bring a gleeful hand down upon his young friend's shoulder.

This time Danaus' voice was a taurine roar:

"Ariston's not old! He's only two years older than I am! And he's not—"

"A pederast? Ha! Then what do you *do*, brother mine, in each other's company? What thing so interesting that you've passed eight or nine years of constant companion-ship without either of you taking time out to get married? Tell me that!"

"We talk. He teaches me things. The verses of Euripides, for instance . . ."

"Did he teach you this one, then, Brother?" Chryseis said; and suddenly the shrillness went out of her voice. It

267

dropped a whole octave, became low, vibrant, lovely, but
so sad that the sound of it stopped Ariston's breath:

Of all the things under heaven that grow and bleed,
That think, reflect—Oh, doubt it not, my masters!—
What creature is more luckless than a woman?
Who else on earth must pay hard cash to
Buy a brute's tyranny over her trembling flesh?
A man she's never seen, is forbidden to look
Upon before the night that torn, outraged
She weeps, despairing of ever learning how
To guide toward peace the hairy beast
Who sleeps, worn out by his bestial labors,
At her side—For this she pays a dowry!
And she, who at the cost of anguish finds
The way to make him resent her presence
Little, counts herself blessed; but she
Who can't, who offends him in the least,
May the kind gods grant her death!
And her lord and master, tired of her person
And her face, marches out as he pleases to
Find a flute girl, a companion, a whore, a boy—
While she waits, in dumb misery chained
To him, and him alone!
Yet men say we're lucky because we sit
At home and do not have to face the
Perils of war—
Ha! I'd charge naked and unarmed into
The whole Spartan hosts, plunge my breast
Against the forest of their spears
Three times, or more than three, before
I'd undergo the giving birth of
But a single child—

"The *Medea*—" Ariston whispered. "You know, Sok
rates, those words are true!"

"Aye," Sokrates growled, but then Danaus' voice came
over to them. He was almost crying.

"Chryseis, I can't! Don't you see! It's against all custom
and all law!"

"Then Hades take custom and law both!" Chryseis said.

268

Ariston pushed open the door and stepped into the dining room so quietly that neither of them heard him.

"Upon my head be the sin, Danaus," he said, his grave, deep voice making music of his words. "For such a woman as this sister of yours, I'll risk the world's anger—and even your own—to meet."

They both whirled, stared at him. Parthenope was right, Ariston saw. The girl was ugly. She was thin to a painful degree. She had no hips nor any discernible breasts. Her mouth was big and startlingly full-lipped for so thin a face. Her eyes had a curiously Scythian slant; and their golden, almost yellow, brown, flecked with tiny motes of green, was a fire in the Egyptian darkness of her face. Her hair was lovely. That much could be said for her. Its blackness was Stygian, yet somehow it conveyed softness, warmth. Her bare arms, and what he could see of her legs through her lamb's wool robe, were pipestems, skeletal, almost without flesh. And now, as she turned toward her brother, he could see that she had breasts, after all. They were tiny, no bigger than little cabbages. His heart sank within him. Not even Parthenope's candid description had prepared him for how totally unattractive this poor little creature was.

Then she spoke, and Ariston's heart not only reversed its downward course, but leaped, lifted, soared. For her voice, saying his name, sculptured music out of naked air.

"Is *this*—your—Ariston?" she said.

"Yes," Danaus said, "to whom I must now apologize for this horrendous breach of all the proprieties. The more so if he heard your fishwife's shrieks through the door. Now get out of here, Chryseis! Haven't you shamed me enough?"

"No," she whispered. "I promised to give him a piece of my mind and I'm going to! That I see *why* you love him, that he is as beautiful as you said—no, more beautiful than you had wit enough to describe—doesn't make it any less horrible!"

"Make *what* any less horrible, my lady?" Ariston said.

Chryseis came toward him, step by step, like a tigress. Like a bony, fleshless tigress, who is starving. The thought was more apt than he knew. She came on until she stood there in front of him so close that had he bent down a foot or more, he could have kissed her mouth. The thought occurred to him. It was singularly appealing. She stood there staring up at him. He could smell her. She smelled of soap, of perfume—of excitement, and of fear.

"What is it you find so horrible, little Chryseis?" Ariston said.

"Homosexuality," she said. "Homosexuals like you!"

"Chryseis!" Danaus got out, but Ariston halted him with a lifted hand.

"I'm sorry," he said. "I'd much rather that you liked me. Enough, at least, to attempt to cure me of that grave affliction."

She stared at him wonderingly.

"Then—then you don't deny it?" she whispered.

"Would you believe me if I did?" Ariston said.

"Chrys—this is outrageous!" Danaus said. "He—"

"—is making fun of me. I know it. I'm quite accustomed to it. Men are so short-sighted. The can't see beyond a woman's ugliness, beyond the fact she's a bag of bones to—"

"Her soul?" Ariston said. "I can." Then he raised his voice: "Sokrates!" he called out. "Will you come in here, please?"

Sokrates came into the dining room. Danaus stared from Ariston to the philosopher. He was terribly confused. This scene was unpardonable, but who truly was to blame for it?

"I give you the Lady Chryseis," Ariston said in his deep, rich voice; "who thinks I am unmanly. Further, she insists that we should examine her soul, instead of her—let us face it!—rather scant and meager flesh! What think you of her, O Sokrates?"

"That she is a spirit of the upper air," Sokrates said gravely, but with a mischievous twinkle in his little black eyes, "wafted to earth on a moonbeam, blown across the world upon thistledown, come to rest at last to grace our polis. My lady, I salute you!"

"And I, you, great Sokrates, wisest of men," Chryseis whispered. "Will you not sit? And talk to me? I have such a hunger for that! Pay no attention to my dullard of a

270

brother! He hasn't even the wit to see that to a creature like me, the mores that govern women serve for nothing."

"Why don't they, my lady?" Sokrates said.

"Because they're designed for the preservation of virtue, of virginity—both, from my point of view, burdens—"

"Chrys—!" Danaus said.

"Oh, stop saying Chrysssssssss—like an idiot, Dan! Both, from my point of view, burdens I'd be rid of, that I'd gladly exchange for the freedom that a man enjoys. But in my case, unnecessary to guard, protect, since who'd bother to have them of me once he's seen me? Wait! Don't misunderstand me! Especially not you, O Ariston, with your beauty more of gods than of men! I am not a she-goat compact of all lechery. I don't even comprehend—desire. I —I have never felt it—"

"The gods help you then!" Ariston said.

"But I'd become an etaira in a minute, had I the equipment."

"And what equipment is that, my lady?" Sokrates said.

"Beauty. Charm. Even enough flesh to awake a man's lust. I've told you I don't understand desire. I don't. But 'm sure—ugly as it is, as it seems to me—it's better than rejection. I go out veiled—as an Athenian lady must, accompanied by my slave girl. I see how men's eyes follow her along the street—her, not me! For it is only by noting what direction my sandals take that men can tell whether 'm coming or going—"

"Chrys." Danaus groaned. "Have you no pride at all?"

"None. For what would it serve me, Brother? What have I to be proud of?"

"A voice that's purest music," Ariston said, "the loveliest, most haunting sound I've ever heard. Don't you know, little Chryseis, that by speaking alone you could enslave a man forever? And then, there are your eyes. The eyes of a wild-timid woods-thing, dashing by night through the forests of your quite imaginary fears. What a flame burns within their depths! What a warmth, a tenderness—"

"Ariston," Danaus said, "I'm not sure that I like this!"

"Spoken before you, my friend, openly, and honorably. Your sister is not beautiful—why should I try to convince

271

her that she is? But what she and you both forget is that beauty is at best, unimportant; and at worse, a curse. It has been for me. All I'm trying to do is to reassure her, rid her of the nonsensical belief that she has nothing to offer. I, who would lay my heart and my fortune at her feet this instant if I could, if I were permitted to."

Chryseis' slim hands flew to the base of her throat. The motion was incredibly graceful. It was like the lifting, the flutter, of wings.

"Why—why can't you?" she whispered. "Have you—secretly—a wife already?"

"Chrys!" Danaus said. "You shame me past all bearing!"

"Oh, shut up, Dan! I won't take your lover from you. I can't. And I wouldn't if I could. I don't mean to marry ever."

"Why not?" Ariston said.

"Answer my question first, noble Ariston! Say I were to—to be even slightly interested, which I'm not—why couldn't you marry me?"

"Because I am a metic, my lady. Even an ex-slave. And that slavery was the vilest kind imaginable."

"Into which you were sold through no fault of you own," Sokrates said, "and before that, you were of one o the highest, noblest houses in Lakonia. Don't debase your self, my boy. The only obstacle's the law. And I think now we should put our heads together to find some way aroun that obstacle. Surely some method can be found to gain o buy you your citizenship."

"Perhaps if you bought and outfitted a trireme, gave i to the polis, came along with us as a trirach—" Danau said.

"Dan!" Chryseis said.

"I could buy and outfit a trireme," Ariston said gravely "but I couldn't command her. A metic cannot give order to citizens, Dan. So I'd have no chance to display my hy pothetical valor. We'd better think of something else."

"Exactly!" Chryseis spat. "Especially that nothing yo did or ever could do would make me marry you! You c any man!"

Ariston stared at her. Then very slowly he smiled.

"Why not?" he said.

"Because—a wife's a slave. A miserable and debased slave. Who must submit her body nightly to—" She stopped, shuddered convulsively.

"Chryseis!" Danaus said. "Will you never cease to shame me?"

"Aye. Now I will. Now I shall retire to the gynaekeia and leave you free to plot my enslavement. Go to it, Danaus! I suppose you *can* deliver my body to this your friend —your beautiful friend—for, oh, he is, he is! But what not you nor anyone else can guarantee is that there shall be life in it!"

Then she whirled, ran from the room—a doe breaking cover, her lance shaft of a body inclined along the plane of terror, flight. Watching her go, Ariston could almost hear the baying of the pack.

"Ariston," Danaus groaned, "permit me to offer you my apologies—"

"And I, you, mine." Ariston said quickly. "I shouldn't have broken in on you like that. But your sister's voice— and, I admit, the things she was saying—intrigued me so that I couldn't help it. After all, if there was any actual reach of the proprieties, it was I who committed it, not he. She only threatened to remain until we came in. I actually did enter the presence of a highborn Athenian maid without the permission of her father or her brothers. And that, according to your mores, is unpardonable. But will you allow me to jolt you with a thought, my dear Danaus?"

"Of course!" Danaus said. He was beginning to feel much better now. Ariston's mere presence had that effect upon him.

"Why do you insult your women so?" Ariston said.

"Insult!" Danaus said.

"Yes. In Sparta, ours have every freedom. As maids, they dance totally naked in the sacred processions before the eyes of all men. They can receive any guest they will in their husband's presence or out of it. A man dropping by unexpectedly to visit a friend will be, in that friend's absence, most graciously received by his friend's wife. We just don't believe our women are panting to hop into bed with the first male who catches them alone. You see, we

273

have faith in their honor, their pledged word, their chastity. And what women in all Hellas have the highest reputation for all three?"

"All right, all right!" Danaus said, "but is that reputation deserved?"

"It is," Sokrates said. "Every visitor to Sparta I've ever met vouches for it. While our Athenian dames have the worst. In all of Hellas, the worst. Can you think of why, Ariston?"

"I think you provoke them," Ariston said slowly. "Prison is not good for anyone, Sokrates. And that's what your gynaekeia are: prisons. There's nothing about slavery that elevates the morals. I know. I've been a slave. Then, having reduced your wives to mindless dolls, superior household slaves, distinguished from your concubines only by the fact that the wives' sons have legitimacy, can inherit, you have to go to the etairai for companionship, for the give and take of minds you miss at home. Minds, not bodies! For Hades take it, Dan! Any Athenian worth his salt is ashamed of frequenting pornai. I've spent ten years almost in the constant company of one of the finest etairai in Athens. Her house is filled with graybeards come to talk! To talk, Danaus! I know total homosexuals who'd vomit at a woman's touch who adore her. I've debated verse forms with Sophokles there; I've heard her sternly rebuke Aristophanes for his constant obscenities. She alone of all Athens has wit enough to see that Euripides is *not* a misogynist, that he loves and defends women instead of abusing them. Which brings me back to the subject of your sister—"

"I'm listening," Danaus said frigidly.

"I am going to try to obtain Athenian citizenship now. Seriously. And if I do, I want your permission to marry her —always with the prior condition that I can win both her consent and her love. I promise you to stay away from her, during your absence, until such time as I've gained the right to offer the Lady Chryseis the honorable estate of wife. My wife. My only wife—with no concubines to share her bed with me. No etairai to amuse me. Because, Dan, the very things that shock you enchant me. She is a person, not a doll. She has a mind, spirit, fire. And great nobility of soul. Do you agree to this?"

"Ariston—" Danaus whispered. "She—she is not beauti-ful —"

"I know. What of it? Her mind is. And I think, her soul. Besides, she'll become pretty enough, Dan, once she loses her terror, stops fleeing life. Can't you even imagine what she'll look like with half a talent—no, say even a quarter of a talent—more of flesh upon these exquisite bones? And that will come. Once she knows what it is to be loved, truly loved, her nerves will quiet enough to let her eat. Besides, what's mere fleshly beauty, anyhow, my friend? I've lost count of the beautiful women I've bedded with. But one has to get up sometimes, Dan. Talk. Have interests in com-mon. Oh, Hades and Persephone both take it, I don't want a brainless idiot for the mother of my sons!"

Slowly Danaus smiled, put out his hand to Ariston.

"I know of no one I'd rather have as my brother-in-law than you, Ariston," he said.

But once having thus pledged away his future, in the following days, reaction against his own folly held Ariston hard in its grip. Chryseis, poor little thing, was so awfully thin and plain. No, more than plain—ugly. He tried to tell himself that her ugliness was interesting, exotic, even excit-ing—as it was, being in sober truth far more appealing than cold and classic beauty; but he needed to see her again to reassure himself of that fact. And that, under the present circumstances was utterly impossible—unless she should de-cide to pay another clandestine visit to Parthenope, as now he rather hoped she would.

His mood of uncertainty, of doubt, even of melancholy was such that he set out in search of Sokrates to ask counsel of that wisest of men. The sailing date of the Syrakusan expedition had been postponed once again, which afforded him the doubtful privilege of joining it and making the desperate effort to gain his citizenship by a feat of arms. That the effort was almost sure to be unsuccess-ful, and if successful, only so at the cost of his life, didn't recommend it as a procedure. Nor did it help his mood to be faced with the embarrassing necessity of saying good-bye to Danaus all over again.

But when he reached Sokrates' house, he heard Xanthippe screaming like a fishwife within it. The object of her wrath was lovely young Myrto, daughter of Aristides the Just, whom some years before Sokrates had also married. The Assembly had legalized polygamy temporarily in order to restore Attica's population—terribly wasted by the great plague that had carried off so many of its citizens, including the great Perikles, and by the slow bleeding away of her young manhood by this ugly fratricidal war that had gone on for almost sixteen years, except for a few months of truce. That Myrto had presented the philosopher with two sons, Sophronikos and Menexenos, against Xanthippe's one, that she was young and pretty and loved her merry old husband with all her tender heart didn't help plain, shrewish Xanthippe's already unlovely temper, especially when this further division of Sokrates' already tiny income among so many was taken into consideration.

"How do I know where he is?" Xanthippe was shrieking. "Go look for him yourself, Myrto! Look first at Parthenope's—or at the house of some other high-class whore! He just loves to advise them—lying down! Or go to Alkibiades' palace! Or to the house of all the idle young wastrels who pick his brains for him without paying him an obol for it, while other Sophists gain fortunes instructing aristocratic youths! Or go to the houses of rich men like Kriton and Ariston, who feed him, let him guzzle all the wine he wants, and introduce him to etairai, but nothing more! I tell you, you simpering little witch, I—"

Sadly Ariston turned away. If Sokrates wasn't at home, as Xanthippe had already saved him the trouble of even asking, Athena in her wisdom knew where he was by now. Searching for him was worse than useless, for Sokrates, obeying that inner daimonion who instructed him to goad men into examining their own heads and hearts to their ultimate benefit, might be anywhere from the port of Piraeus to the boundary stone of the Kerameikos, which was about as far away as it was possible to get and still stay within Athenian territory. He would find no help from that quarter today.

But he had to talk to someone. He had to! But who on earth—

He turned his gaze over the whole broad sweep of the

Athenian landscape. There, far below where he stood, the sea gleamed blue-silver between the Attic hills. The hills themselves were purplish with shadow, their humped umbrella pines silhouetted black against the matchless light, the cypresses stabbing the sky like inky spears, but the sunlight, already dying away from the mainland, rested upon the Island of Salamis like a lingering caress, making that low hump of rocky land, crowned with the white of its houses, the somber green of its trees, glow like a mottled, imperfect, yellowish pearl.

Salamis, where Euripides lived. Surely the one man to whom the gods had unlocked all the secrets of the feminine heart! He'd go to see him, the only human being he'd ever met whom he sometimes thought wiser than even Sokrates. It was too late now to set out; but tomorrow he'd go. Ah, yes—tomorrow.

But as he started downward from the Agora toward his own home, he heard his name being called, and turning saw a group of glittering young officers, most of them clad in armor which his own factories had made. In the midst of them, taller than the rest, was the joint commander of the expedition. Alkibiades, son of Kleinas. With him were several young hippêis whom Ariston didn't know, and two men in civilian dress. One of the two, surprisingly enough, was Autolykos, surprisingly because a matchless fighter like the son of Lykon should have been among the first to join the expedition; but, approaching them now, Ariston saw why his good friend and wrestling opponent wasn't in armor: Autolykos had his left arm in a sling, and Ariston could see the wooden board to which it was bound. A broken arm, of course, was excuse enough to keep the indolent, handsome, and gay athlete at home. The other civilian, Ariston recognized now, was Perikles, son of the immortal statesman of the same name. Surely, Ariston thought, he has been kept at home because of politics. A pity. Men say he's one of the finest naval commanders that we have.

"Ah, Ariston! Ariston!" Alkibiades mocked. "For your chosen role of Hephaestos, you're singularly ill-fitted. Because the blacksmith of the gods was both ugly and lame and had the fair Aphrodite as wife, while you—"

"I'm ugly enough, though not yet lame," Ariston said

277

easily. "Chaire, kalokagathoi! And you, Autolykos, old friend, it would seem you'd play crippled Hephaestros for a fact!"

"Your namesake, Charmides' pet pankratist, did that," Autolykos groaned. "The older he gets, the meaner—and the tougher. Broke my arm for me like a wand. I should know better than to wrestle old Ariston. But you, beautiful young Ariston—tell me, how go all your loves?"

"I'll tell you for him," Alkibiades went on with his raillery. "He disappoints me. He should wed, and thus provide me with an Aphrodite to play Ares to. But not only does he refuse me any opportunity of adorning his forehead for him, but he contents himself with one *very* dull boy—you all know Danaus, son of Pandoros, don't you?"

"I know him," Perikles said, "but that he is Pandoros' son, I doubt. Knowing Pandoros, I doubt it profoundly!"

"Oh, yes, he is," Alkibiades went on solemnly. "It seems that one night the Lady Tekmessa, in despair, went out to the stables, cut off the tail of one of the mounts, and glued it to her chin with a little flour mixed with goat's milk. After that, she clad her fair form in a chiton stolen from one of the stableboys—unwashed for a twelfthmonth, naturally. And Pandoros came home drunk, and smelling his favorite perfume—that gut-churning stink of unwashed oaf —reached out his hand and encountered that thick, new-sprouted beard. So wild with delighted lust, he leaped upon her and—"

"Alkibiades, for Artemis' sake!" Ariston said.

"By Eros, I swear it's true," Alkibiades said gravely. "So well did the trick work that she repeated it three more times, thus providing her august pederast—to his own disgust—with a family. But in any case, Danaus, however got, is the cause of the season's richest scandal. For hear me, friends. For love of Danaus, our Ariston donated to the poet Sophokles the very finest etaira in all Attica!"

"I'd heard that," Perikles said, "but I didn't believe it."

"You were wise not to," Ariston said, "since there's not a word of truth in it."

"Oh yes, there is!" Autolykos hooted. "And now our little Theoris is great with child, which that old lecher Sophokles fancies is his!"

"Then he has my whole-hearted admiration," Perikles said serenely. "Any man who, at Sophokles' age, has any basis to even imagine such a thing, should be crowned with laurel at the next Dionysia."

"Lucky child!" Alkibiades said. " 'Tis sure to be beautiful. For Theoris is the loveliest of women, and Sophokles, even in his winter season, is one of the most beautiful men in Attica. Besides, even if he is mistaken, our Ariston here is sure to have had a hand in its making, and he—"

"A hand, great Strategos?" one of the young hippêis mocked.

"A figure of speech, young friend," Alkibiades said primly. "Let us not be gross, I pray you! Well, Ariston—how about joining us for supper tonight? I assure you it will be a most chaste and pious affair—"

"Like the last time I was at your house?" Ariston said.

Suddenly, surprisingly, Alkibiades reached out and took his arm. Gripped it so hard Ariston was sure the bones were crushed. Looking into the newly elected Strategos' face, Ariston saw that Alkibiades was frowning a warning at him.

"I thank you for the invitation," Ariston said, "but I cannot, Alkibiades. I mean to beard Euripides in his cave tomorrow, and for that I must get up early."

"Do visit him," Perikles said suddenly. "I was over there two days ago, and he speaks of you most kindly. Ever since your late father paid for the chorus of his *Hecuba*, and you played—Hektor, I believe, wasn't it? With those masks it's hard to tell—"

"Yes, Hektor," Ariston said.

"He has bemoaned the fact that you did not become a professional hypokritos. He says you have the voice, the looks, the bearing, and the sensitivity to—have made an excellent actor.

"Besides, your visit will do him good. He's quite ill, it seems to me—worn out by his labors on the new play. He read a bit to me, but he had to stop after a line or two because his voice failed him. Even so, it seems to me a wonder."

"What's it called?" Ariston asked.

*"The Trojan Women,"* Perikles said.

"Ariston," Alkibiades said, and astonishingly, Ariston detected a note of worry in his voice. "Sure you won't come to supper?"

"I can't, Alkibiades. I'm truly sorry, but—"

Then again Alkibiades caught his arm.

"Then walk apart with me a moment, Ariston," he said. "It's imperative that I have a word with you in private. Excuse us a moment, kalokagathoi, please!"

They walked a few rods away.

"Ariston," Alkibiades whispered, "that miserable transvestite affair you mentioned—you'll keep silent about it, won't you? If it comes up again, I mean. I fear it's going to. If it does, I'll be ruined. But he'll need witnesses who weren't themselves involved in it, and you—"

"Who needs witnesses?"

"Thessalos, son of Kimon. I've been paying that miserable sykophantos for years to keep his mouth shut, but now that I'm leading the expedition, his jealousy is sure to—"

Ariston smiled dryly.

"Since I cannot ruin you without also ruining Athens, you may count upon my silence, great Strategos!" he said.

"You mock me," Alkibiades said. "But hear me, Ariston. Listen to my words! Whatever other charges may be brought against me once we've sailed—and sure as Zeus rules on Olympus, something will be—they'll be false! Do you believe me?"

"No," Ariston said.

"I swear it upon Hipparete's grave." Alkibiades said quietly. "Do you believe me now?"

Ariston stood there, staring at him a long, slow time. Then he said, with complete conviction:

"Yes, Alkibiades; now I do."

# CHAPTER SEVENTEEN

WHEN ARISTON GOT OUT OF THE BOAT in the inlet before the cave where Euripides lived, Cephisophon, the great poet's Ethiopian secretary, came down to meet him. Ariston could see from Cephisophon's frowning dark face that the man had come expressly to warn him off, to tell him that the poet was in no mood, or was too ill, to receive visitors today.

Then Ariston saw Cephisophon's face change. His eyes narrowed suddenly, giving a certain speculative cast of his whole aspect. Then they cleared, and the secretary bowed very low.

"Welcome, O noble son of Timosthenes!" he said.

Ariston stood there on the rocky beach of the inlet, looking at Cephisophon. All his instincts told him that something was amiss here. For one thing, that greeting had been excessive. "Ariston, son of Timosthenes" would have been enough. For among the things that Timosthenes, moved both by Ariston's great beauty and his strong resemblance to his own dead son Oebalides, had foregone when he adopted the Spartan boy, was any chance of conveying his own hereditary rank to him. Had Timosthenes adopted a citizen, the new son would automatically have become an eupatridos, a noble, as Timosthenes himself was. But having, in his blind sentimental folly, adopted a lowly metic, he couldn't convey nobility to him any more than he could citizenship.

And all this Cephisophon knew.

Ariston smiled at the dark-skinned secretary a little mockingly.

"This newborn servility of yours ill becomes a servant of such a master," he said. "Besides, I know you of old;

you're not wanting in pride. I'm not a noble, as you know well. I'm simply Ariston the Shield Maker, Ariston the Metic, or, if you will, by the love he offered me, by the love and veneration I bear his memory, Ariston, son of Timosthenes. Now tell me, how goes it with your master?"

"Ill," Cephisophon said sadly. He stood there a long moment, staring at Ariston, doubt and hesitation struggling in his eyes.

"Speak, O Cephisophon!" Ariston said.

"Young Master, I—" the Ethiopian began. "No, I dare not. But—but will you have a word with Mnesilochos, first?"

"Of course," Ariston said.

Mnesilochos was Euripides' father-in-law; and, more important, his good friend. A better friend, Ariston thought grimly, than his wife is, or his three sons, none of whom have come nigh him since that bellowing old demagogue Kleon had him tried for impiety. And even though Euripides was acquitted, no son of his has had the courage to—

He stopped short, his mind digging into the problem. Why, in the name of Athena did people hate Euripides so? Those rumors that Chorile, his wife, had frequently horned him—rumors having not the slightest basis in fact but repeated with bitter satisfaction by all Athens—again why? Why did people swear his mother had been a greengrocer, a vendor of the wild chervil grass that was only eaten in times of famine? And that ridiculous charge that the poet hated women—he whose feminine roles were always stronger and finer than his male?

These things were a mystery, but the mystery was beginning to clear in Ariston's mind. After I've talked with Mnesilochos, Ariston thought, I'll draw Euripides out a little, learn something more of him—who almost never talks about himself—before burdening him with my problems. That is, if he's not too ill. If I even dare—

Mnesilochos greeted Ariston with a worried air, clawing his gnarled fingers through his beard as though to comb it out. As was often the case in Hellas where men waited until thirty or thirty-five to wed and then sought brides just past puberty to ensure, as Theoris had bitterly pointed out, that they were indeed virgin, Mnesilochos was somewhat younger than his son-in-law.

"Chaire, O son of Timosthenes!" he said.

"Rejoice, Mnesilochos," Ariston said, and waited.

Again he witnessed the sad spectacle of a man struggling with himself; though this time, not having Cephisophon's burnt teakwood complexion to hide it, Mnesilochos' perplexity was even clearer.

"Speak, Mnesilochos," Ariston said. "You're troubled— as Cephisophon also was. But this house's troubles are my own. Nothing would honor me more than to share them."

"And to relieve them?" Mnesilochos said.

"That would more than honor me," Ariston said. "That would bring me joy."

Mnesilochos looked at Ariston from under heavy brows. He was, after all, a Hellene; and all Hellenes knew in their bones that craft was better than straightforwardness.

"Even if it costs a great deal?" he said.

Ariston smiled at him, mockingly.

"Ah! So it's only money you want, Mnesilochos?" he said. "You relieve my mind. I thought you were going to ask me something difficult."

"More than a talent? Maybe even two?" Mnesilochos whispered.

"Is it for Euripides?" Ariston said.

"Yes. Yes, of course."

"Will five talents be enough?" Ariston said. "Ten? You name it. Bring me writing materials, and I'll make you out a letter upon my banker Paris now."

Mnesilochos stared at him.

"Without even knowing what it's for?" he said.

"If it's for Euripides, I know enough. Anything I can do for him is by that very token for civilization and against savagery," Ariston said.

Mnesilochos bounced up then and clasped Ariston in his arms. Kissed both his cheeks. Stood back, holding him at arm's length. And now Ariston could see the tears in his eyes.

"You have saved his life!" Mnesilochos said.

"Oh, come now, Mnesilochos," Ariston laughed. "Don't

283

be melodramatic. Euripides wouldn't like it, for he never is. Tell me, how much does he need?"

"I don't know," Mnesilochos said. "And anyhow, it can't be done that way. The Archon Basileos has read the new play. He's passed it for production—reluctantly. He admits it's a work of great genius, but he fears the people will consider it inflammatory and be enraged by it. Therefore, to save his own skin, he won't appoint a choregos for it. We have to find our own—"

"You've found him," Ariston said. "I'll go to the King Archon as soon as I get back to Athens. But may I not see Euripides a moment? That is, if he's not too ill?"

"He was," Mnesilochos said happily; "but surely this news will cure him!"

Ariston sat there looking at the great poet. Euripides' face—terribly worn and gray-hued from his titanic labors—was still singularly beautiful, though not in the fleshly way that Sophokles' was. From a physical standpoint, there was some justification for calling him ugly, as all his enemies did. His forehead was too high, his cheeks too hollow, his lips sunken over gaps where his gums had lost their teeth, and he had two or three prominent moles on his face. But none of these details mattered, Ariston decided. The spirit within him glowed through his thin flesh like a light, transforming that face, making it extraordinarily beautiful.

"So, my young friend," Euripides said with gentle mockery, "you have some ambitions of setting up your little monument in the Street of the Tripods?"

Ariston smiled. When a poet won the prize at the Greater Dionysia, his name, the name of his play, and that of the leading hypokritos—a word that originally meant not "actor" but "answerer," for in the old primitive days when tragedy was just emerging from the Dionysian ritual dances and chants, the role of the hypokritos was simply to answer the chorus, giving back the antistrophe to their strophe—were all carved on stone tablets set in the walls of the god's temple, because for a tragedy to have won the prize was equivalent to winning immortality for its author and its chief interpretor both. But, as for the choregos, a rich man selected by the Archon Basileos to bear the expenses of the production, the honors were much less. He was allowed, at his own expense, to set up a bronze tripod with his name on it, in a miniature temple to commemorate his own contribution to the victory. A whole street had been dedicated to this purpose, and so named. It wound around the eastern end of the Akropolis to the Theater of Dionysus, and was fairly choked with the monuments of small men to their pitiful vanity.

"No, Master," he said. "I only want to give the world the chance to enjoy—no, that's wrong—to suffer genius."

"Suffer it?" Euripides said. "Aye, you're right, son Ariston! They suffer it—but sadly. Immortal gods, how they hate me!"

"They crowd the theater until even an ant couldn't burrow his way in every time a piece of yours is produced. They bellow at you like idiot bulls, invent lies about the chervil grass growing about your cradle. They swear poor dear Chorile beats you—confusing her, I think, with Sokrates' Xanthippe who once actually did give him a drubbing in the market place before all of Athens to their immense delight. You probably could have heard their roars of laughter in Ionia!"

"They say worse than that," Euripides sighed.

"I know. But not even they believe it," Ariston said. "And, for all of that, they come back. Every time a masked and buskined hypokritos treads the boards speaking your words of brine and blood and fire, they come back! Aristophanes has been attacking you without letup for twenty-odd years in every comedy of his. Why, master? May I suggest an answer?"

"I'd be delighted if you would," the poet said.

"Because you are a genius. The greatest that Hellas has ever produced. Greater than Aeschylos, because you've learned all he had to teach and have gone beyond him. Greater than Sophokles—"

"No," Euripides said. "That, no!"

"Yes! Greater, because you have more courage. Sophokles' verse is smoother than yours, more musical, but less powerful. He rubs the truth round and smooth to the touch, so that it doesn't irritate too much. Only once did he truly break out, it seems to me—in his *Antigone*, against the nonsense men erect between themselves and truth's utter horror. While you—"

"While I—flay them, lash them, make them bleed!" the poet whispered.

"Exactly. Which is why your works will live forever. Because you are neither a clown nor a whore, and that's what crowd-pleasers have to be, and why their shoddy wares age and die."

"Aristophanes is no clown," Euripides said calmly. "You go too far, son Ariston! Remember the lines in *The Clouds,* when Unjust Argument attacks even the gods as scoundrels, and having made Just Argument admit that speechwriters, tragic poets—meaning me!—public orators and so forth are all blackguards, he turns, points at the audience and asks: 'Which class among our friends seem the most numerous?' "

" 'The blackguards have it by a large majority!' " Ariston quoted. "And they roared with laughter at their own expense. A comic poet can do that, because people don't really take him seriously. But the great tragic poets aren't so easy to forgive. You give them truth, than which there is no more unpalatable diet; you strip away from them the pitiful defenses they erect against their own meanness, littleness, and their coming, irrevocably final end—"

"Which is cruel," Euripides sighed.

"But necessary. Does not a father beat his son to make a man of him? Can we ever achieve dignity without facing reality, enduring its awful pain? A being setting up stone dolls to babble nonsense called prayers to them, and torturing small animals before them in the idea that primordial savagery and blood lust is pleasing to them, is a backward, primitive child; but he who stands tall against the night that will engulf him, accepting the onrushing dark calmly, unwhimperingly, unafraid—is a man. I prefer manhood, Euripides. And I've had it—the true conception of it—from you as a gift. For which I thank you. Tell me, would you rather be loved than respected?"

"So far, I've been neither, Ariston, my son. But no matter. I've lived a long time and seen all I loved slip away

286

from me. My father, the merchant Mnesarchides of Phyla —the gods deal kindly with his shade!—my good sweet mother, Cleito—need I tell you she *wasn't* a greengrocer, son Ariston?"

"Of course not," Ariston laughed. "But all the same, you're responsible for that story yourself, Master."

"I?" Euripides said. "In Hera's name, how?"

"Remember the line in your *Melanippe?* 'It is not my word but my mother's word . . .'? Add to that the fact that Melanippe, and even more so her mother, were famous for their knowledge of potent herbs, and you have that base fable readymade. And even more so in the case of—" Ariston stopped suddenly, his handsome young face reddening visibly.

"My wife, Chorile," the poet sighed, "who, apart from occasionally taking a leaf from Xanthippe's book and berating me soundly for all my sins, is a good helpmate and a loving spouse, but in whose mouth they put the lines I've written for the most wicked of my heroines and to whom they attribute their vilest acts. That's what you were going to say, weren't you? I know that, son Ariston. What I don't know, or understand, is why."

Ariston smiled. He had noticed this same trait before in Sophokles, and even—more surprisingly—in Aristophanes himself—this curious blind spot in men of genius. Euripides, who indisputably saw deeper into human motives than any other writer who ever lived, could not see at all one of the commonest and shallowest of these motives: the average man's total lack of creative imagination.

"And not only does this average man lack it," he went on, after having said his thought to the poet, "but lacking it, he disbelieves in its existence. You jolt him uncomfortably by putting real women on the stage; and hide it as he will, deny as he does his own experience of wives who don't know their place and won't be dominated, the ache of the knobs sprouting on his own forehead, the welts raised by the rough edge of a female tongue, instruct him that your analysis of feminine character is both penetrating and just. So he asks himself: 'How does Euripides know so much about women?' And answers himself, lacking even a suspi-

287

cion of what the mind of genius does: 'Why, out of his own experience!' You draw a Theseus, so you have to be a cuckold. You draw a Medea and—"

"But my sons live, so they can't hang that one on my poor Chorile!" Euripides laughed. "Actually, speaking of parallels from life, my poor mother was of an eupatride family—of noble stock. I don't suppose she even knew what chervil grass was. I have Aristophanes to thank for that canard! And, as for my so-called bitterness against life, I'm at a loss to account for it. I was born at Phyla, at the very heart of Attica, and no more pleasant village exists in all of Hellas. Though all around us the earth was dry and parched by a merciless sun, Phyla is a place of many earth-born springs and streams, covered with trees, green and fragrant. That's why we have so many temples there. Even the gods, men thought, sought us out for their earthly abode.

"I was cupbearer to the Dancers' Guild who trod the sacred measures before the altar of Delian Apollo—and, if you know anything about Attic society, you know how much chance a greengrocer's son would have of being given that high honor! Even less of being chosen fire-bearer to the Apollo of Cape Zôstêr, which I also was. You know what that means? I headed the troop of naked torchbearers who met the Delian Apollo at the Cape and lighted his way from Delos to Athens—"

"And you were happy?" Ariston said.

"No. I don't think so. I was born with a questioning mind, which precludes happiness, however happy one's circumstances. Oh, I had some hard knocks! When I was four, we had to leave home because the Persians were upon us. I remember even now seeing the smoke rising from the towns and villages of Attica, and at last from the Akropolis itself. How my poor mother wept at that! When I was eight, the walls of Athens were rebuilt, and we could go home again. My father took me to see the first great tragedy—by Phrynichos, for whom great Themistokles served as choregos; but now I don't even remember its title, so little impression did it make upon me. I was more impressed by the paintings of Polygnôtus, which Themistokles caused to be set up in our temples at Phlya as well as in Athens itself. Oh, how I yearned to be a painter! But life and this accursed profession of scribbling had already laid their hands on me, although I knew it not. At ten, I saw the procession bringing great Theseus' bones home to Athens from the Island of Skyros, and verses stirred in me. I set them down, but reading them over afterward, I sadly smoothed the wax of the tablet on which I'd painfully written them with my boyish stylus and consigned them to the oblivion they deserved."

"I doubt that," Ariston said.

"Don't. They were doggerel of the worst sort. At twelve, I saw Aeschylos' *The Persians*, and had found my destiny, though I resisted it. At seventeen, I saw *Seven Against Thebes*—Perikles was the choregos for that—and I was lost. Or I would have been if I hadn't become an ephêbos the next year and had to shoulder my spear and shield and march out against the Thracians. I, too, was strong in body, Ariston, my son—as strong as you are now. I won the long race at Athens and the pankratieon at Eleusis. But I was still mad to be a painter; and unfortunately for me, I found success at that, too . . ."

"Unfortunately?" Ariston asked. "Why unfortunately, Master?"

"Because, if I'd failed miserably at it, I should have been forced to turn to my true profession earlier. There are paintings of mine—quite respectable ones—hanging in the temples of Megara now. I was commissioned to do them, because in those days I was considered a great painter. I wasn't. I was a good, workmanlike painter, nothing more. All my paintings lacked was the essential—"

"Genius," Ariston said.

"Yes. But in those times I had scant excuse for my melancholy, except perhaps my acute sensitivity to the difference between words and deeds, between what men preach and what they practice. Or even what the gods—"

"Demand of men in contrast to what they themselves give," Ariston said.

"Which is little—or nothing," Euripides said. "But Athens herself, or rather her noisy rabble intent upon defending a piety they can neither spell nor define, soon gave me cause enough for grief. My old teacher, Anaxagoras of

289

Klazomenae, was driven out of the polis, forced to flee for his life, despite all Perikles himself did to save him. And Protagoras, who read here in this very cavehouse his great work *On the Gods*—"

" 'In regard to the gods I cannot know that they exist, nor that they do not; many things hinder such knowledge —the obscurity of the matter, and the shortness of human life—' " Ariston quoted.

"You remember everything you read, don't you?" the poet said.

"Or hear. It's a strange gift, for which I'm grateful to Protagoras' dubious gods. I need only to read a thing once or hear it with attention, and I have the bulk of it forever, mostly word for word—"

"Which is another reason why you should have been a great hypokritos instead of a manufacturer of the implements of murder!" Euripides said.

"Of murder?" Ariston said. "I call myself a defender of civilization, of which Athens is the mother—"

"As at Melos?" Euripides said.

"I see. And you're right. *That* had no defense under heaven. But I didn't make weapons for massacring the innocent, Master. You cannot blame me if my products are misused. I was a Spartan. In my native polis, I've seen art, beauty, music, perverted to savage ends and intelligence crushed. That's why I defend Athens. With all her faults, she is the freest polis in the world. But please, about Protagoras—"

"He'd be alive now if 'free Athens' hadn't driven him out for writing what he believed," Euripides said bitterly. "He drowned at sea, and—"

"You wrote: 'You have killed, O Hellenes, you have murdered the Muses' nightingale, the wizard bird who sang no wrong!' " Ariston quoted.

"Aye, so I did. Forgive me my brusqueness, Ariston—especially now that you've come to save my play. But I warn you, we cannot hope to win with *The Trojan Women*. It may even be that you, as choregos, might fall into public disfavor because of it."

"A privilege," Ariston said, "because to so inflame men's minds, it must be great—"

"Strong at the least. I wrote it because of that horrible business of Melos. You see, in Athens, during the summer, I saw a boy, one of the captives, in the slave market. He was as beautiful as a god. His hair was like corn tassels, blond to the point of being silvery; but his eyes were as black as night. He had a sword cut in the shoulder that had healed badly, and now had broken open again. It was dripping blood and pus, and the flies were at it. He made no move to brush them away, but just sat there staring off into space with those unfathomable black eyes. I went up to him and asked him his name. 'Phaedon,' he said; that was all. So I rushed home to get money to buy him, set him free. But when I got back, he'd already been sold. Into one of the bathhouses, I'm told, as a pornos. And he was no more than twelve years old—"

"God!" Ariston said.

"So I came back here and the first lines of the tragedy —I've been thinking about the idea a long time now—began stirring in my mind. I sat down and wrote easily and at once, without having to rub out a single letter my stylus cut into the wax:

> " 'How blind you are
> You who tread cities underfoot, that throw
> Temples down to desolation, lay waste
> The mighty tombs where lie
> The Ancient Dead, You
> So soon
> To die!' "

"Master," Ariston whispered, "may I read it? May I read it now?"

"Of course," Euripides said.

So it was that Ariston departed that cavehouse on Salamis without having mentioned his problems, having forgotten that they existed or that such a maid as Chryseis lived. Dark Cephisophon had to take him by the arm and guide him to the boat, so blinded were his eyes from weeping, so intense the pity, shame, and horror that the greatest single tragedy ever penned by man had awakened in him.

Two weeks from that day, in fact, on the eve of the morning that the often delayed expedition against Syrakuse finally did sail, Ariston sat in the open-air theater with Danaus and Sokrates waiting for *The Trojan Women* to begin. Neither of them knew that he was its choregos, for he hadn't told them that. Them, nor anyone. It didn't seem important to him, against the glory of that play.

But what all three of them knew past all doubt was that Euripides couldn't even hope to gain the prize. Xenokles, against whom he was competing, was sure to win with one of his three tragedies, *Oedipus, Lykaon, Bakchai,* or his satyr play, *Athamas.* Ariston had seen the *Oedipus,* and Danaus had seen all three tragedies by Xenokles but only half the first act of the satyr play, because he had left the theater in disgust at its crude filth. Sokrates hadn't seen any of Xenokles' plays, because he only went to the theater when a work of Euripides' was presented. He made no exceptions, not even for Sophokles, who also was his friend.

But all three of them had seen both the *Alexander* and the *Palamedes,* the two tragedies of Euripides so far presented. And they were going to see *The Trojan Women,* which was today's bill. It was a tribute to their devotion to their great friend that they also planned to endure his *Sisyphos,* though it was a satyr play, one of those outrageously obscene farces that all poets were forced to add to their entries in the festivals in order to appease the Athenian mob's bottomless appetite for filth.

"I've seen all of Xenokles' claptrap!" Danaus raged. "He's not fit to lace Euripides' buskins! And yet—"

"He's going to win," Ariston said sadly. "The reason's obvious, Dan. Euripides will not betray his artistic integrity. He doesn't try to please the crowds. This very play is going to lose him the prize. I know that. I've read it."

"You have!" Danaus said.

"Yes. At Euripides' house—or rather in his cave on the Island of Salamis. I had myself rowed out there because Perikles told me the poet was ill from his labors, had tormented himself into near madness writing this particular play. You know why he did this? Because of that horrible affair of Melos. To teach Athenians that to massacre the whole population of a defenseless island is something less than—honorable, shall we say? That, by so doing, we have sunk past barbarism into savagery. A point of view scarcely calculated to win him popularity, what? He takes the Trojans' side, don't you see? I, when I left him, had to be led by a slave, so blinded were my eyes from weeping!"

"How does it go?" Sokrates said. "Do you remember any of it, kalon?"

"Too much of it. It rips my bowels still. But wait a while and you'll hear it for yourselves."

"No," Danaus said, "I love what your voice does, kalon mine, speaking great poetry. Say some of it for me!"

"Let me see—" Ariston whispered, "let me see . . . This, then:

> " 'Here, beside these unhung, smashed, and broken
>     gates
> where any slave with stomach enough to look at her
> can gaze his stupid fill, Hecuba lies, weeping
> for Troy's uncounted dead, her uncounted tears.
> With Polyxena, the youngest of her daughters
> already murdered
> throat cut and burnt like a she-goat upon
> Achillios' tomb.
> King Priam gone, the children she bore him
> slaughtered.
> But one girl's left: Kassandra
> mad now
> screaming mad
> reeling under the blows Apollo rains upon her,
> mercifully not knowing that a little later on
> the great and pious Agamemnon will force her
> will ravish her
> soaking
> with the blood of her torn hymen
> his secret, swinish bed
> against the gods' will,
> against all pious teachings. . . .' "

"God!" Danaus whispered.

"And this," Ariston said; "this alone will cost him the prize:

" 'For one woman's sake
   for one adulterous coupling in the dark
   these brave ones came in search of Helen
   and tossed uncounted lives away.
   Their strategos, their polemarch—ah, how pious and
   how wise!—
   in the name of that whorish woman cut his own
   daughter's throat
   upon the high altar at Aulis.
   For a favorable wind Iphigenia
   died
   by her father's pitiless hand.
   For a puffed sail.
   A half bagful of air.
   All this to bring home
   his brother's soiled wife,
   this porna
   who went of her own free will
   unthreatened
   to the bed of her adulteries . . .'."

He heard the gasps behind him and turned. But the woman who sat there on the stone seat behind him was too heavily veiled for him to see who she was. Then the tragedy began, and he forgot all about her.

But once again during the performance she gasped aloud. It was at that point in the play where Andromache says:

"Men say one night of carnal play is enough
to rid a woman of her repugnance for any lusty bed;
but I hate and despise the woman who forgets
a great and pious love
to take another in her arms—"

He turned and stared at her. She was dressed in the robes of an Athenian matron. A widow, he decided, for this to affect her so. Probably one who has already fallen from that degree of piety. She seems young—but no. A young woman would never veil herself to that extent. Feminine vanity wouldn't let her.

He turned back to the tremendous drama before him. He forgot the woman behind him, the lover-friend at his side, the embodiment of wisdom at his right hand. When they reached the climactic scene where the victorious Hellenes tear the baby Astyanax from his mother's arm, to kill the child lest great Hektor's valor live on in him, he bent his head and wept, remembering Alkmena, his own mother, remembering Phryne in his heart, his mind, the mother of the sons he'd never have. The awful words sang like whiplashes, lacerating the very air around him:

> "Take him, throw him from the tower.
> Smash his little head like an eggshell on
> the rocks. Stain the earth with his blood
> his innocent baby's brains; eat
> his tender flesh like a suckling pig's
> if you want to.
> It is the gods—the so very kind and gentle
> gods—who condemn us to this horror, and I
> haven't the strength to save my son.
> So, cover my face. Hurl me into the stinking
> bilge of your ship. Lead me to that
> second, flowering, bridal
> bed
> I walk to now
> across the body of my child . . ."

Then he felt her hand on his shoulder. Her voice came to him. It was hoarse from crying, thick and humid with tears, too much so for him to know if he had heard it before, or not. It seemed to him he had. But where?

"You weep for this?" she said. "You? A man?"

"Yes," he said. "For this—and for the mother who died for my father and for me. Who took a blade through her heart to save us both. For the only girl I ever loved. Who was butchered like Polyxena above the tombs of murder-

295

ous beasts. This play has too much of my life in it, my lady. I'm not ashamed to weep—"

"The—gods bless you—stranger," the woman said.

Later in the day, still under the grip of emotions that *The Trojan Women* had waked in him, he went and sacrificed before his adoptive father's tomb. When he had finished that pious act, he turned and saw a veiled woman standing a little way off, accompanied by a slave girl. He thought it was the same one, the one who had sat behind him in the theater. But he couldn't be sure, because, when he approached her, she turned and walked away from him with such immense dignity that to have followed her would have been a grave insult. So he turned away, went home again.

# CHAPTER EIGHTEEN

THAT GREAT CRY AWOKE HIM the morning after the fleet had sailed. It seemed to come from everywhere at once: It vibrated down from the Kolonoa Agoraios; it swept through the columns of all the stoae on the Agora; it echoed down from the Akropolis, screamed down from the Aeropagos, the Hill of Ares, soared up from the port of Piraeus, ran cityward along the long walls in a series of ululate pulsations that sounded as though they burst from the throats of wolves rather than from those of men.

He leaped from the bed, threw on a chiton, ran out into the street. Everywhere people were gathering before the doors of their own houses, weeping, wailing, wringing their hands. Then he turned, and, seeing the reason, was hard put to contain his own tears. For all the protective Hermes Bifontes that were set up in front of every Athenian home—those two-faced ancestral busts in which the two countenances were joined back to back so that they could stare in both directions at once to watch for danger to the household—had been smashed by some savage hand.

Although Ariston didn't believe that stone statues could protect anyone from anything, he'd set up a Hermes before his own door out of his strict policy of respecting other men's beliefs and not giving offense by openly scorning them. And the cause of his own grief was not the Athenians' superstitious horror at what seemed to them a monstrous blasphemy, but the fact that his own protective Hermes was the product of Sokrates' skillful hand.

For, at Ariston's request, the philosopher had returned temporarily to his original profession, that of sculptor, though he didn't need to, since the wealthy Kriton had so well invested his savings of seventy minae for him that

Sokrates was freed from the necessity of having to gain his bread by chiseling figures out of stone. Now he made statues simply to amuse himself, or as acts of piety, such as the Hermes and the Three Graces he had donated to the Parthenon, or, in this case, as gifts to beloved disciples and friends.

And now, staring at the ruined figure, Ariston could hear the shouts:

"Who did it?"

"Who else but Alkibiades, the impious swine! Or agents of his. A man who dresses himself in an heirophant's dress like a woman, a priestess, in his own house, and openly profanes the mysteries there, is capable of anything, I tell you!"

"What to do? Call a meeting! Send the state trireme after the blackguard! Drag him back! Make him guzzle hemlock instead of wine! And to think we made him General!

And then it was that Ariston remembered Alkibiades' words to him some weeks before: "Whatever I'm charged with, it will be false! Upon Hipparete's grave, I swear it, Ariston!"

Slowly Ariston went back into the house and closed the door behind him. As if to drown out madness, as though to muffle pain.

That afternoon he was to attend a banquet given by a circle of Athens' richest men. But now, under the present circumstances, he wondered if any purpose would be served by going. Still he decided to go, after all. What better place to gauge the city's temper?

Charmides turned to Ariston.

"And you, my friend," he said, "surely you have an opinion about these things. Please tell us what you think?"

Ariston looked around the dining room. How strange it is that I should be here! he thought. The banquet was being held in the house of Charmides, son of Glaucon; and the men present, with the two exceptions of Sokrates and himself, were all sons of Athens' oldest and most distinguished families. Reclining on the couches about the table were: Nikeratos, son of Orchomenus' former owner, the strategos Nikias, who yesterday had sailed away with Alkibiades and the fleet they jointly command to attack Syrakuse; Ariston's own good friend and wrestling opponent Autolykos, son of the politician Lykon; Antisthenes the philosopher, who had deserted the teachings of Geogias the Sophist to embrace the dialectic method of Sokrates; both the wealthy Kriton and his son Kritoboulos; Kallias, richer still, but with a reputation for dissipation rivaling that of Alkibiades; and, last of all, Kleinias, Alkibiades' cousin, one of those youths whose stunning beauty made the customary Athenian confusion of the sexes more understandable.

"Come on, Ariston!" Charmides said, seeing his hesitation, "you may speak freely! Even Kleinias knows Alkibiades is a filthy swine. Say what you think!"

Ariston smiled. "I think that you, gracious host, have forgotten that I am not a citizen and that I have no desire to put myself at the mercy of the sykophantoi by saying a thing that could be considered slander."

"That's nonsense, noble Ariston," Kleinias said. "There are no extortionists present"—he paused, gave a long, slow look around the table before going on—"at least I don't think so," which brought a hoot of laughter from the company. "Of course, I have heard that Kallias is in debt now because of his multitudinous and multisexed love affairs, but—"

"I won't blackmail the beautiful Ariston," Kallias said. "For aside from the fact that I have no use for those miserable dogs of sykophantoi who are always after me, who could blackmail a man of such exemplary life? Now that the fair Danaus has set sail to reduce the Syrakusans' pride, he hasn't even a lover. So he may speak freely. Tell us, beautiful Ariston, did someone also knock the nose and ears off the Hermes before your door?"

"Yes," Ariston said.

"And what do you think of that?"

"That I'll never forgive whoever did it. That particular Hermes was my greatest treasure."

"Ha!" Nikeratos said. "An ugly stone statue was your greatest treasure? You who can buy my father and Kriton here, and Kallias all put together?"

"Yes," Ariston said quietly, "because it was carved for me by Sokrates, here."

"Ah!" Antisthenes said, "then you're right. Even mutilated, I'd give you its weight in gold for it—if I had its weight in gold—which I don't, and if you'd sell it which you wouldn't. But come, Ariston; you were once close to Alkibiades, through your friend and fellow prisoner Orchomenus—I never did understand why you and he were not ransomed along with the other Spartan prisoners from Sphacteria."

"Ask Nikeratos, who surely has had the story in detail from his father, the General," Ariston said drily. "Go on, Antisthemes—"

"Tell us: Do you think that Alkibiades engineered the mutilation of the Hermes which protect the doorway of every household in Athens?"

"I don't think so," Ariston said. "In fact, I know he didn't."

"And how could you *know* it, young man?" Kriton said.

"If you put it thus, sir," Ariston said, speaking with that ingrained respect toward his elders that Athenians found exaggerated, just as he and all other Lakedaemonians found shocking the Athenians' total lack of diffidence toward the aged, "I don't know it. But all the same, I'm sure he didn't. Let us agree, if you will, that Alkibiades' morals are unsavory; but who among you would dare call him a fool?"

"You've a point there, my boy," Kriton said. "Remember how he got rid of Hyperboulos?"

"Yes, Father!" his son, Kritoboulos laughed. "Hyperboulos—that Kleon in hyperbole!—tried to have him ostracized. But when the ostraka, the broken pot shards, were counted, Alkibiades and your father, Nikeratos, had so maneuvered that more than twice as many of the clay bits had Hyperboulos' name scratched on them as had Alkibiades' and Nikias' put together. So the lampmaker was ostracized, exiled. Ha! Ariston is right; Alkibiades is no fool!"

"I ask you all this," Ariston said. "What did Alkibiades stand to gain by such a folly? He already had the joint command along with Nikias. What good would it possibly do him to pay agents to infuriate the Athenian people by this sacrilege against the household gods? So now you send that imposing state trireme after him, to bring back to stand trial for impiety, thus falling into the trap the actual perpetrators of this vileness laid for you, thus benefiting the only men who stand to profit by this seemingly senseless mutilation of the Hermes."

"And those men are?" Autolykos said.

"The agents the Syrakusans paid good silver to engineer Alkibiades' disgrace," Ariston said.

"But why think you they'd do that, kalon?" Sokrates said.

Ariston looked around the table until he caught Nikeratos' eye.

"Nikeratos," he said, "will you forgive me for speaking freely? As a man, I admire and respect your father; but as a general—"

"He's a timid old fussbudget with too many superstitions and no imagination at all," Nikeratos said calmly. "That I know better than you, Ariston. I've had the misfortune of serving under the old man more than once. With Alkibiades there to supply the courage and the dash, we'd have beaten the Syrakusans easily; but now—"

"It's in the lap of the gods," Ariston said. "Sokrates, will you carve me another Hermes to set before my door?"

"Gladly," the philosopher said. "But my fee will be high, I warn you!"

"Name it," Ariston said, smiling.

"A duplicate of the present you recently made the poet Sophokles," Sokrates said solemnly. "Only prettier."

The roar of laughter that went up at that made the silverware on the table rattle. The story that Ariston had given the little etaira Theoris to the great poet had spread all over Athens and, he saw now with astonishment, had been seriously believed. A babble of talk broke out among Charmides' guests, ranging from a fevered description of Theoris' charms to the outcome of the trial in which the poet's son Iophon had tried to prove the old poet had grown feeble-minded, to consort with etairai and beget children at his age. Sophokles, it seemed, had won the trial right handily, by reading to the judges the choruses from a new work of his not yet staged. The name of that work Ariston fixed in his memory, so that he could ask the poet for a copy of it when he saw him again. It was called *Oedipus at Kolonos*.

Ariston was listening to Kallias' loud assertion that Ariston should be brought to trial on the same charges, since a man who gave away one of the loveliest etairai in all Hellas was certainly non compos mentis if not entirely mad, when a slave came into the room with a letter on a little silver tray. He bowed to his master and whispered something, jerking his head toward where Ariston sat. Charmides picked up the letter, stared at the seal. But it was meaningless to him, for instead of being the device of any Athenian family, it represented a tiny doe. He lifted it to his nose and sniffed it loudly.

"Ha!" he said. "You spoke too soon, Kallias, when you said that our friend Ariston has no lover now that Danaus has sailed away to war. It would seem he has—and a highborn lady, too, to judge by the daintiness of this script and the richness of this perfume! So, friends and lovers, the mystery of his cruel behavior to the poor little Theoris stands explained: He had to get rid of her! This letter has a prophetic air—of a wedding in the near future, and to such a one as will not tolerate etairai, auletrides, pornai, or even boys! That's it, isn't it, Ariston?"

"I wouldn't know," Ariston said calmly, "since I have yet to read the letter, and have no idea whom it's from. . . ."

"That's easy enough," Charmides laughed. "Take it to him, Nibo—that he may amuse the company by reading it aloud!"

"No, thank you!" Ariston said. "I have not yet become Athenian enough to be so shameless. Tell me, good Nibo, how did the messenger happen to bring me this letter here? I mean how could he know where to find me?"

"Your servants told him, my lord," the slave said. "He had orders to deliver the letter into no other hands but yours and after much argument with them—it seems they greatly desired he leave it with them—"

"So they could steam it open," Sokrates whispered, "or pass a heated knife blade under the seal. You must tell the lady to be careful, kalon!"

302

"Go on, Nibo," Ariston said.

"They told him. He's waiting outside to see if there's any reply."

"Give him this drachma," Ariston said, "and keep this one for yourself. Tell him to tell the sender I will reply tonight. He—"

"Ha!" Charmides said.

"—Or she, will understand why I cannot at the moment."

"Thank you, Nibo. You may go now."

"Thank *you*, my lord," Nibo said.

They were all staring at him with the mischievous eyes of schoolboys. Coolly, without even glancing at the letter, Ariston put it into the bosom of his chiton and turned to the company.

"Now where were we, my friends?" he said.

Being Athenians, they spent the next half-hour speculating upon the identity of the lady who had sent Ariston the letter and trying to pry the secret out of him. Kallias went so far as to suggest that it was Nikeratos' wife, a thing he could do safely for that sweet and noble lady's total devotion to her husband was the talk of all Athens. In a curious way, it caused more comment than the latest scandal: "Nikeratos and his wife are so advanced that they can even be faithful to one another—a new angle, what? Totally unheard of in Athens, my dear!" the wits said.

"I'll beat her when I go home," Nikeratos said solemnly, and everyone roared.

"Sokrates, will you indulge me a moment?" Charmides said. "My nephew is here and wants to meet you. He's only twelve years old, but he has an unusual mind. I've been trying to persuade my brother-in-law to let him become your pupil."

"When he's older, much older. I shouldn't like to be accused of sodomy," Sokrates said. "But bring him in, Charmides, bring him in!"

Charmides sent a slave for the boy. When the slave came back with him, they all stared at the little fellow curiously. He was exceedingly broad and stocky, very muscular for a twelve-year-old. And he would never be beautiful. But Ariston was sure that never in all his life had he seen greater intelligence than that which shone from those dark eyes.

"This is my nephew Aristokles," Charmides said. "But we never call him that. We always call him Platon because he's so wide. I'm having Ariston—the wrestler, not our friend here; god knows the two have nothing in common but the name!—train him; and already he's a terrific little battler! Platon, come meet the great Sokrates, son!"

The boy came over to Sokrates, bowed and kissed his hands. But Sokrates raised the boy up and kissed his forehead.

"Would you like to be my pupil, Platon?" he said.

But the answer to that question, and all that passed between Sokrates and the pupil who afterward would rival even his great fame, Ariston was not to hear. At that moment, Nibo came into the banquet hall again. After whispering to his master, he came straight to Ariston.

"The metic Orchomenus," he said, a little contemptuously, causing Ariston again to reflect that household slaves were the world's worst snobs, "is waiting for you outside, Master. He says it's urgent. And he does look upset—"

"Is he drunk?" Ariston asked bluntly. Orchomenus quite often was, these days. The degeneration of his character since poor Thargelia's death had been marked.

"No sir," Nibo said. "Just—agitated, sir. He's pacing up and down and—"

"All right, I'll come," Ariston said.

Nibo was right. Ochomenus was noticeably agitated. The long scar that remained after the brand of a runaway slave had been removed from his forehead was livid against his flushed face. But he was both clean and neatly dressed. His hair had been cut, his beard neatly trimmed. He smelled of a quiet, rather pleasant perfume. And he was alone. No pretty, effeminate boy accompanied him. Which was the most unusual thing of all.

"You've got to help me, Ariston!" he said, without waiting even for a greeting, "you've got to!"

"Have I?" Ariston said.

304

"Yes, by Zeus Thunderer! All right, I'll admit that by your lights I've been a swine, but that's finished, I tell you! Finished!"

"Is it?" Ariston said.

"Yes. By Aphrodite! You see, boy, for the first time in my life, I've fallen in love. Truly in love. With all my soul!"

"What's his name?" Ariston said.

"*His* name? Ha! This time you're wrong! *Her* name, my friend. My wife's name—my little bride's!"

"You've married again?" Ariston said.

"Yes, yes! To keep her, you see? I couldn't give her up. I couldn't, Ariston! Only even that is not enough now, for—" He broke off, his big voice torn by a sound that was curiously like a sob.

"Calm yourself, Orchomenus," Ariston said. It came to him, with a sudden burst of pity, that Orchomenus was a little mad.

No, more than a little. Suffering did that to a man, sometimes, when he hadn't the interior equipment to take it. "Tell me your bride's name," he said.

"It's Chlodovechia, or Cassevelauna, or maybe both. I don't know, really."

"Chlodovechia? Cassevelauna? She's barbarian, then? Athena witness those aren't Hellenic names!"

"No, of course they aren't. And she *is* a barbarian—the prettiest little barbarian you ever did see! She's one of the Keltai—from Keltia, you know, the land farther west than Sicelia, but not so far west as Hesperia, where we have the city of Massalia? I have a devil of a time understanding her speech. She hadn't been in Massalia long enough to learn Hellenic well. Seems that she was born at a place called Lutetia—a town on an island in a river, and that her people are called Parisii—"

"That's Hellenic," Ariston said.

"No, it isn't. A linguistic coincidence, that's all. She didn't even know who Paris was. And she'd never heard of Helen. Or Homer."

"Athena grant her knowledge!" Ariston said.

"Amen. But she is *so* beautiful, Ariston! Her hair's so blond that it's almost white—"

"Ha!" Ariston said. "They sell those bleaches in every chemist shop."

"No, they don't." Orchomenus grinned at him like a wolf. "You see, being a Keltic barbarian from Keltia, or Galia—the country that the Italiotes call Gaul—"

"I know where Massalia is," Ariston said. "Go on, Orchomenus."

"—she hasn't learned to be completely dainty. Oh, she's clean enough, always smells good; but she hasn't been taught to shave herself or use depilatories the way our women do. And she's that blonde all over. Everywhere, Ariston! Her eyebrows, her lashes, her armpits, her—"

"Please!" Ariston cut him off. "She's your wife, Orchomenus! Have a little respect for her, will you? Don't go roaring out the names of every part of her anatomy in a public street—"

"How delicate you are, kalon! You look like a man now, but you're still girlish, aren't you? No matter. Come on! I want you to meet her."

Ariston stopped.

"This is Athens, remember," he said.

"I know that. But I'm not an Athenian, and neither are you. Besides I trust your confounded sense of honor. Now come on!"

"I suppose," Ariston said drily as they went along, "that within a year, you'll have beaten or kicked her to death, too, as you did poor Thargelia."

Orchomenus stopped dead. A trembling came over his mighty limbs.

"There's—a demon in me, Ariston!" he whispered. "I have a lust—for cruelty, for hurting people. It comes on me when I'm drunk—which is why I haven't touched a drop since I've known her. Even in that, you've got to help me, my friend. If ever I weaken and take a cup too many, may I come to your place to sober up before going home?"

"Of course," Ariston said.

"Because if I ever hurt Chlodovechia-Cassevelauna, I'd die. Eros save me, but I love her!"

"Then don't hurt her," Ariston said.

"Perhaps I—I can't help it," Orchomenus said. "Alkib-

306

iades says there're only 'two kinds of people in this world: those who get pleasure out of giving pain, and those who enjoy receiving it. You, it seems to me, are of the latter class. How you love to suffer!"

Ariston stared at him. Sokrates had said something much the same: "Mind you, Ariston, that your reasons for loving the little Chryseis are not—wrong. Wrong for you, I mean. She is much like my Xanthippe—and you haven't my placidity of temper. She'll make you see Tartarus daily with her way of being. She's of those who can't help tearing the very object of *their* love. Because she's uncertain of herself, ashamed of her lack of beauty, she'll accuse you of a thousand imaginary infidelities, scream at you, throw tantrums. Which matters not, or it wouldn't, if I were sure you're whole, that you aren't still seeking, all unknowingly, to torment yourself, hunting the debasement that something in you craves."

He felt, suddenly, the letter scrape against his bare chest under his chiton. But now was not the time to draw it out and read it. Besides, whoever had sent it—certainly not Chryseis, who'd die first!—could wait until tonight for a reply.

"We'll have to change those hideously barbaric names of hers," he said to Orchomenus. "How do they go, again?"

"Chlodovechia-Cassevelauna," Orchomenus said.

"The only thing close to that in Hellenic would be Chloris. Chloris—greenish. No; that won't do. What's the other one?"

"Cassevelauna."

"How about Kassandra?"

"No! Zeus, no! That's unlucky! In the first place, it means 'She who entangles men,' and in the second, look what happened to the original bearer of that name—to her and Agamemnon, both!"

"You're right there," Ariston said. "Perhaps I'd better wait until I see her before giving her a proper name. In the meantime, will you stop leaping about like a shaggy goat and tell me what the trouble is?"

"I—I bought her off a sea captain named Aletes. He's a cup companion of mine and knows my tastes. When I had money, he used to bring me the likeliest boys and maids first, *before* turning them over to the slave dealers. Now he's been away a long time, so he didn't know you'd kicked me out of the factories, and that I've thrown away almost my last obol—on boys, mostly. They appeal to the cruel streak in me, more than women do. When I saw her, I went wild. I gave him a promissory note and took her, swearing by all the gods I'd pay him the next week. He guaranteed her to be a virgin—and his word was good. Zeus, how she bled, the poor little thing! I had to have the iatros in. But she forgave me when she saw how fearful and contrite I was. Now, she's beginning to get used to me, I think. Given time, I'll teach her to love me. That's what depends upon you, boy! Zeus Thunderer! Who'd ever think—"

*"What* depends upon me?" Ariston said.

"That I have the time. You see, Aletes is trying to repossess her. That's why I married her. As my wife, he can't take her back without an order from the court of criminal and civil affairs. I figured that he'd have to sail away before he could get his appeal in to the judges, or that I'd have her belly pumped up big enough by then to appeal to those old goats' sentimentality. But I was wrong on both counts. We go before the dikasteria tomorrow, unless—"

"Unless I cough up your pirate friend's asking price," Ariston said.

"Exactly. Don't tell me you're going to refuse me, boy! By Hestia and Hera both, don't tell me that!"

"No," Ariston said slowly, "I won't refuse you—but I'm going to make my loan contingent on several harsh conditions, Orchomenus—"

Orchomenus stopped and stared at him.

"Which are?" he whispered.

"One: That you come back to work for me, at my biggest ergasteria, as manager, at which, as you've already proved, you're very good indeed. Wait! I *want* you to be stern with the workers, who've gotten pretty slack of late. But the first time you strike anybody, even with your open hand, out you go. Agreed?"

"Agreed," Orchomenus said. "Two?"

"That you're to pay me back your slavegirl wife's price out of your wages, Orchomenus. I'm past making gifts to you. I won't press you; but pay me back you must. Agreed?"

"Agreed," Orchomenus growled. "Three?"

"That we stop off at the scriptorium of the nearest public scribe *before* I've seen her, so you won't think with that evil mind of yours I'm plotting to relieve you of her, and draw up a paper in triplicate, one copy to her, one copy to me, and the third to the magistrate of your district, in which you give me your solemn promise, sworn to before Athena, to grant her both her freedom and a divorce if ever you hit, kick, or otherwise brutalize her. Agreed?"

Orchomenus stood there, glaring at him.

"You don't trust me, do you, boy?" he said.

"Say I know you," Ariston said evenly.

"Which amounts to the same thing," Orchomenus sighed. "And you're right. Agreed. Come on! Let's draw up your blasted paper!"

The girl—this glorious girl child not yet fifteen—came toward them very slowly, shyly, and Ariston's breath halted. His mind stopped. His heart. There was no word in either Attic or Doric or Ionian for angel. The best he could manage was nymph of the upper air. Or goddess. Eos, rosy fingered bringer of the dawn. Aphrodite, herself, rising from the foam. Helen. For Helen must have looked like this, or else there was no explication for what had happened at Troy.

There was a sadness in him unto death. The words, "Too late, too late, too late!" rang through his stricken mind like a refrain—this aching, haunting, delicate loveliness—to belong to a gross brute like Orchomenus! No! By Eros, by Aphrodite, by love, itself, no! But there was no help for it now. He turned his face aside so as to master himself, to hide the sudden hot salt sting in his eyes. Chryseis didn't exist. He had never known her. The letter in the bosom of his tunic became weightless and without feel.

He turned back again and said, trying to keep his voice from shaking, "I know what to call her, now, Orchomenus—"

"What?" Orchomenus said. "I'd thought of Kalliope, but—"

"No. That's not good enough. Kalliope—Fair of Face . . . True, but not enough."

"What then?" Orchomenus said.

"Kleothera," Ariston whispered.

"Kleothera—" Orchomenus tried it on his tongue. "Kleo—thera—" He rolled the sweet syllables about, ponderously. "Hmmmnnn—" Then he roared out like a bull: "Kleothera—Noble Beauty! By Zeus, that's it! You've hit it, boy! But then I knew you would! Come here, Kleo—and meet your patron! This is—"

Then it happened. With a soft gurgling note, halfway between laughter and a sob, the newly named Kleothera skipped forward and hurled herself upon Ariston, fastening her arms about his neck.

Orchomenus' face went black as the clouds that Zeus sowed. He stretched out his hand to snatch the girl—Girl? Ariston's reeling mind thought. This moonsilver and noonsunlight goddess!—away from Ariston. They both heard her babbling away in utterly barbaric gutturals that on any other lips but hers would have been hideous, but coming from her was a long splendor of exotic and erotic music, contralto deep, and as warm as summer with joy.

"I'm sorry, my dear," Ariston said, "but I understand no tongue that's not Hellas—"

"Oh!" she wailed. Then she released him and backed away. Stood there looking at him, her blue eyes jeweling over with sudden tears. "Forgive me, my lord," she whispered in broken, bad, colonial Hellenic. "I'm sorry—I—I thought you—were one of us! Your eyes—your hair—your beard—"

Orchomenus laughed then in pure relief.

"Ha!" he said. "She thought you were one of her barbaric tribe! Look, Kleo—we do have towheads among us. Not very many, but some. Our greatest ancient hero, Achillios was blond. And Odysseus was a redhead. Even now, in Macedonia and in Thrace—but you don't understand a word I'm saying, do you?"

"No, my lord husband," Kleothera said.

310

"Athena help us! Ariston, how on earth am I ever going to teach her to talk like a human being?"

"Meaning like a Hellene? I'll ask Sophokles to lend us Theoris to give her lessons. No one speaks more beautifully than Theoris now. Not even Parthenope."

"All right—as long as she doesn't teach her any of those etairai vices! They pretend to love men, but—Look, boy, about that loan—Aletes will be here at the tenth hour sharp tomorrow, and I—"

"Send him to me," Ariston said.

He didn't go home. He couldn't. He was a man possessed. He wandered the streets of Athens, not even hearing the angry arguments about Alkibiades' guilt or innocence in the matter of the shocking sacrilege of mutilating the protective Hermes. Finally he stood still, his mind an anguished blaze, his heart in the hands of the most fiendishly expert torturer that ever broke man upon his wheel: black, unrelenting jealousy.

"I'll go to Parthenope's!" he raged. "Get drunk as Athena's owls! Bed with—"

He lurched away as though he were already drunk. He was. But upon the bitter wine of pain.

The little etaira-in-training, Psylla—which, naturally enough, was not her name, since it meant "flea" and had been given her by her companions because of her diminutive stature and the quick way she hopped about—pulled her mouth very slowly away from Ariston's.

"What's the matter, love?" she whispered. "Usually *my* kisses can wake the dead."

"Don't know," Ariston said. "Too much wine, perhaps. No, too much sadness—"

"I'll cure you of that!" Psylla said, and got to work. But try as she would, she could not arouse him.

She sat up staring at him. She was very tiny, and very pretty. The nipples of her breasts had been rouged. The perfume she wore was very heavy and very cloying. He felt sick suddenly.

"Look, Psylla—" he began. But whatever he had been about to say strangled in his throat, choked there, died.

311

Chryseis stood there, looking down at them. She was not crying—yet. What she was doing was a subtler, a more awful thing. She was coming apart, internally. He could see that dreadful process of disintegration going on behind her eyes.

She bent suddenly, picked up something, held it out to him with a wildly trembling hand. It was the letter. The same one he'd had in the bosom of his tunic all day without remembering to read it. The same one he'd forgotten existed, that had fallen to the floor with his chiton when he'd yanked it off.

"Read it, when you have time, my lord Ariston," she said, her voice as brittle as shale rock, hard-bright. "It—will make you laugh—I think. I—I offered you my body. You who have a plethora of bodies—glorious bodies like this little doll's—at your beck and call. But what else you had —and have still of me—she can't give you, because she hasn't one, beautiful, beautiful Ariston! My soul. And— other things. The virginity she's forgotten she ever had. Love—an article not for sale. Faithfulness—a word you don't even know!"

She whirled, took a step, stopped, looked back again.

"At least I'm glad—she's not—a boy!" she wailed, and fled.

"Oh, leave that skinny old Hecate go!" Psylla said. But he pushed her roughly away from him and got up.

He was pulling his chiton over his head when he heard Parthenope scream.

"I tried to stop her!" Parthenope wept. "I tried to, Ariston! Oh, Hera, Mother of the Gods! What are we going to do?"

Chryseis opened her eyes.

"All you did," she whispered, "was to—to make—oh, gods—it hurts, it hurts!—to make me miss—my heart. Now it's going to—"

"Chrys!" Ariston groaned. "Oh God, Chrys!"

"—take me a—a long time to die. And I'm not—not brave. . . . I thought—I was—but—it hurts! Pull it out, Ariston! So that the blood—"

Then she fainted.

"God," Ariston said. "God God God God."

"Ariston—" Parthenope wept. "They'll close my place! The astunomoi, I mean! Maybe put me in prison! I—I'll starve! Oh, lambie, honey—get that little witch's carcass out of here! Oh Zeus Thunderer, why'd she have to kill herself in my house?"

The sudden burst of ice cold contempt that tore through him then had the strange effect of clearing his heart, his mind. He felt utterly calm. That it was the calm of pure shock, he didn't know. But it made no difference, because it served.

"Shut up, you shriveled old whore," he said. "She's not dead. And, if I can help it, she's not going to die. I've enough deaths on my soul already. Now go get cloths for bandages. Hot water. Lint for the blood to clot upon. A needle and thread. *Linen* thread. And boil the needle. I've seen the military surgeons do that. It helps. I don't know why, but it does. You heard me, you miserable old porna! Hop!"

"You—you're going to—to sew her up? Like a torn sack?" Parthenope said.

"Of course. Get going, Parthenope!"

The dagger was embedded in Chryseis' left breast, on a long diagonal slant, so that one edge of it showed almost to the point. It hadn't, he saw now, gone through the rib cage. If he could keep her from bleeding to death, there was a chance to save her. A slight chance—but still, a chance.

"Asklepios, help me," he prayed. "And you divine Apollo. And you, Paeon. Athena. Panacea. Hygeia. Centaur Chiron—all the healing gods, guide my poor hand, that it doesn't shake too much. Oh, divine ones, please. . . ."

He drew the dagger out. The rush of blood was terrible to see. In spite of all the blood he'd seen shed on the battlefield, he almost fainted. Because this was Chryseis' blood—this poor, dear, tender fool's. This fragile, tiny, almost skeletal wild wood-thing—who loved him enough to want to die—as Phryne had died. No! Great Zeus, no! Hera, Hestia, Artemis who loves the chaste, the innocent, the pure—

He picked up the needle. Behind him, he could hear Parthenope vomiting.

Psylla knelt beside him, handing him things as he needed them. Her eyes were enormous in her little face. But she didn't faint, as Parthenope already had, or even vomit. She knelt there, helping him. When it was done, she looked at him, looked at that still, greenish white, blood-stained figure on the bed. Then the tears burst, exploded, jetted from her eyes.

"She's dead, isn't she?" she whispered. "Oh, my lord, every year on this day, I—I'm going to sacrifice at her tomb! In honor of her who knew what love is—and that it's worth dying for. For it is! Oh, it is! Oh, Ariston, I—"

But Chryseis was not dead. Neither the Fates nor the Furies were that cruel.

Or, if you will, that kind.

# CHAPTER NINETEEN

HE BORE HER IN HIS ARMS, wrapped in an himation, through the dark streets of the city to his house. He was lucky: He did not meet any of the Scythian mercenaries who served the polis as a sort of police force. There would have been no serious difficulty if he had met them, for he had money enough in his purse to buy their silence. But they would have delayed him, which could have been serious enough.

Once or twice, in his haste, he jolted Chryseis, and she groaned. That faint, breathgone, tortured sound tore his very heart. He prayed to all the gods he didn't really believe in, not to let her die.

Inside his bedroom, he laid her down, pulled the bell cord repeatedly until he had awakened all the female servants. When they came, he saw the shock, the speculation, that slack-lipped, almost panting desire for scandal, which is the only true lust women have, on their faces; but he ignored it.

"Attend to her," he said shortly. "But gently, you fools. Her hurt is grievous. And send Podargos to me!"

One of them scampered away toward the men's quarters. The rest of them bent over Chryseis.

"Poor little thing!" they crooned. "So tiny—so thin! She's been starved, the little dear. And—this wound! How awful! Someone tried to kill her! Ugh! The blood! I wonder—"

"Don't wonder," Ariston said. "Get warm water and cloths—*clean* cloths, by Hera! Get that robe off her. Bathe her, make her comfortable. Her undervest and bindings, too. Put one of your nightdresses on her—a newly washed and untorn one, if you have such a thing, you she-goats!"

By then Podargos stood before him.

"Podargos," Ariston said solemnly, "can you still run?"

"Have I ever lost a race for you, Master, in any of the games you entered me?" Podargos said, in an injured tone.

"You must run another now, my friend," Ariston said. "The cruelest race you've ever run. The prize is a life. No, two. For if she dies, I cannot live."

"Master!" Podargos said.

"Run to the house of Ophion, the iatros. Tell him I sent you, and that he must come, despite the hour. If he refuses, bring him by main force. I'll pay him enough to make him forget the offense, afterward . . ."

"I go, master," Podargos said.

Ariston turned back to the bed. The serving women had stripped Chryseis now. Her poor little body was emaciated to a dreadful degree. He could count every bone she had. I'll have to find a way to get some flesh on her—if she lives, he thought.

The physician Ophion looked up at him.

"Who dressed this wound?" he said. "Who sewed her up like this?"

"I did," Ariston said.

The iatros smiled. "Then I must welcome you to the synorkeo of surgeons," he said. "It's good work. Better than that of some third-year apprentice iatroi I've seen."

Ariston brushed aside this faint, mocking praise—if it were praise at all, for everyone knew what fearful butchers apprentice surgeons were—and said:

"Will she live?"

"I think so. Ordinarily a wound like this wouldn't kill a healthy woman. If her blood is clean and no mortification sets in, she should. That's not the main problem—"

"Then what is the main problem?"

"Starvation. Didn't you *ever* feed her, my old friend? The rest of your wenches are plump enough!"

"She was not in my charge," Ariston said carefully, "until now. But if she lives, and remains in it, I'll cover these exquisite bones of hers, Ophion—"

316

"Do. In fact you must. The immediate problem is to get enough nourishment in her to overcome her weakness. Soups, broths, wine. Nothing solid for a few days. Ariston—"

"Yes, Ophion?"

"I'm not going to report you. That would be useless in any case, because with your money you'd buy free at once. And I'm not one of the sykophantoi—"

Ariston smiled. That word had not the connotation which centuries later, in Imperial Rome, it would acquire, of fawning, devious flatterers. In classical Athens, it meant very simply, blackmailer.

"Go on," he said.

"But I *am* curious. Why did you stab her, my friend?"

"Ask me another question, Ophion. A more sensible one. For instance, how and where I learned to sew up wounds."

"All right, I will. I do. How and where did you? Jesting aside, the job's really not half bad."

"In the Spartan army. I was a hoplite."

"Meaning?"

"A soldier. An expert at dealing stab wounds. Trained all his life to do it—well."

"Why—I hadn't thought of that! I knew you were one of the Lakedaemonians taken at Sphacteria, but— True. True enough. No man who knows how to handle a dagger would have made a mess like this. Then who—Aphrodite and Eros! Of course! She did it herself!"

"I didn't say that," Ariston said.

"You don't have to. The downward trajectory of this wound is such that you'd have had to reach around her from behind to stab her thus. All you did was to knock aside her arm so that it didn't penetrate, find her heart, as she fully intended it to. And now I know it all. You refused her —she's as scrawny as a crow and uglier than Hecate's daughter—so she tried to kill herself. That's it, isn't it?"

"I didn't refuse her. I love her. I'm going to marry her, if it's possible."

"Apollo, Averter of Madness, save me! You're going to marry this—this—"

"Poor, shamed, tormented creature—who has a lovely soul," Ariston said.

317

He fed her the broths his servants brought him with his own hands. At first she choked on them. After that she vomited them up. But he persisted until he got a cupful into her. Then two cups of wine. He lifted her tenderly into his arms while his servants changed the bed sheets when she wet them, as in her unconscious state she had to. It seemed to him that there was a faint flush of color in her cheeks. That gave him hope.

He watched beside her all that day, and all the ensuing night. Toward morning her breathing became peaceful, regular. She seemed to be asleep.

It came to him then, at long, long last, that he still hadn't read her letter. So he drew it out of the tunic of his chiton, broke the seal, and drew the oil lamp close.

"My Love, my Own," Chryseis had written. "These words will shock and startle you, I know. But how else can I begin? You are that and more: my love, my own, my very life from this hour on. Even, if you will it so, my master, I am your most abject and humble slave. Which is a condition that I hate; but my own blind and treacherous heart has sold me, my wild, rebellious blood.

"You see, my Ariston, 'Best of Men,' Noblest and Best, I eavesdropped brazenly while you were talking to my brother. I raged at you, tried to hate you in my heart, to convince myself that you were making fun of me. But your voice—your grave, deep voice—so sweet to listen to!—was utterly sincere. I wept all that day and all night, but they were tears of joy. The next day I followed you to the theater, saw you *weep* for a woman's sorrows! Learned a little—a very little, of your own. You'll tell them all to me, won't you? I do so long to comfort you! Then afterward I saw your act of piety, and all my pneuma soared on divine wings. I followed you everywhere you went in the ensuing days. I—I spoke with half Athens about you—all those I dared to: the humbler classes, of course—metics, tradesmen, slaves. They all adore you; no man in Athens is so loved, not even Sokrates himself. I learned you'll keep no slaves in your service—all who work for you are by your sweet hand freed. . . .

"Except me. Whom you can never free from your service, your worship, your idolatry; whom only Lord

Hades and Lady Persephone can tear from your side. And now, I, your slave, beg that you, my master, forgive my script, for what I am going to write is so shameful I cannot watch my hand form the letters, must turn aside my eyes.

"I am coming to you, Ariston. This night at Parthenope's. And you must take me in your arms, have of me my virginity. Forgive me! I told you I have never felt desire —and I don't now, except in a vague, fantastic way. But the sacrifice is necessary, because of a curious legalism. I've talked with one of the archons, a friend of my father's. He tells me that there is no way under heaven for a metic, however distinguished, learned, rich, to gain Athenian citizenship now. 'And if an Athenian lady—loved such a one?' I said. He saw through me at once. 'Poor, poor child,' he said. 'Forget him.'

" 'I cannot,' I told him. 'Without him, I would die.'

" 'Then go to him. Become his mistress openly and publicly. Thereafter, if you can prevent your brothers from killing him—and with the only one of them worth his salt absent from the polis, that shouldn't be hard—your status is legal, and recognized—more than a concubine; a sort of semi-wife, as the etaira Aspasia was to Perikles. If he clings to you, and you to him, if neither of you dishonors the other with known adulteries, your state is not without honor. There are many such unions nowadays,' said he.

"Oh, Ariston Ariston—will you have me? Or will you condemn me to death by my own hand? For if you refuse me, having read this, I cannot, will not live a single hour with my shame. Answer this letter if you will, or can. If you cannot, know I will be there from midnight onward. I shall bring a dagger with me. My life or my death is yours to decide. Either way, whether you condemn me or allow me life and joy, know that

I love you,
Chryseis."

He sat there staring at those words, until the beautifully formed letters blurred out of recognition. He bent his head and wept, torn by pity, and by shame.

· He felt then, suddenly, startlingly, something brush his cheek. That touch was feather-light, but even so, it burned

319

him like a brand. He opened his eyes and saw her lying there, staring at her bony fingers. On them, in the lamp light, he could see the sparkle, the glitter of his tears. She raised them to her lips, slowly, reverently.

"How sweet. How unutterably sweet," she said.

But, one hour later, she awakened once more and turned to him with eyes that flamed with fever, with delirium, with—something else, something that was neither, that was perhaps a part of the incurable disease of living, the poison product of the pride of self, without which rational life is not possible, lying dead and festering within her, killed by scorn, rejection, neglect. . . .

"Ariston," she whispered, "about—that girl—"

"What girl?" he said, already knowing, but trying to divert her from this fatal course. "There's no other girl, now—only you."

"Don't lie to me!" Her voice rose, became shrill; her face, which in repose had a certain barbaric attractiveness, becoming hideous, a maenad's mask, an image of Hecate. "That little girl! That tiny, glorious creature who was abed with you! And both of you as naked as the day your mothers gave you birth!"

Ariston smiled at her, a little mockingly.

"Clothes are hardly of use in such delicate situations, Chryseis," he said, "and I've never pretended to you I was a devotee of Artemis. Forgive me, my dearest—but you must understand. I had no idea you meant to come to me, and—"

"Oh no!" she shrilled. "You didn't read my letter! You threw it on the floor when you stripped to make the beast with two backs with that wench! Go to her, Ariston! Go to her! I don't want you! I want to die! To die! To—"

He bent forward then and found her mouth. Her breath was rank and fetid. It smelled of vomit and of blood. But though it sickened him, he went on kissing her, imprisoning her small face between his strong and tender hands until her wild efforts to tear her mouth from his ceased, and her lips slackened, softened, blooming upon his like some exotic flower.

He drew back slowly, peering into her big, warm, wonderful brown eyes. But he couldn't see them now. All he could see was a glitter, a trembling, a spill, a falling flash, reflected in the lamp's glow, brimming endlessly.

"Chrys—" he groaned.

"Ariston—" she whispered.

"Yes, Chrys?"

"Do you—do you love me?"

"With all my heart," he said—and if pity is a part of love, it was almost true.

"Then why—didn't you read my letter!" she wailed.

"Because when it came, I was at a banquet with some of Athens' gilded youths, who tried to force me to read it aloud. So I stuck it in my bosom—"

"And forgot it!" she sobbed.

"Yes. Or rather say I had it driven from my mind. A friend of mine was in trouble. Bad trouble, Chrys. I had to go to his rescue, and—"

He told her Orchomenus' story. He even described the Gallic slave girl to her. She listened very quietly. Then she said, her voice hoarse and strident with horror:

"You're—in love with her! With this Kleothera! With your own best friend's wife! Immortal gods, what have I done! Oh, divine Artemis, let me die!"

He saw then that it wasn't any use; he perceived, heard, recognized inside his mind, his heart, the shape of this insidious torture he'd invented for himself, clasped to his bosom, sought. With Chryseis, happiness wasn't going to be possible; life with her was going to be a new and rarely awful variety of hell.

When she fell back at last, worn out with screaming, her eyes red-streaked and puffed with the terrible burning of one who has used up her store of tears, he got up and walked in the garden. And his thoughts labored through his mind in rhythm with his slow, pacing steps:

What is the nature of sin; and what, of punishment? Do they exist? Or aren't they a part of the monstrous vanity of man? This ant now, crawling across the flagstones in the moonlight, I step on him, and he is not. As I am not. I could have saved Phryne, and I failed her. Did it, or did it not cross my mind that afterward she'd have been unendurable, all covered with scars, and lacking an eye? My mother and my father died because of me. Both of them, because of me. Arisbe. My foster father Telamon. Perhaps Simoeis, too, and Lysander. I murdered Lycotheia. Butchered Pancratis. Whom have I not killed or failed? Who has not failed me?

So now I free slaves, make pious sacrifices, do works of charity, and for what? The legion of shades that gibber forever at my side laugh with fleshless mouths! Did the ant believe he was a great sinner, too? Did he pray, as my heel crushed substance, life out of him, to the mighty pantheon of ant gods for pardon for his antheap sins?

What did I do, what could I have done, that matters a jot in the scheme of things? What do the bawdy, roistering, adulterous gods we created in our own unlovely image care? What am I, what is man, that we merit the attention of a god, or gods? Strew the earth with corpses, pile cadavers up until high Olympus itself is overtopped and all the vultures of the sky glut and sicken, too replete to break, to tear; but Tartarus itself remains a vanity. A mockery, the Asphodel Fields. And vanity of vanities, Elysium!

Chrys, now. How can I explain her, even to myself? I knew what she was, poor, hurt, sick, lost little thing. But did I seek her out of pity, award her my base counterfeit of love out of compassion—or because I need and want to suffer? Because I exult in my own pain?

He stopped at the edge of the pool, looked down at his own distorted, shadowy image, painted upon it by the moonlight.

He grinned at it crookedly.

I should steal Kleothera from Orchomenus, he thought. There's no peace to be gained by goodness or by expiatory acts. One must find out what one is and cease to violate that ultimate self. If this business of Chryseis *is* a violation, if—

He turned and went back into the house.

That next morning, he settled the matter of Chlodovechia-Cassevelauna-Kleothera in less than ten minutes, by paying the pirate Aletes the quite outrageous price he demanded for the Gallic slave girl without a word. But the peace of his house was not to be so easily insured. Four days later, Chryseis' father and her two elder brothers came.

They came without arms, disposed to bluster, to extract what profit they could from this unexpected but boundless source, this living fountain that poured forth silver: the richest man in all Attica.

Ariston looked from Pandoros, his gray beard elaborately curled, perfumed, all his gestures mincing—Athena in her wisdom inform me how such a thing as this *ever* sired children! he thought—to Brimos, his heavy, grossly muscled body melting into fat; to Chalcodon, clearly his father's son, even to the trace of rouge upon his lips, the languid gestures, the blurring of the lines between the sexes, the ultimate outraging of life, of nature, the final destruction of the identity and the continuity of man.

Danaus, poor Danaus, away now facing death in the harbor, before the walls of Syrakuse, loved his sister. But these creatures, one gross brute and two teetering demimales, had come—to sell her. Their debts were legion, their appetites boundless, and poor, skinny, ugly Chrys, whom they'd looked upon as a lifetime burden, since among the three of them there was neither hope, nor desire, nor any real possiblity of amassing a dowry great enough to make a man forget her lack of either looks or charm, had provided them with this unexpected windfall! Ha, the rich metic bastard! They'd make him sweat gold through every pore!

Brimos stood up, heavy and menacing.

"This violation of our family's honor by a dog of a metic!" he began, but Ariston cut him off.

"Let's not talk nonsense, Brimos! And certainly not waste time in discussing a quality you don't even understand. Danaus could speak of honor; but he is gone, crossing the whole Ho Pontos to maintain it. So let's skip the preliminaries, shall we? How much?"

"Metic dog!" Brimos howled.

Ariston smiled.

"That's the second time you've used that expression, Brimos. Coming from you, it doesn't even offend me. For a dog is a noble animal, infinitely better than a swine. Better even than three swine. So stop blustering, will you? I know you have to speak for these two perfumed and twittering practitioners of sodomy, pedication, fellatio, and other assorted abominations, since you, at least, remain mostly male. But I haven't time to waste. You're here to reduce your sister, whom I'd honor as my lady and my wife, to the status of concubine, porna—goods for sale! Remember it's you who so insult her, not I. So on with it, you dimwitted clod! How much?"

"My dear Ariston!" Pandoros squeaked.

"I'm not your dear anything, Pandoros. If I were Tyrannos of Athens, I'd have things like you gelded so that you could no longer do any harm. Though in your case, I'd have to decapitate you as well, because you make use of both ends of yourself for pleasure, don't you? Now, shut up! Brimos, since I see you're still ass enough to think you can threaten me, stretch forth your arm. I'm not angry with you, but it seems to me you'll keep this up forever if I don't demonstrate how empty your threats are— Stretch forth your arm!"

Brimos put his huge right arm out. With a smile, Ariston caught him by the wrist. The next instant Brimos lay flat on his back on the floor. He came up roaring—which was a mistake. From the day he'd been freed from Polyxenus' bathhouse, Ariston had gone every morning year-round to the public palaestra. His physical condition was superb; and he had been trained by both his namesake, the champion wrestler Ariston, and by Autolykos, many times winner at the Panathena, the Ishmanian, and the Olympic games, in the pankratieon, that murderous combination of boxing and wrestling. He quite easily could have killed Brimos by the use of several secret blows he knew. Instead, he simply danced aside, sank his left fist to the wrist in Brimos' lard tub of a paunch, straightened him up with a knee to his chin as he doubled, and as he went down chopped the back of that bullneck with the edge of a hand that was as hard as a blunt ax blade.

Ariston stood there looking down at his fallen foe. Then he turned to pull the bellcord and waited, grinning at

Pandoros and Chalcodon, who were clasped in each other's arms, actually crying from fright.

"My lord?" the manservant said.

"Throw water on—that," Ariston said contemptuously. "Is the magistrate here?"

"Yes, my lord."

"Have him enter to witness the transaction. No, first have Eurysakes and Paktolos bring the balance in. Then have the serving women to assist my lady. The magistrate last of all," Ariston said.

Afterward this transaction became the talk of all Athens, for it was beyond reason to expect the astunomos or the servants who witnessed it to keep their mouths shut. Two menservants came into the hall bearing a huge balance of the kind used in Ariston's factories for weighing crude metal as well as finished swords, spear points, daggers, breastplates, greaves, shields. After them came four more bent under the weight of heavy sacks. Then two, bearing Chryseis on a litter. The pompous and self-important astunomos, or magistrate of the district, entered next and took his seat.

Chryseis' eyes leaped with sudden fear at the sight of her father and her brothers. Chalcodon and Pandoros glared at her with the feline fury of women bested by a rival, which, at bottom, was how they really felt; while Brimos sat there, shaking his head with a dazed expression on his huge, blubbery face, with water dripping off his chiton and pooling between his sandals on the marble floor.

"My lord," Ariston said to the magistrate, "you are here to witness a commercial transaction. These gentlemen have come here for the purpose of selling me their sister—"

Chryseis gasped aloud.

"Conceivably they might have demanded of me my life as punishment for what, not knowing the facts—facts I have no intention of revealing—they might have had some justification for calling an offense against this sweet lady's, and their family's, honor. They chose not to do so. They came, as you see, unarmed, disposed to haggle, to bargain

325

over what can be neither bought nor sold, and what to me is priceless: my lady's love and the possession of her person—both of which she, and only she, can award. So be it!

"But first I must say to the Lady Chryseis that she is in no way a party to this sickening affair. I pay only to be rid forever of a trio of sykophantoi, not ever to insult her by pretending to purchase her favor, her body, or her love. If, when she has the strength to do so, she wishes to leave my side, she is quite free to go. I shall sorrow, of course; but she is not bound by this!"

He turned to her, then said gently:

"Chrys, my love—"

"Yes—Ariston?" she whispered.

"Are you strong enough to stand upon the balance?"

Dumbly Chryseis shook her head.

"Then lay her upon it, litter and all," Ariston said. He turned to Pandoros and his sons and said quietly:

"I offer you my lady's weight in silver for your promise to quit my house forever, make no further demands upon me as long as you shall live, and pledge that you will not oppose a marriage between the Lady Chryseis and me, when I shall have found a means to become a citizen of this polis. Agreed?"

They sat there, staring at him. Ariston nodded to the servants. They opened the sacks, began to pour minae into the balance. Not drachmae, but minae, worth a hundred drachmae each. Brimos' eyes seemed about to burst, so wildly did they bulge from his head. Chalcodon leaped to his feet, executed a dancing step.

"Agreed!" he shrieked, his soprano voice fluting with excitement. "Agreed! Agreed! Agreed!"

"And you, Pandoros?" Ariston said. "Think how many helpless, weeping slave boys you'll be able to commit your abominations upon because of this! And Brimos—why, you can become owner of all the brothels you frequent at Piraeus. . . . What say you, gentlemen? Is not your honor worth this price? Cannot such things as you be bought? You have only to say the word, sign this paper as a guarantee against your going back on your word—worth, I'm sure, exactly as much, or as little, as your honor.

Come kalokagathoi, sophrounoi, promnestroi—come gentlemen, exquisites, procurers—what say you to this?"

The way Chryseis was crying was very bad.

"Father!" she wept. "Brimos! Chalcodon! Don't! Don't shame me like this! I beg you! Don't—"

But their eyes turned away from her anguished, pitiful face to that shower of silver, rattling, glittering, pouring into the scale.

"Agreed—" they whispered. Then their voices rose. "God, yes! By Zeus Thunderer, agreed!"

A month from the night, Chryseis came to Ariston's bed. She sat down on the edge of it and stared at him, her eyes afire in the somber death mask of her face.

"Aren't you ever going to make use of what you've bought?" she whispered. "This apparatus of flesh which men, I've been told, derive great pleasure from? Here I am. I'm yours. You've bought and paid for me. And I'm not so dishonorable as to cheat you of the delights you purchased. Take your slave concubine, Ariston! Tear her clothes! Rip her flesh! Pound upon her! Roar! Outrage—"

He smiled at her, sadly.

"Chrys," he said, "you've got it all wrong."

"I've got *what* wrong?"

"This. A woman can't be bought. Not even the lowest porna can. Those who frequent whores cheat themselves. All they get is a pitiful pretense—a counterfeit of love. I don't want that from you. I don't want even pleasure—in a solitary sense, I mean. For love is mutual or it is nothing. I'm prepared to wait—for years, forever, if need be, until you come to me with your heart between your outstretched hands. With tenderness in your eyes. Desire that matches or overtops my own. I want your body as a gift, but not unaccompanied by your soul. And I want to give myself to you—soul and body, both. I want you never to rise from our bed without having known pure ektasia, without having experienced pleasure far greater than my own."

Her great doe-slanted eyes opened very wide.

"But that's not possible!" she said. "Women can't—"

"A lot you know about it," Ariston said. "Want to try?"

327

She stared at him. He could see the beating of her blood at the base of her pitiful throat.

"Yes—god, yes!" she said.

But in the morning when he waked, she was gone. He sat upright in bed, a prey to icy terror. Had she again tried to—

Then he heard her voice. It soared up like sunlight, as warm, as golden, as filled with joy. She was singing a love song, a part of the chorus of Sophokles' *Antigone:*

"Unconquerable love, all men bow to you,
Whether you lie glowing on a dear girl's cheek
Or roam the shaggy hills, the wild sea's trackless blue,
Oh Love, who holds prisoner the very gods, must men seek
To be free of you, whose dominion is so sweet?"

Then she pushed open the door and stood there, holding out to him a little bowl.

"What's in it?" Ariston said.

"A little goat's milk, some crumbled bread—and all my heart," she said.

# CHAPTER TWENTY

THE IATROS OPHION held the cup out to Chryseis.

"Here, drink this," he said gruffly. "It will make you sleep."

Chryseis took the cup in hands that were like claws of some rapacious bird. Her voice was hoarse from all the crying she had done.

"Every year!" she sobbed. "Tell me, good iatros, is there no way, no way at all that I—"

"—can bring to birth a living child?" Ophion said. He looked toward Ariston, who stood staring out of the window into the courtyard. Something in his bearing, in the weary, bent-forward aspect of his body, moved the physician. He decided to tell the truth. Only—was it? About his profession, at the very best, there was far too little known.

"I think not, Lady Chryseis," he said slowly. "So far the gods have favored you. By which I mean the fact that you always abort within the first three months has very probably saved your life. Considering the way you're built, the slenderness of your hips, the narrowness of your loins, I'm quite sure that being brought to bed of a full-term child would be the end of you."

Ariston turned toward the iatros.

"You know that positively, Ophion?" he said.

Ophion sighed. "If you were only a patient and not my friend, I'd say 'Yes,' Ariston. But the love I bear you constrains me to the truth. I don't know it positively. About the healing arts, no man knows anything positively. Any iatros who says he does, lies."

"Then—then—" Chryseis whispered, "it might be possible for me to come to full term, bear a living child and—"

"One thing at a time, my lady!" the doctor said. "To

come to full term—that surely. All you have to do, once you're sure that you're with child, is to go to bed and stay there for nine months; avoid walking or any effort that causes jolts or strains—"

"Aeschylos bless you!" Chryseis said.

"Wait. Having said that, I must add that I don't advise it. For a woman of your size and childlike structure, labor can be a fearsome thing. I think the child would die before he was fully born; I think the strain would very likely kill you as well—"

"But you only think," Chryseis said hopefully. "You don't know."

"True. There's a chance. A slim chance. So very slim that it would be close to murder for me to permit you to take it. So my considered opinion is, my lady Chryseis, that you should avoid pregnancy at all costs. Do you promise?"

"No," Chryseis said coldly.

"Why not?"

"My—brother died—without an heir. He left no son to perform the funeral rites. So I must provide him with a male nephew to make the sacrifices. If not, his shade must wander forever between the worlds, homeless and lost—"

"Oh, Hades, Lord of Tartarus!" Ophion snapped. "Don't talk idiotic nonsense to me, my lady! Ariston, a word with you, my poor friend—"

The two of them walked out into the inner court.

"She's obsessed with that, isn't she?" the iatros said.

"Yes," Ariston said, "ever since Danaus fell in that horrible debacle at Syrakuse—"

"*If* he fell," Ophion said. "You don't really know."

"The other prisoners came back. Most of them within seven months after the defeat. I was at Euripides' cave-house when a group of them came to thank him."

"To thank him for what?" the physician said.

"For their freedom. Unlike you Athenians, the Syrakusans don't mock at genius. They freed every man who knew a few lines, a verse or two, anything that could be copied down from Euripides' choruses. That's why I'm sure poor Danaus is dead. I'd taught him whole choruses from *Hecuba, Hippolytus, Andromache, Elektra, Medea*— If any man should have been freed for knowing Euripides' verses, it would be he!"

"All right," Ophion said. "Ariston, have you a concubine? An etaira on the other side of the Agora? A flute girl? Even a porna?"

"No," Ariston said.

"I'd advise you to find some such outlet. Of course your —your wife's in no real danger as long as she doesn't come to full term. I could kick myself for telling her how to manage that! But a full-sized child would be dangerous to her. Very dangerous."

Ariston smiled, sadly.

"I'm not one of those satyrs who find it impossible to dominate desire, Ophion," he said. "And poor Chrys—why should I lie to you, my friend?—tempts me very little in that sense. Nor is she, I hasten to add, one of those rare women possessed by lust. She is normal, by which I mean she has to be stroked and petted into desire, like every woman born. Or she did, before she became obsessed with this mad idea that—"

"I see. And now she has become aggressive—in that regard?"

"Decidedly," Ariston said.

"That makes matters difficult. Very difficult. A woman bent upon motherhood is worse than the Furies themselves. All I can say is that you should avoid her all you can. When you cannot, take all the usual precautions. And if in spite of everything she does get pregnant, I'll give you a medicine to put in her wine that will force her to miscarry. Under no circumstances must she be allowed to be brought to bed of a fully developed child. Understand?"

"Yes," Ariston said. "I understand."

"Chaire, then, old friend," Ophion said, and took his leave.

After the physician had gone, Ariston went back into Chryseis' bedroom. He found her sleeping quietly under the influence of the sleeping draught that Ophion had given her. So, with a feeling of relief, he picked up his walking stick and went out into the street.

He wasn't going anywhere in particular. What he was doing, really, was seeking surcease from the funereal sadness that lay upon his house ever since Danaus had failed to return from the Sicilian disaster—a disaster caused surely by the folly of removing the brilliant Alkibiades from the joint command and forcing him to flee to Sparta to escape being condemned to death for a blasphemy he hadn't even committed, that stupid business of the mutilated Hermes. From that all-pervading sadness there was no relief, actually; but still Ariston sought it now—that and some means of evading the mood of weariness that lay upon his life like a blight.

It had been all of five years now since Danaus had fallen —if he had fallen—before Syrakuse. Five years since Dan had disappeared in the heat of battle, to be heard of no more. Another five years of the bitter fratricidal war between Hellenes that had been going on since he, Ariston, was twelve years old, and that now, twenty-one years later, showed no signs of ending or even abating. In itself, that was cause enough for weariness: Time and time again, when he had not been able or—moved by an obscurely suicidal impulse that was scarcely strange considering what his life was now—hadn't even wanted to bribe his way out of the ranks, he had loaded his fine, great-thewed body with hoplite's armor and marched out to the stinking, terrifying, soul-crippling dullness of mankilling.

Besides—and it was this more than everything else that had taken the heart out of him—even the issues weren't clear any longer. Worn out by war, Athens was falling away from her lofty ideals; more and more the enemies of human freedom within her ranks were beginning to show their hand. So low, in fact, had the Mother of Human Liberty sunk, that for several months she had groveled beneath the heel of an oligarchic government known as The Four Hundred. Then—and Ariston shuddered to recall it—force and fraud and political assassination open enough to disgrace a Persian satrapy had been the order of the day.

But, for the moment, the polis enjoyed a precarious salvation engineered by Alkibiades from exile and carried out by the sturdy democrats of the fleet. At Samos, the ordinary seamen had revolted, disposed of their oligarchic officers, elected the able Thrasyboulos and Thrasyllos to the command, recalled Alkibiades from exile, made him Strategos Autokrator, and prepared to sail upon Athens to set things right.

Whereupon the most moderate of the oligarchs, one Theramenes, already derisively labelled "Kothornos," "Buskin," for the rapidity with which he could shift sides to save his own precious hide—the joke being the fact that the Athenian military boot could be worn on either foot—turned against his own colleagues of The Four Hundred, overthrew them, and restored a limited democracy, thus freeing the fleet to attend to its primary concern, which was beating Sparta.

And that right handily it did, at Kynossema and at Abydos. And last of all, this very spring, in a battle in which Ariston himself had taken part with the land forces, Alkibiades had proved the overwhelming quality of his military genius by wiping out the Lakedaemonian fleet at Kyzikos.

So now, standing upon the Akropolis, Ariston could watch the workmen fitting into place the graceful maiden statues which were being used to support the roof of the new Erechtheon instead of the more usual columns. They were called karyatids, and they gave the new building a strange and haunting loveliness. The newest demagogue, Kleophon the lyre-maker, was responsible for this, and for the new temple of Athena being built to the left of the Parthenon. Kleophon wanted to give work to the many unemployed thêtes, and thus supplement the diobelia, the dole of two obols daily given to those workmen whose livelihood had been cut off by the war.

Say what you will of demagogues, they are infinitely preferable to oligarchs, Ariston thought, and started back down the hill toward the city below.

But as he turned homeward, obsessed by the nagging feeling that Athens was still in grave danger, that Kleophon had been a fool not to accept the Spartan offer of peace after Kyzikos, and wondering how Alkibiades' campaign to recover lost Byzantium was turning out, he saw Theoris coming toward him.

333

He stopped and waited, because plump now, becoming matronly, all the glow of a great and perfect love showing in her eyes, Theoris was a pleasure to look upon. It wasn't true, as the wits quipped, that he had given her to Sophokles; but if it had been, he might well have been proud of that act.

"Ariston," she said gently, in that voice that had become pure music, all of its youthful stridency gone, "I've been looking for you for weeks!"

"I'm glad," he said. "I thought you hated me, Theoris."

"Don't be a fool, Ariston. I could never hate you. I've ceased to—to need you; if the quality of my feeling for you has changed, it remains—love. A sisterly sort, perhaps, but love for all that."

Ariston stood there smiling at her. How beautifully she spoke; how liltingly perfect her Attic had become!

"Why were you looking for me, Theo?" he asked.

"Because of Kleothera," she said simply.

Ariston frowned. "Is there anything wrong? Has Orchomenus—"

"Taken to tormenting her as he did poor Thargelia? No. He tries to—mentally—by flaunting before her his sluts and catamites; but physically, because of the way you so cleverly bound him, he doesn't dare. And even mentally he cannot, because only one thing can, and does, cause her untold distress—"

"Which is?" Ariston said, his voice gone tight and dry.

"Your absence. That you don't come to see her any more. . . ."

"Theo—" Ariston groaned.

"I know. You don't dare. Your precious sense of honor! But I'm a devotee of Aphrodite, not of Artemis. I think that what you do is—wicked. I think that the goddess should drag you down to be trampled by horses as she did Hippolytus for his sins against her. Yours are greater. Hippolytus merely defended his asceticism, his chastity, while you live in unlawful union with a woman you don't even love, and leave poor Kleo in the hands of a brute who revolts her. I—I had a dream about you, and that's why I sought you out. I dreamed that you went to Delphi, and I, invisible by the gift of Aphrodite, accompanied you unseen—"

334

"And?" Ariston said.

"You asked the priestess if you'd ever know happiness. She replied: 'Yes. When you learn to laugh with the laughter of the gods!'"

"And what, my dear Sybil of a Theoris, does that mean?"

"That when you learn to give as little thought to the conventions and prejudices of men as the gods do, you'll know happiness. You and Kleothera were made for one another! You're both such beautiful people and—"

"Theoris, please!"

"Why don't you come with me and see her now? For ten minutes—five—long enough to put the light back into her eyes, the glow in her cheeks?"

"Theo, you talk rot. Kleothera has always been kind to me. But never by word or gesture has she—"

"She's a decent girl, Ariston! What do you want her to do—rip off her peplos and fling herself naked and panting into your arms?"

Ariston grinned at Theoris. "Now that's what I call an idea of true, philosophic beauty! Why don't you suggest it to her?" he said.

"Oh, you! Oh, men! She'd slap my face if I did. And she'd slap yours if you openly tried to seduce her. The whole point is you don't have to. All you have to do is to be gentle and sweet to her until one day she can't bear it any more and falls weeping of her own volition into your arms—"

"And you recommend that?" Ariston said quietly. "You say I should gently draw her into adultery, betray—"

Theoris looked at him.

"You're betraying her now, her woman's right to love. You're betraying yourself, your own right to happiness, peace. And you're offending Aphrodite who, when angered, is merciless. So do as I tell you! Come!"

When he walked into the room with Theoris, Kleothera got very slowly to her feet. She was almost nineteen now, and any description he might have given of her, even to himself, would have been in some ways an understatement, a lie. Her body had never been spoiled by childbearing—probably, Ariston realized suddenly, because Orchomenus' own excesses had robbed him of the power of procreation —and to call its lines under the soft cling and fall of her ankle-length woman's robe perfect was to add new dimension and meaning to that word.

Her great blue eyes opened like the sky of morning and all the stars of heaven fell into them suddenly and drowned. He could feel her gaze moving over his face, as tactile as the fingers of the blind.

"My lord Ariston," she whispered, "I—"

Then shyly she put out her hand to him.

He took it gently, raised it to his lips. He could feel it trembling under his mouth, feel the wild sweet vibrations racing up her slender arm. He released her hand and stood there smiling at her.

"Well, Kleo—?" he said.

"My lord, I—I—" she quavered, then for the first time she saw Theoris standing there behind him. "Oh, Theoris!" she laughed, her voice reedy and vibrant with relief. "I *am* so glad you came!"

Every trace of her quaint, childish colonial Hellenic was gone. Her Attic was as pure, as flutelike as Theoris' own.

"But not that *I* did?" Ariston said in a tone of mock reproach.

"Of course I'm glad you came, my lord!" Kleothera said. "What I meant was that I'm gladder that Theoris came with you. Oh! That sounds awful! I didn't mean—"

"*What* didn't you mean, child?" Ariston said.

"Oh—oh, I don't know what I do mean!" Kleothera wailed. "Sit down, both of you! Let me get you some rice cakes and wine. I made the cakes myself. I—"

"Then they will be sweeter than the nectar of the gods," Ariston said in his grave, rich voice.

"Please don't say such things to me, my lord!" Kleo said, and fled through the curtains into the kitchen.

"I'll help you, Kleo," Theoris said, and pushed the curtain aside. She stopped there, holding the curtain open so that Ariston could see into the kitchen.

Kleothera stood there like a Delphian priestess breathing the blue flames that bring mystic communion with the god. She was staring at the back of her own hand, at the place hat Ariston had kissed. Then with trance-like slowness, aching tenderness, she raised it to her mouth.

Theoris let the curtain drop and smiled at him in purest triumph.

"Do you mind if I leave you, Kleo?" she called. "I left he baby alone, and—"

"Oh, Theoris, don't go!" Kleothera almost wept. "I—"

"—don't want to be left alone with this wicked old atyr," Ariston said, "with this son of Goat Pan who is sure o—"

She came back through the curtains.

"It's not you, my lord. It's—it's Orchomenus. He'd be ure to think ill, if—"

"—anyone were to tell him, which no one will," Theoris aid. "Kleo, darling, I have to go. And, anyhow, I've known Ariston a good many years now. He invented self-control, nd he's so perfect a kalokagathos that it can be maddening. So let him stay and chat with you a while. It will do oth of you good. Chaire, now, you beautiful people!"

After she had gone, Ariston sat and ate the little cakes, rank the wine. But they didn't talk, really. Words between them had become great stones to be lifted one by one nd dropped without a splash into vast depths of silence.

It was unbearable. Ariston stood up.

"Good-bye, Kleo," he said.

"You're going? So soon?" she wailed.

Ariston smiled. "You don't seem to be enjoying my company," he said.

"Oh, but I am! It's just that I—"

"That you're nervous, and afraid of me, and—"

Suddenly, wildly, she shook her head.

"It's not you I'm afraid of, my lord," she whispered.

"Then of Orchomenus?" Ariston said.

"Nor of him—" Her voice was the silence beneath all ound.

"Then?" Ariston said.

"Of—of myself!" she wailed, and whirling, dashed toard that curtained arch.

As quickly as she moved, he was quicker. He caught her y the shoulders, turned her with great gentleness until she

337

was facing him. He stood there holding her like that,
staring into her face. It was silk white now, all color fled
from it. She opened her mouth—to protest, he was sure
—but all it formed was his name, making of it a sound like
bells plunged into the wind, drowned silvery notes in mov
ing air.

"Oh, Ariston, Ariston—"

He bent then and found her mouth, kissing it without
passion but with a tenderness more hurtful, searching,
lacerating than mere pain, cherishing her warm, soft
tearsalt lips, as though they were the petals of some rare
flower, infinitely fragile, inexpressibly dear.

Then he dropped his arms, released her. But she didn'
move. She stood there like that, her mouth clinging to his
so lightly, delicately, that touching, it seemed not to touch
Time was lost, suspended upon his breath, herself unbreath
ing still, until he touched her shoulder and brought her
back to existence, back to pain.

She stood there, facing him, and let the great tear
silver-scald her eyes, bead her white-gold lashes.

"Kleo—" he groaned.

"Oh, Ariston," she whispered; "Oh, my lord, my life—
—I love you so!"


No one in Athens, had their secret love been known
would have believed that they kept it free of commo
carnality. Even Theoris, who did know of it, who actively
aided and abetted their meetings, didn't believe that. Yet by
Artemis and Hestia both, that love was almost as innocen
as the games of childhood.

Perhaps, in that Athens where every conceivable variet
of sexual fare was available upon a man's lightest whim, a
any hour of the day or night, abstinence was the only
tribute he had left to pay her. Perhaps, knowing love fo
the very first time since poor Phryne had died, he tended
to enshrine it, make of it an object of worship, and of her
the goddess of all his idolatry. And she—whose knowledge
of physical love was confined to Orchomenus' gross occa
sional taking of her, without preliminaries, often without
so much as a kiss or a caress, forcing himself upon her, so
that to her revolted mind the act had become synonymous

338

with a violation, not only of her bruised, aching, unprepared and therefore all the more violated, outraged body, but also of everything within her that was fastidious, delicate, fine, her very conception of herself, her being, her identity, her soul—was glad of Ariston's restraint, even welcomed it, at first.

But later, being, as she was, a woman in love, having for the first time a gentle, matchlessly tender lover, she gradually became aware that she was of flesh and blood, melting flesh and pounding blood, and nerves that could scream nightlong in bitter anguish.

He found her, soon enough, capable of childish fits of temper, unexplained tears; but loving her wholly, as he did, even these negative sides of her personality amused, delighted him.

Until the night, obsessed with the need to torment him as she was herself tormented, all the more so because she didn't truly know what was the cause of her black moods, so completely had her experience with Orchomenus caused her to separate the idea of love from the thought of physical desire, she met him with downcast eyes and sullen, pouting lips, told him, for the first time since she'd known him, a cold, deliberate lie.

"I'm with child," she said, and had the cruel satisfaction of seeing his lips go white.

"By—him?" he whispered.

"Who else?" she said indifferently.

He turned then and walked out of the house. She ran after him screaming, calling his name, but he didn't so much as turn his head. Very tall and proud, his back held rigid against her cry, he kept walking. And that night, for the first time in many years, he got drunker than one of Athena's sacred owls. He lost all track of time; he could never afterward remember where he'd been.

Nor even how he got home again. But he woke up in his own bed, possessed by a conviction amounting to absolute certainty that if he moved his head it would fall off and roll across the floor. He lay there for a long time, until finally he achieved the major feat of getting his eyes to focus and saw Chryseis lying there beside him, smiling at him with an expression of purest triumph.

"What was the name of the wine you made yourself drunken with last night?" she purred.

"Don't know," he groaned. "Why?"

"So I can buy a barrel of it! Oh, Ariston, Ariston! Oh my love, last night—"

"Last night what?" he muttered.

"You loved me like—a god! Like Dionysus! Or Apollo! Or Eros himself! Oh, my sweet lord, I—"

He turned his head then and was most thoroughly sick upon the bedroom floor.

# CHAPTER TWENTY-ONE

THIS TIME, ONCE SHE WAS SURE, Chryseis kept to her bed. In panic and in misery, Ariston flew to Ophion's house to procure the draught that would cause her to lose the child the iatros was sure would kill her at birth. He slipped it into her wine every day for four months.

It didn't work. It didn't work at all.

Chryseis lay there round and rosy and content, almost pretty with the soft, sweet glow of maternity, while Ariston paced the floor, forgot his business, forgot the war, went, in sober truth, very nearly mad. Until the day—

—that Kleothera came.

She came through the doorway of his house, her pale hair spilling winter sunlight about her shoulders; one of her eyes blackened and swollen shut, the other leaping with all the terrors of Tartarus, her lips puffed, a dried trickle of blood penciling her chin, great purplish whip marks curling around her shoulders, and stood there, trembling, looking at him in a way that he could neither believe nor accept, nor even bear, that tore and healed him at the same time, until he substituted for the words that would not, could not, come to him to define the quality of his anguish, the simple gesture of opening his arms to her.

And, without an instant's hesitation, with a childish skip and scamper, a choked-off little sob, Kleothera came to him.

He stood there, holding her and quivering with the total rage that possessed him, his nostrils filled with the hot, animal-blood stench rising from her robe that was stuck to the multiple stripes from the merciless lashing Orchomenus had dealt her, while she clung to him and soaked his chiton with her tears.

"Kleo—" he groaned.

She raised her battered face, and whatever he was going to say was gone, vanished out of time and mind, lost as that soft, pink flutter inches below his mouth caught and held his gaze, his breath, his life, in utter immobility, in a paralysis so complete that she, seeing it, recognizing it, had the mercy and the tenderness to end it for him.

She went up on tiptoe and pressed her mouth to his until his blood roared like a pride of lions and life, being, strength, and even—strangely—will flooded back in him.

"Kleo—" he said, "what—"

"—are we going to do, now?" she said. She didn't even emphasize that "we." Her acceptance of what there was between them, what there'd always been, was complete. She needed neither the consecration nor the profanation of words for it.

But he, a tortured soul possessed by what Sokrates had called the vice of self-torment, did. He couldn't let what was gloriously well enough alone. He had to dig into it, beat the air about her defenseless head with melancholy questions, logical objections, until she said:

"Will you shut up and go on kissing me? That's what I need, not talk!"

"But Kleo!" he groaned. "The child—your child—"

"My child who never existed," she said impishly. "I lied to you, Ariston, my lord! I wanted to hurt you, because—"

"Because what?" Ariston said.

"Oh, I don't know! No, that's another lie. I do know now. Only I can't tell you—"

"Why not?" he said.

"Because it's too shameful. Now will you kiss me, love? Please? Oh, please, please, please!"

He bent and found her mouth. He kissed her now as he'd never kissed her before. As a woman, not as a fragile doll. Then he felt her hands against his chest, pushing. Instantly he turned her loose.

"That's enough," she said, her voice gone ragged, breath-torn. "In fact, it's too much. I—I—didn't come here for this, though Aphrodite witness I have need of—of tenderness. I only came to ask your help, my lord, because you, of all men I know, are truly kind. I—I'm sorry I lied to you that day. Though Aphrodite and Eros both witness I've been punished enough for that. I mean when you stopped coming to see me. That, lord of my life, was a torture that even the demokoinoi might have envied—for every day that you stayed away, a little piece of me—died."

"Kleo!" he whispered.

"Kleo!" she mocked. "How eloquent you are, my lover! What pretty speeches you make me! But I can't even flirt with you a little now. I—I hurt too much. Orchomenus—he—"

"That monstrous beast!"

She shook her head.

"No, Ariston," she said. "He's not, and you know it. He's a good man, even kind in a rough way, when he's all right, when his demons don't possess him—"

"Which they do too damned often!"

"Yes. Too often now. I—I can't bear it any more—though the fault is all mine—"

Ariston stared at her. At nineteen, she was already all woman, regal, queenly, tall. He didn't know that in the opinion of her wild Gallic tribesmen, she'd have been considered almost a dwarf, and too slender for beauty, for among the Gauls, the women were quite often bigger and stronger than the men.

"In what way is the fault yours, Kleo?" he said.

"I let him catch me writing your name on a piece of parchment. Just your name—nothing more. Theoris taught me how to write. And that was the first word I learned to set down: your name. So I could sit for hours, staring at it. Even the letters of it are—beautiful. Ἀριστων. Alpha rho iota sigma tau omega nu, Ariston. 'The Best.' A beautiful name for a beautiful man. For my love."

"Kleo, you mustn't!"

"I know I mustn't; but I'm going to." She laughed, suddenly. The laughter was a little shaky, he thought. "You see, I do know how to make pretty speeches—to you, anyhow; not being a laconic Lakonian—Theoris says that's where the word comes from, because all you Lakedaemonians are tongue-tied and terribly shy—is it true?"

"Yes," Ariston said. "Most Spartans would rather die than have to make a speech."

"Then don't. Just kiss me—" Then abruptly, without any transition at all, the pain broke through.

"Oh, Ariston, what *are* we going to do?" she wailed.

"Get you free of him," Ariston said grimly. "Can you walk?"

"I walked over here. No—I ran. Why?"

"We're going to the magistrate," Ariston said.

"What good would that do?" Kleothera said morosely. "A man has a right to beat his wife, under the law—if he thinks she deserves it. And if I go to the magistrate with you —that will *prove* I deserved it. If it needed any proof, which it doesn't. I did."

"Don't be a fool, Kleo!" he said; "You have only to present that paper I made him sign, and—"

She stared at him, wonderingly.

"What paper, my lord?" she said.

Ariston smiled.

"I knew that too. That he wouldn't give you a copy of it, I mean. That's why I left one copy with the magistrate and kept one copy myself. Now come!"

But she didn't move. He stopped short, stared at her, said a little lamely:

"That is, if you *want* to be free of Orchomenus. Do you, Kleothera?"

She lifted her gaze, looked at him. Her pale blue eyes cleared.

"Yes," she said. "I want that more than anything—except one thing—"

He stood there staring at her. His breath halted again, his heart.

"And that thing is?" he whispered.

"To belong to you. To be yours," Kleothera said.

"Hmmnnn—" the astunomos said. "Hmmnnn. And what did you do, young woman, that made your husband beat you thus? Wander about the streets? Take other men as lovers? *This* gentleman, for instance?"

Kleothera pulled her peplos back up over her striped, lacerated shoulders.

"Ohhhh, Ariston!" she wailed.

"Nothing of the kind," Ariston said, trying to keep the

344

anger out of his voice. "Her husband drinks. And when drunken, he—"

"A likely story!" the magistrate said. "Pretty as this blonde child is, any man would be tempted to—"

Ariston handed him the parchment roll he'd forced Orchomenus to sign before the previous astunomos, unfortunately out of office now, in which the half-mad Spartan had promised by Athena never to beat, kick, or otherwise torment his bride.

"How do you account for this, then?" Ariston said.

The astunomos read the document.

"I can't account for it," he said. "Why would any man in his right mind, sign a thing like this?"

"Perhaps because he's *not* in his right mind," Ariston said quietly. "Look, good magistrate, I have known Orchomenus nearly all my life. When he told me he planned to wed—for the second time—and asked money of me to buy this girl's freedom from slavery, I forced him to sign this, because I knew him. What's more, I had him sign it, before I'd seen his bride, so that my own disinterestedness should be entirely clear—"

"What's not clear," the astunomos growled, "is why you forced him to sign it in the first place!"

"He'd been married before. His first wife died—largely of his drunken brutalities. I can produce twenty witnesses to the fact that hardly a week passed without his beating her half to death, burning her with hot irons, cutting her with knives—neighbors of theirs, inhabitants of the quarter where they lived. And your colleague, the astunomos Philocotes—he who preceded you in office—will gladly tell you that Orchomenus signed this of his own free will, and was under no constraint at all. Well, magistrate?"

"I'll refer it to the Archons' Court," the magistrate said slowly. "It meets in two weeks. Make sure you have all your witnesses ready, then—"

"Oh, Ariston!" Kleothera almost wept. "Two weeks! Where will I go? What will I do? I can't go back home now! He—he'll kill me!"

Ariston thought about the matter. He could rent a little house for Kleo readily enough, provide her with servants, food, clothing—even an armed guard to protect her in

345

case Orchomenus came and tried to take her home by force.

But—he knew only too well how the Athenian mind worked. To do that would be to compromise the case, even, almost surely, to lose it. Given this opportunity, Orchomenus' speech-writers—for in Athens, the legal profession confined itself to looking up the points of law and working them into discourses which the contending parties had to memorize and to deliver before the dikasteria themselves, hence the profession's rather apt name—would point out all the obvious implications: a rich man stealing a poor man's wife, setting her up in a cozy little house with servants and guards—"Kalokagathoi, I ask you—"

But he couldn't send her back to Orchomenus. He couldn't. Then it came to him. He'd take her home. To his own house. Chryseis, for all her fiendish temper, was a tender soul. He'd tell her the truth—or at least that part of it she could hear without hurt—exhibit Kleo's poor lacerated back to her. It was the best plan of all. Chryseis would never believe he'd bring his mistress to her house; nor would the dicasts, married men all, dream that any Athenian would dare do such a thing considering what sisters to Xanthippe most Athenian women were. Its very boldness would lend it innocence, insure his winning the case against Orchomenus.

He was quite right. Except for one thing.

When he led Kleothera back to his house, the women servants had already, with delighted malice, informed their pregnant mistress of the master's sudden departure with a lovely girl—thus revenging themselves upon Chryseis for the daily round of abuse and not infrequent blows she dealt them. No sooner did they come in the door than she—having been informed of their arrival by one of the vengeful maids and forgetting in the stress of the moment all Ophion's advice—got up from her bed and dragged her grossly swollen body into the foyer.

"Chrys!" Ariston said. "You shouldn't have got up! Ophion told you—"

Chryseis drew herself erect. But, attempting dignity, she missed originality; none of the truly crushing remarks

346

she'd been rehearsing for the last half-hour came to her mind. Instead she uttered those well worn words that nearly every wife in human history has had one time or another occasion to say:

"Ariston, would you mind telling me just *who* this woman is?"

Ariston smiled.

"Orchomenus' wife," he said calmly. "She's come to us under sad circumstances, Chrys. Fleeing for her life, in fact. Show her your back, Kleo—"

Then it was that he saw Kleothera's face. She was staring at Chryseis' swollen belly. Then she turned her great blue eyes upon his face. She didn't say anything. She just stood there looking at him and letting her eyes go blind-scalded, walling their utter anguish behind that sudden sapphire glitter, that wild white rush, that hopeless spill and fall. . . . Then very slowly she turned her back, tugged her peplos from her shoulders, let it slide downward to her slender waist.

"Ohhhh!" Chryseis gasped. "Hera save us! What—what a monster he is! What an utter, brutal swine!"

Kleothera stood there with her bare back turned to Chryseis. She had her head bent, and the huge tears chased one another endlessly down her face. But it wasn't because of the pain of her stiffening stripes that she wept. That pain was as nothing now.

Chryseis saw her shoulders shake. She took a heavy step forward, another; stood there staring at that living statue of Niobe drowning all the world in bitter tears. And the question Ariston had been dreading—because like most men unaccustomed to lying, he did so very badly—was vanquished by her pity, quite forgot. She didn't say: "Was it because of you he whipped her thus, Ariston?" Instead, suddenly, impulsively, she took Kleothera in her arms, kissed her on both her cheeks.

"Oh you poor, poor child!" she whispered, and her own warm brown eyes flooded in their turn. The two of them stood there like that, holding each other and crying.

Three days later, Orchomenus appeared before Ariston's house, armed to the teeth and roaring like a maddened

347

bull. He was, naturally, wildly drunk. He demanded that Ariston come out, announced at the top of his mighty lungs his intention to rend his wife's seducer limb from limb.

Ariston waited until his bellowings had attracted quite a crowd. Then he came out of the house barehanded.

"Go home, Orchomenus," he said quietly. "Your wife is here, yes. She came here seeking refuge from your drunken brutalities. In fact, she shares the gynaekeia with my own, who is tending the hurts you inflicted upon her. And here she stays until she is well, and until the heliaea has handed her down a bill of divorcement. You'll never torment her again. So, if you know what's good for you, go home."

"I'll kill you!" Orchomenus roared. "I'll rip your head from your shoulders! I'll—"

"Oh, don't be unnecessarily tiresome, Orchomenus!" Ariston said.

Whereupon Orchomenus leaped upon him like a lion. Only, the big man had forgotten several things of great importance, to wit: that he was ten years older than Ariston and never exercised; or, conversely, that Ariston was ten years younger than he, and went religiously to the palaestra every day to work out with Autolykos or the other Ariston; that since Sphacteria, he had never again borne arms, so that even his Spartan hoplite's skill with weapons had diminished markedly, while Ariston had served in three bitterly fought campaigns in the ranks of his adopted polis; that drinking, carousing, and eating too much had larded his great muscles over with fat; that drunk as he was at the moment upon both wine and rage, his coordination and his reflexes were nothing short of pitiful; and, last of all, he was facing one of the three supreme exponents of the pankratieon in all Attica.

Ariston ducked under his wild sword thrust, caught his sword arm by the wrist and, using it as the lever and his own broad back as the fulcrum, sent Orchomenus cartwheeling through the air amid the delighted roars of the spectators.

Orchomenus landed upon the cobblestones so hard that the sword flew from his hand and all the breath left him. But he clawed at his belt for his dagger, only to take a kick to the point of his chin that glazed his eyes over. When he came to himself, all his weapons were gone. Ariston had piled them neatly on his own doorstep.

"Go home, Orchomenus," he said quietly.

But Orchomenus rose up, bellowing—whereupon Ariston kicked him in the belly with such force that the big Spartan gave up in libation to all the darker gods all he'd eaten and drunk that day. Then Ariston chopped him across the bridge of the nose with the edge of his hand, thus breaking the cartilage in it and causing it to bleed profusely, and caught the huge man by the neck and hammerlocked him, throwing him with a force that shook the ground. Standing above Orchomenus, he turned to the hooting, howling spectators, and said:

"Athenians! Hera witness that my cause is just! I leave it up to you: Shall I kill this man?"

"Kill him!" the mob roared back. "Kill the black-browed swine!"

Ariston smiled.

"No," he said, "in memory of the friendship I formerly bore him, and the fact that he once saved my life, I give him his. But I'll make it difficult for him to come this way again!"

Then lifting Orchomenus' big, hairy leg, Ariston broke it deliberately across his own upraised knee.

"This way, my friend, you'll leave me and mine in peace," he said, and turning, went back into the house.

So it was that Orchomenus came into the court on crutches, his left leg in a splint. His speech was surprisingly good: He accused Ariston of stealing his wife, both of them of adultery, and asked the court to award him ten full talents from Ariston's purse as compensation for his sorrows and his wrongs, as well as to return his erring spouse to him.

But Ariston's speech was far better, for he had written it himself. His use of irony was studied and effective. He pointed out the existence of the document Orchomenus had signed, offered it in evidence. He called witness after witness to the fact that the brutalities Orchomenus had inflicted upon his former wife, Thargelia, had been without

349

number and without end, to the extent that one could well believe she'd died of them. He told of having purchased the freedom of Kleothera after she'd become the Spartan's bride, and at Orchomenus' own plea, a debt still largely unrepaid.

"So, dikastoi, kalokagathoi, jury, gentlemen," Ariston summed up, "it was natural that the poor child should seek refuge in my house. The astunomos Plillip, son of Thetos, can testify as to the state of her back that day! He saw how it had been lashed into ribbons, was covered with blood! And as for this ridiculous charge of adultery, I ask you this: When, where, and upon how many occasions did this adultery take place? What proof has he presented that would incline you to believe that I have ever carnally known his wife? You are married men, one and all, and hence have a certain knowledge of the sweet docility of Athenian dames. So I, very gently, ask you this: Which of you would dare take a secret mistress into your own house? How many of you, these days, can bring even a purchased slave girl home if she's the least bit pretty?"

The roars of laughter from the spectators drowned his words; even the dikasts joined in right heartily. When the laughter had died, Ariston went on:

"My own dear wife is great with child, or she'd be here to testify in poor Kleothera's behalf. She'd tell you that since, in her delicate state, I have naturally kept apart from her, this poor, abused child has occupied a couch in the same room at her side. This, gentlemen, for our adulteries!

"I ask you, dikastoi, to grant this innocent child Kleothera freedom from this brutal monster! I ask you to place him under restraint, that never again may he harm her. I ask you to uphold Athens' honor and her justice! May wise Athena, her patron goddess, inspire your minds and hearts. I have spoken, gentlemen of the dikasteria, august archons, I thank you!"

He won the case hands down. In a unanimous vote, the heliaea granted Kleothera a bill of divorcement. Further, it placed Orchomenus under restraint, warning him that if he harmed or molested his ex-wife, the free metic Kleothera, in any way whatsoever, he'd find himself chained to the oar bench of a galley for the rest of his life.

Orchomenus heard the sentence with bowed head. Then, muttering curses, he swung out of the court on his crutches.

Outside in the sunlight, Kleothera stood looking up at Ariston in a way impossible for him to bear; as though, he thought, she's been condemned to death instead of freed to live out her life in hope and joy.

"What now, my lord?" she whispered. "I can't go back to your house. I cannot! I can't face Chryseis! I have too much—sin—upon my soul!"

"Sin?" Ariston said.

"Yes. The sin of—of wanting you. Of being more than guilty in my mind, my heart, of—of exactly what Orchomenus accused us of! Of not being physically a sinner only by your tender mercy and the gods! For you, it's different: You have a wife, who—who loves you—who is with —with—with child!_Your_ child, Ariston!"

She bent her head and wept aloud, the sobs tearing up from her throat in wild pulsations.

"Kleo—" he groaned.

"I think I shall die of that, my lord! Of the knowing! That you—you touched her, held her, kissed her, entered her body, her life—Oh, Ariston, Ariston—of that I shall go mad, curse all the gods and die! Of that!"

"Kleo!" he said again, helplessly.

"I—I've dreamed of having your child, my lord. Of feeling it grow within me, so little and warm and round and soft. Of giving it birth with such joy that I'd feel no pangs, not one! Of—of holding it afterward, putting it to my breasts, having its tiny mouth tug at me, melt me into pure delight! It would look like you, wouldn't it—this child can never have—who can never be? It would grow more like you day by day, so tall and strong and beautiful! Oh, Ariston, Ariston! Lend me a blade! A little dagger just long enough to reach my heart, and sharp enough not to hurt too much! Let me die now quickly instead of slowly and by inches! Let me—"

He took her by the arm and shoved her roughly down

351

the crowded street. For the worst of it was that he could neither kiss nor comfort her there before the court, in the face of the grinning mob.

An hour later, they stood in the foyer of the little house he had rented for her. She was very white, but she had recovered her calm. Slowly, she put out her hand to him.

"Promise me, my lord," she said quietly, "that you will not come here again. I, in my turn, will promise not to harm myself. For only thus can we honor what has been between us, and now must be no more! By keeping it pure, by not sullying it. I—I'll endure. As the special priestess of your cult, my life, while yet it lasts, devoted to your worship, your idolatry. The hierophant of your sweet mysteries! There's honor in that, I think! Promise me?"

"You ask more than flesh can bear!" he said.

"Try. You can. It's I who cannot. Which is why I beg you to spare me, my lord. That mercy I ask you, please!"

"If I can," he whispered. "By all the torments of Tantalos, by Prometheos bound, by Sisyphos' stone, I swear I'll stay away, if I can. By the love I bear you, I swear it!"

But he could not. He had nothing to distract his heart, his mind. Chryseis was very great with child, lost in her mad dream that this time, despite all the conclusive evidences to the contrary she had already had, it would live. And even if she had not been preoccupied thus, her poor charms were insufficient to hold him. He tried the obvious remedy; he went to Parthenope's house of perfumed sin. Only to find that what burned in him was no such simple thing as lust; that what he suffered was verily love; that his mind, his heart, his trembling flesh, had been melted in that crucible, refined beyond response to aught else; that he was blind to every other face no matter how lovely, deaf to every other dulcet voice, inert to any other lissome form.

He sat nightlong by his window, listening uncaring to the tumultuous shouting of the merrymakers in the streets. They'd had news at last of Alkibiades, who had set out to prove—

That you can't judge a man from either his behavior or

352

his appearance, Ariston thought wryly, not when that man is a genius. As Alkibiades is. The greatest military genius that Athens has ever produced in all her history. This boy-lover. This mincing, lisping fop. This irreverent blasphemer. This fancier of whores. This drunken blackguard who—

—has won back Thasos and Selymbria. Taken Chryso-polis, established a toll station there so that every ship that rows in from the Euxine has to pay tribute. Besieged Chalkedon, made it tributary to us; and now has starved mighty Byzantium, that queen of cities, into surrender, so that the Athenian Owl screams its triumph over the whole Bosporus once more.

And thus insured the peace, very likely. Thus cutting me off from the only way out I could have taken in honor—to convert a square rod of foreign soil into Attic earth by soaking it with my blood. So be it! Artemis and Hestia both forgive me! Black Hades take my honor! Tartarus, my shade!

Then he got up and went out into the night.

He came up to that little house. Knocked softly, hesitantly, upon that door.

Kleothera opened it. She stood there without saying anything. She had a lamp in her hand. By its light he saw her eyes were red and swollen from crying.

"Kleo—" he said.

She went on looking at him. Then she said, very quietly. "I don't suppose you'd consider going away and not making an adulteress of me, would you, Ariston?"

"No," he said. "I wouldn't consider it."

"Nor that you—you're forcing me to—to despise myself for the rest of my life? That you're making of me the kind of a creature that abuses the confidence of the woman who was kind to me? The only woman who ever has been? Who —who kissed me, wept over my hurts like a—a sister? And who is—who is going to—gods, let me say it! Let me get the words out that are killing me!—Who is going to—"

"Bear my child. Nor that," he said bleakly. "That doesn't matter either. There is only one way you can be rid of me, Kleo."

"And that is?" she whispered.

353

"Tell me—meaning it—that you don't love me," Ariston said.

She went on looking at him a long time. A very long time. Then she sighed. The sound of it was as of a sword of breath being thrust slowly through her beating heart.

"Come in, Ariston," she said.

He saw her face. It was as white as Phrygian marble. Even her lips were white. She wasn't breathing. Her eyes had rolled back into her head like a dead thing's, like a slaughtered animal's. He opened his mouth; screamed at her.

"Kleo! Immortal gods, Kleo!"

But she didn't, couldn't answer him.

He clutched her to him, her naked body inert, boneless, all give, shook her fiercely, crying now, his eyes so blinded with tears he could no longer see her face.

"Kleo! Hestia, Artemis forgive me! Oh, Kleo, mine—"

Her eyes fluttered open. Her mouth. Her breath was a gale storm suddenly, beating against his throat. Her lips were bruised petals caught in it, fluttering wildly, trying to shape sound into words, to say—

He bent and kissed them in an agony of tenderness, molding them under his own until the ragged pulse and jet and beat of her breath slowed, slowed. . . . Then he released her, and her tears were a spill of diamonds on her face.

"How—beautiful. How—utterly—beautiful," she said.

"Oh, Kleo, Kleo! God, but you frightened me!" he moaned.

She smiled at him then, with grave tenderness.

"I died," she whispered. "I died and went to the Elysian Fields. I walked among the ancient women in a field of light. Antigone was there, and Andromache and Penelope, and Hecuba herself, and all the women who have ever truly loved. And, oh, how they envied me!"

"Child," he murmured. "Sweet, idiot child!"

"I wasn't prepared—for this," she said. "All I'd ever known of love—was pain. And sweat, and animal roarings and—the stink of hairy manflesh—and—Oh, Ariston, turn me loose!"

"Turn you loose?" he said. "Never!"

"Please. For a while. I want to get down on my knees. I want to kiss your hands, your feet—"

"Kleo!" he said.

"To thank you—for showing me that what a man and a woman do together is sacred. A high and holy thing. Our bodies are—living temples, aren't they, lord of my life? And love's the flame of divinity within. Oh, Ariston, Ariston—how can you men go to the public women? How can you make a mock, an obscene parody of this, this—"

"—seeking, this finding," his deep, rich voice took up her thought, making of it a litany, a prayer, "this only moment between birth and death that we are not alone? I don't know, Kleo. I never shall again. I'll never be able to. You've set your seal upon my eyes, blinding them to any other face. And it will always be thus while I have breath and blood and longing in me. Oh Kleo. Kleo mine, I—"

"Don't talk. Not now. Not any more. Just hold me. Never let me go. Never," Kleothera said.

But it couldn't last. There are those who lust after evil, who delight in inflicting pain. Someone followed him to that little house, surely. A woman who hated and envied Chryseis, perhaps; or one of the many deviates whose attentions he had scorned. He didn't know, he would never know, who it was. It didn't matter. All that mattered was the appalling cost.

For there came a day that Ariston stood by Chryseis' bed, listening, white-faced and trembling, to her demented screaming:

"You heard me, Iatros! Rip me open! Take my child alive! What care I if I die? It will have a mother! His straw-haired slut will care for it right tenderly! His tow-headed whore! She'll value anything that sprang from his sweet loins, even the seed he wasted upon poor me! So take it! Save my baby! Can't you see I want to die? In Hera's name, what have I to live for now?"

Ophion turned to Ariston, seeing his face, seeing what was in his eyes.

"You get out of here, Ariston!" he said.

And, utterly defeated, his head bent, his gait shambling, Ariston, the Athenian metic, went like a lackey, a slave.

Twelve hours later, Kleothera heard that knocking on her door. She ran to open it, her face flooded with joy, her blue eyes alight. Then she hung there, frozen, a blade of ice probing for her heart.

The woman who stood before her looked like nothing human. Her face was skeletal, a mask of yellowish parchment drawn tight over brittle bones. Her blue, bitten, bruised lips were drawn back in a hideous counterfeit of a smile over a glittering of teeth. Her breath was fetid as fever, the whole of her stank—

Of blood. Her peplos was soaked with it. It ran down her ankles beneath her robe, pooled and puddled on the stair.

She had something in her arms. With a sweep of a hand like a vulture's claw, she raked back the cloth that covered it.

Kleothera's mouth came open. She felt the beginning of a scream tear up like brine and ice and fire through her throat. But Chryseis stopped her cry with a regal gesture.

"Here," she said, "take it. You can have it now. It's yours. This is your doing, Kleothera. This would have been *his* son, had not the agony you caused me killed it."

Then she laid that crushed, blue, malformed, tiny obscenity in Kleothera's arms, and turning, went back up that street, like a ghost, a phantom, a shade.

But like some ancient queen, awful in her pride—like a Medea.

Kleothera didn't know how long she had been wandering the streets. The days and the nights had become but a flickering alternation of light and dark. She hadn't eaten in — She didn't remember that either and it didn't matter, because the very thought of food brought the vile green rush of nausea to her throat.

She'd buried the child. With her own hands, she'd buried it. She hoped she'd dug that little grave in the garden deep enough. But that didn't matter either; she'd never go back to that house again.

She could see the long walls stretching out before her now toward the port of Piraeus. She'd follow them. At Munychia, hard by the port, there was a temple to Artemis.

Artemis, goddess of chastity, whom most especially she had offended; against whose sacred teachings she had sinned most terribly. She would go there. And before the altar of the goddess, she'd offer up her life. She had no weapon, but the cord belt of her robe was stout enough. Wrapped twice about her naked throat and pulled hard, it— If she had strength enough. If her trembling hands didn't lose their grip— Then she smiled. Failing that, she could always starve.

Head bent, reeling with weariness, with hunger, with thirst, she set out. It never entered her poor, half-mad, tormented mind that to get to Munychia she'd have to pass through Piraeus itself, where the sea scum of all the world, the Panhellenic louts washed up upon Attica's shores like flotsam, had one proud boast they always kept:

"Not even a she goat gets through here unplugged!"

And it was toward their taverns, hovels, foul smelling huts, that poor Kleothera went.

She fought them as long as she could with a wild strength born of desperation, sprung from utter horror. This body that had been his—his instrument to touch, to stroke, to caress until it twanged like lyre strings vibrant with delight—could not now be profaned by others! It could not be used by these goats and monkeys, these scourings of the world! No! She'd die first! She'd—

Then she heard the biggest of them scream, his voice gone woman-shrill, and looking down, she saw him writhing on the stones, his bullneck broken by a single blow. Another sank to his knees, clutching at his throat where a hand like an axblade had crushed his larynx; another clawed at his crotch where a kick had rendered him useless to women forevermore.

Then the rest were gone, trailing a ragged banner of curdog yelps behind them. And he stood there as beautiful as a god, towering like Ares in his wrath, muscled like Herakles.

"Oh my lord, my love!" she wept. Then she stopped short, peering into the face she'd never seen before. It was as beautiful as Ariston's own, but it wasn't his. It wasn't his at all.

The man smiled, a little sadly.

357

"I'm not your lord—whom surely all the gods have blessed!—nor even your love, worse luck! But if you, Eos, goddess of the dawn, or some golden nymph of the upper air at the very least, could look with favor upon this poor mortal, you have—"

"Who are you?" Kleothera whispered.

"Autolykos, son of Lykon—and your slave," he said.

# CHAPTER TWENTY-TWO

THREE YEARS FROM THAT DAY, his triumphant campaigns in the Propontis, the Hellespont, the Bosporus behind him, Alkibiades was invited to come back to Athens once again, to receive the honors for the glories he had won and also to be cleared of, or pardoned for, the charges still pending against him: of having mutilated the protective Hermes and having made public mock of the Eleusinian mysteries. The news was on every tongue, was the topic of conversation in every house. Even in that of the wealthy shield-maker, the metic Ariston.

"So they're allowing him to come home at last," Chryseis said. "You knew him, Ariston. Tell me about him. What's he really like? There are so many tales—"

"Alkibiades?" Ariston said. "What you ask is impossible, Chrys. I'd say that Alkibiades invented contradiction. You've met Orchomenus. You've seen how intelligence and stupidity, good and evil, alternate in him—with no middle ground at all, no place where the warring elements of his being can meet and reconcile themselves. . . ."

"You didn't help when you stole his wife," Chryseis said tartly.

"Nor you, when you drove her into the streets like a homeless dog," Ariston said.

Chryseis turned away from the loom, from the bright, many-hued cloth she was weaving, and put her hand on his arm.

"I'm sorry about that, Ariston," she said gently. "But I had to save my own life. And without you I cannot live. You know that."

Ariston stared at her. What had worked this change in

her? For a whole year now, she had been very good, very gentle. Of course, she lost her temper now and again; but she always mastered herself with astonishing quickness, and apologized humbly for her fault. And as a result, he suspected, of her new found quietude, she was much better-looking. She would never achieve anything even remotely approaching beauty; but she had put on flesh, become a rather interesting woman, with the kind of face that's often remembered when mere beauty is forgot. And she hadn't gotten pregnant again. Ophion was of the opinion that she wouldn't any more. The damage to her womb by that last dreadful forceps delivery had been too extensive. The iatros had told her bluntly that he was almost sure she could never expect to so much as conceive, much less bear, a child. She had taken the news calmly, seemed wholly resigned.

"Chrys," Ariston said, "what's happened to you? What is it that has changed you so?"

"Are you complaining?" she asked, a little mockingly.

"No! Hera witness it!"

"That's Sokrates' favorite oath," she said.

"How'd you know that?" he said. "*I* never told you."

"Of course not. I heard him say it. After that—business of—of you and Kleothera. I was losing my mind, Ariston. I used to leave the gynaekeia and wander the streets—alone. I suppose that if I'd been pretty, someone would have ravished me. One day I ran into Sokrates. He too was alone, lost in meditation. I was bold enough, wild enough, mad enough, to interrupt his thought. He took me to his house, presented me to his wives—he has two! No one ever told me that—"

"Xanthippe and Myrto. Yes. Go on, Chrys."

"And talked to me. Or rather he asked me questions. And when he was done asking me things, somehow—as if by magic—he'd led me to see what a wicked, selfish fool I'd been; how I'd driven you into Kleothera's arms. I promised him on my knees I'd be good to you from now on. I swore it before Hera, which seemed to please him. And I—I've kept my word, haven't I?"

"Yes," Ariston said, and kissed her.

"Thank you, my lord!" she laughed a little tremulously.

"I was beginning to think you'd *never* do that again, not to mention—"

"Chrys," he said reproachfully, "you know why."

"There's no danger, Ariston. I cannot conceive—as I'll prove to you tonight. No, I want to talk. You haven't seen Sokrates in a long time, have you?"

"Not alone. In the company of his disciples, yes. The trouble is that Phaedon keeps me away from him. Oh, not by anything he says or does, but by looking at me with such undisguised horror that it makes my flesh crawl."

"Why should he do that?" Chryseis said.

"He didn't at first. Then someone told him that I, too, had been a bathhouse slave. You know the story? Kriton bought him out of Gurgos' bathhouse at Sokrates' request. I suppose I remind him too much of that—horror. I know he does me. He even looks as I did when I was young—"

"Thirty-six is hardly old," Chryseis said fondly.

"It's not young. Phaedon is still a boy. He was taken at Melos. They didn't kill him, because he was under age. The trouble is that he fastens those huge black eyes on me, and distracts me so I can't follow Sokrates' discourses."

"Make friends with him," Chryseis said. "Point out to him that—even that shameful slavery was neither his fault nor yours. Anyhow, it doesn't seem to have done you any permanent harm—"

"It has, though," Ariston said quietly.

"How?" Chryseis said.

"The same kind that your preoccupation with what you insist upon calling your ugliness has done you, Chrys: I cannot—love myself. Or respect myself. I *know* that before submitting to that, I should have taken my own life. So all my years since were bought at that price. It was too high."

"Bless you for paying it, then!" Chryseis said, "or else I should never have known you."

"I doubt that you have," Ariston said. "Let's talk about something else, shall we, Chrys?"

"All right. For instance, Alkibiades. What a fascinating man!"

Ariston smiled at her.

"Trying to make me jealous, Chrys?" he said.

"I wish I could! But no, that's impossible. You no longer love me—if you ever did, which I doubt. No, don't protest. You're kind to me, and that's enough. And you're *here*. Upon such crumbs of comfort I can live. But tell me about Alkibiades. If half what they say about him is true—"

Ariston hesitated; then he said gravely: "I'm afraid it is. But what could I tell you about him that you don't know already? Besides, you'll see him tomorrow. I'm taking you to the ceremonies, Chrys. . . ."

Chryseis dropped her shuttle and clapped her hands like a child.

"Oh, Ariston, are you? How sweet of you!" she said.

The triumphant return of Alkibiades to Athens to be officially absolved of the charges still pending against him since before the disaster to Athenian arms at Syrakuse, all of eight years ago now, was one of those rare festive occasions to which Athenians felt free to bring their wives. For, as a rule, the seclusion in which upper-class women were kept was almost Oriental, though not as rigid as later writers have made it seem.

Chryseis, like every lady, went to the theater in total freedom; she attended all major religious festivals, including, naturally, those for women alone, which neither Ariston nor any other Athenian husband was allowed to attend. She could visit her women friends and, if she wanted to, her brothers; for Pandoros, her father, had died, precisely as one might have expected, in Polyxenus' bathhouse, his arms growing rigid around a terrified, naked boy. But she didn't want to visit Brimos or Chalcodon, for which, considering their outrageous act of selling her, she was scarcely to be blamed. Actually, she could go out by day whenever she felt like it, as long as she maintained the conventions by taking a slave girl along annd veiling her face. For her, this latter was no hardship; in fact, her shame at her lack of beauty made her rather overdo the convention of the veil. Most Athenian matrons wore a transparent wisp of veil, or none at all; but Chryseis really covered her face—which, on that particular day, had its rarely awful consequences.

For, no sooner had they reached the Akropolis, where

the ceremony of purification was to be held, than a hearty bass voice roared out:

"Ariston! Chaire, old friend! You and your lady join us! By Zeus Thunderer, boy, I haven't seen you in years!"

And the next minute, Ariston found himself locked in Autolykos' iron embrace.

He doesn't know! his reeling mind whispered as those huge and horny fists pounded him on the back. He actually doesn't know!

"What injury have I done you," the athlete was saying, "that you've avoided my house like the plague? Our wives could have become friends and our children—you don't have children, boy?"

"No," Ariston muttered, praying to all the gods he didn't believe in that he wouldn't reel, stagger, fall. Or that Kleothera wouldn't. Her face was whiter than the snows atop Mount Taygetus. Even her lips were drained of color. All the life in her was pooled in her eyes. They were twin sapphires, filled with light, sculpturing the very image of his face.

Then Chryseis broke the unspeakably painful silence. She dropped her veil, and astonishingly, kissed Kleothera's cheek.

"Chaire, Kleo!" she said. "Are *these* your children?"

"Yes, Chryseis," Kleo whispered. "They—"

"So you know each other!" Autolykos said. "Wonders never cease! Tell me, how in Hera's name—"

Chryseis looked at Kleothera.

"Haven't you told him—anything?" she said.

"About—Orchomenus, yes," Kleo whispered. "The rest I —I couldn't. Please, Chryseis! I—"

Chryseis put her arms around her, fondly.

"You need not fear me, Kleo," she said.

Autolykos, as open and straightforward as athletes usually are, was far from being a fool. His face darkened. He glared at Ariston.

"So it was you!" he said.

"No, my lord Autolykos," Chryseis said serenely. "I know Kleothera, because she took refuge in our house when that ugly brute of a husband of hers had beaten her almost to death. In fact, I nursed her myself, though I was with child at the time—a child I afterward lost. And it was at *my* urging that my husband procured a divorce and the protection of the court for her. After that we—neither of us—ever saw her again, though we did hear she'd married you."

She turned to Kleothera.

"Where did you fly to, dear—after the trial was over? Poor Ariston! He did look so disappointed when he came home—and told me how you'd dashed away into the crowd! I've always suspected he wanted to imitate Sokrates, with you playing Myrto to my Xanthippe!"

"Later—" Kleothera got out, her voice made an anguished sound. "Chrys—the—the children—"

Autolykos turned aside, clapped his huge hands. A slave woman scurried toward them.

"Take the children away," he said. "The talk's too grown-up for tender ears!"

Chryseis pinched Ariston so hard he jumped.

"If you don't stop staring at the boy so hard, he'll know," she hissed, "though if he doesn't now, he's the world's greatest fool! A Dionysus, sprung from your thigh, as the god sprang from Zeus's!"

But Autolykos had turned back to them. His voice was heavy and sad as he said:

"Now you may speak, Kleo. I too, should like to hear this tale. . . ."

"And I," Ariston said with a calm that cost him agony.

"All right!" Kleothera all but wept. "Since you all insist upon shaming me! Autolykos, kind husband, this will hurt you, I know; but I must say the truth: I ran away from Ariston because I'd fallen in love with him—and I couldn't —abuse the confidence of a woman who'd been as—kind to me—as Chryseis had—"

"No, you couldn't; could you, dear?" Chryseis said.

"Chrys, for Hestia's sake!" Ariston said.

"And this part will hurt *you*, Ariston!" Kleo said defiantly. "I—I almost starved. So finally I—I took a lover. A wealthy man. I didn't love him, but I could endure him because he—he looked like you—"

"How clever!" Chryseis said, staring at the little boy in his nurse's arms.

"But he—had to go back to—to Macedonia. He was of that nation. He wanted me to go with him, but I was terrified at the thought. I'd heard so much about how wild that country is—"

"Wilder than Gaul, dear?" Chryseis said.

"That I can't say, since I've never seen Macedonia, and I scarcely remember my polis, Lutetia, anyhow. I was a little girl when I was brought to Massalia, Chrys. And Massalia is a Hellenic polis, a sort of miniature Athens, even though it is in Galia. And, anyhow—if you want the truth. I was still in love with your husband! What I was terrified of was being taken so far away I'd never see him again!"

"Kleo," Ariston said gravely, "have a little respect for Autolykos, if you won't—or can't—for me."

"Oh, I do respect him!" Kleothera was frankly weeping now. "I love and respect him! He's the best of men—nobler by far than you are, Ariston!"

"Kleo!" Autolykos said.

"Hear me out, my husband! I ran away again. And that was when you found me struggling with that evil smelling monster who was trying to—"

"—rape you, doubtless," Chryseis said icily. "But tell me, dear: Just why were you struggling? Precious little you had to lose by then!"

"Chryseis!" Ariston roared.

Kleothera pointed to the little boy.

"Perhaps—him," she whispered. "You'd already shown me that a woman—can lose an unborn child. And I thought —I knew—he was going to be beautiful—"

"Hera save us!" Autolykos said.

"And Hestia," Ariston said. He smiled at Autolykos. "Are you going to challenge me to a pankratieon—with iron studded gloves, say?" he said.

"No," Autolykos said quietly. "We've been friends too long to end that friendship over a past thing, however grievous. Even if you were Kleo's lover, as I suspect you were, what does that matter now? I know you haven't been near her since she entered my house. I've had great joy of her, my friend. I love my son, whoever his actual father is, since his existence doesn't constitute either a deception or a cheat. Kleo told me from the first she was with child. And

365

she's given me the loveliest little sea foam and sunlight nymph of a daughter in this world. So you and I are quits —if ever you sinned against me, which I doubt. Even if you have, I forgive you. Have you?"

"No," Ariston said. "I have not seen Kleo since she entered your house until today. And, Autolykos—"

"Yes, Ariston?"

"She's right. Accept my homage. You're nobler far than I could ever be!"

"Chryseis—" Kleothera whispered.

"Yes, Kleo?"

"Can't we be—noble, too—you and I? Can't we follow the—the example of our men—kiss each other—and forgive? I want *your* forgiveness so much, so much! I think I'll have no peace until you grant me it!"

Chryseis stood there like one of the statues that support the porch roof of the Erechtheon, so still that Ariston could not see her breathe. Then she sighed:

"So be it!" and kissed Kleothera.

After that she veiled herself again. And it was that simple act of covering her face that caused all the trouble.

Alkibiades, splendid in hippêus' armor, rode at the head of his men upon a magnificent bay. It was difficult to tell which attracted more attention, the rider or the horse, for in Athens, after so many cruel years of war, fine steeds were rare indeed. Behind him, the troop of hippêis cantered, all of them perfectly equipped. But Ariston didn't notice them at all. He was too busy studying what forty-three years of unending dissipation had done to Alkibiades' face.

So it was that the sudden, totally unmilitary motion that the knight directly behind Alkibiades made, his savage sawing at the bit, breaking the rhythm of the parade, almost escaped Ariston. But he was forced into awareness, for this man, somewhat younger than his commander, and a lochagos from his insignia, hurled himself down from his mount, crying: "Ariston! Ariston!" like a madman. The next instant, Ariston was being crushed against that breastplate, his face covered with kisses, soaked with unrestrained tears.

"Dan—" he got out. "In Zeus's name! Dan!"

They stood there, holding each other, both of them too moved for speech. Then Ariston heard the harsh rasp of breathing whistling through locked teeth, and, turning his head, looked into Chryseis' eyes, above the thick swathing of her veil. They were leaping, flaming with pure joy; but in that same immeasurably brief shattering of an instant, they changed. Horror invaded them. Their warm, pale golden brown went greenish, smoky. And before he could open his mouth to say—

What? What was there to be said upon such delightful occasions as this? "Dan, kiss your sister. She lives with me now, as my mistress, my concubine. Hope you don't mind, my friend. . . ."? What words were there, what words at all that could excuse, justify—?

Chryseis had whirled away like a doe-thing that hears the winding of the hunter's horn, plunged into the crowd.

Danaus' gaze flickered after her.

"Who's that little creature?" he said, dropping his voice into a confidential whisper, so that neither Kleothera nor Autolykos would hear what he said. "Somebody's wife, doubtless, to run away like that. Whom are you adorning with the keroesses now, my friend?"

Ariston let his breath out very slowly. It wasn't possible. A man couldn't live all his life at a woman's side, and that woman his own flesh and blood without— But there was no trace of anger or of mockery in Dan's handsome, open face. He hadn't recognized Chryseis! Of course he hadn't seen her in eight years, but—

That was it. That was the heart of it: those eight years. Or at least the last of them. Since her visit to the house of Sokrates, Chrys had resigned herself to life as it was, as it must be lived; had become almost domesticated, tamed. And one of the results of that resignation, contentment, call it what one willed, was physical. Her nerves had ceased to claw her stomach into a strangled knot; she's developed a respectable appetite for food, ate quite well, for a woman as small as she naturally was. In that year she had gained fully a quarter of a talent in weight. So, to anyone who remembered the emaciated starveling of before, her body now, with its very attractive, almost plump, slenderness

367

would be totally unrecognizable, for the robes that a Hellenic matron wore, though entirely modest, did not conceal the lines of a woman's figure at all.

And Dan hadn't—the memory struck Ariston now with all the force of a blow—seen his sister's face! He hadn't, because after that kiss of pardon—was it? had it been?—she had given Kleo, Chryseis had again veiled her face to the eyes. Of course, if Danaus had really studied her, he would surely have recognized her even so. But he had been too occupied with the friend who, in his heart, was more than friend, to pay much attention to anyone else.

"Later," Ariston said unhappily, knowing the problem was only postponed, not solved. For Danaus was an Athenian hippêus and, unlike his brothers, he had never fallen from that high estate or violated its stern code of honor. This—seduction—of a hippêus' sister, by that code, called for a death. *My* death, Ariston thought wryly.

Then Danaus stepped back, swept his helmet off, and Ariston saw the tiny rearing horse—the emblem of Syrakuse—that had been burned into the flesh of his forehead with a hot iron.

"Zeus!" he said.

Danaus touched the brand mockingly.

"The mark of slavery, Ariston!" he said. "But also of bad luck! When I learned how men were being freed for knowing the choruses, I spouted Euripides by the hour at my new master. He told me to shut up, that he couldn't stand verse. 'Makes no sense, and gives me a headache!' said he."

"I quite agree!" Autolykos said.

"Autolykos!" Danaus said, and embraced the athlete, too. "Is this your lady?"

"Yes," Autolykos said, "and those are my children—"

"What beauties!" Danaus said. "You tempt me to marry, Autolykos—especially if I could find a goddess like this your wife—"

"I am not his wife," Kleothera said suddenly, her voice taut. "I hope you will understand this, noble Danaus. I—I am a metic. My lord cannot marry me. But our—our union is honorable, despite that. We love each other, honor the household gods together, bring up our children in total piety. . . . There are many such—arrangements nowadays. The tolerant and the wise accept them. I hope that you—"

Then it struck Ariston. He understood why she was doing this, why she was deliberately sacrificing her good name by telling Danaus something he had no need to know. She was doing it for his, Ariston's sake. And perhaps even for Chryseis'. . . .

"You don't need to give explanations to Danaus, my girl," Autolykos said. "He's no devotee of Artemis, Eros witness it! Come, Dan, tell us how you managed to escape the Syrakusans?"

"My new master decided—with great justice—that I was good for nothing," Danaus laughed, "and sold me into the galleys. At Kyzikos, the trireme that I'd rowed twice across the world, it seemed to me, was taken by no less than Alkibiades himself. In the general slaughter after the boarding, I cried out: 'I am an Athenian! Save me!' "

"And proved it by your accent," Ariston said.

"Exactly!" Danaus said. "Tell me, how was my skinny monkey-face of a sister the last time you saw her, Ariston?"

"Chrys?" Autolykos bellowed jovially. "Why, she was— Ouch! Kleo! In Athena's name, I'd swear you've crushed my toes!"

"And I'll crush them again if you don't shut up, my beautiful, stupid husband!" Kleothera hissed. "He doesn't know!"

"My lady," Danaus said with grave mockery, "stamping upon a husband's foot is a form of censorship unseemly in a democracy. I fear me you've been reading—or seeing— Aristophanes!"

"You can bet she has, Dan!" Autolykos groaned. "Especially the *Lysistrata!* That form of dissuasion she's been practicing for years!"

"The *Lysistrata?*" Danaus said. "I don't know that one. I've seen *The Acharnians, The Knights, The Clouds, The Wasps,* and *The Peace;* but—"

"Which means you've missed *The Birds, The Thesmophoriazusae,* and *Lysistrata,*" Ariston said. "The *Lysistrata* is the best of all." Then he outlined the quite outrageous plot of the comedy to Danaus.

369

"Then I must take your words as hyperbole, Autolykos," Danaus said, "because surely those two glorious little sprites didn't spring full-armed from your brow as Athena did from Zeus'! By the way, both of you, bring me up to date as to what has happened in Athens since I've been gone. . . ."

"Tomorrow, Dan," Ariston said quickly. "Your troop is getting rather far ahead. And breaking ranks like this on your commander's day of glory is scarcely recommendable military procedure. . . ."

"Right," Danaus said. "I'll call on you tomorrow, after I've paid my brotherly respects to Brimos, Chalcodon, and Chryseis, as well as my filial ones to my father—"

"Dan," Ariston said bluntly, "your father—is dead."

"Oh!" Danaus said, and stood there, his head bowed. Then he looked up.

"I'll sacrifice at his tomb then," he said harshly, "although I never loved him. Chaire, my lady Kleothera! Chaire, kalokagathoi, friends!"

"Oh, Ariston, Ariston!" Kleothera breathed as he rode off. "You must go away! You must! He'll never accept that you, that she—"

"Don't worry about it, Kleo," Ariston said.

Chryseis was not at home. Ariston set out, worriedly, to look for her. He went everywhere he thought she might have gone, even to Sokrates' house. But she wasn't there either. Nor was Sokrates.

"Who knows where that good-for-nothing idler's wandered off to now," Xanthippe said.

Coming away from the house, Ariston realized that a logical defense could very well be made for Xanthippe's shrewishness. Living with a genius and a saint, both of which Sokrates indisputably was, must be, for an ordinary woman, terribly hard. For one thing, Xanthippe had to endure the pretty Myrto's presence daily and that of children not her own. Besides, she saw her husband forever surrounded by gilded youths like young Aristokles, called Platon for his great shoulders, already a winner of the pankratieon in the games; by such notables as the great soldier Xenophon; by such beauties as the blond, black-eyed youth Phaedon, rescued through her husband's agency from a house of ill fame—which must have exercised her jealousy, since in Athens the sex of a real beauty mattered not at all, as also must have the widely known fact that Theodote, at the moment the most celebrated etaira in all Athens, was devoted to the ugly old philosopher, constantly sought his advice, and repaid him for it, men said, very well indeed, though not in coin—and, worst of all from Xanthippe's practical point of view, by such rich men as Ariston, from whom her husband would not accept a bronze obol.

Of course, Kriton had invested the philosopher's savings, all of seventy minae, so well for him that Sokrates and his double family could live one cut above the subsistence level, whether Sokrates worked at his sculptor's trade or no, with which that merry old wise man, who called himself a "pimp of ideas," a "procurer of thought," even a "midwife of wisdom," was well content. But Xanthippe, knowing that Sophists like Georgias were being paid as much as a thousand drachmae to instruct a single wealthy youth, could not help but resent her great poverty and her husband's utter contempt for material things.

If only he'd compromise a little for her sake, Ariston thought; but knew Sokrates wouldn't, that compromise wasn't in him. Then he pushed the matter from his mind and renewed his search for Chryseis.

But he couldn't find her. He came at the edge of night to his own house, worn out with worry and with fear. He knew how much Chryseis loved her brother, knew her morbid tendencies. If he didn't find her soon, Zeus alone knew what she might—

Then he stopped. Danaus stood before his door. The young officer had changed into civilian clothes, wore a simple chiton and a chlamys. There were three tall and handsome young men with him, hippêis, surely, by their bearing. Danaus was crying openly and without shame. And he had two daggers in his hand.

"Take your choice, Ariston!" he wept. "You've given me no escape from killing you now. To debauch my sister the minute my back was turned, to—"

"Dan," Ariston said wearily, "don't be an utter fool."

371

"Ha!" Danaus raged. "I have been, but no more! Here, take a dagger! Which one doesn't matter. My word as a hippêus, they're both the same. I offer you an honorable chance at life, for—"

"No, you don't, Dan," Ariston said, "for I could never kill you—not even in self-defense."

Danaus stood there. Then he flipped one of the daggers end over end so that its point bit earth between Ariston's feet.

"Take it up, Ariston!" he said.

Ariston shook his head.

"No, Danaus," he said. "By the love I bear you, no."

Danaus turned to his three companions.

"I call on you to witness I gave him every chance!" he said. "And I'd have your oaths by Athena to stay out of this, no matter what happens. Do you swear?"

"By Athena!" they said.

"Take up that dagger, Ariston!" Danaus cried.

"No, Dan," Ariston said.

Then Danaus sprang, the dagger glittering in his hand. His miscalculation was very nearly total. Even though Ariston was thirty-six years old now, no man in Athens, with the possible exception of the matchless Autolykos, could have beaten him in a wrestling match. Danaus found his dagger hand caught in a vise of iron, bent behind his back, forced upward, twisted, until his hand had to open, or the bones themselves would snap. He unlocked his fingers from around the hilt, let the dagger drop. Instantly Ariston released him.

"Go home, Danaus," he said quietly. "My advantage over you, unarmed, is greater than yours was over me with a dagger in your hand. I beg you—go."

"Ariston—" Danaus whispered, "tell me that they're lies, the things I've heard. Tell me you don't keep my sister as your concubine in your house. Tell me—"

"I keep her as my wife," Ariston said, "or I would if the polis would grant me the citizenship I've sued for a thousand times, in a thousand ways. The sin is neither hers nor mine, Dan. Hestia witness we'd be married if we could—"

"But you can't," Danaus whispered, "and you knew you couldn't. You knew all the time that—"

He stooped with astonishing swiftness. As rapidly as Ariston moved, he was not quick enough. Danaus' blade laid open his left arm from wrist to elbow. The cut was not deep, but it bled frightfully.

Then Ariston did what he had to: He struck like a gale storm on the Ho Pontos, knowing that he must bring Danaus down before the strength drained out of him. A swift kick to the belly doubled Danaus in half, a knee to the chin straightened him up again; grasping his dagger hand in both his own, Ariston whirled, bent, threw Dan over his broad back with such force, that Chryseis' brother cartwheeled through the air and came to earth five rods away, where he lay dazed. He gazed about him, saw the dagger, stretched out his hand to seize it, only to have Ariston's sandled foot pin his wrist to the earth. Ariston kicked the weapon into the gutter.

"Do you give up, Danaus?" he said.

"No!" Danaus lurched to his feet. Whereupon Ariston swarmed all over him like an Eastern god equipped with a hundred fists. The wet, sick, smashing sound of his knuckles striking was terrible to hear. Danaus, who had not been born a Spartan and whose training, while good, was no more thorough than that of any other highborn Athenian, did not land a single effective counterblow.

Seeing his eyes glaze over, Ariston stood back and let him fall, catching him in his arms before he struck the earth. Then he turned to Danaus' comrades.

"Here, take him home, gentlemen," he said.

When Ariston came into the house, reeling a little from fatigue and the loss of blood, Chryseis was already there. She stared at his slashed arm, and her lips went white.

"Did—Dan—do that?" she said.

"Yes," Ariston whispered. "Ring for the maids—"

"And—and he?" she got out.

"In worse shape than I am, I fear."

Three hours later, one of the young hippêis who had accompanied Danaus knocked on the door. He had come to tell them that Danaus was dead.

Chryseis whirled away from the young knight. Her eyes became twin coals of purest madness, flaming in her face.

373

"Beast!" she screamed at Ariston. "Murderous dog! You killed him! You killed my brother! Oh, Hera save me! I—"

Then she was upon him, teeth bared, nails raking for his eyes.

"My lady!" the hippêus said. "He—"

"Beast! Animal! Assassin! Murderer!"

"Chrys—" Ariston groaned; but she drew blood from his face, almost reached his eyes. So again he did what he had to in a world gone totally mad, in which violence had overtopped all reason—he slapped her stingingly across the face. She reeled back, staring at him. Then she ran toward the door.

"My lady!" the hippêus called. "You've got it wrong! He didn't! He—"

But she was gone, out into the enveloping night.

"Let her go," Ariston sighed. "When she's worn herself out, it will be easier to talk some sense into her. Who killed him? Don't tell me I struck harder than I knew—"

"No, my lord Ariston," the hippêus said. "Your behavior was honorable on every point. Ares witness you could have killed him two dozen times if you'd wanted to. You refused to draw steel, defended yourself barehanded against his blade. We've already given testimony before our polemarch, Alkibiades, on that; and afterward, at his suggestion, before the Archon Basileos, himself. No—poor Dan was stabbed—from behind—by his brother Brimos."

"Zeus save us!" Ariston whispered.

"You see, my lord," the hippêus said, "when Dan got home after his fight with you, he was in a foul temper. And Brimos was drunk. They quarreled, and Brimos sneered: 'Why should you fight over that little porna? She went to him of her own free will—though afterward I sweated her weight in silver out of his filthy rich metic's hide—' "

"And then?" Ariston said.

"Dan dragged the story out of him bit by bit: How your —your lady—had followed you to Parthenope's place, had tried to kill herself before your very eyes. How you brought her home, saved her life, and afterward how he, Brimos, his father, and his brother had demanded her weight in silver minae for her, which you—"

"—offered. They didn't demand. They'd have taken far less—which doesn't matter now. And then?"

"Dan knocked him down, made the mistake of turning to walk away. Brimos came up off the floor like a bear and put his dagger through poor Dan's back. We—Akastos, Kerkyon, and I, Laonomos—in case you want to know—killed Brimos. Then we dragged that wilting flower, Chalcodon, who was also present and witnessed it all, before our polemarch, although he promised to let us perform all sorts of what he obviously considered delightful obscenities upon him if we'd let him go—and forced him to tell the truth. That's all. I am here in my own name and on behalf of my comrades to offer you as hippêis and kalokagathoi whatever satisfaction you may desire for our part in this—"

"Satisfaction? Why? You—you've all behaved honorably. I thank you—especially for saving me from having to kill Brimos. Now I—"

Then suddenly, to his own surprise, Ariston bent his head and wept.

The young knight stared at him.

"You weep for him?" he said; "For a man who tried to kill you?"

"I loved him," Ariston said. "He was one of the few beings in all this world I loved. Therefore the Erinyes marked him, too, for death."

"But why?" the hippêus said.

"Because I loved him. Because he loved me. It's always —thus. Now, I must go—"

"Where?" Laonomos said.

"To make the sacrifices. For his pneuma. That it—may rest. If there are any such things—"

"Any such things as *what*, my lord?"

"Souls. And gods to sacrifice to. And even—rest," Ariston said, and bowing, left him there.

Early in the morning, Chryseis came into his bedroom. Her face was gray with weariness. Her lips were swollen, purplish, bruised. There were nail furrows on her shoulders, a blue crescent of teeth marks on her throat. She stank. Of sweat—male sweat, mingled with her own. Of various other carnal odors. She had her hands behind her.

There was something in them. A knife, likely. Ariston didn't move. He no longer cared enough to even defend himself.

He went on looking at her. He didn't say anything. There was nothing to be said. There were no meaningful words to be spoken between them. Not now. Not ever again.

"Alkibiades?" he said finally.

She nodded dumbly.

He went on looking at her until a shaking came over her body, a frenzied, palsied quiver.

"Above your brother's grave," he said.

And then, suddenly, she was kneeling before him with a terrible whip in her hands. It had many strands, and the tip of each strand was leaded. It was the kind the demokoinoi used when slaves were to be whipped to death for such crimes as the violation of an Athenian citizeness or a boy of the hippàs class.

"Take it," she said. "Beat me—to death. I'm going to die anyhow; but I don't want to die—easily, Ariston. I—I promise you I—I won't scream any more than I can absolutely help. . . . Please, my lord—"

"No," Ariston said.

"Shall I command my brothers' slaves to do it, then? Or shall I profane the mysteries and turn myself over to the demokoinoi, the public torturers? Because dying itself isn't enough now. I—I know from before how simple and easy it is. I—I need this death, Ariston. I need to be turned into a bloody horror. To die screaming. Then maybe I can forgive myself. Perhaps the gods—"

"There are no gods," Ariston said. "They don't exist. Only the Furies do."

"I—I went to his house," she said, as though she had not heard. "I bribed a slave to let me in. I went to his room. Took off my clothes—"

"Stop it!" Ariston said.

"Got into his bed. He wasn't there. It was hours before he came. He was drunk. He said: 'Who are you, little mouse?' I didn't tell him.—I—we—"

"I said stop it!" Ariston said.

376

"Afterward I told him—I was—your wife. He looked at me in horror. Said: 'Why?' So I told him that too. Why, I mean. He said: 'You fool, you've profaned me! Destroyed my luck forever!' Then he told me how, and by whose hand—Danaus died. How nobly you'd behaved before. How you'd risked your life to keep from killing Dan. I could see he wasn't lying. I snatched up his dagger, put the point against my throat. He made no effort to take it away from me. He only said: 'Not here. Don't stain my sheets with any more of your vileness. Else I'll have to order them burned. Outside in the gutter where rabid bitch vixens ought to die.' Ariston, please kill me. Please beat me to death. Please. Please."

There was a thing in him now that had no name. But the shape of it was the shape of darkness. And it was as multi-headed as the Hydra. It coiled inside him and made a sickness. And that sickness was a kind of lust. Not the clean, quick, upstanding lust he had felt for many sensuous women and, even before his imprisonment in the bath-house of Polyxenus, for such beautiful youths as the dead Lysander had been, as fair Phaedon was—but an ice-cold, slow-writhing desire to do what she asked of him: to shred the living flesh from her slender bones, splatter all the walls with her blood. And, facing that particular head of the Hydra, he recognized that here was a perversion, as deep, as nauseous, as any of the various sexual acts performed between man and man; the only perversion, perhaps, that was possible between man and woman, for whatever other rarity a couple might do, Parthenope had taught him, was—at least in part—redeemed by their complementary natures, so that nothing heterosexual can be wholly bad. Except this. This desire to rend, to tear, to hurt, to achieve even orgasm by the giving of pain.

Or by the taking! For that obscure, reversed, perverse hunger was what he saw—perceived, recognized, in her face; in her eyes' hard glitter; in the slackening, moistening, glistening of her parted mouth. That was another of the Hydra's heads. And for him, the greatest, the most terrible; for he realized now, it was this that had ruled his life. This ugly, sick, obscene need to suffer—which now, though he didn't know it then, would not realize it for some time yet, she had killed in him, even exorcised from him, by showing him the nature of it, how hideous it was.

And then another demon-god's head rose up—but different from the others, being new: the wild, tormented desire to be free of her at last, to seek happiness elsewhere, to find some way to—to recover Kleo. To thus injure Autolykos, his friend, who had never done him the slightest wrong; who had always displayed the highest nobility, who—

His eyes cleared suddenly. All the writhing, scaly heads sank down, vanished out of time and mind.

"No, Chrys," he said quietly. "You can seek your judge, your executioner, elsewhere. Even your torturer. I'll not join you in such a vileness. All you can have of me are two things you don't want—"

"Which are?" she whispered.

"My forgiveness and my pity. Now get up from there. Go take a bath. Wash his sweat off you at least. It offends my nostrils—"

"Ariston—" she said.

"Yes, Chrys?"

"You—you're crueler than I thought. Perhaps even than you yourself know. You—condemn me to—to life. With this horror in me. Can you—dare you—do that?"

"Yes, Chrys," he said. "I both dare—and can."

She got up then. Stood there, facing him.

"On your head be it, then, Ariston," she said slowly, calmly, "be all the unspeakable wickednesses I shall probably do from now on. Because of this. Because you wouldn't relieve me of—my guilt. And one thing more—"

He waited, looking at her, his response to her a weariness unto death.

"Know I shall hate you till I die!" she screamed and flung down that whip at his feet. Then she whirled from his presence as she had long since departed from his heart.

He went to bathe and perfume his body as if that would remove the feeling of uncleanness that lingered in him still. Then he dressed in fresh robes and went into his scriptorium. There he sat down, drew up before him on the table papyrus, ink, goose quills, a box of dry sand. He sat there

a long moment, lost in thought, before he began to write
one of the pitifully few fragments of his works that have
survived:

> And thus charged she me with quitting her of guilt,
> who have found no way of tearing from my breast,
>     my own.
> How then to heal in her the sickness of which
> lifelong, I have, myself, been dying?
>             This
> O great Sophokles,
> Immortal Euripides,
> is the true stuff of the tragoidia in man.
> It lies within
> and no god from your creaking mechane
> let down from your painted Olympus upon your pul-
>     leys, ropes
> can have it out without a death.
> For, dragged forth,
> it lies beating bloodily a while before it dies
> in his immortal
> or imaginary
> hand. . . .

# CHAPTER TWENTY-THREE

ARISTON WENT VERY SLOWLY up the steep and rocky paths leading to the Akropolis. He had a basket under his arm. In it were a pair of doves he meant to sacrifice to Athena.

I wonder why I have come here, he thought. I am not a believer. And in many ways the gods, if such there be, have used me ill. Or I have used them ill; for what has my life been but one long offense, one unholy stink in Olympian nostrils? Still—

Still he toiled up the ancient goat tracks toward the creamy marble houses of the gods. He didn't know why, but more often than not he found peace there, or if not peace, a certain lessening of his disquietude. Especially in Athena's temple, called by men the Parthenon, the House of the Maidens, since all the priestesses of the Wise Goddess were sworn to perpetual chastity. And even a temporary lessening of the anguish that tore him was, he thought, well worth the climb.

He saw the matchless beauty of the temple lifting before him, the miraculous symmetry that robbed the massive stones of weight. He began to walk faster, the pain in him, the sorrow, the long, slow, never-ceasing ache, beginning to lift too at the sight of—perfection. For the Parthenon was that. It would never again be equalled by the hands of men, he thought.

Then he slipped inside its cool and shadowy nave to say a prayer, sacrifice the pair of white doves he had brought —and hung there frozen, staring at the tall scaffolding the workers had erected around the immense chryselephantine statue of Athena in order to—

—rob her! Commit upon her this outrageous sacrilege,

this blasphemy! His rage-sickened mind, vibrant with a very real horror, despite his unbelief, shaped the words, just below the threshold of sound.

For the workers were busily engaged in stripping away the golden ornaments from the ivory body of the goddess.

His rage found voice, made booming thunder that threw back echoes from columns, nave, and roof.

"In her sweet name, what do you here?" he cried.

The workers looked down at him uneasily. They didn't like what they had to do any more than he liked seeing them do it. In sober fact, most of them were trembling while they worked. Who knew but what the goddess, angered at being thus despoiled, might not—

"Answer me!" Ariston thundered.

The foreman of the workers came round to him from behind the scaffolding. He had a scroll in his hands. He didn't know who Ariston was; but a person of such bearing, even—Apollo witness it!—of such beauty, was sure to be someone of importance. Slowly he handed the scroll to this kalokagathos, at the very least, perhaps even to this hippêus.

"These are my orders, my lord," he said quietly.

Ariston took the scroll. A glance at it was enough. The man had full authority to do what his workmen were doing. The order was signed by the whole Assembly. The Archon Basileos' name headed the list.

"I see," Ariston said. "But why, good citizen? In Athena's name, tell me that!"

"Bad news, my lord," the foreman said sadly. "Of course I don't know the full particulars, but put it this way, sir: We're her people—and this is her polis, ain't it? Well, right now, it seems we need the gold we've offered her more'n she does. Need it to save ourselves from death. Or from what's a sight worse to my way of thinking— from slavery. We ain't robbing Our Lady. We're kind of borrowing from her, for as long as the trouble lasts. Kind of think that afore she'd witness Spartan brutes cutting our throats and straddling our women and our boys, she'd likely approve; don't you agree, sir?"

"Very likely she would," Ariston whispered. "But tell me, what has happened now, good Workmaster?"

"Well, sir, you probably know that after we'd pardoned Alkibiades for that nasty business of blaspheming the goddess Demeter and Kore, he left here and—"

"—beat across the Pontos Adriatikos to Notium and bottled up the Spartan navarch Lysander with the Lakonian fleet of ninety triremes in the harbor at Ephesus. Of course. And also that being Alkibiades, he got bored with the endless rowing up and down, took his flagship and sailed across to Phokaea to watch his fellow strategos, Thrasyboulos, invest that place, leaving—"

"That damned young fool Antiochos to keep Lysander corked up in that harbor. Which was either bad judgment or—"

"Treachery? I doubt it," Ariston said. "Alkibiades has scant reason to love Sparta, and even less reason to go back there."

"You can say that again!" the foreman guffawed. "What with old King Agis fairly itching to de-ball him—at the very least—for knocking up his old lady, Queen Timaea, getting her with child and—"

"Hardly a place for unseemly gossip, this, eh, good Master?" Ariston said pleasantly. "But get on with it. And don't tell me about Antiochos. I know that sad tale, too."

"You mean about his piling into Lysander almost afore Alkibiades was out of sight?" the foreman said.

"Which was roughly equivalent to a puppy dog's taking on a tiger. Yes. And spare me all those street-corner strategoi's theories that he did it at Alkibiades' own orders. He didn't. He was a young man with a young man's hunger after glory, that was all. He violated his commander's orders, not obeyed them. Attacked Lysander—the greatest admiral the Lakedaemonians have ever produced—so great at sea fighting that I wonder if he really is a Spartan."

"Athena's own truth!" the foreman growled. "A fair terror on blue water, ain't he?"

"The best. Which he abundantly proved that day. By murdering Antiochos. No—massacring him. Crippling the fleet. And you Athenians—"

The foreman stared at him. There was a tiny something in this lordly gentleman's accent that'd make a body think—

382

"You mean *us* Athenians, don't you, sir?" he said.

"All right. Us Athenians. I am an Athenian though I wasn't born here. But I refuse to share the common guilt in this. It was criminal folly to listen to the city mob screaming treachery, howling that Alkibiades had taken Persian gold—"

"Well, he couldn't have taken Lakedaemonian gold, now could he, sir? Athena witness they haven't any! Main reason why they—"

"—bartered away all that Hellenic heroism gained at Marathon, Salamis, Thermopylae," Ariston said slowly, his voice remaining even, but a note getting into it somehow that caused the foreman's skin to prickle, "surrendered the Ionic Hellenes to the Persian's iron yoke. For—gold. For bloody, filthy gold to go with this—murder of brothers. This—suicide of Hellas. This putting out of civilization's light—"

The foreman stared at him.

"You're way past me now, kalokagathos!" he said. "Don't understand that kind of talk. Makes a fellow shiver hearing it. Specially the way *you* say it—"

"Sorry!" Ariston said crisply. "But I don't believe Alkibiades was bribed. I know him too well. Money, as such, just doesn't interest him. They'd have had to give him fifty certified virgins—"

"And as many unbroke boys!" the foreman bellowed.

"No boys. He's not that way, truly. But that's unimportant. What's important was that to depose him again, send him off to sulk in his castle at Cherronessos on the Hellespont, was criminal folly, as I said. Because he's the only strategos we have who can equal Lysander at sea—and if the Lakonians hadn't matched our folly by replacing Lysander with this new man, Kallikratidas, we'd probably have a Spartan garrison on the Akropolis right now—"

"If we don't look alive and stir our stumps," the foreman said gloomily, "we're going to. That's what the order is about, sir. You mean you haven't heard?"

Now it was Ariston's turn to stare.

"Heard what?" he said.

"The bad news. Appears this new navarch is better'n Lysander. Picket boat come in last night. This Kallikratidas has swept the seas like a new broom. Took Delphinon in Chios, and Methymna in Lesbos, two weeks ago. But that ain't all. Eight days ago he caught Konon off Mytilene and sunk thirty of our triremes, sir. And right now, he's got the rest of 'em bottled up inside the harbor of Mytilene. So we're fresh out of a navy. And out of luck, unless—"

"Unless?" Ariston said tonelessly.

"—the new measures work. I mean stripping the temples to get the wherewithal to build a new fleet. Promising citizenship to the metics and freedom to the slaves—"

Ariston hung there. "Immortal gods!" he whispered, so low the foreman didn't even hear him.

"—if they'll pitch in and fight. Situation's desperate, sir. Looks like—"

But by then Ariston was gone. He stood there, outside the Parthenon in the afternoon sun for a long time. Then he opened the basket and released the doves. They leaped up, white-winged, arrowing skyward above—

His Athens.

His now. His! He looked down at the city lying there beneath his gaze, the houses white, gray, beige, except for the red tiles of their roofs, with the black-green spears of the cypresses standing up between them, the shimmering verdant silver of the olives, the ragged spray of the pines, and here and there a frosting of almond trees, blossoming now, white with spring, making a loveliness keen enough to cut his breath.

His city! His polis! The one place in all Hellas where his mind and heart were truly at home. This seaward splendid sprawl of pastel cubes and crimson angles, crowned by its matchless marble skyward soar of temples—his! If the foreman hadn't lied, wasn't mistaken. Which was scarcely probable. The man had impressed him as a better sort of thêtes: sober, industrious, intelligent, though unlettered— the kind who wouldn't misuse truth. Besides, he needed only to go to the Agora to confirm the news. It would surely be posted there. And all the world would be discussing the matter. He could hear the oligarchs snarling now:

"Citizenship to metics! Freedom for slaves! Immortal gods! What's Athens coming to?"

Her senses, perhaps, Ariston thought wryly. In any

event, she's mine. Only—only I have to take Chryseis along with this glorious polis; take her, barren, bitter, and shrewish, as my lawful, wedded wife—

He bowed his head, looked up again.

"I promised Danaus," he murmured. "And he is dead. So that promise is sacred, if anything ever is. But what is a man's word? What's a promise? What is, finally, even this thing called honor? A gust of wind. Nothing. As man himself is. Spring snow, gone before noon. Words written on water. Inscribed upon naked air. And yet—"

He turned his steps toward his house.

But when he told her, Chryseis only shrugged.

"Why should you? What difference would it make now?" she said.

"This much. Sokrates insists the souls, the shades, the pneuma of men are—immortal. I don't know whether he's right or not. But if he is, I should like for Dan to know—I kept my word. That I gained my citizenship and married you, as I promised."

She turned to him then, and her great eyes were luminous.

"Ariston—" she whispered.

"Yes, Chrys?"

"I think you're the noblest of all the men upon the face of earth," she said.

That same day Ariston obtained a trireme's hull from the government and outfitted it at his own expense. He had criers go about Piraeus promising six obols a day, twice the official pay, to all who'd sail with him. He found, and put in charge as his nuarch, or second in command, the same old pirate Aletes who had sold Kleothera to Orchomenus. He offered the third officer's birth to Orchomenus, who refused it.

"After the way you've lamed me, how could I fight?" Orchomenus said. "Besides, when all this is over, when there's a Spartan harmost and a garrison on the Akropolis, it won't be a healthy thing to be both a Lakedaemonian and a turncoat, boy! Tell me, why are you doing this, Ariston?"

"*My* reasons," Ariston said.

"Ha! So you can marry her, finally. That ugly, shrewish little witch you should flee like the plague! A question of honor, isn't it, O most noble and honorable Ariston? Take a lesson from my book, friend. At least I abuse my women; I don't let them abuse me. Or do you so love Sokrates that you must imitate him in all things—even to procuring yourself an imitation Xanthippe? I prefer the original. At least she has given him sons!"

"Still so bitter toward me, Orchomenus?" Ariston said.

"No. Who can maintain bitterness toward a fool? If you'd stolen my Kleo from me for your own use, and out of so normal a thing as lust, I could have hated you. But since you relieved me of her for windy philosophic abstractions and ended up by passing her on to another man, I merely—despise you. And pity you. All your philosophy's taught you is new ways of being a fool!"

"All right," Ariston said. "Have it your own way. Chaire, Orchomenus."

"Rejoice, Ariston! But for what?" Orchomenus said.

Ariston came out of the factory and started toward Piraeus, reflecting upon the irony of his existence. All over Athens, wealthy men were being reduced to penury by this war, but his own fortune was triple what Timosthenes had left him. Because, he thought mockingly, I have found my true trade. Haven't I been a merchant of death all my life? Why then shouldn't I gain my wealth out of the instruments of murder? I tell myself I am defending human liberty, man's dignity as man; that when I provide the polis of Athens with the sinews of war, I'm only maintaining these high and holy things.

Which is true—in part. Should my native polis win, she will install oligarchies everywhere, as she has always done. But when I defend Athens, am I not defending the massacres of the Skione and Melos? Am I not shoring up commercial imperialism, the tricks and chicanery of trade, base brigandage?

The answer is, I suppose, that wars are fought between men, not between angels on the one side and demons on the other. So be it! Perhaps if there be gods and they be kind, I shall be freed—of all things, including this slavery that men call life. . . .

At the port, he embarked on his new trireme. With the wealth at his command, it had taken him less than a week to outfit her, since he had paid to have the work continued by torchlight throughout the nights as well as by day. One innovation he had insisted upon: The beak that was used for ramming was of iron instead of the usual bronze. It had been made in his own foundries, and brought to an edge so sharp that a man could shave himself thereupon, as one of his seamen demonstrated to a doubting rival from another ship by rubbing his jaw against it and removing half his beard.

But the reason for Ariston's haste was nothing so simple as an eagerness for war. He meant to gain his citizenship; but to do that, he had to distinguish himself in battle. And, he fully realized, he knew absolutely nothing about naval warfare. Nineteen years ago he'd watched from the shore the siege of Sphacteria; but he had never engaged in a sea battle himself. And he had approximately one month to learn.

During that month, his trireme put back into Piraeus only when her supplies were utterly exhausted. She towed abandoned and rotting bulks out to sea and practiced upon them the art of ramming. The artillerymen who served her catapults used up a ton of stone missiles daily in target practice. Her helmsmen learned to turn her on an obol; the archers, peltasts, and javelin throwers in her rigging perforated straw dummies the size of men which had been flung into the sea, while her slingers, even in these exercises, used the expensive molded leaden bullets instead of stones.

Her oarsmen not only learned to hit the beat the instant the keleustes set it, pounding on a block with their wooden mallets, but also at a command to lift their sweeps high and drag them into the hull as far as space would allow, so that the trireme could plow alongside a Spartan or a Syrakusan man-o'-war, shearing off her enemy's oars on that side like matchsticks while leaving her own intact to maneuver swiftly and complete the destruction of her crippled foe.

His crew grumbled, of course, and cursed him behind his back; but their real feeling toward their trirarch was revealed when the crew of another ship ventured to make mock of him, calling him the Attic equivalent of "Old Spit and Polish." The ensuing fist fight wrecked three whole taverns, and a dozen men had to be carried into the iatreia with broken jaws, arms, legs. It was a tribute to their stern training that Ariston's crew emerged almost unscathed from the fray, and to his understanding of men, that they had come so to love him.

It was not merely a matter of the doubled pay. Among the other intangibles was the fact that the rations were better and more abundant than on any other ship in the fleet. The honeyed wine they were allowed to swill each night after practice was the famous Daprias—the so-called "rotten" wine that all seafarers prized. No oarsman was chained to his bench. They were all slaves, but each bore, in a water-tight oiled leather bag about his neck, a promissory note to his owners, signed by Ariston, guaranteeing the price of his manumission if for any reason the polis failed to fulfill its promise to free him. The wives and children of every man aboard, whether citizen or metic or slave, were already upon a pension paid by Ariston's banker, a pension higher in the majority of cases than their husbands and fathers had ever been able to earn for them—said pension to be continued in case of the death in action by the breadwinner until the children's majority and during the widow's life.

No wonder, then, that the trirarch Ariston commanded the smartest vessel in the whole Athenian fleet. And he himself had learned so much in that month that Aletes grudgingly admitted:

"You don't need me. You could sail her without me."

"No, Aletes," Ariston said. "As sure as Zeus reigns on Olympus, something will come up that you never thought to teach me, the kind of thing that occurs once in twenty years—"

"You'd master it, if it did," Aletes said.

Which, though he knew it not, was a kind of blasphemy. What man can master the Fates, the Furies, or the gods?

Ariston's trireme, the *Phryne*, went scudding hull down through a long trough of gray-green water, already flecked here and there with the white bared teeth of the storm. The weather had turned dirty; the wind had an ominous note in it now.

"We'd best turn back, Trirarch," Aletes said. "Zeus Thunderer witness you've done enough to earn your citizenship ten times over."

Ariston didn't even look at his nuarch.

"Over there," he said, "to the windward—how many of our ships lie wrecked, Aletes?"

"More than twenty," the nuarch said.

"And if we don't get to them in time?"

Aletes shrugged.

"They'll drown," he said. "Now, with your august permission, Trirarch, I'd like to ask you a question: How many are the crews of twenty wrecked triremes?"

Ariston looked at him now, already catching the drift of his second's thought.

"Some—two thousand men, Aletes," he said quietly.

"And how many could we take aboard *if* we get there?"

"Don't know. Say—one hundred . . ."

"One hundred out of two thousand. We've won, my captain. We've sent more than seventy Lakedaemonian triremes down to Poseidon. You've the honor of accounting for six of that number, before the very eyes of the strategoi Thrasyllos and Perikles, not to mention that the trirarch Theramenes also saw our part in the action and his word in Athens carries considerable weight—"

"If he'll give it," Ariston said drily. "I wouldn't trust the Buskin as far as I could throw him. Anyhow, Aletes, if we only save *one* man, that one is still a human being with dreams and hopes and a life before him. Tell the keleustes to increase the beat—"

"But if instead of saving that one, we drown ourselves?" Aletes growled. "Look over there to the leeward, Trirarch!"

Ariston turned his gaze toward the Arginusae Islands, forever after that day to be immortalized as the site of Athens' greatest naval victory. He could see a squadron of Syrakusan triremes bearing down upon them with a quartering wind behind them. Of course they bore no sails—triremes always left their masts and sails ashore when going into battle to avoid the fire weapons and entangle-

389

ment—but even so, a wind astern helped the rowers' speed.

Then he smiled and pointed in his turn.

A much bigger Athenian squadron led by the trireme of Theramenes was slanting across on a long diagonal to intercept the Syrakusans. He'd have time and to spare to save some of the men who were clinging to broken planking in the water, time at least to give hope to those he couldn't save, so that they'd hold on until the rescue squadron arrived; for surely that was what the troop ships, commanded by the taxiarchs, or troop commanders, were clawing up from the South to do.

Then he saw it. There were three Megarian vessels between him and the wrecked Athenian triremes. Their peltasts, archers, and slingers were amusing themselves by slaughtering the helpless Athenians in the water.

"Triarch!" Aletes bellowed. "In Poseidon's name!"

"Full beat," Ariston said. "Have the enomotarchs ready to relay the signal—"

"In Zeus's name, Trirarch! What signal? Tell the helmsman to put her hard over or—"

"No. See how close those two Megarians lie together? Full beat ahead, Aletes!"

"Oh, my poor widowed wife!" Aletes groaned. "Oh, my fatherless sons!"

"Shut up, and give the orders!" Ariston said.

The oars bit water and dug in, flashing dripping foam. The two Megarians grew before them, getting bigger with every stroke the oarsmen made. So intent were these allies of Sparta about their murderous sport that they hadn't even left a lookout on the aft poop deck.

"Now," Ariston said.

"Diekploy!" Aletes roared. Below decks the enomotarchs repeated the order in a single voice. And Ariston's perfectly trained oarsmen, with one smooth motion, lifted their sweeps skyward and held them there. Deprived of her propulsive power though she was, the sleek-hulled trireme scarcely slowed. Carried by her own momentum, she plowed between the two Megarians, shearing off all three banks of oars on the port side of one and the starboard side of the other as she went. The sound of the breaking timber was thunder-loud; but the Megarian oarsmen's screams were louder still.

Ariston shut his ears to them. He couldn't afford pity now. The Megarian oarsmen, slaves all, chained to their benches, couldn't escape. And the great beams of the oars, broken, sheared off, crushed by the *Phryne's* beak and hull plowing between the two Megarian triremes, whipped back with murderous force, knocking those poor devils' brains out, jerking the arms of some of the men completely out of their sockets, splintering and disemboweling others. Below the Megarians' decks, the carnage would be fearful; but he had no time to think about that, nor would anything be served by compassion now. Clear of the two Megarians, his own oarsmen took up the beat.

"Put the helm over," he said to Aletes, "hard to port."

"Good!" Aletes grinned, looking at the third Megarian, which was racing away as if black Hades and the Furies were pursuing her. "We'll periploy her, eh?"

"Exactly," Ariston said.

His crew performed that maneuver, too, with textbook precision. The *Phryne* came halfway round, then leaped forward like a hard-flung spear. Her iron beak bit into the Megarian's timbers like a knife through cheese, three-quarters aft, opening her up to the rising seas.

"Back water!" Ariston cried.

The oarsmen reversed their stroke. The beak tore free of the Megarian, leaving a fearful gap. Through it, Ariston could see her oarsmen fighting to free themselves of their chains. On her deck, her officers and fighting men were stripping off their armor, diving into the choppy waters. Then the sea poured into that rent. The Megarian plunged straight for the abode of Poseidon, taking with her all hands.

"Those other two," Aletes said, "shall we take them in tow, Trirarch? Fine prizes! We can ransom the officers and—"

Ariston looked up into the lowering skies, listened to the note of the wind. The *Phryne* was pitching violently now.

"Sink them," he said. "Weather's too dirty for towing."

The two Megarians, with no oar left intact on one side of each, were absolutely helpless. But they knew better than to expect mercy. So they put their catapults into action, concentrated their archers, slingers, peltasts on the side from which the *Phryne* was bearing down upon them. But the sea was rising every second now. The pitch and roll of their disabled vessels spoiled their aim. Ariston rammed them fatally one after the other, backed the *Phryne* off and watched them start to sink.

It was then he heard his lookout's despairing cry.

Turning, he saw a thing that brought the sick rage leaping to his throat. Theramenes had turned his squadron to leeward, avoiding the Syrakusans' attack, leaving a gap in the Athenian line between his squadron and Thrasyboulos', through which in their wild dash to escape the Syrakusans poured, so that now there was only the *Phryne* to impede their gaining the open sea.

Alone and outnumbered twenty to one, Ariston fought his ship like Ares himself. But valor counted for nothing in such a situation; the only thing that could have saved the *Phryne* would have been for Theramenes to lead his squadron to the rescue. And that "Kothornos" Theramenes had no intention of doing. That militarily and strategically he was correct, that it wasn't prudent to risk his squadron to save one ship in a rising storm with the battle already won, didn't help the way Ariston felt. Strategy be damned, Theramenes should have thrown his squad into the breach, fought the Syrakusans, made some effort to save Athenian lives.

Four Syrakusans rammed the *Phryne* at one and the same time, sending her over on her side. She didn't sink at once. Ariston saw that all his men got off, attaching themselves with ropes to the oar shafts and what other planking they could hack free. Then, stripping off his armor, he dived into the gray sea and swam over to where Aletes and twelve of his strongest men clung to a raft-like slab their own iron beak had torn free of one of the sunken Megarians' hulls. They clung to that, waiting for Theramenes to lead his squadron to pick them up. Then, lifting their heads, they saw it: the whole Athenian fleet, scudding to leeward toward the islands, leaving them to drown.

Throughout the night, Ariston did what he could to kee

up the spirits of his surviving crewmen. Four times he released his hold on the timbers to swim to the rescue of men who'd lost their grip, been swept away. He got his men ashore alive. But as he gazed around him, he saw that his problem was going to be to keep them that way.

The barren, deserted spot where they were now, Ariston guessed, was somewhere on the shores of Phrygia, one of the domains of King Darius the Great of Persia. Formerly all this coast had been Ionian and all the cities Hellenic. But since Sparta had bartered away the freedom of the Asiatic Hellenes for Persian aid and gold, Ariston didn't dare lead his men, naked and shivering, parched and starving as they were, into Antandros or Roeten or Sestos or Abydos, because of the near certainty that they'd fall into the hands of the soldiers of the satrapy, especially since both Tissaphernes and Pharnabazus, the former satraps, had been replaced by Prince Cyrus, Darius' son, who was known to be madly in love with the Spartan navarch Lysander.

But Ariston did what he could. He procured arms and armor for his men from the bodies of dead Athenians and Lakedaemonians who had been washed ashore, marched them inland in good order, and surprised a hamlet. Then, at sword's point, he obtained food and drink. A week later, his band of fourteen were mounted on stolen horses; by fall of that year so great was the fame of these brigands that a whole detachment of Persian cavalry was assigned to the sole duty of capturing them.

Which served for nothing. All through that winter their numbers grew, as daring Ionic Hellenes sneaked out of the cities to join this gallant handful who dared to rob the mule trains and otherwise make war on the great king. By spring of the following year, Ariston commanded two hundred mounted men.

But Aletes and Ariston knew that it couldn't go on forever, for King Darius was dying and the young Prince Cyrus had been called to his bedside.

Knowing as he did the propensity of his own race for taking bribes, the elasticity of their honor, Cyrus left Lysander the Spartan as his satrap in command of all the Ionian coast. The plan that Ariston and Aletes had contrived, of buying or stealing at least a penteconter and sailing with all they could crowd aboard across the Aegean to Attika, now had to be put into effect in all haste and without the precautions they ordinarily would have taken. It was one thing to outride and outfight Persian horses, but to face Spartan cavalry was another. In fact, it would be suicide, and they knew it.

"Look you, Captain," Aletes said. "I have a far better plan, if you'll allow . . ."

"Of course, Aletes," Ariston said. "Most of your plans have been good up until now. Speak of it."

Aletes knelt down and began to draw on the ground with the point of his sword. Like most professional sea captains, his knowledge of geography was very good indeed. A map of that part of Phrygia grew under Ariston's gaze.

"Here's where we are," Aletes said. "And here's the coast. You know that coast by now, Captain. There's not a stade of it that's not filled with cities, villages, hamlets—and the individual houses of fisherfolk in between. Our chances of getting through to the sea without an outcry being raised are frankly nil. And to steal a vessel after that? Even a triaconter?"

"I see," Ariston said grimly. "Then what do you propose?"

"We ride further inland, east and north, hit the shore of the Propontis somewhere between Kyzikos and Kios. That's wild country—houses are few. There're almost no settlers—"

"And consequently almost no boats," Ariston said drily.

"Hades take me! I hadn't thought of that!" Aletes said.

"The plan's still good," Ariston said slowly. "Only we change it a bit. We strike for the shore of the Propontis farther west—between Lampsakos and Kyzikos. There the risks are greater, but so are the chances of capturing a sizable vessel. A triaconter won't do. I mean to try for at least a bireme, or, at worst, a penteconter."

"Maybe we could even take a grain ship there," Aletes said. "And even if we fail, we can always ride for Byzantium. They're still an Athenian ally, aren't they?"

"Who knows by now?" Ariston said.

The plan worked beautifully—except for one thing: As they pushed their stolen penteconter—for they had had to settle for a mere fifty-oarer after all—into the eastern end of the Hellespont, they met the whole Spartan fleet of more than one hundred triremes boring into it from the western, the Aegean, end.

There was nothing to do but to run for it, so they headed diagonally across the strait toward the Cherronessos; but the Spartan triremes were accompanied by picket boats, light triaconters and penteconters as fast as they were. They made the shore, almost in the shadow of a great castle, with the Spartans hard on their heels. On land, vastly outnumbered, they did what they could in a running fight. Which wasn't much. In fact, they were down to twenty men when a troop of cavalry led by a big man on a magnificent bay came out of the gates of the castle and forced the Spartan peltasts and marines to race for their boats. That done, the cavalry captain galloped back to where they were and boomed out at them in a great voice that no longer had any trace of a lisp:

"Athenians—or allies of my polis, for such you must be! I offer you refuge in my fortress! Come!"

Ariston stood there. Sometimes the gods overdo their ribaldry, he thought. Then he sighed.

"I give you thanks, Alkibiades," he said.

That night at supper, Alkibiades suddenly stretched out his mighty arm to Ariston.

"Don't hate me, Ariston," he said quietly.

"Why should I hate you who've just saved my life?" Ariston said.

"Because I know women. She told you. She came to me burning with the desire to revenge herself upon you for a thing you hadn't even done. Had I known she was your wife, I'd have kicked her from my bed—"

"As you kicked Queen Timaea?" Ariston said.

Alkibiades smiled.

"You're not King Agis. I have never hated you. Besides—"

"Chryseis is not Timaea, who men say is beautiful. All the same, Alkibiades, you owe me some recompense. I hereby demand of you exactly what the matter's worth."

Alkibiades studied him.

"Which is?" he asked.

"One obol," Ariston said.

Alkibiades went on staring at him. Then he threw back his head and roared.

They, the two of them, stood on the quay before the city of Sestos and watched the Athenian fleet pouring into the Hellespont.

"Beautiful!" Alkibiades breathed.

Ariston turned and looked at him. There was so much—longing—that was it!—so much hopeless longing in the exstrategos autokrator's voice. For all the wild zigzag of his life, Alkibiades loved Athens. If only he'd been able to discipline himself enough to serve his polis the way her citizens would have allowed him to; or, conversely, if only the Athenian Demos had been wise enough to permit him the outrageous irregularities which were but another facet of the genius he indisputably possessed, while making use of that genius itself, all of recent history might have been different. Splendidly different. Too much to ask. And now —too late. The saddest words, Ariston thought, in any language spoken of men.

He turned back toward the fleet. It was a glorious sight: The picket boats, little triaconters and pentaconters, fanned out before the majestic triremes, and they, with a fair wind filling their sails taut as wineskins, the shields at their gunwales blinding, their pennants striping the air with color, were coming in now, all one hundred and eighty of them, to trap that sea wolf, Lysander.

"Lysander has taken Lampsakos, on the other side," Alkibiades said worriedly. "A town with a harbor as good as this one. No, better. I only hope they know, they realize—"

"We'll tell them, when they put in here," Ariston said.

But the Athenian fleet didn't put into Sestos. Majestically, slowly, the great triremes crawled on by the one spot on that side of the Hellespont where they might have been reasonably safe, where even the most elementary grasp of logistics demanded that they anchor: in a harbor before a town with fresh water and food to supply their needs,

396

iatroi to attend their wounded, sound conscripts to replace their dead.

"Do you know where they're going, Ariston?" Alkibiades roared. "Do you?"

"No," Ariston said.

"Think! What's the absolutely worst place they can put into? What site on this coast is totally untenable before an attack of punting skiffs manned by effeminates, women, and boys? I ask you—what?"

"Aegospotami," Ariston said. "Oh, no! Don't tell me that! In Hera's name, don't tell me they're going to anchor off 'Goat Rivers'! I don't believe—"

"I don't ask you to believe," Alkibiades said. "Mount you now—and come and see!"

He was right. Terribly, sickeningly right. The two of them rode into the midst of the Athenians busily engaged in setting up a camp upon that naked beach designed by nature as a slaughterhouse for fools. Ariston sat there on his horse and looked at them. He almost wept—this doomed, deluded army was his one slim chance of getting back to Athens; he had no choice but to join them.

But Alkibiades roared like a wounded lion:

"Fools! Dolts! Have you no eyes! What have you here? I'll tell you! Sand to soak up your pitiful asses' blood. Rocks to break your legs when you try to flee! But fresh water? Ha! Food? Again, ha! Help of surgeons? Nursing women? Conscripts? . . . Athena, look down upon your sons! Why, O Divine One of All Wisdom, did you not grant half a brain to any Athenian born?"

Tydeus and Menandos, the two strategoi in charge of the camp, came up to Alkibiades, followed by an enomo-archy, of thirty men. And every man of the thirty had his javelin ready to throw, or his sword already drawn.

"Get out," Tydeus told him coldly. "Traitor to Athens! Blasphemer! Taker of Persian gold! Leave this camp or be buried beneath it! The choice, O Alkibiades, is yours!"

Alkibiades surged forward, but Ariston caught his great arm in an iron grip.

"No, my friend," he said quietly. "They are not worth our death."

"Aye, but Athens is!" Alkibiades raged.

"Yes," Ariston said. "She is—when your death might, or could, or would, serve her. But now? Think you that dying at the hands of these fools would change anything?"

Alkibiades sat there on his horse. Slowly, his great muscles relaxed, then slackened into what was very close to—defeat.

"You're right, Ariston," he said. "Come . . ."

That night Ariston reluctantly told his great, brilliant, erratic friend, that he would be leaving him to return to the encampment of Aegospotami.

"You're right, of course, Alkibiades," he said. "They're fools. But how else will I ever get back to Athens? I have interests there—even a wife, of sorts, faithless though she is. And I can go. I'm not under banishment. So—"

"You risk your life to go with them," Alkibiades told him harshly; "but the choice is yours. Can't say I blame you. At least try to join Konon's squadron. He alone has some brains in his head. . . ."

After the lookout had called him, the strategos Konon stared down at the armored men standing breast deep in the water. They had waded out that far in order to hail his flagship.

"You were at Arginusae, you say?" he growled.

"Aye, by these scars!" Ariston roared back at him.

"Then how came you here?" the strategos said.

"Marching and fighting!" Aletes bellowed. "After Poseidon had spared the broken planking on which your cowardly Athenian dogs had left us to die!"

Konon stared sadly down at them. His eyes went dark with trouble. He knew that story only too well. And these men, if they spoke truly, had been in part responsible for saving his own life.

He turned to his nuarch.

"Throw cords down to them," he said.

In the next week, Ariston was constantly at the strategos' side. Since his involuntary exile had lasted almost two years, he was hungry for news of Athens, of those he loved, of Kleothera, Chryseis, of his friends. The first day he questioned Konon as often as he could, seeking information to quiet his heart.

And when he had it, much of it was sad: Euripides and Sophokles were both dead—Euripides, in exile in Macedonia; Sophokles, at Athens—out of grief, men said, at the loss of his great friend. On the other hand, Aristophanes was alive and in good health, as was Sokrates. Ariston could not, of course, ask directly after Kleothera; the conventions surrounding a woman's life in Athens were such that unless she were of the fallen sisterhood, the strategos wouldn't even know her. And since Kleo's relations with Autolykos were the same as his with Chryseis: a form of semi-legal marriage that centuries later would be called morganatic, the chances that Konon had ever heard of her were very slight indeed. So he contented himself with asking after Autolykos and, having received the reply that the athlete was alive and well, took comfort from the near certainty that while Autolykos lived, no real harm could befall Kleo—if his own separation from her were not a harm, a kind of slow and lingering death.

He was aware now that the strategos was staring at him with questioning eyes.

"What is it, great Strategos?" he said.

"You puzzle me, Trirarch," Konon said. "I know everyone you know, all of them outstanding citizens of the knightly class, and yet I can't place—you. Why is that?"

"Because," Ariston said, "I am not a citizen, general, but only a humble metic who happened to have enough money to outfit a trireme at my own expense when the polis, in her great need, finally allowed me to. I did so in order to gain Athenian citizenship, which is a thing greatly to be prized. When I get back, I mean to sue for it. After all, the polis promised that reward to metics who would enlist in her services. Besides, I have two excellent witnesses to my feats of arms on behalf of Athens: Perikles, son of Perikles, and Thrasyllos—both of them strategoi, my general, so their word should carry some weight . . ."

Konon looked down at the planking of the deck, then looked up again.

"No, you don't, my boy," he said quietly. "They're dead, both of them. Do you have any other witnesses?"

"Well—surely the trirarch Theramenes and possibly Thrasyboulos. Theramenes wasn't fifty rods off my port bow when the Syrakusans rammed my vessel, sending us plunging down to Poseidon. Surely he—"

But Konon shook his head. The gesture was slow, and freighted with sadness.

"Athena witness you have no luck!" he said.

Ariston stared at him.

"Don't tell me that Theramenes and Thrasyboulos are—"

"Dead, too? No. They're both very much alive, the swine!"

Ariston stood there looking at the strategos. He waited. He had to wait a considerable time, for Konon seemed to be struggling with his own thoughts.

"You were—a victim of that action," the general said at last, "so I'll put it to you fairly: How do you feel about the fact that you and your men were abandoned, left to drown? Tell me that."

"Well," Ariston said slowly, "as a man, I resented it. I do still. But as a soldier, I understand it. For greater considerations override lesser ones, don't they? The objective at Arginusae was to break Sparta's growing sea power, destroy her fleet, make ourselves once again supreme in the one area where truly we can be hurt, even destroyed, which is on blue water. Men always die in battle. To have attempted to save us would have been to jeopardize the victory. And that we couldn't afford. I say that despite all the brave men, comrades, friends that decision cost me. . . ."

"Spoken like a sailor!" Konon said, and brought his huge hand down on Ariston's shoulder, hard. "Your analysis is both correct, and what's more, professional. But as a matter of fact, you weren't abandoned because of strategical considerations. My good friends, the eight strategoi who commanded at Arginusae, were true Athenians as well as naval men, Trirarch. They weren't inclined to let the crews of twenty-five triremes, more than two thousand men, drown—"

"So many?" Ariston said.

"So many. And they died because of that pair of swine, Theramenes and Thrasyboulos. Though Thrasyboulos' sin was less—he merely kept his mouth shut and let six brave men die in his stead, while Theramenes actually accused them—"

Ariston stared at the strategos.

"I'm afraid I don't understand you, General," he said.

"I know you don't. How could you? The point is, Trirarch, that Theramenes and Thrasyboulos—who was only a trirarch himself at Arginusae, because those fools at Athens had broken him from strategos' rank because of his association with Alkibiades—were ordered to take the ten troopships commanded by taxiarchs instead of true seamen, and thirty-seven triremes more and go to the rescue of the drowning men."

"They didn't do it," Ariston said grimly. "That I can vouch for!"

"Again I know it. But, back in Athens, when the city mobs began howling for blood because of such a shocking loss of life, Theramenes accused the eight generals of the cowardice of which he himself was actually guilty. And Thrasyboulos at least kept his mouth shut and let six of them die—for Protomachos and Aristogenes didn't come home at all—in the most outrageously unjust and illegal trial in Athenian history! You know there should have been eight separate trials, don't you? Or at least six, since only six of the strategoi were present—giving each man the right to defend himself individually and in detail upon the merits of his particular case?"

"Yes," Ariston said. "That is one of the safeguards of Athenian law."

"Yet, it was set aside," Konon said harshly. "Thrasyllos, Perikles, Aristokrates, Diomedon, Erasmides, and Lysias were all tried at one and the same time, condemned by what was no more than judicial murder. In fact, so absolutely illegal was the procedure that Sokrates, who happened to be president of his prytany on that day, flatly refused to even put the motion for the death sentence to the vote. You should have seen him, Trirarch, standing there like a rock and smiling down at the mob that raved and shrieked and demanded his blood along with that of the six strategoi—"

401

"I'll wager he never put it to the vote," Ariston said. "He'd die first, if I know my mentor!"

"He came close to dying for it," Konon said. "What saved him was that too many men have sat at his feet and imbibed the wine of philosophy from him. That, and the fact that his prytany's term in office automatically expired in another two days. So they waited. The president of the next prytany was less brave. And six of Athens' bravest and best died—"

"Including the two who were close enough to me to witness my modest feats of valor in behalf of the polis," Ariston whispered, "leaving—"

"—only those two cowardly swine who had every reason *not* to testify in your behalf, to whom your very existence is now a threat," Konon said. "So now you have only your own unsupported word and that of your surviving crewmen upon which to base your suit for citizenship, Trirarch. I wouldn't wager much upon your chances. I'll do what *I* can, of course; but—"

"Thank you, my general," Ariston said.

He was aware then that Konon was studying him again very carefully.

"Strange I can't place you," the Strategos said. "You were a metic, rich enough to outfit a trireme, and yet—"

"I was the noble Timosthenes' adopted son," Ariston said.

"Of course! No wonder you moved in such exalted circles!" Konon's face changed suddenly, became grave. A worried look tugged at his brows. "Look, Ariston, my boy," he said, "I despise men who delight in bearing evil tidings and Hera witness you've troubles enough already! So I will not bear them. But you are Ariston the shield manufacturer, aren't you? I have you placed at last, haven't I?"

"Yes," Ariston said. "Why, my general?"

"No reason. Only—if you do get home, one word of advice. . . ."

"Which is?"

"Look to your wife!" Konon said.

In the days that followed of fruitless maneuvers by both

the Greek forces and the Lakedaemonian fleet, Konon grew very fond of Ariston. He greatly regretted that the gods had not granted him such a son.

"General," Ariston said during a lull in the fighting on the fifth day, "will you pardon me if I say a thing to you?"

Konan looked at the younger man.

"Of course," he said. "Speak, Lochagos!"

"That beach is untenable. All Lysander's feints have been designed toward just one end—"

"To wear us out, make us go ashore to rest, and then— to slaughter us. You think I don't know that, son?"

"So?" Ariston said.

"We keep to the sea. No matter how the men grumble. Even if I have to put down a mutiny, we keep to the sea!"

So it was that at dawn while the whole Athenian fleet lay beached upon the sands, Konon's eight triremes and the state ship, *Paralos,* moved a stadia or two off shore. And, as he came out on deck, Ariston heard the lookout's despairing cry:

"The Spartans! By Hera! The Spartans! All of them! The whole obscene obscenity of the Lakedaemonian fleet! To starboard! There! Bearing down on us!"

Ariston turned then and stared into his strategos' eyes.

"Well, Lochagos, what shall we do?" Konon said with weary mockery. "Die like heroes—or fly like men?"

Ariston weighed the alternatives. Nine triremes wouldn't make the slightest difference. Lysander would detach a squad of twenty of his own to take care of them, and still would have more than one hundred beaked prows to smash into the helpless Athenian fleet. Dead, Konon and his men would be useless to Athens. Make a run for it, and some of them at least might get through to warn her.

"I'd take evasive action, great Strategos," he said.

Now Konon's eyes were boring into his.

"Why?" the strategos said.

"To stay alive long enough to warn the polis. To defend her to the last from the long walls—"

"Good!" Konon said and turned to his second. The nuarch's face was gray with terror.

"Give the keleustes the racing beat," Konon said. "Tell

the helmsman to bear hard to port. Run up the signals for the others to follow us."

"To port!" the nuarch all but screamed. "But that's—"

"Away from Athens. I know it. We sail for Lampsakos, Nuarch! Go give the orders!"

Ariston stood there, staring at his commander. Then he smiled. At that moment, his admiration for Konon was boundless.

"Lysander's—sails, great Strategos?" he said.

"Exactly. The sails that are always left ashore when a sea fight's brewing—as ours are left, upon that miserable beach where we have no chance to retrieve them—so enemy catapults can't hurl fire missiles into them, so they don't get fatally entangled in the rigging of friend or foe while in the midst of battle. So now, to borrow Lysander's sails. Which will serve us well—to lend wings to our keels. To drive us so fast that no oarsmen alive can catch up with us—"

"Athena has blessed you with her wisdom, Strategos!" Ariston said.

So it was done. Konon's squadron scudded to leeward past the Spartan fleet, drove arrowlike upon helpless Lampsakos. Lysander hadn't even left a garrison there. They captured the sails, hoisted the nine they needed, burned the rest. Their canvases bellied, ballooned; the wine dark water foamed white beneath their prows. They stood out to sea, keeping half the Hellespont between them and the Lakedaemonian fleet.

But even so, they could see the black smoke pluming Zeus's heavens, shot through with sullen tongues of flame from where the Athenian fleet burned on the beach at Aegospotami, smell even, when the wind shifted, the stench of charring man flesh making an offense in the very nostrils of the gods.

That.

And one thing more: Before they could escape that acrid smoke, that obscene smell, they heard a hail, heard Athenian voices screaming:

"Help! Save us in Zeus's name!"

Ariston saw it then: a little picket boat, a triaconter, hull down and half awash. He saw the glancing rent a Lakedae-monian prow had made amidships, saw the triaconter's crew were already doomed unless—

He turned and stared at Konon.

"Stop the beat! Backwater!" cried that great commander.

They drew them aboard, those blue, trembling, bleeding wretches who had been men. Konon himself questioned them.

"We—surrendered. The strategoi saw it was hopeless. So they—"

"Threw themselves upon Spartan mercy?" Konon said.

"Aye, great Strategos! Only—"

"Only what?" Konon whispered, already knowing, as Ariston also knew. "What, in Hera's name!"

"That's a word Lakonians don't even know how to spell, sir," the spokesman said, "if they even have it in Doric, which I doubt—"

"No!" Konon said. "Don't tell me—"

"They're slaughtering the prisoners? At Lysander's orders, sir. Three thousand men. Burning the bodies inside the ships. That's how we got away. Takes time to kill three thousand men. Takes Tartarus' own time even—"

"—at the hands of such professional butchers as the Spartans are," Konon said. Then he bent his head and wept.

Ariston stood there and watched him stonily. The rage he himself felt, the nauseous, bottomless shame at what his fellow countrymen were capable of, lay far too deep for tears.

Three nights later, he stood on the foredeck and gazed at the stars. The conviction that those stars were in the wrong places grew upon him. Even his slight acquaintance with navigation enabled him to recognize that. Besides, they should be able to sight the lights of Athens by now. He looked ahead toward where the city should be. No lights. Only the blue-black sea, quiet, whispering. He looked at that sky, those stars. And knew. Very completely and perfectly he knew.

He sought great Konon out.

"Look you, Ariston," the strategos said, "have you already forgotten what I told you of the fates of the six strategoi after Arginusae? And one of them Perikles' son, at that?"

"No, I have not forgotten," Ariston said.

"Then do I have to point out to you what the Athenian mob will do to a defeated strategos who puts in at Piraeus bearing such tidings?"

"No," Ariston said.

"I want to live," Konon said. "Never acquired a taste for hemlock, my boy—"

So, then?" Ariston said.

"We're headed for Cyprus. Pleasant island, Cyprus. What's more, her king, Euagoras, is a friend of mine. There I can live out my days in peace."

"But—Athens! She must be warned!" Ariston said.

"I'm sending the *Paralos* to warn the polis, my boy. Fat lot of good that will do them with no fleet, no money to build another one, no—"

"Great Konon—" Ariston said.

"Aye, Ariston?"

"Send me along aboard her! I have to get home! I have to! It's been two years—"

Konon looked at him, pityingly.

"Don't be a fool, Ariston," he said.

" 'Tis a condition I was born to," Ariston said. "Please, my lord!"

The strategos sat there staring at him.

"Oh, all right!" he said at last. "I'd hoped to keep you at my side, but there's no gainsaying what I see in your eyes. But one thing more, my son—"

"Which is?" Ariston said.

"Send a herald ahead to your house to announce your prompt arrival before you land," Konon said.

Ariston looked at him.

"Why should I do that?" he said.

"Why? In Athena's name! To spare yourself grief. Useless and unnecessary grief, Ariston. You understand *that* much, don't you?"

"Yes," Ariston whispered.

"Then get out of here and leave me in peace!" great Konon said.

# CHAPTER TWENTY-FOUR

ARISTON AND AUTOLYKOS walked back from the market place, with their two menservants carrying their purchases as the custom was in Athens. For there, indeed in most of Hellas, the duty of shopping for the household fell upon the husband, not the wife. Since the Hellenes held that for a decent woman to leave the shelter of her home on any but festive occasions, or in some emergency such as the sickness of a relative or close friend, was unseemly, Athenian gentlemen found themselves burdened with many small tasks habitually done by women in most other parts of the world.

On this day, truth to tell, they could have carried their purchases themselves and in one hand at that, had custom permitted them to do so. For though now the siege was over, Athens totally defeated, the long walls pulled down, the Akropolis occupied by a Spartan garrison, the oligarchic exiles—notably Kritias—recalled and ruling the polis without mercy, and enough food was coming into the city again to keep her populace from starving, no Athenian was getting fat. Athens was a conquered city, and the victors had no intention of letting her forget that cruel fact.

"I wept for him," Ariston was saying, "for though I spent a goodly part of my life disliking, even hating, Alkibiades, in the end he saved my life, was both noble and just to me. He was a libertine, a mocker, a scoffer at pious things. His vices were legion, but so were his virtues. I tell you, Autolykos, he was one of Athens' greatest men."

"I don't know," Autolykos said. "Something less than great, I'd say. Because, as Sokrates says, you can't divorce greatness from morality, Ariston. A man who is not good cannot be great."

Ariston smiled.

"In some ways, my old teacher is naïve," he said. "Greatness has nothing to do with goodness—or very little. In fact, in a real sense, I'd say a strain of true goodness in a man would bar him from greatness. Alkibiades, now, died not for his treachery to Athens, but because he'd repented of that treachery. When we exiled him and he went to Sparta, became our enemy, his life was safe. But in the end, when we removed him again from the command through no fault of his but because of the insolent folly of a subordinate in defiance of his orders, he had every motive for once more turning against us. Yet he didn't. He risked his life to advise our commanders in what grave danger the fleet lay. He was right. I was there and saw their folly. Had they listened to Alkibiades, we would not now be slaves of Sparta—"

"And of The Thirty," Autolykos said grimly.

"And of The Thirty. So it was of his virtues, not of his vices, that Alkibiades died. Lysander ordered him murdered —reluctantly, I'm told. Kritias—now there's evil for you, and look how secure he is!—told Lysander that there was always danger of revolt as long as the democrats had hopes of Alkibiades' return. So Lysander procured his death."

"But Lysander was also pushed by King Agis, who sits there on his throne and stares at Leontychides and is reminded that Alkibiades tumbled his wife—"

Ariston stood there. Wild and bitter laughter tore through him silently. And I, that he tumbled mine, he thought. Though I had of him what the matter was worth. One obol. But you wouldn't understand that, would you, Autolykos, in your beautiful world of blacks and whites and no shadings in between?

"That, too," he said slowly. "In any event the assassination was a monumental piece of cowardice and dishonor. Alkibiades had to leave his castle when Lysander's fleet took ours. He couldn't hope to stand against the crews of one hundred and forty triremes. He got away. And he was living in peace in a little village in Phrygia with his mistress Timandra—"

"Always a woman!" Autolykos said.

"He was a man," Ariston said quietly. "Would you have preferred his being a homosexual like our Kritias? Remember in the days before the Assembly banished our noble leader of The Thirty for writing that outrageously atheistic play, how even Sokrates, usually the most tolerant of men as far as the follies and the lusts of humanity are concerned, was forced to rebuke Kritias to his face for rubbing up against Euthydemos like a swine against a stone? If Kritias loved women, he'd have less evil in his heart, I think."

"I remember how you threw him head over heels when he tried to caress you," Autolykos said. "Strange he hasn't had you arrested by now. Athena witness he never forgets an injury!"

"He's waiting for me to make another mistake. Or perhaps I'm of too little importance these days for him to bother. Doesn't matter anyhow. As I was saying, the manner of Alkibiades' death was thus: Lysander sent a message to the satrap Pharnabazus, who, knowing Lysander's influence with Prince Cyrus, was happy to obey. Pharnabazus turned the matter over to his brother Magacus and his uncle, Susamithre. They came in the night with a band of archers, javelin throwers, and slingers, and set Alkibiades' house afire. When he came out naked with a sword in his hand, they shot him down from afar, because none of them had the valor to engage him hand to hand. And afterward Timandra buried his body with loving grief, with piety, with respect. I'm glad he had that little, at least, Autolykos. The love of a good woman compensates for many things."

"True," Autolykos said. He looked at Ariston, and his simple, candid face was troubled. "True enough—when he really has that love, and when the woman in question is really good. Ariston, I—"

Ariston stopped, put his hand on the athlete's shoulder.

"You want to tell me what happened during my absence, don't you, my friend?" he said. "Don't. I beg of you not to. I had the good fortune to return at an hour when he who was probably profiting from my supposed death was not in my bed or even in my house. And afterward, I think—for, mind you, I *know* nothing—Chryseis got word to him.

Upon which he, being a cowardly swine who surely did not love her, or at least was less impressed with her person than with her wealth, disappeared. Conjectures, Autolykos. Do not think ill of me, my friend, if I prefer them to certainties. You have great happiness; I, a poor and shoddy counterfeit thereof. But better that than nothing. I was dead. My widow's grief was short-lived. All right. So be it. I resurrected myself. And now it's the past that's dead. Let's leave it buried, shall we?"

"All right," Autolykos said, "if that's what you want, Ariston."

"That's what I want," Ariston said.

And it was then that they heard the flute players. The music was a dirge, slow, solemn, sad. Turning, they both saw the funeral procession coming toward them, with the slaves carrying two biers, not one, on which lay two swathed and covered figures with myrtle and olive wreaths upon their breasts.

"Ariston!" Autolykos said. "Those slaves! They—they're Nikeratos'! I've seen them at his house too many times not to—"

Then he was off, dashing toward that solemn procession like a madman. Ariston followed him more slowly. Nikeratos, son of Nikias, the general who had now paid for his own timid blundering at Syrakuse ten years ago with his life, had never been a close friend of his. Ariston had found his leanings far too oligarchic for his taste, had, in fact, envied him the celebrated devotion of his wife, his great domestic happiness which contrasted so cruelly with the eternal alternations of love and war he'd had to endure with Chryseis. But Autolykos, that simple, noble soul, was capable of loving men whose views were diametrically opposed to his own, as Nikeratos' had been.

When Ariston came up to the athlete, Autolykos was already crying, tearing his hair and clothing, throwing dirt upon his head and beating his breast in sign of grief.

"They killed him, Ariston!" he raged. "They forced him to take the hemlock at home, before his poor wife's eyes! But—she—what a lesson she read them! As his limbs grew heavy—you know how the poison works? You walk and walk until your legs grow heavy, cold—and then you lie down to die—she whirled and snatched a dagger from one of The Eleven or their guards and plunged it through her heart before their evil faces! The gods granted him a wife unequalled by any—"

"Save your own," Ariston said.

Autolykos looked at him sadly.

"No, Ariston," he whispered. "For you—Kleo might die. For you, whom she loves still, she would surely. For me, no. I know the screaming Tartarus you endure with Chrys, though you're much too gentlemanly to speak of it. But I wonder if it's worse than the quiet hell I support each day, pretending I don't see through Kleo's pretense! Since the day of Alkibiades' return, of Danaus' fatal homecoming, it's been like that. Would god I really were the fool I seem!"

"Autolykos—" Ariston said, "I'm sorry. There are no words for this, I know; but I *am* sorry. Truly."

"I know. Life is an untidy mess, isn't it?" Autolykos said.

And now, though their way did not lead them in that direction and they could have avoided it, they went up the hill to the Akropolis to have a look at the city from that high, cool, lovely vantage point. In their shock over the tragic deaths of Nikeratos and his wife, they'd quite forgotten the Spartan garrison quartered there.

Despite the fact that it was late in the month of Beodromion, it was still hot, and Kallibos, the Spartan harmost, as the garrison commander of an occupied city was called, was in a foul temper. In sober truth, the heat had less to do with his temper than the Athenians did. A Spartan out of Sparta was not a fish out of water, he was something else again. It was as if a Circe touched him, as she'd touched Odysseus' men, for the moment he entered the gates of another polis, he became a filthy swine.

Before the war, like all Hellenes, the Athenians had had an awed admiration for Spartan bravery, dignity, discipline, and sobriety—an admiration that had lasted until they had had to live under the Spartan yoke. For, while it was entirely true that the Spartan, at home, guided by the multitudinous rules that controlled every aspect of his daily conduct, was an impressive, even an admirable human being, away from home, under different circum-

412

stances, the damage those rules had done him by robbing him of adaptiveness, improvisation, even, actually, the power to think, showed. Confronted with Spartan boorishness, the sickening filthiness of his speech, his mindless brutality, the Athenians' first reaction had been stunned shock. Then, seeing what an utter oaf, a hopeless bumpkin, a mindless clod the average Spartan was, the Athenians proceeded to bait him with exquisite wit and subtlety, so that the Spartans became aware that they were being baited but were never quite sure how. By that late fall day, the hatred between Athenian and Spartan was far worse than it had been at any time during the war, perhaps because neither side had any longer the active relief of killing.

And, as such things have the utterly unspeakable habit of doing, everything went wrong at once. Kallibos was alone, having found even the company of his own junior officers unendurable; his temper was at its notorious worst. When he turned from staring out over this maddeningly beautiful city that ground the shoddy poverty of his own into his very soul, this city filled with maddeningly beautiful people, all of whom, men and women alike, rejected his clumsy advances, his gaze fell upon the two Athenians, both of them tall and exceedingly handsome men, not yet in their fortieth year. The disdain, the contempt that showed on their faces—or that his grinding sense of inferiority to any Athenians whatsoever caused him to read there—set the harmost wild.

"Athenian dogs!" he howled. "What do ye here?"

Autolykos bristled. But then he controlled himself.

"We're looking over our kennels," he said icily. "Have you such in Sparta, Harmost? I think not. I've been told that a pig might well mistake your dwellings for his sty."

Thereupon Kallibos lifted his staff and struck Autolykos full in the face with it. The next instant the Spartan was cartwheeling through the air, to land in a clanging clatter of iron a little way down the hill.

He scrambled to his feet, drew his sword, and started up toward them. But, suddenly he stopped short, raised his sword to his helmet, and made the Spartan salute with it.

Ariston turned. A tall man, wearing the insignia of a

413

Spartan navarch on his armor, his lips twitching in an effort to control his laughter, stood just behind them.

"Did you throw my harmost down that slope?" he said to Autolykos.

"Yes, great Lysander," Autolykos said.

"And if I hadn't been here, and he'd gotten to you with that sword, what would you have done?" Lysander said.

"Taken it away from him and made him eat it," Autolykos said.

Lysander studied him. No men in the whole Spartan army had bodies that even approached the muscular development of these two. In all his life, he had not encountered such absolute physical perfection. He was aware at once that Autolykos was not boasting, that he very probably could have done exactly what he had said.

"I see," the navarch said gravely. "Now, tell me how all this started."

Ariston, who was much more ready of speech than Autolykos was, told Lysander the story.

"Your harmost," he said smoothly, "seems to feel that Athenian citizens have no right upon this Akropolis which our fathers built. He struck my friend here in the face with his staff because he—and I, great Navarch!—resented being called dogs. From his treatment of us, the harmost actually seems to think we are canines. Which puzzles me. In Sparta, do dogs build such temples as these?"

"Not even men do, I'm afraid," Lysander said quietly. "They are—glorious. And they are one of the many reasons I would not let our allies persuade me to destroy this city. Chaire, gentlemen! You will not be troubled again."

"But, but—" Kallibos spluttered, "he struck me! He threw me down! He—"

"Oh, shut up, Kallibos! You don't know how to manage freemen," Lysander said.

"Where are you going now?" Autolykos said to Ariston as they came down the hill of the Akropolis together.

"Home," Ariston said.

"And then?"

"Nowhere else now. To the Bouleuterion—day after tomorrow," Ariston said.

414

Autolykos stopped and frowned at him angrily.

"To sue again for your citizenship," he whispered, "which already they've twice refused you. So that you can marry *her*. Marry that filthy, unappetizing little porna—"

"Autolykos!" Ariston said.

"Sorry! 'Tis the love I bear you that speaks, Ariston. Tell me, to whom are you going to present your petition now, my poor friend?"

"To Kritias. Or to Theramenes. Or to both. They're my last hope," Ariston said.

"Then you have no hope," Autolykos said. "Kritias, noble son of the noblest possible line. Great-grandson of Dropides—"

"Pederast. Hater of women. Scoffer at pious things. Atheist. Multiple murderer. Leader of The Thirty. Do you know what they call them now, Autolykos?"

"Aye. The Thirty Tyrannoi. What makes you think Kritias would hear your suit? Or failing him, that 'Buskin' Theramenes would either?"

"I don't think they will—although Kritias was—fond of me, once. But I have to try it."

"Hera save us! Have you sunk so low? You'd even lie with that—that—"

"Practicer of fellatio, sodomy, and other assorted abominations? No. Besides, you're forgetting one thing—or maybe two, Autolykos—"

"Which are?" Autolykos said.

"I'm almost forty, an age which doesn't appeal to pederasts. And—I once tumbled Kritias into the dust, just as you did the harmost, today—"

"Aye, so you did! I remember that. And that murderous swine—tell me, how many people has he ordered to their deaths now, Ariston?"

"More than three hundred," Ariston said.

"And he never forgets an injury. So, knowing all that, why do you persist?"

"Because I have to. I pledged my sacred word—to Danaus," Ariston said.

"I see. And I'm sorry. You can't imagine how sorry I am," Autolykos said.

That day, as Ariston reached the Bouleuterion, he met Sokrates coming out of it. The old philosopher put a finger to his lips in a wonderfully comic burlesque of a conspiratorial air.

"Tell me, Ariston," he whispered, "are you more than thirty years old?"

"Nine years more," Ariston said. "Why?"

"I am forbidden to talk to anyone under thirty, lest I corrupt him. Kritias has so forbidden me. And Charikles. Tell me: Did I corrupt you when you were young?"

"Dreadfully," Ariston said. "You taught me to think. There's nothing worse!"

"I fear me you are right," Sokrates sighed. "For among those I also taught to think were Alkibiades, and Kritias himself. Now look at the results! Chaire, Ariston; I go. Phaedon awaits me with a group of friends. I say—why don't you join us?"

"Today I can't. Another time, perhaps. But take a message to your beautiful Phaedon, will you, Master?"

"Which is?" Sokrates said.

"That I am no more responsible for what I remind him of, than he is, for what he reminds me of. He'll understand. And that I'd be his friend. Nothing more. Chaire, Sokrates!"

As he went up the stairs into the Bouleuterion, he wondered why Sokrates had never seen precisely where his teachings could be said to have erred. Which was in the area of politics. For the philosopher had always scoffed at the basic idea of democracy: that it was, and must be, a government of amateurs. How many times had he heard Sokrates say: "You wouldn't hire a flute player to carve a statue, would you? So why then do you call in, by the mere method of counting noses, men who know nothing about governing other men?"

Because, O Sokrates, Ariston mused now, the men who do know something about it are too dangerous! The very type of mind that is inclined to govern, to manipulate men, is nearly always coupled with an ambition more ravenous than a wolf's hunger. For one Solon, one Perikles, you find a thousand of the type of Kritias. And who has harmed the polis more—Alkibiades or Kleon? For despite you, master, despite that comic mocker Aristophanes, we were better governed by the tanner, the lampmaker, and their kind than by your specialists. The analogy of the flute player turned sculptor does not hold, because it is based upon a logical premise. And what, in God's name, has logic got to do with men or their affairs? We're ruled by passion, superstition, madness, fear, even lust, my Master—not to mention greed. You've been blinded by your own nobility and your lofty thought. You forget that you deal with— swine!

"Oh, yes," Theramenes said to Kritias. "He most certainly did perform the feats he claims. I witnessed them. And so did Thrasyboulos of Steiria, though, thanks to *you*, he's not here to testify in Ariston's behalf. The trireme that Ariston outfitted—"

"And commanded," Ariston snapped.

"Oh come now, Ariston! You had that old pirate Aletes as your second, didn't you?" Theramenes said.

Ariston looked at the ex-trirarch, Theramenes. He had depended upon his help, because all the world knew that Theramenes had come to oppose Kritias' unbridled—and murderous—use of power. There had been the slim chance that Theramenes would support his bid for citizenship in order to gain a supporter he conceivably was going to need when the falling out among thieves everybody expected finally occurred. But now, Ariston saw, he had miscalculated. The "Buskin" had shifted feet again.

"True," he said quietly; "But I did outfit the trireme, and though you seem disinclined to believe it, I commanded her in action. Aletes was outraged at the chances I took. It was because he knew better that he counseled caution."

Kritias smiled.

"You're very skilled in dialectics—for a metic," he said. "One would almost think you frequented Sokrates in your youth."

"And frequent him still, which is the only point on which we differ, Kritias!"

"A most dangerously stubborn old man, Ariston," Kritias said. "You'd better advise him to mend his ways, for if not—"

"If not, what?" Ariston said.

"I might find myself obliged to place him under some sort of restraint," Kritias said smoothly.

"You'd be wiser," Ariston said, knowing it was hopeless now, "to place yourself under at least the degree of restraint he tried to teach you, long ago. Did you really believe you could force him to take part in your judicial murder of Leon of Salamis, Kritias? Didn't you know when you ordered him to arrest that blameless man, he'd refuse—at any cost? Did you think you could so easily destroy his influence among the wise, the just? *You* at least should have known better, Theramenes! For you've already faced the fact that Sokrates is prepared at any hour to die for his honor when he defied you in the trial of the six generals, including your cousin Perikles, whose blood is on your hands. But I see I waste my time here—and yours. Chaire, kalokagathoi! I go—"

"Wait, Ariston!" Kritias said. "Don't be so hasty. You were promised your citizenship by a government that no longer exists, that has been overthrown. We have no power to honor the promises made by that—rabble. But, if you were to display some evidences of loyalty toward us . . ."

He left the phrase hanging languidly upon the air.

"Display it, how?" Ariston said.

"For instance, you might pick up a guard of four men outside—tell them you have my authorization—and go arrest the athlete Autolykos for insulting the Spartan harmost two days ago. It seems he tumbled the Lakedaemonian commander into the dust—a ruffianly act, what? Though I faintly recall that *you* were not above such practices, once. . . . But that was long ago, when you were young and beautiful and foolish, shall we say? I'm told you witnessed that unfortunate affair. Did you?"

"I did," Ariston said, "and so did the Spartan supreme commander, Lysander—"

"Ah, but Lysander is no longer with us! Didn't you know that? He has been recalled to Sparta, for consultations, say. So you'd be wise, if you wish to become a citizen of Athens—"

418

Very slowly, knowing he was sealing his own death, Ariston shook his head.

"I've changed my mind, Kritias," he said. "For the Athens whose citizenship I desired no longer exists. I equate citizenship with freedom, not with slavery—"

Kritias glanced at Theramenes. Then he turned back to Ariston.

"You have a most dangerous gift of eloquence, especially in a metic, Ariston," he said. "Tell me: Are you also prepared to die—for your honor?"

Ariston looked him up and down from head to heel.

"Yes, Kritias," he said, "but not as a sacrificial lamb—"

"Then how?" Kritias murmured, mockingly, "are you prepared to die, beautiful Ariston? For you are that, still. . . ."

"As a lion," Ariston said, "who is always prepared to make his dying costly. Chaire, august Statesmen, honorable men! I go!"

Because he knew what they'd do, he did not go immediately to Autolykos' house to warn him. First he went to his own, and armed himself. He could not send another with a message to his friend, because any man he spoke to today would be likewise noted and marked for death.

Despite the persistent heat, he put on a breastplate and donned a himation to hide it. So far, the metics had been safe from The Thirty's political murders, but now, with Theramenes wavering, who could tell how far they'd go?

He strapped on a sword and a dagger, picked up a small bundle of javelins and a shield, making no attempt to cover them, for beyond the defense of the breastplate, he wanted the cowardly dogs whom Kritias hired to know he went armed. As he did so, he heard the long, long exhalation of breath, and turning, saw Chryseis standing there.

"So—you already knew?" she whispered.

Ariston stared at her.

"I already knew what, Chryseis?" he said.

"That—that they're after you, too. This morning, while you were away, a note came from Lysias the speech-writer, advising you to flee. He left the city last night. It seems they—they're arresting metics, too, now. Not for political

419

reasons, but to despoil them of their wealth. Polemarchos, Lysias' brother—you know him, he runs that small shield manufactory not far from yours—is dead, Ariston. I sent servants all over Athens this morning to find you, and every one of them came back with the most appalling news—"

"So?" Ariston said.

"Nikeratos was executed day before yesterday. His wife —committed suicide when she learned of it. Autolykos—"

"Good God!" Ariston said.

"—was killed not an hour ago, when he resisted those who came to take him. But you needn't worry about dear Kleo—she'll only imitate Nikeratos' wife—upon learning that The Thirty have killed *you,* my dearly beloved husband! So, if you don't want that on your conscience, you'd better fly, Ariston. Lysias was quite sure that—"

"And you, Chryseis," Ariston said, "if they do take me, force me to drain that gentle cup, how long will you wait *this* time, before finding another to warm my bed?"

She looked at him, and her eyes were very bleak.

"Not an hour," she said flatly. "So now you know. Fly, Ariston. Whatever there is, or was, between us—I—I don't want you dead. . . ."

"Chrys," Ariston said, "go pack a few things. I'm taking you with me."

She shook her head.

"Don't be a fool, Ariston," she said with a dry and bitter little laugh. "I am quite safe. First, because your worst enemy, Kritias, doesn't even like women. I'd have to be a boy to please him. And, secondly, ugly as I am, who'd bother to even ravish me? I'd only be a burden to you in your flight. Less of one, of course, than Kleothera, your son, and Autolykos' daughter, will be. But even one person fewer will be a help, don't you think?"

Ariston stood there. He was tempted to deny that she was right, that she had so easily and accurately read his mind. But now lying was not only dishonorable, it was futile.

"So be it, Chryseis!" he said.

She stood there, and quite suddenly, her eyes were flooded with tears.

"Since it is very likely we shall not meet again this side

of Tartarus," she whispered, "would my lord condescend to grant his erring wife—a kiss? In parting, Ariston? In token of the love I bore you, and—God help me!—bear you still! The Fates were against us, that was all. And I—"

Ariston took her in his arms and kissed her. A long time. A very long time. With pity, with tenderness, with the lingering ghost of a love long dead. With sorrow and pain.

Sobbing, she tore free of him at last and fled.

He could see the guards before Autolykos' door. There were only two of them. Kritias had never dreamed that any man in Athens would be bold enough, mad enough, to attempt what he was going to do.

He threw back his cloak. Laid the bundle of javelins down at his feet. Took one of them. It didn't feel right. The shaft was a trifle crooked, so slightly that another wouldn't have noticed it. Besides, it was too heavy. He could only throw once, he knew. The first cast must be perfect.

He selected another, then another. The third one was right. It balanced almost weightlessly in his hand. He stood there waiting and sweating a little although it was no longer hot. The two guards, hippêis both, of the most extreme oligarchic leanings, stood there chatting. Then one of them turned, and Ariston threw.

The javelin hurtled across the intervening space, blurring sight; its blue steel point flashed like lightning on the naked air. Ariston heard the sodden thud as it bit flesh—exactly where he'd aimed it—in the base of the hippêus' throat, just above the breastplate. The man stood rooted to earth in an astonishment that under other circumstances would have been comical to see, with the wandlike shaft protruding from his throat. Then very slowly he went down.

The other one screamed, his voice wailing, woman-shrill. From the sound of it, the two of them had been lovers, Ariston guessed. That one high scream was all he had time for, because Ariston was already upon him.

The hoplite fought with desperate fury, but he was too unnerved to be effective. Ariston banged his shield against the young knight's, shoved him backward half a rod,

421

slashed his bare thigh above the greaves to the bone. The pain and shock of that caused the hoplite to drop his guard the barest instant.

It was enough. With one sidewise stroke, Ariston all but beheaded him.

Thereafter, he bent and traced a tiny figure of a lion on the foreheads of his fallen foes with a twig dipped in their own blood. It was, he recognized, a melodramatic, even a puerile, gesture; but he wanted Kritias to know who had struck this defiant blow.

Then he entered the house, to find Kleothera and the children praying beside Autolykos' bier. He stood there, all his breath caught in his throat at that sight. When he had first met Kleo, on the eve of Danaus' sailing for Syrakuse with the ill-fated expedition, she had been no more than fourteen years of age. Now, eleven years later she was but twenty-five, in the very early bloom of her womanhood still and absolutely glorious.

No. More than glorious—divine. For the years, her sufferings, the quietude she had known with Autolykos, the peace and contentment, if no more, had refined her fair Nordic beauty into something ethereal, almost unearthly. He wondered whether the awe, the worship, he felt for her now, would not forever destroy desire in him, as far as she was concerned.

But there was no time. He couldn't even allow her, his son—how beautiful the boy was!—and her daughter the solace of their prayers. He hated to interrupt this scene of perfect piety; but he had to.

"Kleo—" he breathed.

She turned, still on her knees. He put out his hand to her, drew her to her feet. Her face was very white. The tears on her cheeks were jewels in the lamplight.

"Ariston!" she whispered. "You must go! You were with him when—Surely they're after you, by now!"

"They are," he said. "But they'll find taking me quite a task. I've come for you and the children, Kleo. Just as you are; there's no time to—"

But she shook her head.

"I—I can't leave him unburied, Ariston," she said. "I—and the son you gave him, must grant peace to his shade!

Fly, my love. We'll be all right. No man will harm us, for not even The Thirty dare outrage the widows of the men they've murdered. So go, I beg of you, Ariston! Save my life the only way you can—by saving yours. . . ."

She took a quick step forward, went up on tiptoe, fastened her mouth to his.

"Mother!" the boy said, his voice shaking with outrage.

"I have every right to kiss your father, Aristides," Kleo said. "For, as you know, poor, dear Autolykos was not; I never lied to you about that. Now you kiss him, too—who has been separated from us by fate, not by his will—"

The boy Aristides got up sullenly and came to Ariston's arms. Ariston crushed him to his breast and wept.

"Now you, Phryne," Kleothera whispered.

"Phryne! In God's name, Kleo! Why—"

"Orchomenus told me the story of your life, Ariston. What better name could I have given her? I—I deprived her of the glory of being your child, so I wanted to link her to you in what way I could—"

Wordlessly, being beyond speech now, Ariston took the lovely little sprite in his arms.

"I'm sorry you're not my father, Lord Ariston," Phryne said. "I—I loved mine. But now that he's gone— that they—they've killed— Oh, immortal gods! How can such things be? I—I—"

"You are mine," Ariston said. "Forever, Phryne. Kleo, by all the gods, he'll understand! Come with me, bring the children—"

"No, Ariston. I owe him too great a debt for enduring, knowing, the lack of the love I couldn't give him, because you had—and have—it all. Besides, there's Chrys, whom I've injured far too much. Go! Go while I can bear it still —unburdened by us who would only slow your flight enough to cause your death. I beg you, go!"

And, because she was right, because there was no hope otherwise, because only by staying alive could he return to—

What? By all the ribald, merciless monsters on high Olympus—what?

He turned then, on his heel, and fled.

But he had no sooner reached the street than he heard the shouting:

"To the Bouleuterion! To the Senate House! Kritias is accusing Theramenes! He asks 'The Buskin's' death!"

Ariston stood there. A light came into his eyes. Kindled. Made a blaze.

I have no love for "The Buskin," he thought. Let Kritias make him pledge the polis' good health in hemlock! But then? If, at that priceless moment someone were to poignard Kritias himself? For what would The Thirty be without him? Nothing, or less! When he lies in his blood, the Demos will rise and rend them limb from limb, as surely as Zeus rules on Olympus! So now, to add my diobolia's worth to confusion!

He lifted his great voice:

"To the Bouleuterion!" he roared. "Citizens, to the Senate House!"

He did not seek the childish device of a disguise, or even make the simple concession to prudence of hiding his face in the hood of his cloak. The world had gone mad; and in a mad world, audacity was what counted. He was sure that The Thirty would be too busy for the next few hours to concern themselves about the two hippêis he had slain; that is, if anyone even dared report the killings. He saw a little knot of thêtes about the dead men. The commoners were talking in whispers, their faces ashen with fear. So he bellowed at them like a hoarse-voiced old enomotarch:

"Leave those stinking lumps of carrion, citizens! To the Senate House! Follow me!"

At the head of the mob, he marched boldly into the Bouleuterion and took his seat among the thêtes. The crowd was, he realized, a perfect protection. Who, from among all that gaping, garlicky, sweating mob, could distinguish a single face?

By the time he got there, Theramenes was on his feet defending himself. And, after two minutes of listening, Ariston decided that his defense was masterly.

"The gentle Kritias accuses me," Theramenes sneered, "of having engineered the generals' deaths after Arginusae. I, friends? I? I should laugh, were not the accusation as sad as it is ridiculous! I accused them not! *They* accused me! They swore I'd been assigned the duty of picking up the shipwrecked men. So I was! So I was! You see I do not lie! But I put forward, and this august body accepted, the plea that the storm off Lesbos was too great to make it possible to save the men. If the six great strategoi were honestly convinced that rescue was possible, why did they not make the attempt themselves? Why did they leave two thousand Athenians to drown? Perhaps the winds *were* lesser in their quarter! I tell you, citizens, their own words condemned them.

"And, naturally, Kritias has no firsthand knowledge of this matter. For at that time, where was he, senators, gentlemen, knights? He is tongue-tied, I see, so I shall answer for him. The gentle Kritias was in Thessaly, setting up a democracy—Yes, you heard me right—a democracy, friends!—along with Prometheos, and arming the serfs against their masters! He who calls me 'Kothornos,' shapeless Buskin, claims that *I* change foot every fortnight. But this, gentlemen, oligarchs, is *his* consistency!

"I deserve death, says he—for preaching moderation. What then deserves he for arming all the world against us? I stood with him when he proposed that the sykophantoi and informers be put to death; but what gained we when Leon of Salamis was foully and guiltlessly slain at his orders? The condemnation of all men, a public rebuke at the risk of his own noble life by the great sophist philosopher Sokrates! Why was Nikeratos slain? Why was this son of a man of our own class, gentlemen, done to death? What gained we when that noble lady, his wife, killed herself out of grief? What effect did it have upon our enemies' chances when Antiphon, who had supplied our beloved polis with not one but two triremes at his own expense, was murdered? What gained we by condemning the beautiful athlete Autolykos, beloved of the Demos, the people?

"And what honor do we win, kalokagathoi, gerontes, hippêis, gentlemen, senators, knights—when we stoop to murdering and despoiling even the resident aliens, the metics, who have no political force and cannot remotely be considered a danger to our cause? Who, in the hand of this madman, is safe? I ask you, who?

"You, say you? You dare think it? Safe from the grasp of this monster who exiled Thrasyboulos, Anytos, and Alkibiades, thus providing our foes with three matchless captains—No, two now, for through his agency also has great Alkibiades now been slain!

"I tell you—"

But the applause of the whole Ekklesia drowned out "Buskin" Theramenes' words.

And thereby condemned him.

Ariston saw Kritias nod. At once fifty young men broke out of the press of the crowd and stood at the rail, naked daggers in their hands.

Ariston bowed his head. Tears of pure rage stung his eyes.

Fool! he thought. To believe you could get near him! To so underestimate his intelligence, his cunning! Didn't you know he'd have half a hundred hired murderers at his side? Didn't you even dream he'd—

But Kritias was speaking now.

"Senators!" he cried. "As your leader, it is my sacred duty to prevent you from being deceived as now I clearly see you are! Besides, my friends here—stout oligarchs all —are young, and somewhat—impulsive, shall we say? Believe me they'll not suffer this mockery of justice to go unpunished! I know! I know! You'll now raise the interesting point that Theramenes' name is on the roll of the Three Thousand Elect, and thus he may not be put to death without your vote. Ha! Thus do I deal with that!"

Then, like a dancer, Kritias whirled, turned to the rostrum, dipped a pen into ink, spread out the roll of parchment bearing the names of all the accredited oligarchs of Athens, some three thousand strong, and drew a line through Theramenes' name.

"I hereby," said he, "strike off the name of Theramenes from the roll, and with the approval of all The Thirty, condemn him—to death!"

Theramenes leaped to the altar.

"Gentlemen!" he almost wept. "I ask bare justice! Since when has it been in Kritias' power to strike a name from the rolls? I stand here on sacred ground, but I know they

426

won't respect it! What does this monster of impiety fear from the gods he was banished for scoffing at? And what can you, gentlemen of the aristocracy, expect from him? Are your names more difficult to blot out with blood than mine?"

The stroke was a telling one, Ariston realized; but Kritias was prepared for even that. He clapped his hands and the dread Eleven, the public executioners, filed into the room, attended by their servants and led by the vile and shameless Satyrus, their captain.

Kritias towered up above the trembling Senate and smiled. Then he said with theatrical gravity:

"We hand over to you this man Theramenes, condemned according to the law. Do you, The Eleven, take him to the proper place and do that which follows."

Ariston got up then. For the moment, even for the next day or two, he was in absolutely no danger, and he knew it. Kritias was too intelligent to stir up the populace by ordering more seizures, more executions, for a while. No, he'd let the Demos, the mob, calm down, forget.

And I, Ariston thought, can leave Athens this night without peril. Tonight. After I've called on "Buskin" in prison. To pay my final respects. Because, turncoat, coward, traitor, mountebank—he's earned them. By his stand today, he's smoothed the tablet. . . .

Ariston was admitted to the prison at once. For one thing, he was widely respected, even loved; and no order had yet been given for his arrest. The slaying of the two guards had not even been reported, had, in fact, gone all but unnoticed in the general uproar.

When he came into the cell, Theramenes was sitting there, gray as death, holding the fatal cup in his shaking hands.

"Theramenes—" Ariston said.

Theramenes looked up. His eyes widened.

"You!" he said.

"Yes," Ariston said, "I. Who've come to render you the homage that's your due. You've struck a blow for liberty today, my friend. . . ."

"Friend?" Theramenes whispered. "You call me that? I, who left you to drown at Arginusae? Who helped Kritias deny you your citizenship, gallantly earned? Who—"

"Aye, I do," Ariston said, and bending, kissed him.

Theramenes got up then. The gray left his face. His dark eyes sparkled.

"Take up that basin, Ariston!" he said.

"Take up—?"

"That basin! Aye! I hearby appoint you Symposiarch. Know you not how *Kottabos* is played?"

Ariston glanced at the others: The guards, the members of The Eleven, the curious who crowded the cell as always at the hour of a notable's death. Then it came to him— *Kottabos,* the game he'd seen played at Alkibiades' house the night that wild genius had mocked the mysteries, blasphemed against the gods. Orchomenus had been Symposiarch then, had held the silver basin on his knees to—

—catch the far flung drop with which the player pledged his dearest love.

He bent then and picked up the dirty little washbasin.

Theramenes smiled at him, fully in control of his nerves now, his domination of self absolute, and awe inspiring. Then "Kothornos," "Buskin," turncoat, coward, traitor, lifted the cup of hemlock to his mouth. Ariston could see his throat working as he drained that bitter draught.

He drew the cup from his lips, smiled once more, said: "Ready, Ariston, my friend?"

"Aye," Ariston whispered, and held the basin high.

Then, with a masterly flick of his wrist, Theramenes flung the dregs of his cup across the entire cell, so that they splashed into the basin.

"This drop for my beloved Kritias!" he said.

So, in the end, did Theramenes, "Buskin, Who Fitted Either Foot" rise to dignity.

And riding forth from Athens on the road to Thebes that same night, under the high, bright stars, Ariston swore his solemn oath:

"Mine shall be the hand that pours that last drop down Kritias' throat!"

Which was one of the two oaths he broke in all his life. The other was the one he made to the departed Danaus.

# CHAPTER TWENTY-FIVE

ARISTON SAT BEFORE THE FIRE in the little inn, cupping a bowl of heated, honeyed wine between his hands to warm them a little. The inn was in Boeotia, just inside the frontier between that state and Platea, so naturally it was much colder than in the southern peninsula of Attika.

He turned his head to stare at the people crowding every nook and cranny of the inn. That they were nearly all Athenians he could tell at once, though never before had he seen men of his adopted polis so silent, dust-covered, weary, beaten, cowed. . . .

He called the innkeeper, put the question to him.

"Who be they?" that good Boeotian said. "Why, refugees they be, my lord—running away from the Thirty Tyrants. Seems the Athenians have got themselves a new law: Any poor devil whose name ain't on the list of The Three Thousand, oligarchs all, aristocratic and knightly as all getout, can be hauled off to jail quick as a wink, where they wets his whistle right off with a flavorful sip o' hemlock. And this without wasting the public's time on such frills as a trial."

"And these—*all* these were so condemned?" Ariston said.

"No, my lord. Or else they wouldn't be here now. They just sort of had reasons for believing they were next in line for a little hemlock guzzling. Don't take much in Athens these days, I'm told: Maybe they'd been seen giving a coin to a beggar in public, or hadn't never beat a slave o' theirs to death, or never even jostled a thêtes off the sidewalk into the gutter—"

"Or failed in some other way to manifest their perfect

430

aristocracy, their matchless rightist sentiments?" Ariston said.

"Right. And you—if I may be so bold as to ask—what's your problem, good my lord?"

"The same as theirs. Only I got away a little earlier, before this new law you speak of, friend. But, judging from your words, you're a liberal for all your heft, bulk, and well-filled belly. Rare. Anyhow, maybe you can help me. Suppose I—wanted to do something about this—"

The innkeeper's eyes narrowed with sudden suspicion.

"A knightly looking gentleman like you?" he said.

"I thank you. But I am neither hippêus nor kalokagathos. I am a metic. A rich metic, if you will—or I was before they confiscated my factories, and murdered my best friend to boot—"

"Who was your best friend, my lord?" the Boeotian innkeeper said.

"Have you ever attended the games?" Ariston said. "Either the Ismanian or the Olympics?"

"Both," the innkeeper said proudly.

"Then you know—or at least have seen—Autolykos the athlete."

"Him! The great pankratist? Broke Promethian's arm like a wand, threw him so blamed far that— You don't mean to tell me they—"

"—have killed him? Yes," Ariston said.

A fire came into the innkeeper's eyes, leaped, blazed. Like many simple men, he worshiped feats of strength and skill and the brawny, beautifully muscled people who could do them.

"Was I you, my lord," he said, "I'd head for Thebes. Thrasyboulos of Steiria is there. Got himself one damn fine troop of swordsmen, they tell me—"

Ariston sat there, staring at the innkeeper, held motionless by pure astonishment. Thrasyboulos, Theramenes' silent partner in the crime of the judicial assassination of the six strategoi! Where had such a one found the courage to—

But he halted his half-mocking thought, sent his memory winging further back in time. Six years ago Thrasyboulos had gained fame when he had been the partner of Alkibiades in the brilliant sea action against Kyzikos; again, three years later, he had taken thirty triremes and reconquered all those cities in Thrace that had revolted against Athens. Even at Arginusae, smarting though he must have been under the affront to his dignity that the Athenians had gratuitously dealt him by reducing him to trirarch's rank—probably because of his long association with Alkibiades—Thrasyboulos' performance had been at least respectable. Could a man be called a coward because his nerve had failed him once? To face death in battle in all the heat and clamor of one's blood was one thing. But to face it in a damp and slimy prison cell by means of poison was another. Less—bearable, surely. And now—

And now to play sykophantos! Ariston thought mockingly. I'll extort from him who *was* a brave and gallant commander, and whose shame surely drives him now, a leader's place in his ranks, at the price of my silence, of my overlooking what he knows only too well he's guilty of. So be it. To Thebes!

"I thank you, good innkeeper," he said. He rang a coin down on the boards to pay for his meal, his drink, and went outside in the courtyard to find his horse.

"You want a command in my ranks?" Thrasyboulos said. "You—a metic?"

"Hasn't Athens already suffered enough because of the divisons between men and classes?" Ariston said. "I could defend my birth—which is high enough, Thrasyboulos—and explain how I came to be a metic in Athens instead of holding the rank natural to me in my native polis. But I won't. I don't owe you explanations. The kothornos, my General, is on the other foot! Where were you, noble Thrasyboulos, when the trireme I outfitted at my own expense was rammed and sunk by four Syrakusan vessels at Arginusae after having performed feats it ill befits my conception of either sophrune or modesty to even name lest I seem to boast? Where were you when I clung throughout the night to the splintered wreckage and listened to the death wails of my drowning men?"

"You were at Arginusae? You commanded a trireme?"

432

"Ask Theramenes!" Ariston said.

"You direct me to Tartarus, then. Theramenes is dead. But it seems to me I do remember his speaking of the bravery of a certain metic. Aristides—Aristokles—Aris—"

"Ariston—I. Who was the only metic triarch in the fleet. Will you receive me in your ranks, Thrasyboulos? You'll find I know how to fight."

The General looked at the tall man before him. He could see the silver at Ariston's temples, the strands of white in his burnt honey-colored beard; but he could also see that this man no longer young hadn't an ounce of superfluous flesh upon him, that the muscles of his arms, legs, chest, were those of a Herakles.

"You were a professional athlete, weren't you, Ariston? It seems to me I've seen you somewhere . . . I have it! Wrestling with Autolykos—"

"—who is dead, murdered by The Thirty because he repaid Spartan insolence by tumbling the harmost Kallibos in the dust. Which is why I'm here—to avenge him. But I am not a professional pankratist. Rather I follow Sokrates' doctrine that the body is the temple of the soul, and should not be unworthy of her. . . . Well, Thrasyboulos?"

"I have but seventy men. Anytos is second in command. Will you be satisfied with third?"

"Abundantly. All I want is a chance at Kritias," Ariston said.

And now, having crossed the frontier during the night, they were in Attica again. Fat lot of difference that makes, Ariston thought, feeling the icy winds roughening the skin of his bare arms and thighs. Ahead of him, Thrasyboulos and Anytos stopped. Thrasyboulos lifted his arm and pointed.

"What do you think of it, Anytos?" he said.

"Useless," Anytos said. "In that broken jumble of rocks we'll freeze, not to mention the fact that walls in such condition are useless for defense. Kritias' forces would push them over with a willow wand, not to mention a ram."

Ariston stared down at the ruined fortress of Phyles.

433

He's right, he thought. Anytos is right. Hera witness we have no luck at all.

But then something caught his eye: The stones from the fallen section of the wall were unbroken. A ground swell had thrown them down, a spring freshet very likely, tumbling them quite gently. Four days of backbreaking work would put the ruined fortress into a state where the seventy men they had could stand off an army, due consideration being given to the pious hope of that army's being led by a man rash enough to launch a frontal attack, instead of simply surrounding their rude fortress and bottling them up in it to starve.

Is Kritias that rash? he was thinking, when Thrasyboulos' gruff voice jolted him from his reverie.

"And you, Ariston, what think you?" the commander growled.

"I don't know," he answered honestly, "but I ask of you a boon, great Polemarch."

"Which is?" Thrasyboulos said.

"That you give me half the men, the other half being held in reserve as lookouts and to take their turn when I've worn the first group out, and let me see what I can do with that wall."

"Hades!" Anytos began. "We'll never—"

"You know any other shelter hereabouts, Lochagos?" Ariston said. "Another place where we stand a chance of holding off The Thirty's hosts?"

"No," Anytos said. "But—"

"No *but's* about it! He's right," Thrasyboulos said. "Go to it, Ariston!"

In four days he had the wall rebuilt, having employed the simple expedient of shaming the men into heroic efforts by working through both turns himself, and outdoing the strongest of them. The seventy Attic hoplites looked at him in awe.

"Surely he is the son of Herakles himself!" they whispered. "No mere mortal could lift such stones as these!"

Ariston wasn't looking down the goat track to where Kritias and his three thousand men toiled upward over the

434

jagged mountainside to attack the fortress. He was too busy studying his companions' faces. They weren't a reassuring sight. Thrasyboulos looked worried. Anytos' face was gray with a quivering panic he was barely managing to control. The rest of the hoplites were in no better state. Worse, some of them.

He looked down at Kritias' host, coming on. The broken terrain was playing havoc with their formation. He smiled grimly, turned to the hoplite at his side, said:

"Javelins. Two bundles of them. You, Simonides, and you, Gaonikos, stand here and pass them up to me—"

Then, in one great bound, he sprang to the top of the wall.

"In Ares' name!" Thrasyboulos roared. "Have you gone mad? To expose yourself like that! They'll—"

"—learn a trick or two," Ariston said. "Notably, how easy it is to die!"

He stood there waiting in full sight of his foes. Seeing him, the younger, more agile of them, broke into a clumsy run, pounding upward toward him, their armor clanking audibly now. That was one of the two things he was counting on, that they should exhaust themselves, hauling all the weight they bore up the mountainside on the double.

The other was a subtler thing. He stood high above them so that every javelin they hurled at him would have to fight its way upward against the whole ponderous downpull of the world, while his own would be aided, be lent speed, by precisely that same force. He knew from long experience that missiles thrown downward on a long arc generally exceeded the range of those thrown upward by a good many yards, even when the strength and skill of the opposing spearmen were equal.

Which, be it said, they weren't. No one in The Thirty's forces could hurl a javelin with anything like the force or the accuracy that he, an ex-Spartan hoplite, had been trained to do.

One of the young hippêis was in range now, he judged. At the extreme limit of range but still, in range—which would make the feat all the more impressive.

Good! he thought. Something has to be done for the morale of our men.

Without seeming to take aim, he threw. The javelin made a long, long singing arc, yellow bright against the mist-pearled skies of morning, then it whistled downward, gathering speed every instant.

The knight stopped as though he'd run into an invisible wall. His hands came up, clawing at his throat. Then they saw it: the javelin shaft protruding from the hippêus' neck.

The seventy stood there frozen, staring at that sight. A moment later, they split deaf heaven with their cheers.

"Pass me up another javelin, Gaonikos," Ariston said.

He threw twenty javelins in slightly under that many minutes. Eight oligarchs died and twelve fell badly wounded by his matchless hand. It was too much. Kritias' gallant young aristocrats broke and fled.

And sword in hand, all alone, Ariston leaped down from the wall in pursuit of them. It took Thrasyboulos a full five seconds to find his voice:

"Dogs!" he thundered. "Follow him! Let the one *man* I've got be killed like this and I'll—"

Ten Attic hoplites hurdled the wall and clanked like so many infuriated armored beetles after him. Among them, the metic and his ten slaughtered more than twice their number of the oligarchs. When Ariston came back, wiping the blood and sweat from his face, the men within the fortress racked sound out of existence with their exultant roars:

"Not Herakles' son, but Ares'! Sired by the War God himself, by thunder!"

Thrasyboulos embraced him publicly before them all.

"In Zeus's name, where did you learn to fight like that?" he said.

Ariston smiled.

"By the banks of the Eurotas," he said.

"Then—then you're a Spartan!"

"Say—" Ariston said quietly, "I was. Until I was eighteen years of age. I was captured at Sphacteria. And there were reasons I could not go back to Lakonia when the prisoners were ransomed. I have spent the rest of my life trying to become an Athenian. I outfitted that trireme in order to gain Athenian citizenship; but—"

"When we return, you have it!" Thrasyboulos said.

"If we return at all," Ariston thought, as he stood there on the ramparts, gazing down on Kritias' host, encamped on the slopes below. The wind came whistling down from the peaks above him and he shivered. It was late in the month of Poseidon now; and here in the mountains it was very cold. Ariston could see his own breath pluming like smoke upon the frosty air. He drew his himation closely around him, but that did little good. The cold stole in upon him, making his armor icy, penetrating to his very bones. Then he heard the clank of metal, and, turning, saw Thrasyboulos striding toward him.

"Think you they'll attack again, Ariston?" the commander said.

"No," Ariston said. "They don't need to, and they know it. Kritias is nobody's fool, my general."

"You think they'll sit there with all Attica at their backs to feed them and wait until we starve, don't you, Pentecostye?"

"Exactly," Ariston said. "There's one slim chance though, if you'll permit it, noble Thrasyboulos—"

"Speak, Ariston," the general said.

"That I—and one other—slip into their camp tonight, and cut Kritias' evil throat. Believe me, it would demoralize them completely. I'd do it alone, but for one thing: Kritias has his catamite along to share his hammock. The beautiful Nikostratos, who, though somewhat effeminate, is very brave. I could take care of both of them, but not quickly enough to prevent an outcry. With another dagger-man along to poniard the Pornos, I—"

"No," Thrasyboulos said.

"Why not?" Ariston said.

"You'd die, and I need you," Thrasyboulos said. "You're a source of inspiration to the men."

Ariston looked upward toward the peaks. He couldn't see them any more; the clouds had sunk too low. His lips moved, forming words.

"What did you say?" Thrasyboulos said.

"A prayer," Ariston said; "to the shade of Euripides—"

"The poet?" Thrasyboulos said.

"Yes. I asked him to send the god down from the mechane, as he used to in his plays. To perform a miracle, Thrasyboulos. That's what we need now," Ariston said.

And, even as he spoke, the first great white feathery flakes began to fall.

It snowed all night without let-up. And, in the morning, when it stopped, they gazed from the ramparts down upon slopes totally empty of human life. The north wind and the snow had been too much. Kritias and his crew of knightly effeminates had fled before the storm.

"I thank you, immortal Euripides," Ariston said

And now the mountains were behind them. They lay on their bellies just outside of the oligarchs' camp. Ariston looked at the faces of his men. At their eyes. Or at least at the faces, the eyes, of those nearest him—he had more than three hundred men under his personal command now. On the other side of the camp, Anytos lay hidden with a like number.

Which was a miracle. A miracle that could be explained, of course. What had happened was very simple: The defeated hippêis had talked. And being men, they weren't going to attribute their defeat, their rout, to one brave spearman aided by less than half of one of the two enomotarchies Thrasyboulos had actually had at his disposal at Phyles. The unknown javelin thrower became a giant, so tall that his head was shrouded in the clouds. And this superhuman, this Kolossos, had thrown his javelins with both hands simultaneously. And, at the last, at the very moment they were finally about to take him, cut him down, he had clapped his hands, whereupon thunder had rolled, and all the world had disappeared in blinding sheets of snow. . . .

As a direct result of their arrant lies, Thrasyboulos now had more than seven hundred and fifty men. For ardent democrats who before that day hadn't known where to go, now did. And even prudent men cast their prudence to the winds before such direct manifestation of the favor of the gods. They came trooping, flocking into Phyles; and with them came hope, so that now what Ariston saw in the faces of his men was enough to make his heart lift with pride.

They were like boarhounds on the leash. Their eyes glittered; their lips were drawn back over wolfish teeth. He could count on them now. He was very sure of that. And especially could he depend upon his two seconds, Simonides and Gaonikos. They were like young lions at his side. His chief difficulty was restraining them.

"Take off your scabbards," he whispered. "Leave them behind. Shields, too. Ready?"

They nodded grimly. They'd understood instantly the reason for this strange order. Scabbards had a maddening habit of clanking against the thigh plates. Shields banged against each other, made a rustling as they were forced through the undergrowth. And what they had to do was very simple: It was to poniard the two sentries on this side of the oligarchs' camp so swiftly and silently that no outcry of theirs, no dying scream, could wake the sleeping hippêis within their tents.

For if the knights were awakened, given time to saddle their horses, Thrasyboulos' band was done. Even seven hundred and fifty men had no chance against the two full divisions of cavalry Kritias in his terror had sent out against them.

It proved pitifully easy. Even the two sentries were half-asleep. Gaonikos clapped his hand over the mouth of the first one, while Simonides found his life with one swift thrust. Ariston broke the second one's neck with an expert pankratist's blow. He stood there, looking down at his victim. A sudden scald of tears misted his eyes. The dead sentry was only a boy—very young and very beautiful.

They stole into the camp, followed by ten men who bore no other arms than daggers. All ten had unlit torches well smeared with pitch in their hands. Simonides carried an iron brazier filled with glowing coals.

Ariston nodded. All ten of the incendiaries thrust their torches into the brazier. Then they scattered through the camp trailing fire. They came to the pine bough and brushwood stables the hippêis had made to protect their mounts against the cold, set the torches to them, to the tents of the knights, of the hoplites who accompanied them.

The flames leaped up, crackled, stood tall. Then both

439

Anytos' men and Ariston's poured into that camp at Acharnae.

An aide brought Ariston his helmet, breastplate, scabbard, greaves, and shield; helped him to arm himself, he who had gone into that camp clad only in a chiton, with but a dagger in his hand. And just as he drew his sword to lead the charge, he heard the horses scream. They dashed through the camp, their manes and tails afire, screaming like women in childbirth, high and shrill, in a perfect agony of pain.

The hippêis and hoplites stumbled out of their burning tents dazed, half asleep, unarmored. Pitilessly, Thrasyboulos' forces cut them down.

Ariston found himself confronted with a young knight as beautiful as a god. A face of Apollo upon a throat like Ares', atop shoulders of Herakles. His first impulse was to spare the youth, disarm him, let him go free. But it wasn't possible. This highborn young Athenian was a swordsman as good as any foe he'd ever met. Better than most.

So coldly, efficiently, Ariston cut him down. He used the old, old Spartan tricks: the shield slammed against his opponent's hard enough to rock him off balance, the crippling slash to the upper thigh, the long upward thrust that caught the beautiful young hippêus full in the throat.

He stood there above him, looking down.

"Your name, brave foeman?" he said.

"Nik—Nik—Nikostra—" the beautiful youth got out on a rush of blood and died.

Nikostratos. Kritias' beloved. Ariston stood there. Then he sighed. The boy was dead. And making use of his corpse to demoralize Kritias the more might save many lives.

He bent above the dead boy, dagger in hand.

So it was that when Kritias in person came out with the Athenian garrison to retrieve the bodies of the one hundred and twenty Spartan hoplites and more than sixty oligarchic knights left strewn not only in the camp at Acharnae but for seven stadia beyond it—for the pursuit and slaughter of the oligarchs and their Lakonian allies had extended so far—he found a bloody lion cut into his beloved's forehead with a dagger point. Men said his cry at that sight rent the very sky.

Which may, or may not have caused the terrible thing he did next. The refugees pouring out of Athens brought the news into Thrasyboulos' camp. The character of nearly half of them confirmed it. For slightly less than half of the new group of refugees flocking into Phyles were themselves oligarchs, driven into their enemies' ranks by pure outrage.

For Kritias had seized Eleusis, where the famous mysteries were performed, in order to have a place of refuge for himself and his murderous crew should Athens fall. Eleusis was sacred to all Hellas, respected until that moment by every warring band. And when the priests and the citizens of the holy city had protested, the icy homosexual, who knew neither god nor law, had butchered three hundred of them.

They had one thousand armed men now. Thrasyboulos called his two lochagoi to his side. He said but one word, only half in tone of questioning:

"Piraeus?"

"Aye, Chief. Piraeus!" Anytos and Ariston said.

That same night they marched down and occupied Athens' port. No man opposed them. Then they waited there at Piraeus, knowing that the oligarchs had to attack. There was nothing else The Thirty Tyrannoi could do.

That morning Ariston saw Thrasyboulos' soothsayer, sitting despondently apart from the others. And he approached the seer because, still being of a skeptical turn of mind, he wished to test the man's powers.

"What's going to happen, good seer?" he asked. "Are we going to win?"

"Aye," the seer said, "we are."

"Why so despondent, then, O Hpatskopikos?" Ariston said.

"Because my life ends tomorrow," the seer said. "In this battle I must die. The gods have willed it so; there can be no escape for me. You have our commander's ear, noble Ariston. Tell him not to let a man of ours advance until one of our own dies. Then he is to strike with all his forces —and the victory will be ours."

The naked sincerity of the man's tone got over to Aris-

441

ton. Whether it were true or not, whether or not such a thing as the gift of prophecy existed, this man obviously believed what he was saying. Ariston stood there staring at him. Then, because he too was after all a child of his age, he laid his hand on the shoulder of the seer.

"And I, great Hpatskopikos—will I die tomorrow?" he said.

Without hesitation, or any of the grave mummery designed to impress the credulous, the soothsayer, the "reader of livers," answered him at once.

"No, noble Ariston. Your life will be long. You will see twice as many years as you have now. You will die in peace, with your hair snowed with age, surrounded by the sons of your sons, full of honors. And you will know great happiness—but only if you desist from what now you seek. If you pursue it, you will gain it—but at the cost of blighting all the coming years. If you seek it not, happiness will be yours—except for one great unavoidable sorrow, which you will share with many men. And one thing more, my son—"

"Which is?" Ariston said.

"Have you learned to forgive? Much depends upon that. . . ."

"Forgive—whom?" Ariston said.

"Those who have injured you. Foremost among them—yourself!"

On the morrow, Ariston stood in the forefront of the ranks there on the hill at Munychia, before the temple of Artemis and that of the Thrauian goddess Bendis, and watched The Thirty in person lead all their forces up that hill. Which was a measure of their desperation. Neither he nor any man in the ranks moved or lifted their grounded shields, or poised their spears to throw. In obedience to the orders Thrasyboulos had given them, following the prophet's advice, they stood there like statues watching their foes come on.

Then, when the oligarchs were very close, the hpatskopikos gave a great cry and hurled himself down that slope alone. A dozen spears from the enemy ranks found his life, and all the men of Thrasyboulos' forces picked up their arms. The general had placed his peltasts, javelin throwers, slingers, archers, farther up the slope so that they could shoot over the heads of their own heavily armed companions. And now, as with a roar Kritias ran forward, they transformed him into something resembling a porcupine. Ariston drew back his own heavy spear to throw, to have the wild and terrible joy of pinning the dying Kritias to the earth. But then he remembered the dead seer's words and stayed his arm.

"I forgive you, Kritias!" he called. "Witness it, immortal gods!"

It was over then at that precise moment, Kritias fell, the fighting lasted an hour more. Hippomachos, Kritias' second, who had replaced the murdered Theramenes, was slain shortly after his leader. Kritias' nephew Charmides, son of Glaucon, died bravely fighting for the oligarchic principles he believed in. That same Charmides who in turn was uncle to the boy Aristokles, called Platon because of his wrestler's shoulders, who later was to be one of the glories of Hellenic philosophy. The noble, aristocratic Charmides, whom Ariston had numbered among his own friends. Seventy of the oligarchs died that day. Then The Thirty's forces broke and fled.

Ariston stood above Charmides' broken body and wept.

Ariston lay on his litter, locking his teeth together in order not to cry out. He had a sword wound in his lower abdomen just above the groin. It wasn't very deep, because it had been dealt him by a Spartan hoplite already dead on his feet from Ariston's own thrust; but it was wide and ugly, and abominably painful.

Yet it was not from pain that the tears, the groans, he had to fight back, came, but from a crueler thing. And the name of that thing was—despair.

When we had it won! he all but wept. When they'd disposed of The Thirty, elected The Ten—oligarchs still, but moderates all, men of sense and honor—who'd have thought that they'd—have done what they did—send to Sparta to beg Lysander's aid.

He smiled bitterly where he lay, feeling the stitches with which the surgeon had pulled the gaping, ugly wound together biting into his flesh like so many threads of fire.

And I believed the gods favored the right—or I was beginning to, he thought. To concede there could be gods, after all. That the universe conceivably could make sense. Ha! The gods, if such there be, are on the side of the Lakedaemonian phalanxes; the gods sent fair winds and smooth seas to Lysander's forty triremes! And now—

And now he lay there with that painful, dangerous wound in his belly, he who'd taken not even a scratch during the entire campaign against The Thirty. But then, this time he'd been facing not aristocratic Athenian gentlemen, but whole phalanxes of Spartan hoplites, trained exactly as he himself had been trained, and far, far younger than he was.

Even so, because of his greater experience, his incomparable skill, he'd matched them, overmatched them, beaten them. But his men hadn't had the Spartan training he had had. Gaonikos and Simonides were both dead now. Anytos was wounded, though slightly. And all the Lakedaemonians—and their Athenian allies, who actually counted not at all—had to do was to make one more attack upon Piraeus and—

He bent his head and wept. For freedom lost. For hope gone. For Kleothera whom he'd never see again, for the son he'd never teach to love him, for the stepdaughter who already did, for Chryseis whom he couldn't even pardon or forgive—because nothing he knew about his ex-fellow countrymen inclined him to believe they'd give up their delicate and delightful custom of butchering their prisoners.

If only I could get up, fight, he thought, die on my feet like a man, standing tall! If only—

Anytos came through the door. He had his arm in a sling. His eyes were big with wonder.

"Ariston," he whispered, "it wasn't Lysander! It was—"

"Who?" Ariston croaked.

"Pausanias! King Pausanias! The—the Lakonians deposed Lysander! They don't—"

"—trust him," Ariston said. "They never have. And with much reason, Anytos. Lysander is too brilliant, too brave—and too ambitious. A bad combination, even to my

444

way of thinking. He'd make a Tyrannos from whom only death could free Sparta—free all Hellas, for that matter. But you don't mean they deposed Lysander before—"

"The battle? Yes! Ten minutes before. Pausanias arrived at the moment that Lysander was preparing to march upon us, his ranks already formed! Hades, Ariston! You don't think any of us would be alive now if Lysander had been leading those hoplites!"

"No," Ariston whispered. "I don't suppose we would be. . . ."

"But wait!" Anytos exulted. "You haven't heard it all! You know that Pausanias never saw eye to eye with his fellow monarch, King Agis. He's never had Agis' motives for hating all things Athenian—"

"You mean *his* wife failed to catch Alkibiades' discriminating eye?" Ariston said with tired mockery.

"I don't know. All I know is that Thrasyboulos says King Pausanias has democratic leanings, that he's a lover of philosophy, an admirer of Sokrates, a lover, even, of Athens—"

"Ha!" Ariston said.

"He *is*. He must be! He—he's withdrawn the occupation garrison. He's granted us—full pardon. And the right to arbitration. He swears that if the Athenians elect a democratic government, he'll personally see that that government is seated. He's quoted as having said in public that oligarchies do too much harm!"

Ariston lay there, staring at his fellow lochagos. Then slowly, softly, he began to laugh.

"Why do you laugh, you fool!" Anytos roared.

"Because the gods have such a clumsy sense of irony," Ariston whispered, "and are such bad, bad playwrights. Euripides, my old friend, you stand vindicated now! No man can jibe at your gods from the machine again, when History—"

"What are you talking about?" Anytos said worriedly.

"—History herself—uses that shabby device you employed so often—too often maybe—when she lets the god down upon the skene upon such obvious, visible, and creaking ropes! What dramatist could get away with this,

445

Anytos? We were beaten, broken, waiting for Lysander to smash down with his horny fist and—"

"It was a miracle, Ariston," Anytos said solemnly. "The gods—"

"Oh, get out of here, Anytos!" Ariston said.

King Pausanias of Sparta—the only one of Sparta's two monarchs who mattered now, since King Agis sat in Sparta, staring in helpless fury at the royal bastard Leontychides, whose resemblance to the departed Alkibiades increased with every passing day—was as good as his word. He governed Athens with wisdom, justice, and royal calm for two full months until new elections could be held, and respected honorably her citizens' choice once it had been made. The Thirty had taught Athens a hard lesson; but the polis had learned it well. The oligarchs were exiled; the new government was democratic.

And Ariston, the metic, was free to come home again.

Worn out though he was, sick with wound fever, and trembling from fatigue, Ariston's first act upon entering the city was to go and sacrifice at Autolykos' tomb, at Danaus', at Timosthenes'.

His second was to pay a call upon the athlete's widow. That interview was painful beyond all belief. For Kleothera stood two rods away from him and wept, but would not let him take her in his arms.

"No, Ariston," she said. "You'll be awarded your citizenship now. By tomorrow night you will be both a citizen and a member of the hippàs class—or so I have been told. Is this not true?"

"It is," Ariston muttered. "But Kleo—"

"Listen to me, Ariston! These twelve years Chryseis has been waiting—for you to—to lift her out of concubinage—to make her your wife. I have no right—no right at all to—"

"Is not our son a right?" Ariston said.

"No. Because I'd not have even him—legitimized upon —a deceit. A cheat, Ariston, a failure of your sacred promise! I'm afraid, my dearest. No good can come of you and me—of us. No good at all. I can't. I simply can't—"

Ariston stood there, looking at her.

"Because you don't love me," he said.

"I—I don't love you!" she whispered. Then in no interval at all, no elapsing of time, not even half a heartbeat, a firefly's flash, she was in his arms. Her mouth on his was scalding; it tasted of tearsalt. It clung and clung and moved on his, searing and tender, murmuring wild, voiceless, anguished things she had no words for, didn't know how to say. So she branded her meaning into his very flesh with that agonizing, self-destructive tenderness.

He pushed her away from him. Stood back. His head ached damnably. Wound fever did that. Even her features weren't entirely clear to him now.

"There must be a way," he groaned. "There must be!"

Her voice was a flute note, breathing wild laughter through her tears.

"She'll—just have to share you, that's all!" she said. "For I won't let you go, my love. I can't. It's abominable. But there it is! Come—"

But slowly he shook his head. He thought, with bitter self-mockery: How often noble resignation is born of the weakness of the flesh! If it isn't always. Were I to lie down now, even at the side of this glorious child, in two minutes I'd be snoring the roof off. Or shivering with chills and fever. Or even raving—I don't know. But I can't say that. What can I say? What are the words? The empty, puffed-up, meaningless words to hide the fact that this night my aging, broken body is incapable of love? What can I tell her that—"

"I won't divide my life between you and Chrys, Kleo. She's not worth it; and I won't put you in second place. I'll have to—to work this out somehow. I'll ride to Delphi, consult the Oracle. Will you abide by that decision, knowing it is sacred?"

She smiled at him then through her tears and nodded.

"I will," she said, "but will you?"

"What do you mean, Kleo?"

"The Oracle doesn't give dishonorable advice, Ariston. Nor immoral counsels, which is what you're asking it to do. And, since all I can be to you is your—concubine, you'll have to leave me then, or disobey the god. I think it's better that you don't go, that—that we sin now—while it's still only sin and not impiety. So come, my love. Oh, Ariston, Ariston, I want you so!"

"And I want you," he whispered, knowing that he lied. Because he didn't. Not then. Not at that rarely awful moment when he had ecstasy offered him and was capable only of—sleep. He was forty years old now, and he had been through Tartarus. Even his great-thewed, Heraklian body had passed the limits of its endurance and its strength. He loved Kleothera with all his heart, his mind; but his body was a trembling jangle of utter weariness whose every tortured nerve begged and screamed for rest. Besides, his wound, that sword thrust in the lower abdomen sewed up by a half-trained surgeon on the field, had healed badly, so that he was far sicker than he knew.

"Kleo—" he began. But then he felt the sudden iron chill that was one of the symptoms of his lingering wound fever rise up from his buskined feet along all his limbs. His whole great-muscled body shook. He heard Kleo's voice coming from leagues away, crying: "Ariston! Ariston! What—"

But he didn't see her. He couldn't. She wasn't there. What was there now was beyond human understanding, one of those signs and portents and powers that are conjured up perhaps by that ghostly thing in man that Sokrates called his daimonion, a guiding, or a forbidding spirit—or, if you prefer, the reflection of fatigue, wound fever, illness, overtortured nerves, confused, conflicting will, fleshed out for a momentary flickering in a memory returned, reembodied, restored to life in the form of—

The old seer who had died before the ranks on the hill at Munychia.

Ariston hung there, his face graying out of life.

"I don't see you!" he whispered. "I'm overtired, my imagination—"

"You don't see me," the seer whispered. "You're overtired, your imagination—"

"Ariston!" Kleothera wept. "Your face! Your face!"

"Forgive—" The voice was the rattle of hailstones, the drifting of snow, the soundlessness beneath all sound. "—yourself—seek not—"

448

"That which I want, for I will gain it at the cost of blighting all my years—"

"Ariston, Ariston, dearest, you're ill! Your face—"

"But if you/I (was that voice from without? Or wasn't it interior and his own?) pursue it not, happiness—"

"Ariston!"

"—will be, will be, will be—"

He whirled then, already running. Kleo stood there a long moment. Then she sank down into a chair, hid her face in both her hands, and wept. She cried a long time, until her eyes were swollen almost shut, until she had no more tears. Then, worn out, her body weakened by the fact that for months she had had not one decent meal, having given most of the food she'd managed somehow to obtain to her children, as mothers will, she drifted off into sleep there in that chair.

How long she slept she did not know, but she waked at last, her body one long ache, dreaming she'd heard his voice speak her name, and looking up saw him standing there. She saw too that whatever had possessed him before, whatever weakness, illness, madness, or even demon, was gone from him now. His eyes in the lamplight were once more cool and serene, and filled with a quiet joy.

"Come with me, Kleo," he said. "There's something I have to show you that you must see for yourself. Because you wouldn't believe it if I told you. Come—"

Wonderingly she took his arm. Outside in the darkness of that still, blue, fading hour just before the dawn, he lifted her slender figure up on his horse, mounted himself, rode through the silent streets. He pulled up his mount before a certain house, got down slowly and carefully—for truth to tell his half-healed belly ached damnably—put up his arms to her.

"Why," Kleo said, "it—it's your house, Ariston! In Hera's name, what—"

"Come," Ariston said, and lifted her down. He pushed open the door, tiptoed across the court, opened still another door and stood aside, holding it open so that she could see into that bedroom where the lamp still flickered fitfully.

449

"Immortal gods!" Kleo gasped. "You—you've killed them!"

Ariston smiled, and shook his head.

"For so slight a thing? No, Kleo. Those stains are wine, not blood. Lovely, aren't they? Orchomenus, Hephaestos whom I lamed—this gross, big-bellied, hairy sweaty lout. And this skinny vixen, this bag of lecherous bones, who warned me that my bed would not stay untenanted one hour beyond my departure from this house. She kept her word, it seems. The seer got it right, only I didn't understand him. What I sought so long, my citizenship—"

"Ariston!" Kleothera hissed. "They'll hear you!"

"With all the bacchic cups they've sipped, not even Zeus Thunderer could wake them now. Eros give them joy of one another. You'll grant me the cheat, deceit, is not mine? Nor on my head the sin? So now to Hestia's temple to wake the priestess, to be wed before someone makes me a citizen at sword's point and we can't—while we're both still outcast metics and the law—"

Kleo stopped then, faltered:

"Ariston—dearest—are you—sure?"

He threw back his head and roared.

"But, Ariston—you—she—"

"—were never wed, remember. She was a highborn Athenian; I, a lowly alien. For which now Hera and Hestia both be praised!"

She heard then the eerie echo booming back from all the hollow halls, and shivered as with sudden cold.

"Ariston—" she whispered, "what's that awful noise?"

"The gods' laughter—and my own," he said.


There remained but one more prophecy to be fulfilled: that of the great sorrow Ariston was to share with many men. Four years from that day, he who prided himself upon his calm, his iron control of self, burst like a madman into Anytos' house. He found his former comrade-at-arms reclining at the dining table with Meletos and the aged Lykon, father of his own beloved and martyred friend, Autolykos.

But none of the three was actually eating. They lay there, heads bent, gazing at the rich foods with unseeing eyes.

450

Ariston stared at them, his rage choking his voice until it burst through the corded muscles of his throat with the feel of tearing, with the taste of brine and blood.

"You!" he roared. "All three of you! Celebrating what you've done, Charon and Cerberus witness it! To accuse him! To accuse Sokrates! Immortal gods! To take his life! His! A life unequaled in all of memory!"

They didn't answer him. Their faces were still and sad.

"Meletos, I know you not, so what reasons you had for this infamy escape me! But you, venerable Lykon! Do I have to remind you of the love Autolykos and I bore each other? Do you dare gainsay me when I tell you your dead son adored Sokrates, worshiped his master—"

"No," Lykon said bitterly. "Had he loved that windy old fool less or sought better company than yours, metic, he'd be alive today."

Ariston hung there, trembling. His rage was an actual sickness now. He bowed his head, his mighty fists clenching and unclenching, the veins at his throat and temples like great cords that beat and beat, until he had mastered himself a little.

"Your white hair protects you, O Lykon," he whispered. Then his great voice boomed out again: "But you, Anytos! My comrade-in-arms! I, who fought at your side, bled—"

"I don't deny that, Ariston," Anytos said wearily. "Besides, it's hardly at issue here. Sokrates corrupted my son—"

"Sokrates corrupted nobody! Especially not that drunken lout of yours, too witless even to follow your tanner's trade! What reason, Anytos, what reason at all did you have to murder the greatest man Hellas in all her history has produced?"

Anytos got up then, took Ariston's arm, said calmly, quietly:

"Come outside into the courtyard, my friend, and I'll explain it to you. Only, cease to shout, will you?"

They stood in the courtyard, facing each other. And, be it said, Anytos had the best of it.

"I fought and bled for—democracy, Ariston," he said quietly, "as did you, my friend. My son—bah! You're

451

right. He's not worth quarreling over. But—democracy is. The right of men, however poor, unlettered, simple, to govern themselves. Even to govern themselves badly, if it comes to that. And who were democracy's greatest, most terrible foes? I'll name them: Alkibiades, who called it 'organized folly'; Kritias, who all but murdered it; Charmides, son of Glaucon, who aided and abetted Kritias in his crimes. All co-disciples of your master!"

"He didn't teach them that!" Ariston began. "He—"

"Didn't he? Who invented the simile of a flute player hired to carve a statue? A mason called to navigate a ship? Who, during The Thirty's rule, never raised his voice—"

"As in the case of Leon of Salamis, Anytos?" Ariston said.

"Aye. That I'll grant you—if you'll also grant me that during the democracy he equally defied our howling mobs on behalf of the six strategoi. I don't deny his bravery, or his honor. What I do deny is his wisdom—at least his political wisdom—"

Ariston stood there sorely troubled. In this, his ex-comrade was right, and he knew it.

"But hear me out," Anytos went on, "when you say we murdered him, you go too far. It—was not our intent that Sokrates be executed, Ariston. We asked the death penalty in the hope, no, the belief, that it would provoke the dikasts into decreeing a lighter punishment—exile. Ariston, Ariston! This polis we have built, you and I, with our blood, our sweat, at the risk of our lives, is still too weak to endure his merciless attacks upon its guiding principles! His tongue's too well honed; his wit too biting. But I— Hera help me—wanted him silenced merely, not dead! Absent from Athens, exiled to some far off polis, where he could not undermine all you and I almost died for, my friend!"

"And yet—" Ariston whispered.

"He condemned himself! With his arrogance, his mockery! Had he proposed exile in his speech to the jury, I know for a certainty the whole dikasteria would have leaped to apply that lesser sentence. But he— What did he propose, Ariston?"

"That he be crowned like a victor at Olympia, supported in the Prytannery at the expense of the polis," Ariston said slowly, recognizing now how telling Anytos' arguments were. "But he was jesting, Anytos; he didn't mean—"

"Then he was a fool! You note that the second vote for his death was greater than the first?"

"Aye," Ariston said.

"Then that ridiculous fine of three hundred minae! Had he proposed a talent, or five, or ten—"

"All of which I, alone, would have gladly paid for him," Ariston said.

"Exactly. Now, listen to me! The reason I brought you out here is because I mean to propose a thing that neither Meletos nor Lykon would approve of. Kriton is—raising money. He has thrown his whole fortune into the scales. Simmias of Thebes arrived this morning with his money bags full. Kebes and others are prepared to—must I say it, Ariston?"

"Bribe the guards, silence informers, arrange for his escape?"

"Exactly. All of which I could put a stop to by a lifted hand. You notice I don't lift that hand? Five hundred minae from—an unknown donor—reached Kriton this morning. And you, old friend?"

"My last obol. The bread out of Kleo's and my children's mouths. Every drachma I can beg, borrow, steal— For this, at least, I thank you, Anytos! I go!"

Kriton sat there looking at the draft on a local banker Ariston had given him. His tired old eyes misted over.

"One hundred talents. Your entire fortune, my boy?" he said.

"Yes," Ariston said.

"I thank you," the old man said. "I doubt we'll need even a tenth part of this. But thank you. I've already bought off the sykophantoi who'd surely betray his flight. The guards are bribed. I'd procured horses—but with your money, a ship might—"

"Get one!" Ariston said.

"There's time. First I must obtain the hardest thing of all: his own consent. . . ."

Ariston stood there, staring at the ancient plutokrator.

"You think he—he'll refuse to—to escape?" he whispered.

"He has no fear of death and he is very old. We are of the same age, Ariston. And you know him, know his principles—"

"I'll go to him! I'll speak, persuade—"

"You can't," Kriton said. "The guards will only let his family in—and me, as his legal adviser—until the last day. Then, as the custom is, all his friends may come. You wait here, Ariston, my son. Sleep, if you can. I'll have the servants prepare you a chamber. At dawn I go to him. I'll bring you back his answer. . . ."

What that answer was all the world knows from Platon's immortal pen. Sokrates refused to be saved from death, to negate the laws of his beloved polis, even though obeying them cost him his life.

"We are born condemned, Ariston, my son," he said on that final day. "What land is there that death does not know? You'd have me go to Thessaly? Has no man ever died there? I beg you cease to weep! Your tears unman me. Phaedon weeps less, and he's little more than a boy still. I've forbidden him to shave his golden locks in token of his grief. Did you know that, Ariston? And I forbid you to shave yours, though they're more gray than golden now. Now stop bawling like a calf, will you?"

But, try as he would, Ariston could not halt his tears. He sat there, making not a sound through it all with tear stains streaking his face—while Sokrates went to the bath so that his women would not have to wash his body after he was dead, and after that Xanthippe and Myrto and Sokrates' grown son by Xanthippe and his two younger ones by Myrto came and were kissed, blessed, by the master and sent away.

They were all weeping now except Kriton. Phaedon sat beside Ariston, his arm about the older man's shoulder and tried to comfort him. At their side was Kritoboulos, Kriton's son, and beyond him Apollodoros, who outwept them all. There were many people there, several of whom

Ariston didn't even know. Men from other cities, such as Simmias of Thebes. But Platon, the greatest of Sokrates' disciples, was absent, likely because he could not bear the sight. So was Xenophon, who at the moment was making his immortal march upcountry, in far-off Asia.

Then Kriton asked Sokrates if there was anything he wanted them to do, any care he'd charge them with for his wives and children, and the master said:

"No. Just take care of yourselves. That's service you'll be doing me as long as you live, whether you promise or not, for are you not the heirs of my thought?"

"Aye, Sokrates," Kriton whispered. "But—how—I mean in what way—shall we bury you?"

"Make sure you catch me first," Sokrates quipped, "for I shan't be here. Only this ugly worn-out carcass of mine will be. What you do with that matters not at all—"

And it was then that the jailer's servant came, crying like a child and bearing the cup in his hands.

When it was over—when Apollodoros had screamed like a woman in his grief, shaming them all into silence; when Sokrates had looked up and whispered: "Kriton, I owe Asklepios a cock. Will you pay the debt?" and then gone away from them, but not from their hearts, their thoughts, their memories, which would preserve him forever, hand him down intact as a precious legacy to men and nations as yet unborn—the beautiful Phaedon brought Ariston home, because the older man was too blind by then to even find his way. Once there, Ariston wrapped his face in his cloak, lay upon his bed, and wept without ceasing four days and nights. For eight whole days neither food nor drink passed his lips, until Kleothera, great with her fourth, and their third, child, despaired, convinced that he was going to die of his terrible inconsolable grief for the great man who'd formed and shaped his life. But on the ninth day he sat up, cool and sane, and took a little bread and cheese and wine. Kleo was astonished at his calm, his look of joy.

"He came to me in a dream," Ariston said, "and bade me live. So live I must, for never yet have I disobeyed him. But one thing, Kleo: We go from here. I will not live in a polis that kills such men as Sokrates, nor have our children grow here! So pack our things, for we—"

And nothing would change him from this stand. He sold his factories—except the one he had already given to Orchomenus and Chryseis, along with his former home, as a dowry, for he had sternly forced them to legalize their state, even using his influence with Thrasyboulos to procure for Orchomenus the citizenship he had himself refused—and bought a lovely farm in Boeotia, near Thebes. And there he and his wife and their children lived in mutual love and respect and peace, until he was very old.

And, on a day when he was older than Sokrates had been when he died, his hair whiter than the snows atop Mount Taygetus, and even his grandchildren were almost of an age to wed, Kleothera came into the garden and found Ariston writing very slowly and painfully upon a sheet of parchment.

"What do you write, my love?" she said.

"The story of the life and death of Sokrates," Ariston replied.

"But Xenophon has already written that, and Platon too," Kleothera said.

The old man stroked his snowy beard and smiled.

"They didn't get it right," he said. "Neither of them knew him as I did."

Then he bent again to his table and his task.

The gods were not kind. Except for a fragment of parchment not quite four centimeters square on which only the words "ω Σωκρατες ἐφη Αριοτωη," are legible, this work has not come down to us.

# THE AUTHOR

FRANK YERBY, who was born in Augusta, Georgia, in 1916, now lives in Spain. He was educated at Haines Institute, Paine College and Fisk University. In 1947, the publication of his first book, *THE FOXES OF HARROW*, brought him instant recognition and he has since published eighteen other best-selling novels, several of which have been made into films. *GOAT SONG*, his twentieth book, is the product of intense and dedicated research in Greek history and literature.